MW01045148

The Misunderstood Ally

Dearest Iveta

Best wishes &

happy reading

Fara Z

The Misunderstood Ally

Revised Edition

Faraz Inam

Library of Congress Control Number: 2013913943
ISBN: Hardcover   978-1-4836-7932-7
               Softcover   978-1-4836-7931-0
               Ebook   978-1-4836-7933-4

Rev. date: 08/22/2013

To order additional copies of this book, contact:
Xlibris LLC
1-800-455-039
www.Xlibris.com.au
Orders@Xlibris.com.au
504044

CONTENTS

This book is dedicated to the resilient men and women of Pakistan endeavouring, against all odds, to make this world a better place for all.

Thank you my adorable Mom and Dad for your untiring prayers and love for me.

Thank you my darling Wife and children for your unstinting support and patience with me.

Thank you my dear sisters for your persistent encouragement and trust in me.

Thank you my cousins and in-laws for motivating me in my endeavour.

Also my gratitude goes to my sincere friends for their inspiration in formulating this narrative.

~

Author's Note

It is an open secret that Pakistan and the USA share a very complicated relationship. While people in Pakistan perceive the USA as the world's bully, an Israeli ally, an Indian partner, a 'fair weather friend', or even a frenemy, Americans perceive Pakistan as a hot bed of fanaticism, untrustworthy, complicated, the birthplace of Islamic fundamentalism, and the launch pad of terrorism worldwide. However, the bottom line is that both need each other because their interests are intertwined.

Pakistan needs economic assistance for its much-battered economy, a consequence of entering the 'War on Terror'. Pakistan also needs the USA to meet their security needs vis-à-vis their larger neighbour India. Similarly, USA also needs Pakistan to maintain access to Afghanistan and further to the mineral rich states of Central Asia. Besides, the USA needs to keep Pakistan engaged to maintain security in its own homeland. After all, it were the follies of these two allies that gave birth to the ancestors of the Taliban and Al-Qaeda in the Afghan Jihad of the 1980s; then affably known as the 'Mujahideen'.

Despite the entire riposte by their respective security analysts and armchair alarmist, fact of the matter is that people of both these countries share the same human instincts primarily in social values, religious conservatism, and a common desire to live in harmony, to provide a good life for their families through a decent livelihood, a life free from terror, fear, and the danger of meeting an unnatural end.

Sixty-five years into her existence and the Pakistani nation is facing identity crises. The voice of the innocent, peace-loving, and progressive masses has been subdued by a vocal, fanatic, determined, but small minority who otherwise make the bulk of the news from Pakistan, thus signalling a skewed perception of the country to the world. But they have their reasons.

This novel attempts to understand different perceptions that have become extremely deceptive over time. This story attempts to understand different views on sincerity, friendship, and loyalty. It is an attempt to recognise that while we all have a common goal, we need to reach that goal via mutually acceptable means.

The Misunderstood Ally may be a novel, but the environment it reflects is real. Its characters may not be original, but the personas they represent are real. The events may not be precise, but the motives behind their occurrences are real. The story may not have all the solutions but can help to make the reader understand all the perspectives.

So let us understand these perspectives and join our hands together to make this world a better place, where people from all over the world can live a decent life: a life with our loved ones in peace and tranquillity.

Prologue

It is a little past dusk. The last light of the autumn sun has dimmed on the western horizon over the hills snaking into the territory of Afghanistan. Twilight is in the offing, and the majestic Evening Star is proving its dominance in the sky over all other stars. The moon is yet to make its mark on a dark blue horizon that is craving to show more stars as the evening matures.

Underneath this magnificence is a rough rugged, hilly terrain gradually sloping into a small assortment of disorganised man-made mud huts clumped around a relatively larger village mosque, the only cemented structure in the area. This mosque has a unique history. Built in the early 1990s, the mosque was constructed by the Arab fighters who had migrated from the Middle East in the 1980s to fight the Soviet occupation of Afghanistan. After the defeat of the Soviets, a large number of Arabs preferred to settle down in this border area between Pakistan and Afghanistan, and as a symbol of brotherhood, unity, and love towards the local populace, they constructed and gifted their local hosts a mosque—now simply called the 'Masjid Al-Itihad—The Union Mosque'. Stretched outside the mosque was a large earth-hardened courtyard used for Friday congregations, political rallies, and other public gatherings. Al-Itihad Mosque was traditionally used for marriage ceremonies, especially when the marriage was between children of Arab families and the local Pakhtun Tribes.

This evening, the Union Mosque is under the vigilant eye of Lt. Col. Dhilawar Hussain Jahangiri, commanding officer, 9th 'Crack' Commando Battalion of the Pakistan Army. A scion of the proud Hazara region in north-east Pakistan, Dhilawar, affectionately known as 'Dhil' by his friends and family, is cautiously nestled in the distant highlands about 900 metres from the village square overlooking the village. Accompanying him are twenty-three of his men, anxiously awaiting his orders to undertake the mission at hand.

Dhil, forty-one, was a pure commando in form. Strong, well-built, with deep brown intense eyes, thick black moustache cutting across a hardy facial structure; good looks were now a thing of the past. In fact, his current demeanour reflected years of robust lifestyle half of which was spent in challenging terrains undertaking death-defying missions all in the name of performing his duties for his country. Conscientiously following the commando tradition of leading his men from the front, the almost two metres tall commander stood out among his subordinates, acting as their beacon of success thereby enjoying their trust, respect, and loyalty. Such was the effect of his commanding personality that his men's morale would boost at the mere sight of him, and they were ready to follow him even in the most difficult of missions. Despite such a strong exterior, Dhilawar still had the heart of a child that needed to confide in a loved one, that needed to be cajoled and caressed from time to time for him to gain motivation and encouragement in undertaking his duties. And so while the men of his battalion came to him for their morale boosting, he, in turn, sought emotional support from his wife Rania, whom he lovingly called 'Rani' meaning 'Queen' of his heart.

Some distance below from where Dhil and his men have taken positions for the past two days for the impending assault, a marriage procession is in full swing in the Union Mosque. The faint sound of 'duff' — a local hand-held drum is audible muffling the traditional marriage songs being sung by women in a separate room adjacent to the mosque. There is a group of children belonging to both Arab and Pashtun families playing soccer in the village square in front of the mosque. Some local men dressed in their traditional long shirts and baggy trousers with black waistcoats stand outside the empty mosque waiting for their guests to arrive for the marriage. All are completely oblivious of Dhil's men keenly monitoring the situation and awaiting their commander's orders to initiate their assault. Their objectives are clear.

Intelligence reports had revealed that tonight the senior militant commanders of the banned 'Lashkar al-Mujahideen'[1] — LaM and

---

[1]   Army of Muslim soldiers.

Alqaeda, were to attend the marriage ceremony of the son of LaM Commander-in-Chief Maulvi Najeeb Mohammed with the daughter of Mullah Abu Sayyaf—the Alqaeda Regional Chief. Some other high-ranking individuals were also expected to attend this function. They were all deriving security cover provided by the topography of this region, a small valley deep inside the hinterland of a militant-governed area, on the border of Afghanistan and Pakistan. With hilltops all around, commandeered by militants, the writ of the government was simply not enforceable. The surrounding area had been thoroughly checked by the local militant commander Mullah Baaz Jan. While Baaz was tasked with maintaining security of this area, where his leader was coming to celebrate his son's marriage, Dhil's mission was to attack the militants, arrest the top leadership, kill the rest of the militants, and call in the helicopters for air support and evacuation—all to be concluded within sixty minutes.

Mullah Baaz Jan, who claimed to have counted thirty-four winters from the time he learnt to count, had fought one enemy or the other since he was an adolescent. Son of a mujahid,[2] his early childhood memories were of his father bearded, with a traditional metre-long cloth wrapped around his head, carrying a Kalashnikov assault rifle and bullet belts strapped across his body, heading out on fighting expeditions against the Soviet Army in Khost Province of Afghanistan. He would come back home jubilant and triumphant carrying some souvenirs or war booty comprising Soviet firearms, army boots, clothes, a helmet, or personal belongings of a soldier. A young Baaz would eagerly await his gifts—this war booty. By the time he reached the age of ten, he had made a collection of Soviet artefacts. Then one day he saw his father being brought on a stretcher, badly injured and fighting for his life. He remembered his father's last words:

> *Son, you are now the guardian of your mother and siblings and custodian of your motherland. For centuries, we have defended our homeland from foreign invaders, be it the British Empire or the Soviet Army. I entrust you to carry on the family legacy of defending your honour, your family, and your country. Remember, guard your homeland till the last*

---

[2]   Muslim warrior who fought Soviet occupation in the 80s.

drop of your blood. Prefer death to dishonour. May Allah be
with you!

These parting words had resonated in Baaz's mind for the past
twenty-seven years, charting the course of his life. Just like his father
fought the Soviets, he felt it to be his moral duty to fight off the
foreign forces currently in Afghanistan, hence honouring his dying
father's last wish. He had his fair share of encounters with death. He
also wanted to settle a personal score with the Americans, since, in
one of his skirmishes with them in Helmand Province in Afghanistan,
a shrapnel hit his face blowing away part of it, rupturing an eye in
the process. He now covered his eye with a patch and grew a beard
to cover the scars from the disfiguring facial wound. This fascia fell
in sync with his hair, reaching his broad shoulders leading down to
a stout physique. By way of his family heritage and his reputation
of being a fearless fighter, Baaz had progressed in the ranks of the
militants and was now a senior commander and in charge of the
security of Maulvi Najeeb Mohammad in LaM. This tough militant
fighter had cleared this area after thorough examination. However, he
remained unaware of Dhil or the men who had sneaked into caverns
within this area earlier, camouflaging themselves before Baaz could
secure it. This was a once-in-a-lifetime opportunity to apprehend,
dead or alive, the high-value targets attending this function, and
Pakistan Army was not taking any chances.

Night crawls over the clear evening sky, where hundreds of stars
are now twinkling against a navy blue backdrop. The North Star is
lit up, still proving its supremacy over all others, giving direction
to voyagers. Dhil is completely disinterested in the heavenly bodies
while watching, through his night-time infrared binoculars, the arrival
of half a dozen SUVs from three different dirt tracks surrounded by
other vehicles carrying their bodyguards. He counts the arrival of
four high-value targets distinct by their demeanour. The LaM Chief
is wearing the traditional beige long shirt, baggy trouser dress with
a waistcoat; his Arab counterpart wearing his traditional long white
robe and brown gown. The last prayer of the day has been attended
to, and dinner is underway. The cold, dry October wind blows the

aroma of roasted sheep towards the hillsides, where Dhil and his men savour the smell of the feast for now.

Maj. Saifullah Dar is crouched next to Dhil. Major Dar, thirty-three, belonged to Lahore and was a true Lahori at heart. A character full of life, he lived for the day and had a reputation of taking action first and thinking later. Still unmarried, this six-foot tall, rust-haired, able-bodied hunk famous for his romantic escapades was widely popular among the young ladies. Drawing his lineage from a Kashmiri[3] family, his fair complexion, good looks, coupled with a flirtatious personality, earned him the nickname 'Playboy' among his comrades. Miraculously, he always escaped the wrath of the army disciplinary committee since his flings were never made official. But he was also a daring soldier and a respectable leader. He recently joined Dhil's unit. This was his choice posting after he had successfully conducted an operation against the local militants of Swat in 2009. A hero of Operation 'Path to Riddance', he received a gallantry award for his valour and was given the option of a choice posting. He had then opted to join Dhil's Battalion since Dhil also enjoyed a heroic reputation among the young guns in the army.

Dar gets impatient as time passes. He whispers eagerly to Dhil, 'Sir, please give us the go ahead to initiate the operation now. We have waited long enough and I'm afraid that our targets may leave before the women and children do.'

Dhil looks at Dar and growls, 'Major, when the time comes, you'll be given your orders.'

Dar implores, 'But, sir . . .' when he is interrupted by Dhil, who shoots back. 'This mission is tough, and we've waited this long just to avoid killing their women and children, 'cause it's not their war, and their killing would only aggravate the locals' hatred towards us. Saif, you are aware that the army has taken so many casualties just

---

3   In the 1800s, Kashmir was caught in the grip of a prolonged famine and thousands of Kashmiri families migrated south to the fertile lands of Punjab, where they rehabilitated themselves. Most of them have tried to maintain their Kashmiri lineage by marrying among Kashmiri families, prominent among which are Dar, Sheikh, Kitchlew, Khawaja, and Butt. They are known for their handsome demeanour and jovial personalities and traits they want to maintain in their successors.

to avoid collateral damage. Otherwise, it's easy to bomb the whole area and kill them all. So hold your horses and wait for my orders. We must avoid unnecessary killings to the max. Now join your men, and wait for my orders since it won't be long.'

*   *   *

Time: 0815 hrs. EST
Location: USAF[4] Control Room for CIA Drone Operations
Area: Classified but somewhere deep inside the Nevada Desert

Spl Agt Samantha Albright, thirty-four, is engrossed in conducting a Drone Operation over the Af-Pak border area. The target is the leadership of LaM and Alqaeda reportedly gathered in the Union Mosque.

Samantha Albright, code named 'Sam', was single but claimed to be married to her job. Belonging to the mid-Eastern State of Arkansas, patriotism ran in her blood. Her family heritage was to protect America from her enemies. Her grandfather was a soldier of 101 Airborne Brigade in WWII, whereas her father was a Vietnam veteran. Her prime objective was to continue the family tradition of making America a safe place to live, free from any fear or terror. She could not see her country held hostage by anyone else in the world. Her emotional detachment and motivation to conduct any operation without hesitancy made her an ideal candidate for her present assignment. However, covering such a complex range of emotions was an attractive façade. She caught the fancy of her male counterparts who, though enamoured by her chiseled features, auburn wavy tresses, supported by a statuesque figure, more an outcome of rigorous exercise and disciplined routine rather than any beauty regimen, were afraid to ask her out due to her fiery temper which gave her the nickname — 'Balls Buster'. In fact, it was because of this that she could not maintain a steady long-term relationship in her life. She graduated from Harvard University with a degree in Law and International Relations just after 9/11 but, instead of continuing a career in the same field, opted to join the CIA with the desire to follow in her ancestors' footsteps.

---

[4]   United States Air Force.

Today is an important day for her, and she wants to make sure that the mission is a success. She is standing firmly behind the 'Super' Predator Drone pilot. On another screen in the room are the pictures relayed from the drone's cameras to the control room. The room is cold and dimly lit by the light of screens covering the front wall. The drone pilot announces to the room:

'Hunter has taken off . . . bearing 045 degrees, speed 150 Knots, ETA 0845 hrs.'

Sam replies coldly, 'Roger, that . . . maintain altitude at 13,000 ft. Hover on reaching point until advised further.' She then turns her attention to the camera operator, 'Eagle-eye, talk to me.'

The operator responds, 'Image gathering is good, zoom is working, resolution is sharp, visibility is clear, camera rotation is acceptable. All systems are checked, and we are good to go.'

There is an eerie silence in the room for the next twenty minutes while this latest technology drone with its night flying capabilities, makes its way to the circuit area. On reaching the airspace of Paktika Province, the drone pilot declares, 'Hunter has reached its designated area, commencing circuit pattern.'

Sam looks at the camera operator with an inquiry. 'Advise the situation at the target area.'

To which the operator replies, 'Visual is negative, area is blocked by hills . . . request to climb.'

Sam then gives the instructions to climb to 15,000 ft. The drone pilot affirms, 'Revised altitude 15,000 ft, no report of any other aircraft in the area. All is quiet. Commencing circuit pattern.'

Sam, this time, seeks the situation from the camera operator, 'What's the status now?'

'Eagle-eye has target in sight, activity in the mosque is affirmative, counting . . . one, two, three . . . fifteen men outside the target.'

Sam, for the record, queries their weapon status to which the operator responds after seeing the grey silhouettes of what looks like weapons in the hands of their handlers, 'They are carrying weapons . . . That's an affirmative. RPGs,[5] AKs[6] and one LMG[7] . . .

---

[5]   Rocket-propelled grenade.

[6]   Kalashnikov assault rifles.

[7]   Light machine guns.

hold it . . . Eagle-eye sees children . . . one, two . . . twelve children playing soccer in the compound.'

*   *   *

Meanwhile, Dhil is waiting for the right moment to launch his assault. Dar crawls back to him and implores once again, 'Sir, these bloody cowards are hiding behind their women and children, and I'm sure will leave before their families. This is their shield. Please reconsider your decision.'

Dhil had been anxiously waiting for the time when the families would have vacated the area, but it is becoming obvious that they are not going anywhere and the possibility of the men leaving first has only increased with time. He relents. 'Okay, you take your section to the designated launch pad, while I'll take my men from the left flank. Captain Atif will cover the north while Captain Zarrar will hold ground here with reinforcements as planned. On my hoot, commence operation. But', he admonishes, 'make sure no collateral damage and no firing on the mosque unless fired upon. Remember . . . there is still some method to this madness.'

Dar concurs with Dhil and crawls back to his section of men ready to commence their assault.

*   *   *

Sam is contemplating her next move. The presence of children and possibly women has changed the complexion of this mission. Rules of Engagement clearly state—call off the mission on finding presence of non-combatants in the area, but—with a caveat that the operation commander has the final say and if the trade-off is worse than Standard Rules of Engagement, he or she may press ahead with the operation citing non-combatants casualties as collateral damage.

In such a situation the drone pilot asks Sam, 'Ma'am, I've a lock-on target, what are my orders?' Sam prefers to remain silent. She is still contemplating the repercussions of incurring civilian casualties, especially of children. While her mind tells her that a child of today is America's enemy of tomorrow, her heart dissuades her from attacking the congregation.

The camera operator's yell interrupts her chain of thought. 'I see HVTs[8] vacating the mosque. They are outside! They are outside!'

At which the pilot yells, 'Please advise orders? I've the weapons switched to armed!'

*   *   *

The marriage ceremony is over; the noise of duff has ceased and the Nikah[9] ceremony has just been concluded. Children have since joined the women in the adjacent room, where they are anxiously whispering to each other over dinner. The men in the mosque are done with their dinner and are now preparing to leave the area prior to their families.

Baaz stands about seventy-five metres away from the mosque compound on the dirt track leading to Afghanistan, where he is supposed to drive his leader away. With his back towards the party, he keenly gazes into the darkness of the night. He is anxious since the wedding has taken longer than planned. He has already sent the message twice to his leader about leaving the area, but these entreaties fell on deaf ears both times. Amid the silence of the night he hears a faint hum of the drone circling in the far distance over the western border. Meanwhile, his leader and Mullah Abu Sayyaf along with two other senior leaders come out of the mosque with their men and make for their Japanese SUVs parked a distance from each other. Baaz, who is not comfortable with the situation, decides to precede his leader's convoy by about 100 metres so as to clear the area in front. He sits in his Land Rover truck, captured from the Pakistan Army, with a machine gun fixed to it, and gestures the driver to start driving as he instructs his deputy to join the Chief.

*   *   *

Back in the control room the camera operator yells again, 'Lead vehicle is moving! Lead vehicle is moving!' But Sam still resists knowing that the presumed HVTs are still there.

---

[8]   High value targets—normally meant for people who are high on target priority and even have a prize money.

[9]   Islamic marriage vows.

*   *   *

Dhil is now sure that the HVTs are using their families as human shields and intend to leave before the families depart. He signals his men who have already taken their assault positions to standby. Their weapons armed, their hearts beating fast, and their emotions running high, the time has come for which they were crouched for the past thirty-six hours. This may be a most physically taxing mission for them but their motto — 'Do or Die, Don't Say Why' resonating in their minds keeps their spirits high.

Dhil counts the HVTs. One, two, three . . . four, all are outside and now making their way towards their SUVs. Adrenalin starts to rush in his body. He quickly runs a pre-operation check in his mind — primary weapon armed . . . check, auxiliary weapon armed . . . check, targets . . . in sight, radio wireless . . . check, time . . . synchronised, positions . . . check. He shouts at the top of his voice, 'Allah o Akbar[10]!' A call keenly awaited by his men who, as planned, fire six RPGs from their positions at the SUVs parked in the compound. All are direct hits, which blow up with a resounding blast along with all the occupants. His other men start firing machine guns and lobbing grenades, creating mayhem among the militants who struggle to take their positions to return fire at the commandos. Another salvo of RPGs finishes the rest of the vehicles of the militants, which explode like tin cans.

In the meantime, Major Dar, under the cover of fire, guides his assault platoon to the base of the hill towards the village square to get hold of HVTs who have run back to the mosque with their bodyguards. Dar's job was to secure the area around the mosque before reinforcements arrived from behind. The initial element of surprise is successful with most of the militants incapacitated and their vehicles destroyed. Others, however, have taken refuge in the mosque; Dar has taken his position about 100 metres from the mosque, awaiting reinforcements as planned. There is a brief lull in the fighting.

---

[10]   'God is Great' in Arabic. Call sign of Pakistan Army commandos to commence attack.

All this has been achieved within seven minutes and forty-six seconds as planned.

*　　*　　*

Baaz is slowly and carefully moving down the track. The headlights are switched off. He is well aware of the American drones, their surveillance techniques, and night-flying capabilities. He has already come 800 metres down the dusty track at the corner of the hill range heading in a westerly direction of the Af-Pak border. The village is not in his sight for now. Concerned about this gathering, he wants to get out of here as soon as possible as instructed to his number two, whom he left with Maulvi Najeeb.

As Baaz waits for them to join him round the corner, he hears the roar of Dhil's 'Allah o Akbar' in the distance, followed by devastating explosions and rat-a-tat of machine-gun fire. He shouts at his driver to rush back, ordering the machine-gunner to arm the gun. He repents of the moment he left his leader behind. He prays 'Oh Allah, Forgive me! I was only trying to secure the route. Please save my leader and give me a chance to kill the attackers.'

*　　*　　*

In the control room, Sam is busy contemplating the release of the Hellfire missiles when the camera operator yells, 'Ma'am, Eagle-eye sees action on the ground! Some kind of assault has begun. One . . . Two . . . Three . . . six SUVs under fire.'

Sam orders, 'Broaden the scope.'

The operator zooms out the camera of Eagle-eye and observes, 'HVTs are running back to the mosque, other militants being liquidated, secondary explosions underway.' He then zooms in on Dar's platoon, making its way down the hill; the soldier's silhouettes lit up against the black backdrop by the night-vision camera on the drone.

'Assault party seems to be the Paks,'[11] the camera operator states. 'There are more on the hill.'

---

[11]   Americans's short form for Pakistanis.

The drone pilot interjects here, 'Ma'am, what are my orders?' He is wary of the collateral damage that Hellfires would cause on the target. He voices his concern to avoid a needless bloodbath. 'Paks seem to be doing a good job.'

But Sam does not want to take any chances. She knows that HVTs are still alive and there are still chances of militant reinforcements reaching, or resistance from villagers arising, thus spoiling the Pakistan Army's mission. Disregarding the safety of the children, she shouts back, 'Fire Hellfires!'

The pilot responds quickly with, 'Roger that. Missiles unleashed!' and within the next second, the missiles pounce on their designated target—the Union Mosque. Their flight path is clearly visible on the Operation Room's screen with two other screens showing the terrain from the on-board camera of the flying missiles.

Sam smirks softly, 'Go to hell you fundos.'[12] Then with a slight touch of sarcasm in her tone, she tells her Predator team, 'Let's help our Pak allies here by finishing what they started.'

*   *   *

The assault phase of Dhil's mission is successfully over. The targets' escape vehicles have been neutralised, the principal objectives have taken refuge in the mosque with a few diehard bodyguards, the advance party has secured the area and taken position to enter the mosque, civilian casualties are nil, no commando fatalities, and heli support has been called in, expected time of arrival is no more than thirty minutes. Dhil and his men have fought their way to the plains, neutralising the enemies. He joins Dar, who now has the mosque in sight. Meanwhile, Atif and his section of men have also surrounded the mosque from the north as per plan, whereas Zarrar covers the rest from higher ground. Just when Dhil is about to order the objectives to surrender or face death, commencing phase two of the mission, he hears the banshee scream of two Hellfires approaching their target.

---

[12]   Derogatory term for Islamic fundamentalist.

* * *

Baaz turns the corner from the south-west end and, from a distance of about one kilometre, finds his comrades neutralised. What were once prized SUVs are burning wrecks, the bodies of his fellow militants strewn all around, and Pakistan Army commandos surrounding the mosque. A fire now rages lighting up the area for all to see. Just then, Zarrar's vigilant men from the other end of the valley spot Baaz and fire two RPGs in his direction. While they do not score direct hits, they manage to fend off Baaz, preventing him from coming any nearer. He knows he has been spotted, and for him, this battle is all but over since one truck is very vulnerable in this situation. He calls for help via his satellite phone but knows that even the nearest allies are at least hours away. Helplessly he sees the situation unfold, still contemplating on the right course of action to save his leader, but a barrage of fire coming his way stops him in his tracks. Just then, he hears the banshee scream of incoming Hellfires coming from the west.

* * *

There is a flurry of activity in Samantha's Operation Room. In the background are officials humming over procedures underway for this mission. Her immediate superior Assistant Director James Cumming, who was anxiously monitoring Sam's mission, has just joined her. All eyes are now fixed on the two Hellfires on-board cameras, which show that while one missile has zeroed in on the mosque, the other's target is the adjacent room where the families are in-situ.

Time to target is ten seconds . . . the pilot counts down, 'Ten . . . Nine . . . Eight . . . Seven . . .'

* * *

To his horror, Dhil can now see the missiles streaking in at the mosque. He yells at the top of his voice and all duck for their lives, 'In comiiiiiiiing! Take cover!'

* * *

Inside the mosque, Mullah Abu Sayyaf, Maulvi Najeeb, and their men realise that their time of reckoning has come. They nod at each other and then signal their men to open fire at Dhil's men. If they have to go down, they will go down fighting. They proclaim, 'La Ilaha Ill Allah[13] . . .'

*   *   *

In the drone operation room, the pilot continues, '. . . Six . . . Five . . . Four,' his voice rising with each count, '. . . Three . . . Two . . . One . . . we have impact!'

'Eagle-eye' — the operator yells from his work station, 'That's a direct hit! Confirmed.'

The drone pilot again counts down for the other missile as he guides the homing beam for the missile towards the neighbouring room[14], '. . . Five . . . Four . . . Three,' the excitement in his voice growing with every count '. . . Two . . . One . . . missile on target.'

The 'Eagle-eye' operator confirms, 'Second hit, confirmed! Mission accomplished,' and then lets out a cowboy howl, 'yeeeee . . . haaaaa!'

*   *   *

Before the men inside the mosque are able to finish their chant, in comes the missile through the window with precision, followed by a deafening explosion. The cemented roof of the mosque, complete with a large green dome in the middle, caves in as all inside are blown to smithereens. Moments later, in front of Dhil's surprised eyes, the other missile lands a direct hit on the adjacent room; another thunderous explosion occurs, and the complete structure of the mosque gets destroyed, taking with it the militants, their women, and — their children. All falls silent seconds after the whole structure

---

[13]   La Ilaha Ill Allah, Mohammad ur Rasul Allah — There is no one Sovereign but Allah, (and) Mohammad is the prophet of Allah. This is what Islam teaches and is the belief of every Muslim. This mantra is often used in wars and battles to encourage the men into fighting for Islam.

[14]   Places his laser 'homing' beam on the target for the missile homing sensor to follow

is demolished and engulfed in a plume of dust and smoke, with fire raging in some parts of the rubble.

*   *   *

At the other end of the world, inside the Drone Operation Room, the crew breaks into a cheer of delight. High-fives are thrown all over the room. Both the camera operator and pilot walk up to Sam to shake her hand in congratulations. She gets a pat on her back from James, who contentedly smiles at the conclusion. Another few bite the dust—he smirks at Sam, who nods in affirmative while maintaining a straight face. Another mission may be successful, but the war is not yet over—with these thoughts she quietly exits the room after a long night's work.

*   *   *

Baaz, devastated on seeing this destruction from a distance, lets out a blood-curdling cry, yelling at Dhil's men who themselves are dazed from this close call. 'I'll kill you all if it's the last thing I do!' and with that, his driver accelerates out of the range of Zarrar's men before they are able to score a direct hit on Baaz's fleeing Land Rover.

*   *   *

Dhil is aghast!
This mission is over.
    While the secondary objective of liquidating the militants has been met, the primary objective of capturing the HVTs alive is a failure courtesy of his American allies. Adding to this complication is the complete non-coordination of the mission. He had no prior knowledge of any US plan regarding this event and thinks that if his troops were any closer to the mosque at the time of impact, they would have also perished in the explosion, and nobody would have known the real reason. He is further disturbed to see the loss of so many innocent lives of women and children, who will only become part of statistics. Last, but not the least, is his concern for the utter destruction of the Union Mosque which held substantial emotional value for the people

of this region, and its demolition will now create more hatred and resentment against Pakistan Army from its own people.

His mind is perplexed. He does not know where this war is going. His chain of thought is broken by the sound of 'Hueys'[15] circling in to land, to carry his men back to base. Dar, Zarrar, and Atif have gathered their men in neat files ready to board the helicopters. In terms of search and rescue, there is nothing much they can do since all the militants in the area have been liquidated, the mosque destroyed, and the people inside killed. They leave the battle area for the villagers who in time would cautiously sneak out of their huts to collect the dead and bury them around the village. They will be ready to tell the story of mayhem to other people in the area, thus further tarnishing the repute of the army among the local populace.

Dhil's men share the same feelings as that of their commander. Although content that the operation is over, their exhilaration on a mission well done is overshadowed by the dismay caused by witnessing the death of so many non-combatants. There is a tired silence in the helicopter on the return journey. Physically exhausted, after five arduous days, Dhil lands back at the Forward Military Base near Bannu with his men, ready to prepare themselves for the next such mission for their nation and country.

---

[15] Bell UH 1A Huey Cobras, US made 'close support and assault' helicopters supplied to Pakistan Army to conduct anti-terrorist operations.

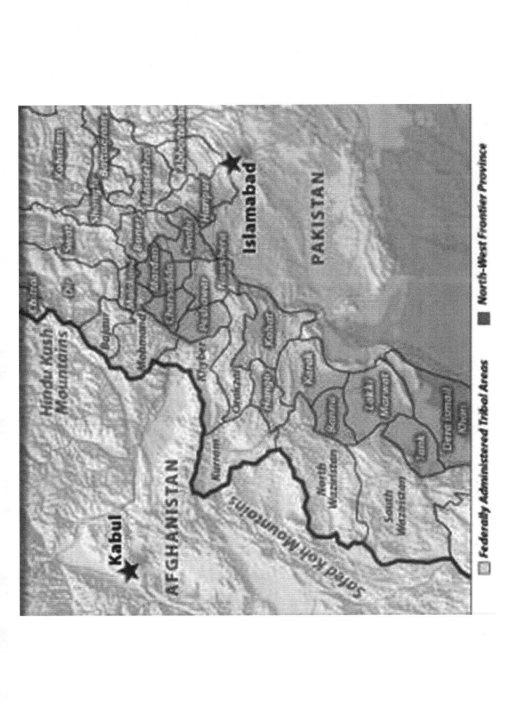

Federally Administered Tribal Areas   North-West Frontier Province

Chapter 1

THE POSTING

It is 1200 hrs in Nevada. Sam writes her mission report on last night's destruction of the Union Mosque. Her primary and secondary objectives of this mission were achieved. Leadership eliminated, a number of militants killed and building structure—destroyed. However, one aspect of the event needed to be elaborated further in order to meet the legal and moral justification of this mission. After giving it a long and careful thought, she concludes her mission report with the following words:

> *Intel on this event termed it as one of the very rare opportunities where Maulvi Najeeb, chief of Lashkar al-Mujahideen, his spiritual guide, Maulana Abdul Ghafoor, Mullah Abu Sayyaf, regional chief of Alqaeda, and his number two Sheikh Fahad Al Marri would be getting together in the Union Mosque for the marriage of Najeeb and Abu Sayyaf's children. This, for us, appeared to be an ideal opportunity where all these four important individuals could be eliminated together.*

> *Considering the involvement of LaM in undertaking suicide bombings both in Pakistan and Afghanistan and their threats to carry on with terror attacks on American soil itself, it became all the more important for us to eliminate this threat by aerial strike at the first opportunity. Moreover, both Najeeb and Abu Sayyaf were wanted by the CIA with prize money on their heads. It was evident from their planning that they were using their women and children as human shields on the presumption that USA/CIA would not conduct a missile attack to avoid collateral damage. Furthermore, we could not wait for the HVTs to leave the premises due to the following reasons:*

1. *They had all planned to travel individually in different directions.*
2. *We were unable to identify the targets once outside.*
3. *The possibility of decoys imitating HVTs, thus confusing us, could not be ruled out.*
4. *We did not have sufficient fire-power to engage multiple targets going in different directions simultaneously.*

Under such circumstances, our most favoured option of liquidating all four HVTs in one strike was to destroy the Mosque complex itself. While we were cognizant of the unfortunate loss of civilian and non-combatant lives, the trade-off of aborting the strike outweighed the executed option. Hence, we proceeded with the mission. The loss of innocent lives, which may be considered 'collateral damage' in this war, is greatly regretted.

Sam looks over the report. She feels that by writing down her justification, she has morally and ethically absolved herself from any wrongdoing. She is confident that she followed the Rules of Engagement and that she will not be held accountable. On the contrary, she expects a commendation for a successful mission. Although she is a little saddened by the unnecessary death of children, she consoles herself by thinking that the children of today may turn out to be enemy combatants of tomorrow, and she has done a service to her country by eliminating such future warriors before they could bring any harm to Americans.

Tired after a long night's work, she yawns, stretching herself, presses the print button to take out the report and shuts the computer before leaving her small office, which gives more appearance of a file room than a special agent's office. Files on various Alqaeda key suspects and other enemies of the State are neatly stacked on one side of her desk. There is another set of files that pertains to various critical CIA operations conducted in the Af-Pak region. Her forte was to go through each individual's file and, based on his personality assessment, historic background, movement record, and contacts, with reasonable degree of accuracy, plot the suspect's future movements and course of action. Her unit carried out many operations successfully based on her 'hunches', and this ability of hers also gave her the nickname of 'Ghost Whisperer', since her colleagues teased her about talking to the ghosts of dead agents in order to predict the future. Sam took such comments in her stride and didn't care much as long as she delivered.

Her body is a little stiff from the previous night's action. She makes her way down the narrow corridor to the office of her boss, Assistant Director James Cummings. His secretary is not around, so Sam goes straight to his door and knocks.

'Yes! Come in . . . ,' his voice reverberates from inside. James Cummings worked for twenty-five years in the CIA. Now, nearing fifty, he spent most of his time sitting behind a desk in the safe confines of his offices in the USA. He specialised in manipulating the careers of his colleagues and subordinates for meeting his own objectives, having sent a few to their imminent death to countries in South America and the Middle East. His utter disregard for the personal safety of agents dispatched to dangerous assignments abroad made his subordinates understandably wary of his motives. They had accordingly nicknamed him James 'Cunning' Cummings. However, James, regardless of his reputation, had the knack of selecting the right people for the job, and in most cases, the mission would be accomplished at whatever cost, a feature appreciated by the decision makers at Langley and Washington.

Having spent three years in her present job, Sam feels that James is considering some kind of assignment for her in the near future. He has recently been asking her more often than usual about her goals in life, her level of patriotism, her family background, and her degree of dedication. Inquiries about her private life, whether she is dating someone or is planning to get married anytime soon and other such questions had become a regular topic of discussion nowadays.

Sam's mind is a little numb now as she enters the room to the beaming smile of James who gestures at her to sit down on a seat across his table. Sam is familiar with this smile. Something weird is cooking; James clearly seems up to something but she prefers not to ask just yet.

'Congratulation on a job well done, Sam,' exclaims James. 'This was a one in a thousand opportunity, and you made their elimination possible. I've advised Langley about it, and they are delighted to hear it. You might be getting a personal call from the 'secretary' himself.'

Sam gives a subtle nod, acknowledging her boss's accolade. Her motivation for undertaking drone missions was not derived from 'blue endorsements' or 'calls of praise' from higher officials. She derived the desire to eliminate the enemy from the personal vow she took on the grave of her father. All the words of praise coming from her boss did not mean much to her. She says a complimentary thank you to James and seeks permission to leave for the day.

'You know, Sam, with such dedication and motivation towards your job, I see a very bright future for you in this organisation. You have progressed very fast up the chain', professes James, 'and I'm sure you'll go places with this kind of attitude. Keep up the good work and God be with you.'

Sam gets up from the chair and makes her way to the door when James calls from behind, 'Sam! Take a couple of days off . . . You might hear something good soon when you return.' Sam stops in her tracks, turns back, and walks up to James, curiosity plainly written all over her face. James, who expected this response from her, gestures at her to sit down.

This time, however, Sam prefers to keep standing. 'Sir, could you kindly elaborate a little on that, I must confess, I am a little intrigued now,' she pleads, excited, apprehension running down her spine.

'Your name has been recommended for an overseas assignment,' replies James. 'It could be either Afghanistan or Pakistan.'

'Pakistan!' Sam exclaims, 'Sir, I mean, are you sure?' She cannot hide her anxiety. In Afghanistan, she knew what was coming, but Pakistan to her was always an enigma. On the one hand, an ally in the Muslim world with a Western-oriented democratic government and a powerful nationalist military armed with nuclear weapons, it was also home to religious fanatics and terrorists adamant on destroying America and its allies. With such an opinion, it was no wonder Sam considered Pakistan to be the most dangerous place on earth.

James had been reluctant to break the news upfront realising he was the one who recommended her name, and knowing well from her history, experience, and attitude that Sam was the right person for this coming assignment. She was to be part of a 'unit' tasked with reorganisation of human assets in the Af-Pak border area. Her new job included collection of intelligence data from these field assets and tabulating that into relevant information for onward transmission to CIA Headquarters at Langley, for the relevant drone strikes. However, since James felt that she may not be comfortable with the idea of going overseas, he would have preferred to break this news gradually.

With this thought in mind, he responds with a smile, 'Well, you take off for now, and by the time you come back next week, the final posting will be out. Wherever you go, I'm sure you'd do well and don't look so anxious,' he tries to console her. 'In either of the two places you are sent, you'll be based in their green zones, and those are pretty safe places. Samantha . . . ,' he concludes, 'this assignment would look good on your dossier too.'

Sam returns these observations with a feeble smile and slowly drags herself to her beaten-down dark blue Ford Mustang, with two words echoing in her mind — Pakistan and assignment. In the car park, she meets Oscar, the drone pilot with her in last night's mission. He is also making his way towards his vehicle — a brand-new Honda Integra Type 'R' that he recently bought from the local dealers.

'Hey, Ma'am,' he greets Samantha. 'You know, Honda is giving some attractive offers these days,' he glances towards her Mustang. 'They are even trading in your older car for a new one. You might want to have a look at that. I recently bought this Type 'R', and she's a real babe on the roads . . . accelerates faster than our drones.' He lets out a laugh at his own joke.

'Yeah . . . Honda is good, but it's not American yet,' Samantha smiles at the youngster, 'Lemme know when we take Honda over and perhaps then I'll think about it,' she concludes leaving behind a confused-looking Oscar who curses himself for initiating a conversation with the 'Balls Buster'.

Samantha settles herself down in her Mustang and drives off to her apartment about twenty-five minutes' drive from base. It is Wednesday, and she has two days off. That, coupled with the weekend, means she can start planning her small vacation. The thought of the mission and the silhouettes of those children on the Hawk-eye screen reverberate in her mind. One moment they were alive and cheerfully playing soccer, completely oblivious of the lurking danger — the next moment, they were all gone, perished, dead, blown to smithereens. Adrenaline now settled, the gloom of losing young lives seeps into her heart; she feels the need to take her mind off this chaos that has currently engulfed her world. With such conflicting thoughts, she reaches her home to be joyfully greeted by 'Lia', her trusted old German Shepherd dog.

*   *   *

It is midnight in Pakistan. Dhil's Huey has reached the forward base close to Bannu. Dhil is standing tall, making sure that each of his men is accounted for and is settled down before taking the day trip back to their unit near Attock.

When all have disembarked, and are standing in a neat file, Dhil walks up to them and inquires about the condition of each one. His men's chests swell with encouragement. While en-route, he had ordered the base to prepare a few roasted chickens, naan,[16] and mutton qorma.[17] He knew that after having spent six days on minimum basic ration, his men would be ravenous enough to devour anything that came their way. This was also a good way of wiping off any sceptical thinking that might have engulfed the soldiers while conducting this operation.

Dhil and his officers join their men over this late-night dinner. But before starting the feast, Dhil feels the need to deal with his soldiers. He knew that there were doubts simmering in their minds, and these needed to be eradicated. The last thing he wanted was sagging morale and confused subordinates questioning the whole purpose of this 'war'. So, before breaking off for dinner, Dhil addresses them directly.

'Soldiers!' he roars at his men, who all become alert while standing in a neat file. He now has their attention. 'How's the morale?' he inquires loudly, infusing energy in a voice which pierces through their disconsolate thoughts—his gaze firmly locked on their eyes. The attitude exuded is contagious, and the men try to respond with equal enthusiasm.

'High, sir!' comes the response, loud but not loud enough hence reflecting their inner feelings. Dhil feels the response should have resonated across the base. He follows through, this time further increasing the decibels of his roar. 'Up to!?' He bellows. This time the men give a more heartened reply and yell back at the top of their voices,

'Sky, sir!'

Dhil knows that he now has the attention of his men, who, reeling under emotional pressure, are desperately in their subconscious minds seeking a word of encouragement from their leader to justify their actions and help them atone for any guilt arising from this operation.

---

[16]   Similar to Mexican tortillas made from flour.
[17]   Pakistani feast mutton cooked in curry.

'First of all, let me congratulate you for a job well done,' begins Dhil. 'It is not easy for anyone — even a soldier to tread undetected for three nights under extremely hostile territory, lay down in camouflage for another two days, and then', he adds coming to the final stage of the Op, 'carry out the operation like true professionals — with valour, dignity, and dedication to your belief, duty, and country.'

He knows he is now treading on sensitive territory and that each and every word of his has to be calculated and well thought out so as not to create any controversy or contradiction with the ethos of the army, which is ingrained in each and every person in the organisation.

'You have fought well tonight and have maintained the highest traditions of a commando, and — a commando of the Pakistan Army.' His officers standing next to him silently nod in agreement so that the message is conveyed in uniformity to the soldiers.

'We must remember one thing; anyone who raises an evil eye on our motherland will be considered our enemy. That enemy could be a person, a group of people, or even a country.' He continues, 'In our lives, we have been trained and raised on the thought that we have only one enemy and that is sitting on our eastern border. We all joined the army to save our motherland from the nefarious designs of that enemy country, and I'm proud to say that we have all done an outstanding job in keeping those infidels at bay.'

By this time, he notices that he has the full attention of his men who are intently listening to each word he says.

'Now when that enemy could not destroy us overtly, thanks to brave custodians of the country like you, they have covertly hired this bunch of criminals and terrorists who in the name of Allah and Islam are trying to destroy the very fabric of our national unity.' He knows that involving India in any issue will create an unprecedented level of patriotism among the ranks, making the soldiers do anything to achieve their objective.

'But we will not let this happen!' he yells commandingly. 'We will destroy our enemies be they from the outside or within, I say, let them come,' he pauses for a moment. 'We will destroy you wherever you are, and whoever you are!' He shouts at the top of his office.

'Naara e Takbeer!' [18] chants the Subedar Major[19] and the men respond at the top of their voices.

'Allah o Akbar!' [20]

'Naara e Haideree!' [21] the Subedar Major continues in the same spirit to complete his battle cries.

'Ya Ali!' [22] comes the reverberating response from the officers and men as if they have been injected with a high dose of electricity.

Dhil can see that the motivation level of his men has risen and depressed postures have given way to pumped chests and taller statures. He knows that this is the perfect time to close since the morale, for now at least is at its peak. So without any more words, Dhil concludes with a resounding cry of 'Pakistan!'

'Zinda-baad!' [23] comes the customary response from all corners of the ground.

'Pakistan Army!' he roars again, the sound coming out of his hollow stomach, breaking all previous records of intensity.

An equally intense response of 'Paa-inda-bad'[24] comes followed by a short burst of machine-gun fire in the air to lend impetus to Dhil's morale-boosting address. The entire base is awakened with these deafening salutations in the dead of the night, which are customary on concluding such events.

With this, Dhil gestures to the Subedar Major to dismiss the congregation and lead them towards the feast, which the men and officers proceed to devour after days of subsisting on minimal diet.

---

[18]   It is the first part of a battle cry, meaning, 'proclamation of faith'.

[19]   Equivalent to US Army's 'sergeant major'.

[20]   It's the second part of the same battle cry, which the group then responds to meaning 'God is (the) Great(est).

[21]   Continuation of the battle cries, meaning, 'proclamation of valour'.

[22]   This is the second part of the second battle cry, which the group then responds to, meaning, O Ali—Ali was the cousin of Prophet Mohammed (pbuh) and was known to be the most loyal and fearless warrior in the times of advent of Islam having numerous incidents of gallantry to his name. His stories are revered even to this day.

[23]   Long Live (Pakistan)—customary salutations while concluding a morale-boosting speech.

[24]   Thrive forever (Army).

There is elation now in the gathering while they are feasting on Pakistani cuisines. Atif and Zarrar walk up to Dhil and enthusiastically shake his hand to declare their unflinching support and trust in his command. They share the same sentiments as does every person under Dhil's command. Dhil joins the company of his men. He feels that his speech has been effective for now but, while he is convinced of it at a tactical level, he has his doubts about the strategic implication of this campaign. Furthermore, he is also frustrated with the Americans for conducting drone attacks with such complete brazenness, often resulting in the death and destruction of innocent lives and property. He is well aware of the effects it is having on Pak Army operations, but tonight's incident becomes too much for him to bear. Apart from causing unnecessary deaths, this uncoordinated attack almost cost him and his men, their lives. He foresees the danger of a retaliatory response from the militants. He feels the need to discuss these aspects with his superiors and also air his grievance against the American action and its repercussions on Pakistani soil.

* * *

It is midnight in North Waziristan. Dhil and his men have left the smouldering remains of the destroyed structure. Baaz, who had earlier escaped from their wrath, cautiously creeps back to the battle site. He is devastated at the loss of his leader and his spiritual head. Moreover, he is furious at witnessing the death of so many of his comrades, their women and children. On seeing that the site is clear now, he starts to sift through the debris in desperation hoping against hope to save his people. He weeps and swears out of frustration like an adolescent schoolboy who just lost his marbles to bigger bullies of the school.

He had already, via satellite phone, called his comrades, the nearest of whom were still a few hours away from Baaz. The drive would be slow and hazardous without lights so as to reduce the chances of being detected by a Predator Drone. Baaz, for now only has his driver and machine-gunner to help him.

The villagers, who heard the whole skirmish, are too afraid to come out at night, fearing vengeance of the militants upon them. These unfortunate souls were caught in the crossfire between these militants and the Pakistan's Armed Forces, each accusing them of being the other party's spies. They considered it prudent to just stay away from both sides. Furthermore, it was night, and with no electricity in the village, they were not of much help to Baaz, who also did not think much of these people, suspecting them of giving in to the Pakistani State. Baaz was such a terror in the area that innocent village people were afraid to confront him, lest they find themselves at the receiving end of his raging temper and end up being shot.

Body perspiring, breathing fast, heart racing along to keep pace with his activity, adrenaline running high in him, Baaz picks up brick after brick of what once was the Union Mosque, praying to God that he may see some signs of life from underneath the rubble. But to his great dismay, there is nothing to see. With only three lanterns to give him light, it was difficult to lift the heavier concrete pieces. Again he lets out a blood-curling scream of frustration and fires a volley of bullets into the air to vent his fury. Even his driver and gunner are afraid to face him and take cover behind the ruins of the mosque to escape Baaz's wrath.

Fatigued and in anguish, Baaz finally breaks down on the ground. It was obvious that there were no survivors and that he needed to wait for his allies to join him by dawn. Only with their assistance could he at least take out the dead bodies or whatever was left of them, from beneath the rubble and give them a proper burial.

A few questions spin around in his mind. He wonders who leaked the news of these high-profile men congregating last night over here; could it be an inside job or could it be one of the villagers who was privy to this information? He rattles his brain; could it be possible that all these people were tracked simultaneously before they all gathered in one place?

He blames the Pak Army for his loss. It was the Pak Army who had somehow infiltrated under heavy camouflage into the area. It was the Pak Army that attacked the marriage party. He also presumes that it was the Pak Army who directed the American drone to attack them. Going further down this line of reasoning, he wonders what unit of the Pak Army could have carried out this operation? This must have been a Special Forces job since it had the telltale signs of a highly professional group, that is, a commando unit based close by. Various ideas creep into his mind for taking revenge, but they all seem too ambitious for now, given the limited resources of his network and the latest loss of his commander. However, he promises to avenge their deaths. He feels that only by exacting revenge will he be able to allay these angry impulses and also prove his loyalty to his people and their cause. With these tumultuous thoughts raging in his mind and body exhausted from all the activities, he dozes off only to be abruptly awakened by a strong tug on his neck by someone very powerful.

*   *   *

It is Wednesday evening in Nevada. Sam is in a deep sleep, exhausted from the last few days of intense work in her office, which finally culminated in a successful execution of the mission at hand. Her trusted pet Lia patiently waits for her mistress to take her out.

Every evening, Sam would take Lia out for her evening walk, where she would run around to refresh herself. When this does not happen today, Lia quietly creeps up to Sam, whines and licks her face to wake her up. Sam awakens to realise that the desert sun is already at the horizon ready to bid farewell to the day and leaving behind a dark yellow wilderness in the sky.

She drags herself out of the bed still feeling the heaviness in her body. Washing her face, she changes into her slacks and pullover and goes to her small neat kitchen to prepare a snack and a mug of coffee.

Sam lived in a one-bedroom apartment on the outskirts of Nevada City. Her kitchen counter faced her living room that was neatly furnished with minimal furniture of contemporary design. Not much into interior decor, she maintained a very basic look in her apartment. Off-white drapes covered the windows, whereas comfortable beige sofas surrounded a brown centre table, and on one side was placed a small wooden dining table with four chairs. Even these were hardly ever used since Sam did not have parties at home except for the occasional small dinner with her close colleagues at the Agency.

On one of the walls in her living room, and visible from the kitchen, were a sequence of family photographs neatly hung. These pictures included her parents' marriage photo of 1972, her childhood photos with her parents and brother Alex, and her graduation in 2002. One particular picture always catching the attention of her guests was that of her father dressed in battle fatigue along with his three fellow soldiers standing in front of a Huey Bell UH-1 helicopter in the deep green jungles of Vietnam. The year was 1970 and her father, a young lieutenant of twenty-three years of age, was about to conduct an operation for which he later received the Purple Heart [25] for undertaking a search and destroy mission behind enemy lines and saving his comrades' lives by putting his own life in danger. How proud Sam was of her father and his feats of valour. She made it a point to show each of her guests this particular picture and also tell them the story behind it.

Sam did not like the hustle and bustle of downtown life and preferred to spend her free time sitting in the wilderness of the Nevada Desert with her dog, reading some book or magazine on world affairs. She liked keeping herself abreast with happenings around the world. Not only was this her job requirement, she was personally interested in world affairs. Her degree in International Relations was born out of a desire to get to know and understand the different people, cultures, religions, and customs of the world.

Sam takes Lia out for her routine walk down the footpath to a park nearby. By the time they reach the park, the sun has already set on the horizon, and the sky has turned a few shades darker. She walks across the park to the jogging path that is now near empty since most of the people on an evening stroll have left already.

What do I do for the next four days? – she thinks to herself. She reaches her usual spot where she unleashes Lia, who eagerly dashes to the nearby bushes. Sam settles herself down on the green grass, the chill of the October evening setting in, she takes out her snack and the hot mug of coffee to enjoy the evening wind blowing across her auburn hair, cooling her mind after last night's incident. The serene environment and the quietness of the evening is occasionally broken by a greeting from a walker, most of whom regularly visited the park like Sam and knew each other. The snack coupled with a shot of caffeine brings her mind out of its lethargy, and she feels more alert in her thoughts. *So, what do I do?* Her mind returns to the problem. *Should I go to Los Angeles and catch up on old college friends who were working there or should I just go visit Mom back in Arkansas?*

It had been quite a few months since she paid a visit to her mother, Catherine who, after the death of Sam's father, had shifted back to her hometown of Jacksonville in Arkansas. There she lived in a two-bedroom extension of the house she and Sam's father had

---

[25]   Gallantry medal awarded in US to recognise feats of valour.

built after their marriage. A major comforting factor for Sam was that Catherine had subleased this house to her cousin Mike Forester, forty-seven, who lived there with his wife Angie and two teenage children since their own home was repossessed in the sub-prime crisis of 2008. This way Sam was satisfied that her mother was not alone and at least had company. Catherine was also happy that she had some family close to her.

Catherine, now nearing sixty, was the epitome of a true American homemaker from a small town, who had spent her life tending to the needs of her family, ensuring that they always had a congenial atmosphere at home, where virtuous values and family traditions were inculcated in the hearts and minds of the children. She did not have a life beyond that.

Sam's father Lt. Col. (retired) David Arthur Albright never settled down after his return from Vietnam. He finally took voluntary retirement from the US Army in 1983 to follow the path of goodness, preaching piety, kindness, and forgiveness and eventually became a pastor in 1985. He felt he was part of the death and destruction caused in Vietnam during his tenure there, and for him, this alternative path was a natural progression to cleanse himself of all the sins he felt he had committed. His friends called it 'post-traumatic stress disorder' whereas he termed it a 'route to salvation'. While David and Catherine settled down in their new life in this town in Arkansas, David's last assignment took him to New York, where he met his demise.

Sam decides to visit her mom. She felt that after losing her father and brother before time, she was the only family her mother had, and she wanted to spend as much time with her as possible. Also, with James's words nagging at her, and the fact that she might be getting posted overseas makes her anxious to see Catherine. Lastly, she needs to share the conflict going on in her mind with the person she loves the most. She knows that what she is doing now may be justified from one aspect, but it still is cruel; she craves to get this guilt out of her system by sharing her thoughts and taking guidance from the person she considered as the pillar of her emotional strength.

With these thoughts in mind, she slowly walks back to her apartment with Lia close on her heels. Lia, with tail wagging from left to right and tongue hanging out, was pleased to have her daily dose of exercise and outing and was now ready to go back to the apartment to have a good night's sleep.

*   *   *

It is dawn and the sun peaks through the eastern horizon. In the distance, the village rooster is heard giving his ceremonial calls of the morning. Baaz is helpless, since he is being dragged by his neck by two burly Arab warriors who were the first ones to reach the sight after last night's event.

Baaz tries to speak but can only manage a strangulated cry due to the chokehold on his throat. He tries to break free from the grip of his captors, but they are too strong for him. He is dragged to the town square where Abu Khalid, a senior commander of Alqaeda, stands with a furious look in his red eyes piercing Baaz's body. He is greatly saddened at the death of Abu Sayyaf and has grave doubts about Baaz, since Baaz was the sole survivor of last night's fight. Baaz sees that his own gunner and driver have both been tied with ropes and are being savagely beaten by the Arab fighters with leather lashes, while being interrogated about the name of the spy who revealed this secret meeting to their enemies. Both of Baaz's men scream with pain, swearing their innocence on this matter and pleading for mercy, but all cries fall on deaf ears. Having come across from the Tora Bora Mountain of Afghanistan, these Arabs were in no mood to go back empty handed. They literally wanted the head of the spy on a platter, and this platter was what they intended to take. Their prime suspect being Mullah Baaz Jan.

*   *   *

Back at the base bordering North Waziristan where Dhil and his men rested after five days of strenuous activity and a sumptuous dinner last night, a soldier of his unit wakes Dhil up from his brief nap at 0700 hrs. Dhil's body has stiffened after last night's operation as his subconscious relaxes letting the real fatigue set in. *God* — he thinks to himself — *I am getting old for this now* — but immediately counters his dejection — *But I still like it.*

Stretching as he gets out of bed, Dhil is still attired in his combat dress, since they need to report back to their unit in Attock and debrief his higher command before the operation can be finally concluded.

After a light breakfast of tea, toast, and butter, Dhil walks to the parade square where Dar is overseeing the loading of their men and equipment into three trucks. Dar salutes Dhil who smilingly responds.

'So, partner, where are we?' he inquires pleasantly from his second in command.

Dar replies, 'Sir, all twenty-three men have been accounted for. The six injured have been attended to, and they are on LD.[26] Sir, as per your advice, Captain Atif will be in Truck 'Charlie', Captain Zarrar will man Truck 'Bravo', and I will command Truck 'Alpha'. We will keep a separation distance of thirty metres while en-route. Loading should be complete by 0830 hrs, sir. We will await your orders.'

Dhil pats Dar on his shoulder, a smile of acknowledgment on his face. 'Dar', he begins, 'I appreciate your motivation and dedication to your job. Your assessment of the situation was correct. These buggers were using their family members as human shields. Unfortunately, the mission ended the way we had not planned, but', he added, 'had that not been the case, we could have missed out on our opportunity, had I not considered your suggestion.'

Dhil pauses for a moment—'You are a brave soldier' he continues . . . 'Keep it up!'

Dar, who had started having doubts about his equation with Dhil after yesterday's episode, smiles. His confidence level back up again, his body stiffens, and with chest out, tummy in, he gives out a proper salute to Dhil and thanks him for his appreciation. Dhil had a way with his men. He had a knack of catching the right wavelength of each of his subordinates and getting the best out of them—a trait acknowledged by his superiors who repeatedly put this to good use.

When all the men and their equipment are on board, the three huge Nissan Army Trucks, Dhil takes a final look and gets on his command vehicle—a military version of the British Land Rover Defender, locally produced in Pakistan and considered a favourite in the army. With the driver at the wheel and a guard standing out of the roof with a machine gun perched on top, they begin their three-hour journey back to Attock from this Forward Base situated in the middle of the mountains bordering Waziristan. While their route was free from Taliban control, the possibility of an ambush could never be

---

[26]   Light Duty—Military term for people who are excused from rigorous duty.

ruled out; therefore, the four-vehicle convoy maintains a high state of vigilance as it cautiously makes its way on the single-track dual carriageway snaking through the arid hills of the north-west region, up east towards the fertile plains of central Pakistan, farmlands stretching across the horizon. The day may be bright and sunny, but the atmosphere is dry and dusty.

Along the way, they pass through a few villages with roadside shops selling groceries, hardware stuff, and basic home accessories. Others are roadside restaurants offering the traditional cuisines of the region including pulses, chicken curry, beef kebabs, and wheat bread. People wearing their traditional baggy dress with a yard of cloth either wrapped around their heads or placed casually on their shoulder sit on charpoys[27] gulping down tea as they talk animatedly over biscuits, about their regular day-to-day lives. Although conscious of the fact that a hundred miles towards the western borders lurked a violent threat to their way of life and properties, they do not let this fear spoil their congenial environment and continue living their normal lives providing sustenance to their loved ones. A few of them even wave at the passing convoy showing support for the army. Dhil smiles and waves back at times. He holds great respect for these hardy and resilient people of the north-west whom he considers patriots and the first line of defence against the militants and religious extremists castling themselves along the Af-Pak border.

The journey is pleasant and free from surprises. Looking at the peaceful situation, Dhil even allows the convoy to make a stopover at a gas station near Kohat Town, where they all grab quick refreshments. Such stopovers were out of regulation, but Dhil was aware that a rebellious streak in a commander only increased the respect from his battle-hardened men. He also realised that sometimes within the norm of safety, taking action out of approved parameters generated allegiance from aggressive subordinates, who then did not consider their commander to be a 'proper chap', a term abhorred among the smart cookie fraternity in the military.

Dhil disembarks on finally reaching their unit in the Attock Military Cantonment at 1330 hrs, where their fellow comrades,

---

[27]   Locally made beds with wooden frames and base made from thick sugarcane threads tied neatly into a net.

relieved and jubilant to see all of them safe and sound, receive them all with applause and enthusiasm. They had heard about the incident beforehand and were eager to know the details from their fellow soldiers who had gone on the mission. Dhil meets his unit officers and, after exchanging pleasantries, delegates the command to the unit's 2nd OiC[28] Maj. Umar Rathore, affably called the 'mother of the unit' for his considerate nature and accommodating attitude.

Dhil gets hold of the command vehicle and drives across to the office of Brig. Haider Khan. Brig. Haider Khan is the brigade commander of commando units situated under the North-western Command.

Haider, forty-six, also a commando by profession, belonged to the frontier city of Mardan situated close to the provincial capital of Peshawar. A volunteer of the undeclared Battle of Kargil[29] in 1999, he had led his forces with such ferocity and aggression across the Line of Control in the name of hot pursuits, that he got the nickname of 'Kargil Tiger' by his fellow men. However, one of the most distressing moments in his life was when he was ordered to retreat despite holding good their position. His predicament was, as a then serving Major, to obey orders while not wanting to leave behind some Kashmiri militants who had decided to stay back and fight, preferring death to dishonour. Retreating from the occupied hills of Kargil and leaving behind diehard combatants, who preferred to be called Kashmiri Freedom Fighters, left a scar on his conscience that was hard to erase even after eleven years.

---

[28] Second officer in command of the unit.

[29] In 1999, India and Pakistan had an undeclared war in the disputed Kashmir region on the Kargil border. While, Kashmiri combatants and volunteer regular troops from Pak Army successfully occupied the peaks in Indian-controlled Kashmir overlooking the strategic Kargil Drass and Kargil-Ladakh roads, notwithstanding the Indian counter-attack, they, under US pressure, eventually had to retreat from that area back into Pakistan-controlled territory. Hundreds of combatants preferred to stay back eventually meeting their death in the wake of cut off supply lines and advancing Indian Forces — overall a victory for India and an exercise in futility for Pakistan despite the entire valour of her people.

However, the stark practicalities of life had mellowed him down over the years, and he now found peace in his family life. Married with four children, his eldest son having recently joined the prestigious Pakistan Military Academy[30] in Kakul to carry on the family tradition, Haider still respected his junior officers' courage and passion to serve. Now, however, he understood the reality, that it is not just courage and heroism that win wars, pragmatism also plays a very important part in meeting strategic goals.

Haider's room was a true reflection of a brigade commander's office. It had a large wooden desk on one side, covered by a green velvet cloth and a glass sheet. A computer was placed on the side table. There were three coloured phones for different purposes. Some files were neatly placed on the left side, seeking his attention; others that lay on the right side of the table had been attended to. His name HAIDER KHAN written in bold brass capital letters, attached to a wooden placard, was placed on the table, facing his visitors. On one side of the room was placed a leather sofa set, two singles and one three-seat unit. An old vase formerly presented to the brigade by a foreign dignitary sat atop a wooden table that was kept in the middle. On the wall behind Haider, hung a wooden board reflecting the Roll of Honour, spelling out the names, ranks along with the tenure of all officers preceding Haider. The paint on the names of his predecessors becoming fainter the older they were; his name was freshly painted at the end, with 'from' date clearly written out, but the space for 'to' date left blank. Old group photos of the brigade and unit officers adorned the left wall of the office; the sideboard accommodated different trophies and crests various units under this brigade had won over the years. After spending a set period of time here, these were then returned to their respective units. Haider looked forward to meeting Dhil for the 'debrief', and knowing Dhil, he knew what was coming and had already prepared himself for the discussion.

His phone bell rings and his personal staff officer seeks permission for Dhil to enter Haider's office. A customary ritual, which Haider affirms and gets up from his chair to greet Dhil at the door.

---

[30] Equivalent to US Army's Westpoint Military Academy or British Army's Sandhurst Military Academy.

Dhil enters the room, 'Assalam u aleikum, Sir!' He firmly salutes Haider, who walks up to Dhil, nods in response, and greets him with a warm handshake.

'Walekum Assalam, Dhilawar, and welcome back,' he gestures at Dhil to take a seat. Both men walk up to Haider's desk, Dhil takes off his beret and sits on the chair across from Haider's table while Haider settles down on his chair. Dhil's back firmly straight, his hands on his knees — he held great respect for Haider and his mannerism reflected as much.

'Congratulations for a job well done, Dhilawar,' Haider acknowledges Dhil's part in the mission. But Dhil is not comforted. If anything, he is a little surprised at the wishes knowing well that they did not fully accomplish their objective.

'Sir!' his tone reveals the query in his mind. 'But the mission did not go as planned.'

Dhil tries to clarify himself. 'Our Intel was correct, those high-value targets were there, we did take the bloody militants by surprise, the objective was in our grasp, but just when we were about to launch our primary attack to capture Maulvi Najeeb and Abu Sayyaf, the Americans destroyed them all by two missile strikes,' he pauses. 'In fact, sir,' he ends on a complaining note, 'we barely managed to save our own lives, had we gone in the mosque or even close to it, even we would be dead,' by now his voice rises with exasperation.

'But look at the bright side,' Haider tries to lighten the tension. 'You and your men are safe.' He tries to inject some humour into the situation. 'These CIA strikes are pretty accurate. See how they identified the friends from the foe and targeted only the foes before the friends would get any closer?'

But Dhil doesn't find this amusing. 'Sir, there were women and children too who died from this strike', he tries to sombre down the discussion, 'and this happened in front of my men. Such damning incidents take their toll on the fighting spirit of my soldiers. They did not sign up for this, and I'm afraid a time will come when they may crack.' Dhil attempts to put his feelings across without sounding insubordinate. He still was loyal to his organisation and getting accused of dereliction of duty was the last thing he desired.

Haider intently listens to Dhil and stops him when he feels Dhil may be implying too much. 'Lieutenant Colonel Dhilawar,' Haider's tone becomes serious, 'let there be no doubt that we are in a state of war. This is not a conventional war for which we were mentally prepared and physically trained. This is a different kind of war where the enemy is not outside but within. But in any kind of war, some things do not change and collateral damage is one of them.' He tries to calm Dhil down. 'As conscious human beings, none of us like unwarranted killings, but at times, it happens and unfortunate though it may be, we have to move on and bring our mission to its logical conclusion.'

By now Dhil is clear where this discussion is going, but before concluding, there is one thing that he needs to get off his mind so as to clear his conscience. He reacts to Haider's explanation, 'Yes, sir, I agree, but can we not stop the Americans from carrying out these drone attacks? Today's incident can be used to explain how much of a damning effect it can have on Pakistan's fight against these terrorists.'

'Well, you are free to write in your report what you feel, but it is not our job to stop them. It is the job of our government which has other priorities at present. We as professional soldiers have our own job to do, and for now, it is to rid our country of these disillusioned, misguided scum of the society, who have taken on the mantle of saving our great religion from us.' Haider pauses for a moment as his gaze wanders to the side. 'Bloody idiots,' he mutters as an after-thought.

There is another pause; this time, of a few seconds, which sends the signal to Dhil that this meeting over. He gets up and wears his beret, feeling that he has put the message across, and knowing Brigadier Haider, he is confident that it will be conveyed up the chain of command to the generals in GHQ,[31] Rawalpindi. His mood still sober but conscience clear for now, Dhil seeks permission to leave.

'Dhilawar!'

Haider has some parting words, 'When we wore this uniform, we promised to defend our motherland from any threat whatsoever, be it external or internal. And for now, that enemy is among us.' He tries to pep up Dhil. 'I've known you since you were a cadet', his voice becoming more conciliatory, 'knowing you, I'm sure you'll keep the men under your command fighting fit, ready to take on the next mission whenever it comes . . . wherever it comes,' he concludes.

---

[31]   General Head Quarter, equivalent to the Pentagon of USA

'Sir, yes, sir! There is no doubt about that,' Dhil assures Haider.

'Go home, Dhilawar, spend some time with your family,' Haider suggests. 'Take rest . . . you need to wind down.'

Dhil nods in affirmative, salutes, and leaves Haider's office. He suddenly feels tired after five days of tribulation; his body now aching with exhaustion, he decides to call it a day and find solace in the welcoming chatter of his cheerful kids and tender embrace of his beloved wife.

*   *   *

It is Thursday morning in Nevada. Sam is awakened by the radio that dutifully starts at the affixed time of 0630 hrs. Sam had felt sluggish last night and retired early. She now felt much lighter and fresher after a good night's sleep.

Lia, who had been anxiously waiting for her mistress to wake up, is delighted to see Sam. She barks with delight, tail wagging: her usual happy self.

Sam greets her with a vigorous rub on her neck, sets down Lia's breakfast, and also prepares some cereal for herself. While doing so, she reaches for the phone to call her mother, Catherine, in Jacksonville, Arkansas.

The call tone is followed by one of the sweetest voices reaching out to Sam, 'Hello, Samantha!'

Sam pauses for a moment to enjoy the soothing voice of her mother, who, upon hearing silence, inquires, 'Is that you, sweetheart?'

Sam breaks out of her trance. 'Hey, Ma! It's me, all right,' she confesses. 'How are you?'

Catherine continues in her calm and elegant tone, her voice emitting the motherly warmth Sam always longed to hear, 'I could be better if my little girl comes over and gives me a warm hug.'

On hearing this, Sam's voice cracks with emotions, her heart suddenly yearning for her mother's embrace, she responds, 'I'm coming over, Ma, it's been a long time, and I wanna see you,' she continues, 'I have four days off, and I would like to spend the time with you.'

Catherine is ecstatic. 'Well, then what's stopping you my child? Fly over by evening, and I'll have your favourite medium rare rib-eye steak with mashed potatoes and peas ready for dinner. Just the way you want it,' Catherine encourages Sam to ensure she comes over, her heart bristling with joy just at the thought of her baby coming to stay.

'Sure thing, Ma!' Sam responds excitedly. 'A Globemaster'll be leaving for Little Rock from here at noon. I'll see if I can hitch a ride on that and be with you by evening. These Air Force boys are real gentlemen,' she chuckles. Having spent time with Air Force personnel manning the Predator Drones, she was sure to get a favour from them. She is ecstatic after speaking to her mom. All the worries about her current job, overseas posting, and reassignment take a back seat while she plans to leave Lia with the neighbours, an elderly couple who dote on Lia anyway, and make her way to the Air Force Base in time to get on the Globemaster. She looks forward to spending some quality time with her mom because this could be one of her last meeting with her for a long time to come.

Chapter 2

PRELUDE TO ADVERSITY

Thursday evening, 1630 hrs in the Cantonment near Attock Town

Having returned from Brigadier Haider's office, Dhil finalised his 'mission report' and called it a day. His home was ten-minute drive on a narrow two-way road running inside the cantonment. He sat alongside his driver in the Land Rover Defender and advised him to begin the final journey of the day.

After driving for about five minutes, they entered the residential area of the cantonment; off-white-coloured army houses of the same type, meant for officers of Major to Colonel ranks, were neatly positioned next to each other in designated blocks. Separated by small boundary walls, some with thick, high bushes running alongside offered a sense of privacy. An occasional tree planted inside some gardens provided shade and enabled the occupants to hang a makeshift swing on the branches for the children to enjoy. Standardised nameplates for every officer meticulously advising their rank, name, and unit were bolted proudly on the front gate pillar of each house.

The children playing outside on the narrow streets caught Dhil's flagging attention. Fallen autumn leaves were strewn throughout his path. He enjoyed the pleasant wind blowing across the open windows of his SUV while his driver dutifully proceeded within the lower speed limit of the clean cantonment. This serene environment was a far cry from the atmosphere he was in less than twenty-four hours back. Every mile covered made him more anxious to meet his family, around whom his whole world revolved.

He remembered the day he had bid them farewell before leaving for Waziristan. Like any other mission, this one too was dangerous and the fear of never coming back alive had prevailed over the parting scene. It was about the same time in the evening six days back when he had said his goodbyes with long, loving hug to his children and an even longer affectionate hug to his wife, taking in their prayers and wishes for success and a safe return. However, that danger was over for now. Before starting for Attock, he had called his wife and allayed her fears about his safety. So now he looked forward to a delightful reception on his safe return.

In another couple of minutes, which seemed like hours to Dhil, he reaches the gate of his home where his wife Rania and children Ayesha, Taimur, and Hamza were anxiously waiting for him in the garden. Before Dhil's Defender could stop fully, his ten-year-old son Taimur dashes up to him with jubilation, shouting aloud—'Baba'.[32]

Dhil gestures to the driver to stop the SUV at the gate and allows Taimur to get up on the side rail of the vehicle to open his door. Taimur opens the door and, elated with happiness, jumps on his rugged father, giving him a big hug while Dhil is still seated inside.

'Assalam u aliekum,[33] Baba!' Taimur shouts while clinging on to Dhil.

'Wal-e-kum salam', Dhil cradles Taimur in his arms, 'how is my big son doing?' he asks, his heart gushing with emotions. Behind Taimur, waiting impatiently for her turn, is Ayesha—Dhil's twelve-year-old daughter.

'Assalam u aliekum, Abbu,'[34] she excitedly cuts in with a protest, 'it's my turn now!'

Dhil smiles and gets down from the Defender, Taimur still clinging on to him.

'Wal-e-kum salam, my princess,' he lovingly responds to his daughter and puts Taimur down to give a daddy's hug to his daughter. 'And how is my big bubbles doing?' he jokingly asks, referring to her chubby figure while placing a kiss on her forehead before realising that his little four-year-old monster is already embracing his leg, trying hard to get his big daddy's attention. On

---

[32] An affectionate term for father in Urdu

[33] Islamic way of greeting each other. While 'Assalam u aliekum' means 'Peace be with you', the response 'walekum assalam' means 'and peace be with you too'.

[34] Daddy.

seeing this, Dhil lets out a guffaw, 'Ah, here is my little devil,' he smiles as he picks up little Hamza and tosses him in the air only to catch him in his firm grasp—an action loved by Hamza. He then gives Hamza a warm hug and showers him with kisses on his plump cheeks, his bushy moustache tickling Hamza. Intently watching this emotional welcome scene, as always, is Rania, Dhil's beloved wife, and pillar of his emotional strength, his confidant, his friend, and the love of his life. Dhil, while carrying Hamza, walks up to Rania and gives her a warm loving hug. Rania responds by nestling into the tall broad chest of Dhil, weeping with happiness; a sense of calm and satisfaction engulfs her mind on seeing her husband safe and sound back into the warmth of her company. Each moment spent without her husband when he is out on a mission seemed like the darkest moment of her life, full of anxiety and uncertainty, but keeping her strong are her prayers for the only man she ever loved.

Dhil places a slight kiss on Rania's forehead, more romantic emotions prudently kept for the privacy of the room. Then, with Hamza still snuggled under his right side, he wraps his left arm around Rania while they slowly make their way into their house, with Ayesha and Taimur cheerfully jumping in the background, eagerly asking their 'hero' Dad to tell them the whole story.

How good it feels to be home—Dhil thinks, relieved to be back among his loved ones while having a slight pang of remorse on remembering similar families he left to die back in Waziristan.

*   *   *

It was Thursday night in Jacksonville. Sam had made it in time to catch the Globemaster flying to Little Rock Air Force Base. She and her mother Catherine enjoyed a sumptuous home-cooked dinner of steaks, mashed potatoes, and boiled peas topped off with red wine—just as Sam liked it. They finally settled down comfortably on the cushions, in front of the fire in the living room talking about old times. The room was dimly lit from the fire and two table lamps placed on side tables. A set of couches was meticulously positioned around the room with a couple of floor cushions casually placed on one side of the fireplace. Family photos adorned the top of the fireplace, and sketches of the four seasons of Arkansas hung on one side of the room draped with brown, beige, and golden wallpaper. The curtains covering the glass doors were drawn back giving the view of the back garden, dimly lit with garden lights that, for Sam, added additional allure to the cosy surroundings. She enjoyed this homely environment. All the while, Catherine talked about the time when as children, Sam and Alex would wear some part of their dad's uniform and play battle zone. How Alex would end up making his kid sister a 'Charlie',[35] he would then become GI Joe. Sam would come to Catherine crying most of the time since she would be the one getting killed by Alex in the game.

A tear trickles out of the corner of Catherine's eye while she reminisces about the sweet memories of David and Alex. She makes Sam realise that, with three full glasses of wine already in her mother's system, she is drowning in the abyss of emotions. Sam makes an attempt to pull Catherine out of it by changing the topic. She knows that by crying over lost relations, her mother's health will only deteriorate, and this was not acceptable to Sam.

'Mom! I've some news for you,' she interrupts. There is a moment of silence as Catherine tries to shake off the wine-induced haze and returns to the present.

'Well, sweetheart,' Catherine slowly recovers some of her composure, 'are you seeing someone?' is the first reaction that comes to the mind of a mother that wants to see her daughter married.

'No, Ma!' comes the agitated response of a daughter sick of being asked by her mother to settle down. 'It has to do with my career.'

'Yes, of course, Sam, how could I have missed that?' replies Catherine, sounding less interested in Sam's career progression. She was always against Sam joining the CIA, citing danger and insecurity as the biggest demerits of the job. Catherine was of the view that a woman's first priority should be to have a family with husband and kids. *Concentrate on raising a good family and leave the perilous jobs for the men folk.*

There is silence in the room. Sam expects Catherine to ask her the dreaded question. Catherine feigns disinterest in Sam's career.

'Well . . . don't you wanna know?' Sam finally blurts out.

'If you insist,' quips Catherine, still desperately trying to act indifferent while getting more curious with time. Sam, for her part is

---

[35]   US term for a Vietcong guerilla fighter.

familiar with these tactics and decides to play along. 'Well, it ain't that important, Ma,' she shrugs, 'if you don't wanna know, it's all right.'

Catherine's imagination is now going haywire. 'Okay, Sam! Come out with it,' she finally gives in. 'You are not doing anything dangerous, are you? I never liked you joining the Agency, you know,' Catherine echoes for the 100th time. 'They make you do dangerous things over there . . . all in the name of service to your country,' she continues raising the histrionics. 'Your father would have never approved', she pauses for a moment before concluding, 'his little Cherry-pie putting her life in harm's way.'

Sam is glad to at least get her mother out of her earlier glum mood. She seldom minded when her mom criticised her joining the CIA because intuitively she knew that Catherine's protests were never very serious. She moves over to her mother and wraps her arms around her from the back, giving a slight kiss on her wrinkled cheek; Catherine still acts a little displeased at her girl's choice of career.

'Ma! You know I love you,' Sam confesses trying to appease her mother. Catherine, bitter after losing her family members prematurely and trying to preserve the only family she has left, is not yet ready to give up—'Yeah and that's why you don't care about how I feel.'

Sam feels that this sweet talk is going nowhere and decides to come to the point. She gathers the courage to face her mother and begins, 'Ma, I might be getting my first posting overseas,' unable to break the news in one go.

Catherine, surprised to hear this statement, pulls herself together. 'And where would that be?' She asks, trying to maintain a brave facade.

'Well, I don't know yet', replies Sam, still trying to break it to her mother in bits and pieces, 'but it could be either Afghanistan or . . . ,' she pauses before blurting out, '. . . Pakistan.'

An uneasy silence falls in the room, with only the noise of crackling wood in the fireplace.

Catherine is dumbfounded. She doesn't know how to react. This is probably the last thing she wanted to hear. As it is, she never approved of Sam taking up this profession, and the idea of her last surviving family member headed into harm's way was too much to bear.

But Catherine is careful about how she reacts. In her tipsy state, she just wanted to get up, start crying and shouting or protesting, passionately entreating Sam to leave her job and come back to her to be within the safe confines of her hometown where she could finally settle down and have kids. But the situation was serious now and the posting for real. In a situation like this, Catherine, despite her divergent views, had the challenge of maintaining a caring attitude towards her daughter who, while cherishing different aspirations, had come to her mother to seek emotional support and encouragement.

God! Catherine thinks to herself in exasperation. *This is too much hypocrisy for me to bear. How will I do it?*

Unable to come to terms with this news, and fearful of reacting honestly, she gets up from her cushion, places a kiss on Sam's sweaty forehead, and says, 'It's getting late now. You must be tired from your day's travel.' She tries to conclude before her emotions get out of control. 'It's so good to have you here with me, my child. We'll go around town tomorrow, and you can meet your uncle too, he was asking about you . . . Goodnight, sweetheart.' With these parting words, she slowly trudges out of the room, suddenly feeling a hundred years older and climbs up the wooden stairs—each step making a creaking noise somehow relaying to Sam the distress her mother felt.

Sam is left all alone in the room. She knows perfectly well how her mother is trying to hide her real feelings. *Yes, that's my mom, all right, a citadel of support,* she admits to herself, *always there when you need her but never imposing herself on you in reality.*

Sam's mind goes in a state of flux as all this is too much for her to handle. She whispers 'Good night' to her mother who by then has already exited the room. She picks herself up and goes to her own room, tired and confused about how to resolve the matter in the next three days.

*   *   *

It is Thursday evening in Attock Cantonment. Dhil has finished his dinner in the soothing company of his family. Rania is busy advising the servant on some chores in the kitchen, while Dhil enjoys the animated stories of the past week from Taimur and Ayesha, while little Hamza sits in his big daddy's lap busily playing with his 'Iron Man' action figure; feeling protected in his dad's scent, he is completely oblivious to the excited narrative spilling out of his brother and sister. Taimur is proudly telling his dad how he saved Ayesha from falling off a galloping horse two days back.

'. . . And, Baba,' Taimur continues excitedly, 'on seeing this, I raced Hector up to Baji's[36] Blue-ray, who was galloping out of control. Baji was screaming for help!'

At this Ayesha interrupts, 'I wasn't screaming for help,' she contradicts vehemently. 'I was just wondering aloud that Blue-ray wasn't stopping.'

Taimur, not to give in easily, insists, 'Come on, Baji, you were shouting, and you were hysterical 'cause Blue-ray wasn't in your control.' Both argue their stance.

Both Taimur and Ayesha had been riding army horses at various army cantonments Dhil was posted to, since they were in kindergarten. Taimur, over the years, had become an expert rider and had won some local show jumping competitions in the children's category. He was also quite famous among the children for his riding skills, a fact grudgingly accepted by Ayesha. Because of the sibling rivalry, the last incident seemed as embarrassing to Ayesha as it seemed fulfilling to Taimur.

Dhil, enjoying every moment of this harmless squabble, now feels the need to end this deadlock.

'Okay, Ayesha was in control, but she was testing her little brother's courage and love for her,' he tries to create a diversion, 'Wasn't that the case, dear?' He winks at Ayesha.

Ayesha, who was looking for a way out of this impasse, takes the cue from her daddy. 'Yes, of course,' she quickly agrees with a mischievous smile. 'And I have to say that Taimur made me proud.' She feels this is the best way of saving face, by giving her brother his due for actually saving her from a nasty situation, but not overtly agreeing to Taimur's version of events.

However, Taimur wants to tell the story till the end since the best part is yet to come. 'So, Baba, I reached up to Baji, Hector and Blue-ray galloping side by side. I held Hector's reins in my left hand and got hold of Blue-ray's rein in my right hand', he continues proudly, 'and then I pulled at both of them with all my strength till both the horses

---

[36] Baji—respectfully used for elder sisters in Urdu language instead of taking their names.

stopped.' He concludes, 'It's good that Baji held on . . . she's good at that at least,' returning her sister's compliments.

Ayesha, being the elder sister, has to have the last say, 'But had you not stopped Blue-ray, I would have had to do it all by myself,' ending the debate.

Dhil, who had been listening to the last part intently, encourages his children. 'Well, then, Son, that was very brave of you.' He refers to Taimur who, while knowing what is going on, is just happy with the accolade he is getting at the moment. He is also happy that the showdown is over, with him now viewed as the hero of the story. 'I'm also proud of you, Bubbles, for not losing your cool and holding on to Blue-ray,' continues Dad, this time referring to Ayesha so as to balance out the equation between the two of them.

Dhil looks at Taimur and compliments, 'I know my family is in safe hands when I'm not around.' Taimur's body pumps up with pride on hearing this from his 'ideal'.

'What about me, Daddy?' protests Ayesha. Dhil gives out a laugh, and before he could put in his words of encouragement for her, Rania, who has just joined the party, takes the lead. 'Sweetheart, when I'm not around, you are the manager of the house, the senior person, whereas Taimur is the guard with the rusty gun, standing outside,' she consoles. At this, they all let out a hearty laughter, while Taimur jokingly objects. Although he would much rather be a guard than a manager, since the guard has the gun, and he gets to fight off the bad guys.

Hamza, who had been busy so far in his own world, suddenly looks up on hearing all the laughter and declares proudly in his sweet husky voice, 'And I'm Iron Man!' as he holds up the Iron Man figure in the air. At this, the whole room erupts in a cheer of laughter reflecting the carefree and jovial atmosphere of Dhil's home, contrary to what he has to encounter in his job from time to time.

'Okay, kids, time to hit the bed. It's already late . . . It's school tomorrow,' Rania announces like a warden, clapping her hands in the process to enforce her command. The kids hurriedly get up and kiss their daddy goodnight before going off to their rooms, Taimur and Ayesha still arguing over the details of that incident.

Dhil enjoyed every moment of this time spent with his family. As they leave for bed, there are a few minutes of isolation in the living room when Dhil regresses from the jovial high he just experienced, back to the battleground in Waziristan almost twenty-four hours earlier. The images of similar children sent to their deaths bombard his mind. He shakes his head to get rid of the gory thoughts circulating within. But he can't seem to make them leave. Feeling suffocated, he gets up and walks outside to catch some fresh air, taking deep breaths in the process.

Damn it! he curses himself, *What's wrong with me? I wasn't like this . . . What's happening to me?* While still looking at the grass and pressing his sweaty forehead with his hand, he tries to shake off the sorry feeling and act strong. He is struggling with his emotions when he hears the sweetest voice his subconscious mind had been longing to hear.

'Dhilawar,' Rania softly calls out to him. 'Dhilawar . . . what happened?' she inquires delicately. Dhil, who had been waiting for this moment since reaching home, turns around and hugs his wife intently, feeling the energy transmitted from her warm body to his, a feeling of comfort, security, and ease transcending his turbulent emotions. 'My Rania,' he sighs contentedly, 'how good it feels to be back with you! You make me forget my uncertainties,' he confesses.

Rania, seeing her husband's emotional state, hugs him gently and pats him on his back. 'My dear,' she responds, 'I also miss you a lot when you are not around,' mirroring the feelings exuded by Dhil. 'I have full faith in you and what you are doing,' she adopts a consoling tone aware of what Dhil is about to share with her. 'Rest assured you are doing the right thing. It's getting chilly out here', she breaks off abruptly, 'why don't we go inside and talk,' she suggests, conscious of the prying eyes possibly lurking in the surroundings, enjoying this intimate scene. Dhil, now out of his trance, consents as they slowly walk inside the house.

Now in the privacy of their room, Rania has changed into her nightgown; she comes up to Dhil who is sitting on the side of their bed, gaze focused at their family photo hanging on the wall across the room. She sits beside him, puts her arm around him, gives him a slight kiss on his cheek to get his attention, and speaks softly, 'Anything on your mind?'

Dhil looks at her, gives out a faint smile, and lies down on the bed, emotions back under control and feeling relaxed in the warm company of his beloved wife who cuddles next to him on the bed. 'When I joined the army back in the eighties, things were very clear to me,' he muses. 'We had only one enemy, and it was my desire to defeat that enemy and conquer Kashmir from them.' His reference is obviously to India.

'When I took the Sword',[37] he continues referring to his first position in his course on graduation, 'I could have opted for Armoured Corp, Artillery, Air Defence, or any other branch but I opted for Infantry, and if that wasn't enough for me, I joined SSG[38] – do you know why?' he asks his wife.

Rania knows the answer but being the considerate listener that she is, lets Dhil get it all out. 'I wanted to fight the Indians, I wanted to set my foot in Srinagar, and I wanted to raise the flag of Pakistan in the whole of Kashmir. I take pride in saying that I fought them in Siachin, I fought them off LOC,[39] I bloody well fought them off whenever I got the chance, and you know who would be beside us?' He doesn't want to stop. Angry at the situation he finds himself in, he springs out of the bed. Rania stays silent but looks at him with inquiring eyes.

'These very same militants we call terrorists,' he answers his own question.

'Back then, they were our comrades, partners in our cause . . . our assets', he continues viciously, 'and today they are terrorists?' he pauses '. . . enemies?'

'How can I justify to myself what I'm doing?' he asks Rania, 'how can I face myself in the mirror?' confusion written all over his face. 'And last night I helplessly witnessed . . . women and children getting blown to smithereens, for what?'

He pauses, and this time waving his clenched fist in the air, he shouts, 'For bloody what?' He thinks for a while. 'Nothing is clear any more', and then concludes in a calmer tone, 'I didn't sign up for this.'

Rania had been through such situations before. Dhil had been sharing his feelings about his missions, his skirmishes with militants,

---

[37] 'Sword of Honor' is given to the overall best cadet in a batch on Graduation Day.

[38] Special Services Group (SSG) are the commandos of Pakistan Army equivalent to Rangers or Delta Force of US Army.

[39] Line of Control is the working boundary dividing the State of Jammu & Kashmir between Pakistan and Indian-administered areas.

and even his tactical successes in his fight against terrorists. But so far, the missions involved search and destroy militants' camps, raid their depots and shelters, or fend off their offensive. The fights would be between combatants only, and Dhil would find enough moral justification to come out victorious in his missions. Although cognizant of such a possibility, it was the first time that he had to command a mission that ended with undesired results, an incident too taxing for Dhil to bear.

Rania knows that countering him at this moment would only aggravate the whole situation. But she also knows that letting him go down this path would eventually lead to his self-destruction, a fate Dhil did not deserve. She quietly walks up to Dhil caresses him and speaks softly, 'Darling, for now we can only pray for the souls of the innocent dead. As Muslims, it is our faith, that time and date of death for everyone is written, which we cannot change.' She tries to comfort Dhil, 'There's nothing you could've done for those poor people.' Then so as not to end on a defeatist note, she asserts, 'But it is also our belief that in this war, the innocent dead are martyrs, and I'm sure they must be in a much better place now,' referring to heaven. He looks back and inquires, 'Thanks for your naive efforts, jani,[40] but should we be doing what we are doing?' referring to the Pakistan Army's war against militants. Rania is convinced that her husband needs to be reassured that he is doing the right thing because any discouragement from her side would only make his life miserable.

'My darling, you have never been wrong. Please be assured of that,' she responds to his query. 'You have always wanted to defend your country from our enemies. With time, enemies change. Those who were your foes yesterday could become your friends today and your friends of yesterday could turn foe today.' In the end, she pleads, 'Please take life as it comes and don't think too much about things you have no control on. You will only turn yourself into a mental wreck.' She then tries to cheer him up, 'Leuitenent Col. Dhilawar Jahangiri, Tamgha Bisalat,[41] has always been my hero, my knight in shining armour . . . and married to you, I feel I'm the luckiest wife on

---

[40] Urdu term for 'my beloved'.
[41] Bravery medal in Pakistan Military.

earth,' with these words she wraps her arms around Dhil's chest and snuggles again into him, content to have him safely by her side.

Not entirely convinced but appreciative of his wife's seemingly earnest efforts to soothe him, he hugs her back. The warmth of her body calming his intense mood, he plants an affectionate kiss on his wife's tender lips. 'My Rania,' he speaks softly, 'Rani[42] of my heart,' he continues, 'where would I be without you?' continuing to hug her, 'you give me all the comfort I need,' he cajoles, 'don't ever leave me . . . okay?' he gives a soft command, 'without you, I'll lose my bearings,' justifying his demand.

Rania, who is happy to calm her husband down, responds lovingly knowing that a light-hearted conversation would eventually bring Dhil out of the morass, 'Colonel Sahib,'[43] she replies wittingly, 'don't worry, I'm not going anywhere as long as I'm alive,' giving out a jovial-hearted warning.

Dhil doesn't like the talk of life and death and responds softly, 'You will live, my love . . . more than me', he continues, 'you'll live even after I'm long gone and see the children of our children's children grow up.'

Rania, upon seeing that Dhil is now relaxed, lets off a giggle, 'Darling, that's a bit too long, let's just pray that God gives us all a healthy, safe, prosperous life, free of any tragedy and that we may see the happiness of our kids together.' She lies down back on the bed.

This seems to be a good compromise for Dhil who is in no mood for talking but just wants to love his adorable wife for the rest of the night. He smiles at her while settling himself down next to her on the bed, kissing her again, and feeling much more relaxed, he switches off the table lamp and finally calls it a night.

* * *

It was a Friday evening in the dry rugged mountains of Paktika Province, Afghanistan. Baaz's Alqaeda captors, who eyed him with suspicion, had brought him just across the border from Waziristan

---

[42] Queen.
[43] Sahib's close equivalent in English is 'mister'. Between spouses, this term is often used to air their witty respect.

to the mountains in Afghanistan. Badly beaten up and tortured by his interrogators to accept their accusation of his collusion with the enemy; he now lay in a semi-conscious state in a cell made deep inside the caves of rocky mountains spreading across the horizon. A perfect hideout for Alqaeda operators, far out of ISAF's[44] reach where the writ of Kabul Central Government was not established.

Despite all the beating, Baaz had not succumbed to his captor's demands. In this state, he hears footsteps coming towards him and people talking in Arabic. Hungry, tired, and badly bruised, Baaz is also angry at the state he is in. He does not blame his captors for his situation. He feels that they are justified in suspecting him of treachery. After all, he was the only important person who survived Wednesday's attack and that also in suspicious circumstances. His anger is targeted towards Pakistan and especially the Army. *These bloody traitors!* He thinks, *Stooges of America! It's all because of them that I'm in this mess. If only they had not joined forces with hegemonic America, we would have driven these pigs out of our country!* He laments, thinking of America as the occupation force in Afghanistan; but for now his prime concern is to get out of this quagmire.

He is still lying down on the damp ground smelling of cow dung when the steel door opens with a long creaking noise and in walk the two burly Arabs who had gotten hold of him in Waziristan. The first one comes and kicks Baaz in the abdomen, 'Ya Hammar!'[45] He yells. Baaz lets out a groan since each part of his body hurts from the beating he received earlier. He feels lucky not to have apparently broken any bones. The other warrior holds him by his neck and drags him out of his cell. Baaz, unable to get back up on his feet, tries to release the hold on his neck, but is too weak to free himself. He feels humiliated. As Mullah Baaz, he had enjoyed respect, loyalty, and stature among his Afghan comrades. He had bravely fought many a pitched battles with US Forces, ISAF, and even the Pak Army over the years to establish his credentials as a gallant warrior and a patriotic son of soil. It was this stature that had finally secured him the position of chief security officer to Maulvi Najeeb with his name in line for

---

[44] ISAF stands for International Security Assistance Force comprising of mostly troops from NATO and English-speaking countries.

[45] Ya Hammar — O donkey in Arabic.

leadership of the Lashkar al-Mujahideen. He feels he did not deserve the treatment being meted out to him.

With frustration, anger, and a sense of helplessness, he is dragged by both captors, all the way down a 15-metre long, narrow, dark tunnel to a hall inside another cave. Senior and important personalities of Alqaeda, the Afghan Taliban, and Pakistan Taliban are gathered. They all constituted the United Shoora for Liberation of Afghanistan.[46] While Maulvi Najeeb's Lashkar al-Mujahideen was not a key member of this council, Baaz was to face trial on the case of aiding and abetting the occupation forces in eliminating Abu Sayyaf and Al Marri, who belonged to Alqaeda.

The hall, carved within a cave, was large enough to accommodate three dozen people. It was dimly lit with kerosene lamps hung across the walls on all four sides. There were some ventilation ducts, but the odours of sweat, damp socks, and 'ittar'[47] still made a strange mix adding gloom to the proceedings. On one side of the room, with their backs to the wall, sat the three representatives of the major members, next to each other. They represented the decision making body of judges. On their left side, facing them, was a small cage into which Baaz was dragged and locked up. His two burly captors stood on each side of the cage.

Baaz had never felt more humiliated in his life than he feels today when he is shoved inside the cage like a dog. A bottle of water is duly thrown inside to help him clear his vocal chords.

Across the cage, on the other side of the room to the right of the judges, sat the witnesses, who had been called upon to testify. The 'waqeel', that is, prosecutor, sat across from the judges facing them; behind him could be housed about two-dozen attendants. The defendant had the right to either defend himself or appoint a waqeel who then would sit next to him outside the cage.

Today, there are about twenty people in the room. Baaz has not been given a chance to seek a lawyer for himself. He has to defend

---

[46]   United Council for Liberation of Afghanistan—a loosely knit assortment of various organisations fighting off ISAF occupation.

[47]   Ittar—is non-alcoholic perfumes preferred by devout Muslims over alcoholic perfumes.

his name and integrity, and he is ready to do this despite being in a weakened state.

The judge, belonging to Alqaeda, calls his name, 'Mullah Baaz Jan—son of Hakimullah Jan, resident of village Kudakhel, Khost.' He continues with the accusation, 'You have been charged with treason by aiding and abetting the enemy in coordinating a missile strike killing Mullah Abu Sayyaf, regional chief of Alqaeda, Sheikh Fahad Al Marri, senior member of Alqaeda, Maulvi Najeeb Mohammad, chief of Lashkar al-Mujahideen, and Maulana Abdul Ghafoor, the chief cleric of Lashkar al-Mujahideen. Not to forget the thirty-six other warriors who lost their lives in this event too,' he concludes and then asks. 'Do you admit your guilt on this charge?'

Baaz, half dazed from the beatings and hunger, is unable to pull his thoughts together. He gulps down the whole bottle of water to quench his thirst. Clearing his throat, he gathers all his strength to sit straight and speak aloud.

'No, sir!' he tries to plead, 'I swear by the name of Allah, I am not guilty.'

Not to give in easily, the Alqaeda judge refers the question to the prosecutor who by now is itching to fire a salvo of accusations towards Baaz. Belonging to Alqaeda and being close to Mullah Abu Sayyaf, the prosecutor is convinced that Baaz had a part in this tragedy.

'Ya Saeedi,'[48] he begins, 'the defendant is lying,' and continues with his logic, 'the defendant was the chief security officer of Maulvi Najeeb Mohammad, chief of LaM. He should have been, if not inside, then at least in close proximity of the mosque. Then why is it that moments before the joint attack of the infidel enemy from both sides, this coward left the place for safe cover?' he inquires and continues, 'All but this man, his driver, and his gunner died in that attack . . . Should we call this coincidence or collusion with the enemy?' By this time murmurs start among the audience, all discussing this logic and accusing Baaz of treason since circumstantial evidence pointed in his direction.

When the prosecutor rests his case, the second judge, belonging to the Pakistani Taliban group, observes, 'You yourself are answering

---

[48] 'Ya Saeedi' translated into English means sir.

your own question.' There is silence in the hall at this remark since for most people this seemed an open and shut case with Baaz guilty as charged.

'Either the defendant survived through a miracle, or he actually aided the attack . . . there are two possibilities. What proof do you have that he actually aided the infidels?' The judge queries the prosecutor.

The Alqaeda prosecutor is visibly perturbed at this question. Alqaeda enjoyed a privileged status among the local Pashtun populace. By virtue of their Arab lineage and access to vast financial resources to aid the local Pashtun clans, their words were seldom ever challenged in this region. Moreover, being Muslims directly from the land of the Prophet,[49] they had, in a way, subdued the local populace who did not even question their state of affairs attributing it to blasphemy against religion. They were instilled with the duty of serving their foreign guests in their cause, whatever the outcome may be.

In such circumstances, when an Alqaeda prosecutor is challenged by a Pakistani Taliban, who ranked third in the hierarchy of Mujahideen in the region, he loses his cool. 'Ya Qazi!'[50] he shouts, 'All the circumstantial evidence is pointing in the direction of this wretched traitor,' he points at Baaz. 'Are you telling me that my reading of the situation is wrong?'

The judge, who had put across this question, does not like the attitude of the prosecutor. 'Abu Waleed!' he growls at the prosecutor. 'The defendant deserves a fair trial, and you need to provide us with concrete proof of his involvement, not some hunch.'

The deadlock between a powerful prosecutor and a third-tier judge creates an atmosphere of unease in the room. The murmurs start again. The burly Alqaeda bodyguards begin staring down the Pakistani judge craving for his blood; their blood-soaked eyes relaying the message. They also do not like the idea of their revered prosecutor being challenged by a judge, whose people lived on the money thrown by the mighty Alqaeda.

The judge is unfazed. An elderly figure, he remains adamant at his stand. The Afghan judge, looking at the stalemate, intervenes.

---

[49]   Prophet Mohammad (peace be upon him).

[50]   Qazi translates to judge in Arabic and Urdu.

He refers to Baaz who is glad to see some support coming from somewhere, 'Mullah Baaz Jan, are you in a position to speak for yourself or do you need time for a lawyer?'

Baaz was a tough nut, and he had used this time to collect his senses. He attempts to speak, still trying to gather the remnants of his strength.

'Your honour, I am innocent.' He starts his defence. 'I am Mullah Baaz Jan, son of Hakimullah Jan. People who know me know of my feats of valour against the Americans, the ISAF, and the Pakistan Army. I made my way up the respect ladder not from anyone's favour but on my own merit. In my fight for liberation, I've been injured many a times.' Referring to his eye, he says, 'For God sake, I even lost one of my eyes from an American shell. Half of my face is distorted from the hit.' He inquires of the judges, 'You think I'll side with the people who gave me this!?' He removes his torn eye patch and pulls his scruffy hair back, pointing at the black hole which was once his eye, showing off his disfigured features. On seeing his face, a unanimous sigh of disgust escapes the majority of people present. The room breaks into another pandemonium, people now taking sides with the two parties.

'Silence!' roars the Afghan controller, who thus far had been sitting silent behind the prosecutor, enjoying the discussion. There is a hush in the room when the judge belonging to Alqaeda directs a question at Baaz, 'All that you have said is fine, but what proof do you have that you did not aid the enemy? Remember,' he continues, 'in our court, you are guilty until proven innocent.'

What can he say here—Baaz thinks hard, trying to remember any incident, any clue, that could substantiate his claim of innocence and then it strikes him like a bolt of lightning. He remembers telling his subordinate twice to go inside and ask the party to disperse since it was well beyond the scheduled time. But that subordinate was dead. That brings him back to square one. He is in deep thought when a loud voice breaks his concentration.

'Mullah Baaz!' shouts the judge representing Afghan Taliban. Not wanting to be left out, he issues a stern warning—'We haven't got all day!' This judge is aware of the position the other two compatriots have taken. While the Alqaeda judge was inclined towards the prosecutor, the Pakistani judge asked for concrete evidence. In a split vote, eventually it would be his vote that will decide the fate of Baaz.

An elderly figure, he had once known Baaz's father. Being younger to him, he had fought some battles alongside Hakimullah Jan against the Soviet occupation in the 1980s. Although he had heard about Baaz, this was the first time that he saw him in person. Seeing Hakimullah's son in the cage hurt him dearly. But the law had to take its course.

Baaz thinks again and remembers something. He exclaims, 'The second time when I asked my subordinate to call the respectful leaders out, I was in my truck with my driver and gunner', he defends himself, 'I was to take the lead in the convoy, and I had told my subordinate to plead with the leaders to leave since we were already late.' 'I didn't abandon them, in fact,' he continues, 'I actually went ahead to clear the way, and I didn't want them to stay, I wanted them to leave as soon as possible.'

There is a hush in the room; the prosecutor, not one to give up easily, airily dismisses this statement with a contemptuous wave of his hand. 'Ya Saeedi,' he asks, 'who can validate his claim?' And before the judge could relate the question to Baaz as per protocol, Baaz quickly responds, 'Please bring my driver and gunner, they will testify for me.' Again there is a murmur in the hall while the three judges discuss among themselves to figure out what to do.

'Silence!' roars the controller again, and the Afghan judge asks the prosecutor, 'Where have you kept his gunner and driver?' since it was Alqaeda members who had arrested all three. At this, the prosecutor looks at the bodyguards, who exchange uncomfortable looks. They murmur something among themselves, not happy with how the case has proceeded. With the clout their organisation enjoyed in the region, the verdict against Baaz was never in doubt. But seeing the tables turned, they appeared perturbed.

One of them walks up to the prosecutor and whispers something in his ear. The prosecutor gives him a disturbed look and, feeling deflated, addresses the judges. 'Ya Saeedi, the gunner and the driver tried to escape and were killed in the process.' With this he bows his head in embarrassment.

Baaz, on hearing this, lets out a shriek, 'No . . . ! Barbarians!' he yells at his captors, gaining strength from the anger flowing in his body. 'How could you do this!' he pleads in disdain, his chances of freedom dwindling in front of his eyes, he collapses again on the floor, exhausted and frustrated over how to prove his innocence against overwhelming odds.

This news clearly disturbs the judges too, who begin debating the fate of this case. After careful evaluation, the Afghan judge, who by now had taken the position of an arbitrator between his other two colleagues, addresses the gathering, 'The prosecutor's claim is based on circumstantial evidence, whereas the witnesses who could testify in favour of the defendant are also no more, may their souls rest in Jannah.'[51] He continues, 'This has put us in a very peculiar situation whereby justice should prevail but undue sentencing is also against the teachings of our great religion.' He pauses for a moment before concluding his address, 'In view of the situation at hand, the Shoora[52] would need more time to come to a decision.' The hall again starts buzzing with people talking out loud, at which the judge ends with these closing remarks, 'Judgment will be given after noon prayers on this coming Monday,' thereby giving two days for them to come to a decision. 'Court is adjourned for now,' he concludes.

Baaz is left wondering about his fate. His ticket to freedom in jeopardy, he has no one to prove his innocence. He looks up to God and pleads, *Oh God! Please save me, you know my feelings.* He goes on—*I didn't do anything to deserve this.* With these thoughts, he is taken back to his cell. This time, he is allowed to walk rather than being dragged, but his fate still hangs in the balance.

*   *   *

It is Friday evening in Jacksonville. Catherine's cousin, Mike Forester, who lived with his family in the main house that Catherine rented to them, has invited both Sam and Catherine for dinner. They feast on roasted turkey, boiled vegetables, and an assortment of different breads, a cuisine Angie considered to be her specialty, and indeed was a favourite all around. Wine is also there to complement their food. Catherine and Sam spent the day in Jacksonville, shopping, meeting Catherine's old friends over a cup of coffee in the local market, and simply spending time together. They did not talk about the looming possibility of Sam's posting for their own reasons. While Catherine just didn't want to talk about it, hoping against hope that

---

[51]   Heaven.
[52]   Council.

if she ignores this topic, it would perhaps go away; Sam, simply felt uncomfortable at the thought of bringing up a subject that might mean revisiting the same tense conversation from the night before. She did not want to upset her mother again unless Catherine herself initiated the discussion by giving her blessings to Sam, as she always eventually had done in the past.

After dinner, Mike's two teenage children help out Sam and Angie with the dishes. They are eager now to break loose and join their friends for late-night fun at the local bowling club followed by a trip to the discotheque — a favourite haunt for youngsters their age. Sam, Catherine, Mike, and Angie settle down with glasses of champagne for some post-dinner chitchat in the warmth of each other's company.

Mike, being the kid cousin of Catherine, was always affectionate towards Catherine's family. Bald, with grey-brown hair barely visible around his scalp, Mike had a lean physique coupled with a thin pointed nose complementing his thin eyebrows and small-buttoned eyes. He knew Alex and Sam from the time they were born and had his own fond memories of their childhood.

'You know,' Mike looks at Sam, 'I'm very impressed with what my niece does,' he announces proudly sharing his feelings with the innocent-looking blonde wife Angie, who sits next to him in their living room with a glass of champagne in her hand. 'So, how long have you been terminating those roaches for us now?' the question is directed at Sam.

'Well, it's been about three years,' replies Sam, thinking with mixed feelings about all those drone missions she participated in till now.

'You know, I'm really proud of you for making America a safer place to live,' Mike continues with his accolade, 'in fact, we are really proud of all our fellow Americans who've put their lives in danger to let us feel safe at home.' Mike had spent his life in Arkansas — and most of his time in Jacksonville. His views about world affairs were courtesy of the local news networks.

'But tell me one thing, dear,' asks Angie, who so far had kept silent, earnestly listening to her husband's patriotic outburst of emotions, 'when you are out there doing your stuff and . . . ', she pauses, 'and a situation comes when you are not sure of your target, do you still carry on with it?' Angie's views were different from those of her husband. A 'flower child', she had childhood memories of her parents protesting against the Vietnam War in Washington and New York.

Sam prefers to remain silent—a slight smile playing on her face. Knowing Angie's aversion to violence, she knew where this question came from. Mike, looking at this uneasy silence, decides to respond. 'Surely, you look at the odds?' he persists, to which Sam simply nods in the affirmative, clearly unwilling to comment on such a sensitive question.

To avoid discouraging his favourite niece, Mike declares, 'Well, we surely wish you all the best and let me tell you, Sam,' he pauses before starting again, his voice rising with emotions, 'you make me proud! You make us all proud.' And not wanting to leave it there, he shouts with emotions, 'By George, you make the whole of Jacksonville proud.' He raises his hand holding the glass of champagne, 'Let me make a toast here,' he says. All raise their glasses to support Mike, who by now is on a high, 'Here is to our beloved Samantha, for your success . . . Cheers!' He gulps down the drink in his glass in one go.

Catherine, who, so far, was just going with the flow, her mind preoccupied with Sam's posting, can't take this fervour any more. She goes for another toast, putting her glass up, looking at Sam with an anguished expression, 'Another toast for GI Jane of Jacksonville, who's going half way across the world to fight those terrorists herself.' Angie, thinking of it to be a joke, lets out a laugh, which quickly dies down on seeing Sam's ice-cold expression at her mother's remark. Meanwhile, Mike, confusion evident on his face in trying to decide whether or not to treat it as a joke, is unable to ascertain his reaction to Catherine's statement.

Catherine was tired of acting the supporting role throughout her life. She now wanted everyone else to know what she actually felt about Sam's job. She sticks to her stance.

There is a moment of silence. Angie feels sympathetic towards Sam and tries to ease the situation, 'Well, is it so?' she asks Sam, who nods softly. To lighten the situation, Angie responds, 'Well, that's . . . kinda good, isn't it?' She looks helplessly at Mike, who is still stunned from the obvious cold vibe between mother and daughter.

Mike, taking the cue from his wife, comes back to life. 'Yeah, that's aaaaa . . . good, isn't it?' He asks Sam, but before she can respond, Catherine interrupts, 'What's good about it?' She protests, 'My girl's going to the most dangerous place on earth?' Both Mike and Angie are startled by her vehemence; eyebrows raised, they look towards Sam for clarification.

'I might be going to the Af-Pak region soon,' she replies softly.

Unable to hide their concern, the couple goes into deep thought, both thinking of Sam's safety. Then Mike turns to Sam with the intention of pacifying Catherine, 'I'm sure you'd be safe wherever you go.'

Before Sam can respond, Catherine interjects, 'I heard they kill Americans on the streets.'

Mike tries to allay her concern. 'Catherine, it's not that bad. I'm sure we have taken precautionary measures, and our personnel are based in, what they call, green zones, which are highly guarded areas by our own Marines,' he throws an inquiring look at Sam, 'Am I right, Sam?'

Sam now gets her chance, which she had longed for since last night. 'Yeah,' she responds quickly, 'We are not the Army or Marines. I'll be working in the safe environment of a green zone in a city like Kabul or Islamabad.' She continues hurriedly, not wanting to give her mother the chance to interrupt, 'I've been trying to tell that to Mom since last night, but she would not listen . . . Well, hello!' trying to match her mother's last night's histrionics, 'I came looking for my mother, the one I knew . . . the gentle and supportive kind, but here is a different mother meeting me,' trying to put her point across. 'My real mom, where are you!?' she makes a weak attempt to draw humour out of this situation.

Both Mike and Angie let out an uneasy laughter, trying to help Sam out, but Catherine is still not amused. 'You know they kill Americans on the streets there,' Catherine reinforces her earlier statement in an attempt to scare Sam, who not wanting to back down responds with, 'Well, they kill Americans on the streets of Chicago too, Ma!'

Angie makes a vain attempt to divert the conversation, 'Why would these people want to kill Americans?' She inquires innocently. 'We do so much for these poor countries. We support them in their development, we look after their poor people, and we help them out with financial support . . .' 'Yeah, with our tax payers' money,' Mike interjects before Angie completes her question. '. . . So instead of being thankful to us', she continues ignoring the interruption, 'why would these people wanna kill us?'

Before Sam or Mike respond to Angie's query, Catherine, remembering David's views on Vietnam War, retorts, 'When you go to an alien land, to the other side of the world, and try to enforce your way of life on them, most of them are sure not gonna like it.' She then attempts to put her point of view across. 'We did that in Nam, and . . .' she concludes with a shake of her head, 'we are doing the same in Afghanistan.' Years of sagacity reflected in her views.

Sam, not agreeing with her mom, counters, 'But this time it's different . . .' Before she can complete her sentence, Catherine interrupts.

'It's never different, my child,' she says helplessly, 'it's never different,' she continues, 'no matter what you say, when you put your boots on someone else's soil, you become the aggressor.'

Mike, who is listening intently to the discussion, tries to help his niece out, 'So what do you expect us to do?' He asks Catherine, 'Take all the shit from those terrorists and sit in fear?' — mirroring a commonplace sentiment in the country.

Angie, not ready to be left behind and appreciating Catherine's point of view, intervenes, 'Well, you could talk to them?' she suggests innocently.

'Talk . . . Huh . . . talk with whom?' Mike smirks. 'Those barbarians?'

Catherine is not quite ready to give in just yet. 'Yeah, talk to them, negotiate with them, we have spent billions and billions fighting them out. With just a few millions, we could have talked them into it and saved thousands of lives,' she pauses and concludes, '. . . American lives.'

Sam replies, 'You know, Ma! We don't negotiate with terrorists.'

'Yeah, we destroy a country, kill their people and have our own killed too, but we don't negotiate with terrorists,' Catherine snaps back, 'this is all barbaric.'

Sam stubbornly holds her ground. 'So be it, Ma, but we will be victorious this time, we will deal with those terrorists and will make America safe, and I will play my part in doing that.'

Seeing the determination on Sam's face, Catherine finally relents, 'My dear, we said that in Korea, in Nam, even in Iraq, and now we are saying this in Afghanistan.' Exasperated, she concludes, 'God help us and . . . God be with you too, Samantha.'

The uneasy silence returns, now broken by Angie, 'I guess that settles the matter, how about another round of champagne,' she offers trying to break the tension, 'that was quite an interesting discussion.'

Mike agrees to another glass, while Catherine prefers to remain silent; her head resting on the back of the sofa and gaze fixed on the wall in front, she tries to come to terms with the latest development. Meanwhile, Sam gets up to fetch a glass of water. Her throat is all dried up from the tension. Not satisfied with the way this discussion ended, she wants to ease her mother's anxieties before leaving for Nevada on Sunday.

Chapter 3

DESTINATION PAKISTAN

It was sunrise in Paktita Province of Afghanistan. The sun's glow spread across the dry and desolate hill range stretched across the border of Waziristan. The day Baaz impatiently waited for had begun. It was judgment day for him, the day his future was to be decided. Despite all the torture and beatings, he had stuck to his plea of innocence throughout but had remained afraid of the authority Alqaeda maintained in his country. No one dared to go against the wishes of their Arab guests, and it seemed they were adamant on making an example of him. Their financial clout, their origin from the Land of the Prophet,[53] and the perceived legitimacy of their cause, had made them heroes in the eyes of Afghans. Under these circumstances, Baaz prayed to God for help, yearning to believe that his prayers will be answered, and that he'll be spared. At least, for the past three days, his thrashings had stopped, and he was given one decent meal a day, which helped him regain some of his strength.

While he prayed in his cell, in another room carved at the other end of the cave network, the three judges exhaustively discussed the verdict based on the available evidence and statements. There was discord between the Arab judge from Alqaeda and the Pakistani judge from Taliban Pakistan. They solidified their positions as the judge belonging to Afghan Taliban keenly listened to both views. Traditionally, the judgment in such cases was given once consensus was reached among the members of the Judicial Shoora.[54] This showed the unity among these organisations and also eliminated the

---

[53]   Prophet Mohammad (peace be upon him).

[54]   Council.

possibility of rifts and doubts among their rank and file. However, this case had become unique in the way that the judicial council refused to reach a consensus as time for the judgment arrived.

Unable to convince his colleague, finally the Alqaeda judge softly yet sternly addresses his Pakistani colleague, 'Brother, your attitude towards this case is certainly not appreciated.' He continues, 'Are you cognizant of the implications this disagreement can have between our two organisations?' His question gives out a veiled threat to his Pakistani colleague who knows that most of the financial aid and training is imparted to them by Alqaeda.

However, not ready to budge from his position, the Pakistani Taliban replies, 'Brother, if this issue becomes a reason for tension between our two brotherly organisations, whose goals are the same, so with regret I have to say,' he pauses for a moment, thinks, and then declares, 'so be it.' But before anyone else can respond to this, he clarifies his position. 'I would let go a hundred accused for lack of evidence than convict one person who is innocent.' Their Afghan counterpart is disturbed from what he sees happening among his comrades. Older and more sagacious of the two, he had witnessed many a large conflicts arising from such trivial incidents. He is wary of the anger and grievance smouldering within Alqaeda, but he could not let them dominate the proceedings knowing well that the conviction lacked evidence.

He feels the need to interject and calm things down before this disagreement trickles out of this room and escalates into full-fledged infighting between two groups. With this in mind, he refers to his Alqaeda colleague, 'Brother, I request you to restrict the discussion to this case,' he implores, 'no individual can take preference over our organisations and no case is more important than our united cause.'

On seeing the tilt of his Afghan counterpart towards the Pakistani Taliban member, the Alqaeda judge tries to justify his position, 'My brothers,' he addresses both of them, 'Abu Sayyaf was very close to our supreme commander,' he continues, 'their association dated back to the time we all fought off the Soviets together as one. He was also a very important and revered leader among all of us. Somebody needs to pay for this incident. If nothing else, this should create a horrible example for other traitors among our ranks. The supreme commander himself is extremely disturbed to hear about this loss, and he needs justice to prevail, otherwise . . . ,' he pauses for a moment, 'otherwise, seeing two judges from Afghanistan and Pakistan releasing a convict from this region against the desires of Alqaeda would create doubts about your loyalty towards us.'

Not willing to take these threats lying down, the Afghan member responds, 'My respected colleague, it is indeed regrettable to see the inferences being drawn from this incident.' Wary of such situations where Alqaeda would eventually prevail, he reacts, voice filled with controlled rage, 'We sided with you against the country which helped us get our freedom from the Soviet Empire. We preferred to be with you than be with the country that promised us wealth, development, and a secure future for our children. When the whole world turned against you, we took you in our fold and accepted you as one of us. We had our country destroyed, our nation divided, and our society deprived for you, and this is how you return the favour', he inquires, 'by giving us veiled threats and telling us that the supreme commander will be annoyed?'

Refusing to back down, the elderly judge continues, 'Well, you can tell your supreme commander that we did not sentence your accused since there was no evidence against him and after that if you want to forget about our favours and alliance and turn against us, so by God let me tell you this,' there is pin-drop silence in the room and this time, it is the Pakistani Taliban judge's turn to observe the altercation going on between his other two colleagues with bated breath, 'when we can fight off the mighty British Empire, the great Soviet Union, and now the superpower America, fighting you in our own backyard would be a walk in the park.'

There is uneasy silence in the room; not expecting this, the Alqaeda judge is stunned by such an outburst from a man whom he thought would side with him. His threats were meant for his Pakistani associate to fall in line with his point of view. He knows that his bluff has been called but, not ready to cave in easily, he makes one final desperate attempt to have his way. 'I acknowledge your position,' he addresses the elderly associate, 'but there was sufficient doubt from the clean condition of his vehicle and of his men that he never participated in the battle. We at least need to hold him accountable for leaving the battlefield and comrades behind?' he implores.

The elderly Afghan judge, trying to settle down, looks at his Pakistani colleague inquiringly, 'For the sake of our unity and friendship, I'll go with this request to punish him for not participating in the battle, which he himself claimed not to have done for reasons already stated. However, we may say that a man of his repute and calibre could have tried harder to engage with the enemy.' Seeing that a consensus is building this time, the elderly judge inquires' from his Alqaeda colleague what kind of punishment he deemed suitable for this act.

'For showing cowardice in the face of danger,' he pronounces the sentence, 'death by firing squad.'

*   *   *

It is Monday afternoon in Attock Cantonment. Last weekend was well spent by Rania with Dhil and her children at the serene hill station of Thandiani, north of Abbottabad. This fun-filled outing had given enough reason for Dhil to unwind — something that Rania cheered about.

Today she is back at her work. Being the wife of the CO[55] of a Commando Battalion, she also represented her husband's 'unit' in the Cantonment Welfare Association, attending to the needs of soldiers' families. She also taught in the cantonment's Army School in the mornings and attended to welfare work at the Association three times a week, in the afternoons.

The school bell rings for pack up, and the Grade 5 children itch to rush out. Rania kindly advises them, 'Okay, kids, you were great today. Please make sure you read through pages thirty to thirty-five, and we'll meet again for an exciting class of historic stories tomorrow. Go and have fun.'

Taking the cue from their lovely teacher, the children first make a row to exit the class quietly, trying to hide their excitement of packing up, and once out, rush to their buses and gates as if they have been let out after serving life imprisonment. Rania smiles at this daily routine; she then collects her books and makes her way to the Principal's Office to discuss the arrangements of a function to be held on 25 December.

On her way to the class, she hails her close friend, Ismat Asim, who is also heading towards the same office to attend the same meeting. 'Hi, Ismat!'

---

[55] Commanding officer.

'Hello, Rania!' comes the bright response from Ismat, a dusky, slender, and charming lady from Multan.

'Looking forward to taking over the arrangements again?' Ismat naughtily asks Rania, who smiles in return as both reach the Principal's Office. The principal, Mrs Hafeez, was an elderly lady. An educationalist by profession, she had grown very fond of Rania over the years for her modest and ever-so willing attitude. Ismat knocks at the open door. 'Ma'am, can we come in?'

Mrs Hafeez, who is on the phone, gestures at them to come in. Rania and Ismat settle themselves on the chairs across Mrs Hafeez's table.

'Yes . . . Hmmm . . . yes,' Mrs Hafeez intently listens to someone on the phone while she smiles at her two guests seated in front. 'This is indeed very good news, and I'll certainly share it with the girls,' being a middle-age lady herself, she referred to her younger colleagues as girls, displaying an aura of a benevolent superior. 'Okay, Begum[56] Tariq', referring to the wife of the corps commander — Lt. Gen. Tariq Hashmi, 'Thank you very much and God bless you too . . . Allah Hafiz.'[57]

She puts down the phone and smiles gracefully at the two ladies sitting in front of her. Her elderly personality, with grey combed-back hair, going in perfect sync with her sagacious tone. 'Well, girls, that was Mrs. Corps Commander on the phone as you must have reckoned by now,' she continues, 'she was all praise for both of you for your efforts in generating 400,000 rupees from the funfair held for the families of our soldiers in the cantonment. Your stalls for dresses, games, fast food, and the stage dramas were all a great success.' Mrs Hafeez then looks at Rania and compliments, 'Rania, while I don't want to take the credit away from Ismat, I must commend you for putting your heart and soul into making this project a success despite having your husband away on a tough mission. Now that we know where he was, it must have been very taxing for you mentally.'

Rania responds, 'Thank you, Mrs Hafeez. It is nice of you to say that, but I am no different from the wives of all our brothers out there.

---

[56] Begum is equivalent to Mrs used as a sign of respect.
[57] Allah Hafiz stands in Urdu for 'God be your guardian'.

I guess anyone in my position would have acted the same,' modesty written all over her statement.

Not wanting to be left behind, Ismat praises her best friend enthusiastically, 'Ma'am, this is Rania for us, the epitome of modesty, sincerity, and benevolence,' she chirps, 'that is why she is referred to as farishtae[58] by the wives of our soldiers.'

Ismat had known Rania from the time they both got married to two course-mates at about the same time. They shared happy memories together at various stations, where their husbands coincidentally got posted together. While they shared similar interests, their natures were poles apart. Ismat was more chirpy and jovial, whereas Rania preferred to maintain her poise most of the time. However, their friendship had made them famous among the ladies at any cantonment they went.

'Well, that is the reason why you both are here,' smiles Mrs Hafeez. 'I have selected you two to arrange the Parent's Day function on 25 December[59]. I leave it to you two to decide between yourselves the jobs that you need to do, and you may select your own teams for the chores. As always, I want a memorable function on that day.' She concludes, 'Of course, I'm here for any support, guidance, or approval required from the authorities.'

'Thank you, Mrs Hafeez, for the honour,' Rania replies respectfully while Ismat nods in concurrence. 'We'll try our best to make this function a success and make you proud of us.' At this, Mrs Hafeez gets up from her seat, thus signalling the conclusion of this meeting and shakes the girls' hands wishing them all the very best.

As Rania and Ismat walk out of Mrs Hafeez's office down the corridor, Ismat asks Rania, 'So, Farishtae, what do you have in mind this time?'

Rania smiles at Ismat and responds after taking a moment to think, 'Something patriotic,' she thinks again staring at the Pakistan flag flapping from a distance at the school gate, 'the struggle of our innocent and the poor people caught in the crossfire.'

---

[58] Farishtae is Urdu for angel.

[59] The birth anniversary of Pakistan's founding father, Mr Mohammad Ali Jinnah, is celebrated on 25 December.

Ismat looks back at Rania, the idea sinking in her mind and her eyes brightening up, she quips, 'So shall it be written,' at which Rania joins in, knowing well what line comes next from Ismat; they both let it out, 'So shall it be done!'

Both exchange a high five and then turn the discussion to the project as they walk down the school corridor.

*   *   *

It is Tuesday morning. James Cummings sits in his office in Nevada with his colleague Asst. Director Jack Springs. They are busy discussing Sam and her latest assignment.

'James, still I personally think that Sam is too junior for this job,' he opines. 'You shouldn't have recommended her for this position.'

James maintains a discreet silence and only smiles back at Jack while reclining on his chair, rotating slightly, keeping one hand on the chair's arm rest and other on the table, where he plays with the stapler.

'I have known Sam from the time she was a trainee in the Academy.' He defends his recommendation, 'There is something about her which puts her way above her batch-mates. Not only is she clever and sharp, but there is also some personal vendetta that she wants to fulfil. There's some torment in her, some kind of impatience which, despite my asking, she hasn't shared with me . . . ,' he muses. 'She is good at her job, though, and considering that our own intelligence gathering in Af-Pak is still not up to the mark, I recommended her, hoping that she might do something which our guys have so far been missing out on.'

Jack listens attentively to James but counters, 'I don't want to sound sexist here, but . . . ,' a smirk creeping over his face, 'sending a pretty girl like her into the hornet's nest . . . she'll need to cover her butt all the time?'

James ignores these innuendos. 'That's also the reason why she was hot on that list,' referring to the final list of nominees for this post. 'Beautiful, sharp, motivated, with no strings attached, and a girl . . . where else would you have gotten a better person than her to do this job?' In the end, absolving himself of this nomination, he states, 'Anyway, Jack, I didn't make the decision here. I only recommended her to Langley.' With a mischievous grin spread across his face, he looks straight at Jack. 'Are you sad a hottie like her won't be around any more?' followed by a suggestive laugh, enjoying Jack's embarrassed self-defence.

'Well, she was a pleasant sight here in the wilderness.' At this, they both laugh out loud when the intercom bell rings. His secretary is at the other end.

'Yes?' James retorts.

'Sir, Special Agent Albright is here to see you.'

'Okay, let her in.' Both men compose themselves as Jack prepares to leave.

Sam had been anxiously waiting for this meeting since last week. By now she had mentally prepared herself for the news and was looking forward to her next assignment. The prospects of going to either Pakistan or Afghanistan now looked a bit brighter since she felt it would take her to the battle zone and closer to her enemy. She enters the room while Jack makes his way out. They exchange nods before James greets Sam and gestures her to take a seat.

'So how did your break go, Sam?' James tries to create a more congenial environment before giving the news.

'It was okay, visited my mom back in Jacksonville . . . spent some time with her.' And unable now to stay formal any longer, she blurts out in the same breath, 'So where am I going, sir?' impatience written all over her face.

Knowing that the pleasantry stage is over, and Sam doesn't need any more coaxing, James replies in the same manner, 'Islamabad . . . Pakistan.'

An uneasy silence prevails in the room.

*   *   *

The Taliban's cave network in the Paktita Mountains. Monday came and went, and Baaz was not called. Tuesday came and went, and Baaz was still not called. His pleas for an update fell on deaf ears. Not having seen the light of day for a week, he got disorientated and completely lost his sense of time. Succumbing to his fate, he sat in one corner of the cell, waiting to be given the death sentence. He found comfort from the thought of meeting his dead wife and little children, who were brutally murdered by the advancing army of the rival Afghan factions after 9/11. His family's only sin was that they were related to a Taliban warrior. Over the years, Baaz had tried to overcome his grief attributing that tragedy to the will of God; this loss was also the driving force behind his fight against the American military and their Afghan partners. But now, he felt betrayed. He felt that his destiny played a cruel game by making him accused of colluding with the people whom he had sworn to eradicate from the soil of Afghanistan.

It is now Wednesday morning. His two Alqaeda captors walk up to the door of his cell and unlock it. 'Yalla!' shouts one of them at Baaz. Gathering all his strength, Baaz feebly gets up on his legs, feeling the strength all but gone from his body, yet trying to be mentally strong to walk on his own. His captors take their place, one on each side of Baaz, and hold him by his arms to assist him in walking. Baaz shrugs them off while trying to find his inner strength. *I may have lost my power, but I haven't lost my self-esteem yet* — he thinks, while making feeble efforts to move on his own, his stride gaining power with every step he takes. The trip down the dimly lit tunnel to the court room seems to be the longest walk he has had in days, but by the time he reaches the courtroom, he is erect, unruffled, and confident enough to face any verdict that comes his way.

He walks into the courtroom and nods at the three judges already perched on their seats. The room is abuzz with discussion on Baaz's fate, for the decision to be delayed by more than two days has never happened in all the history of this court. People talk about the proceedings of last week and are eager to know what consensus the judicial council has reached.

Baaz himself walks up to the cage and settles himself inside it, self-contentment now showing on his face. One Arab captor closes the cage door behind him, and the room automatically quiets down on seeing that the proceedings are about to begin.

The Afghan judge gestures at the Arab prosecutor to begin his proceedings.

'Assalam u aliekum, Saeedi,' he greets the judges. 'We recommend the death penalty for the accused Mullah Baaz Jan based on our earlier plea explained to you in the previous hearing. We have nothing more to say.'

The Afghan judge then refers to Baaz and asks him whether he has anything new to add. Baaz responds in the negative, having already made his case clear to the judges.

The Afghan judge then addresses the court, 'On charges of aiding and abetting the enemy in conducting the treacherous drone attack, which resulted in martyrdom of Maulvi Najeeb Mohammad, Abu Sayyaf, and other comrades and not to forget their women and children, we find the accused,' there is a pin-drop silence as everyone concentrates on the judge, self-analysing their own assessment of the case.

'Not Guilty!'

There is a tremendous sigh of relief among the majority of people in the room. Some of them shout out 'Allah o Akbar'[60] and 'Al Hamdo Lillah'[61] while the Alqaeda prosecutor ferociously stares at his judge, not wanting to believe that his mighty organisation's stand has been overruled. Baaz cannot believe his ears. He had given up all hope and was ready to face death in the eye when suddenly, out of the blue, came this breath of fresh air.

The murmurs in the courtroom lead to pandemonium as people with differing views start arguing with each other inside the court itself.

'Silence!' comes a long roar from the Afghan controller of the proceedings. A hush instantly falls over the room as if they were school kids under the command of their teacher. The Afghan judge, who is visibly perturbed at this interruption, has not finished with the verdict.

'However,' he proceeds, 'the judicial council has taken suo-moto notice of Baaz's cowardly exit from the area of battle.'

'Yessss,' the prosecutor hisses, while Baaz prepares himself for the dreaded words.

'It is felt that while he did not collude with the enemy, he could have certainly participated in the battle and brought harm to the enemy forces fighting our comrades. He chose not to do that and exited the area of battle instead and for this he stands', the judge pauses to get the attention of everyone in the room, 'guilty.'

Baaz has no defence against this assessment. Knowing that the judges will not understand his position and that the verdict has been given, making a plea at this time would only degrade him in his own eye as well as the eyes of the people around. There is silence in the

---

[60]   God is Great.

[61]   All thanks to God.

room since the people are shocked to hear this turn of judgment. However, this time, it is the Alqaeda prosecutor and his comrades turn to smile victoriously.

'And with this, the judges will pronounce their punishment for Mullah Baaz Jan, starting from Ameer Abu Eisa followed by Maulana Kareemullah,' concludes the Afghan judge. People eagerly look towards the other two judges to pronounce the punishment for Baaz.

Ameer Abu Eisa—the judge from Alqaeda, who had so far been sitting silently, now has his chance to appease his people.

'Mullah Baaz Jan, by running away from battle, you have brought disrepute to the cadre of Muslim commanders. This act of cowardice has no place in our legion of Mujahideen, and hence I pronounce for you the punishment of death by a firing squad.'

The slight murmur erupts again in the courtroom, which is immediately silenced by the controller as the judge from the Pakistani Taliban, Maulana Kareemullah begins his verdict. 'Mullah Baaz Jan,' he addresses Baaz, 'You have been accused of cowardice by my honourable colleague for which he has my concurrence.' Baaz continues staring at the floor in front, expecting to hear the same death penalty from the second judge as well. 'However, keeping in mind your previous track record of courage and valour,' he continues, at which Baaz looks up at the judge with a look of disbelief, 'I pronounce for you exile from your country, Afghanistan.'

This was unprecedented in the history of this court to have divergent punishments pronounced by the judges. This development takes everyone by surprise and before the judge could complete his sentence, the room is once again abuzz with discussions, completely disregarding the decorum of the court.

The controller loses his cool and yells at the attendants, 'Silence!' He roars, 'If now I see anyone talking in this court, I'll have him arrested for violating the decorum of this honourable court.' A hushed silence falls over the room just at the thought of this possibility. There is complete silence in the room as all eyes fix themselves on the elderly Afghan judge whose verdict would decide the fate of Baaz.

The whole onus of the final decision falls on the elderly judge. On one side, the life of a helpless man was at stake. A brave warrior and a credible commander, Baaz had made a reputation for himself among the Afghan Taliban ranks and one folly did not deem it sufficient for him to be put to rest permanently. Whereas, on the other hand, relations with Alqaeda were at stake, depending on his stance in this case. The options fell between saving the life of one at the cost of adversely affecting the lives of many others, or sacrificing the life of one to avail the support of their bigger partner, for the greater benefit of their struggle.

*   *   *

It is Wednesday, daytime in Attock. Seven officers from Dhil's unit, from the rank of Lieutenant up to the rank of Major, are gathered in the common room over their tea break, enjoying the latest escapade of Maj. Saifullah Dar—the 'playboy' from Lahore. The room resonates with their bursts of laughter as Dar jovially takes them through the story.

'She took me to her room and started showing me her family album by sitting close to me. The smell of her perfume started turning me on and, considering the last week we spent in mud and water in Waziristan, this situation made me think I'm in heaven with a Hoor[62].' His story is interrupted by the whistles of the younger officers who cannot control their excitement listening to their 'master' at work.

'I looked less at the album and more at her, anticipating my next manoeuvre to commence operation. This officer was hot like fuel on fire, man!' The room echoes with whistles and guffaws.

Maj. Umar Rathore, the 2iC of the unit eagerly listens to Dar's conquest, knowing well where it will lead.

'And then, sir?' pleads a young captain, his eyes wide with anticipation, fantasising about the elusive girl of the tale.

'I held her cold soft hand, placed it on my thundering chest, and looked her straight in the eye relaying my innermost feelings—*for heaven's sake let's stop talking and let's get rocking . . . Now!*' continues Dar sensually, 'she hesitated, showing me that she is not that type of a girl and a good conversation is all that she wanted. But I'd heard many such stories and knew what she really desired . . . a rugged commando.'

'Ahh . . .' sigh the bachelors in the room, completely engrossed in Dar's story much like children are transfixed by fairy tales. Rathore,

---

[62]   Beautiful angelic women of the heavens.

the most senior officer in the room, looks around, smiling, and thinks—*Who could say that these are the 'commandos' of a professional army!*

'Temperature reaching boiling point, just when she surrendered to my advances, I heard the most unwanted noise I could think of!' There is silence in the room, as all wanted the suspense to end.

'It was the bloody honk of her daddy's car! Her dad and her two brawny brothers who had gone hunting for the weekend were back already on Saturday of all days!' Dar exclaims, all animated and taking fun out of the story at the same time. 'And guess what? They had their shotguns with them!'

'Hearing them outside, she went into a frenzy, and I, in only my knickers, frantically tried to put my clothes on, in my hurry wearing my pants inside out.'

'Hahahaha!' at that, the room again bursts into guffaws, and this time, Rathore interrupts, 'Dar, when will you get serious?' he smilingly asks, 'Do you want us to believe this story?'

'Sir, it didn't end here,' Dar tries to stop himself from laughing. 'She tried to push me into a large steel trunk in her dressing room, and I had to dive in under the blankets to avoid detection . . . Her brothers had smelled my cologne in the house and suspected a man inside with their little sister. Just imagine, three big men with guns prowling in the house, looking for the intruder. I was in thick shit, sir!' Dar responds to Rathore's insinuation.

'Hahaha! I can't believe it, Dar,' Rathore mocks back, 'Maj. Saifullah Dar, commando of the Pakistan Army, Hero of Swat Battles . . . hiding in a trunk under the blankets like a timid rat?'

Dar cleverly responds, 'Sir, discretion is the better part of valour. Hiding under the blankets was my only survival option.' He laughs.

Not wanting to be sidetracked, one of the officers pleads with Dar to continue.

'I spent the whole day there in the suffocating heat, cursing myself and praying to God to get me out of there alive and that I would never do it again. Believe me, my professional training came in handy in this situation. But by night, I was paranoid and just wanted to get out even if I did end up getting shot.' The officers were amused, but their faces now showed concern. The story had taken a serious turn. Rathore, having heard many such stories, anticipated the punch line to come anytime now.

'She came to me at midnight and slowly opened the trunk lid to let me out. Huhhhh, I was dazed, man, it all looked like a dream to me,' he consoles himself. 'So much for a lovely weekend after Waziristan, eh? Anyway, I pulled myself together, rushed straight to her toilet, my bladder was overflowing by now . . . and then I was all ready to make good my escape.'

'Did you try the main door, sir?' jokes one of the captains sitting there.

'Yeah sure, and get neutered?' at which the room again erupts into laughter. 'I obviously couldn't get out the main door, so I tried the window. It was the first floor, and the window had grills. Nope, okay then, I tried the toilet exhaust fan. I slowly took it out, and the cavity was large enough for me to squeeze out. It was all dark and silent outside, an odd dog barked in the neighbourhood. I got hold of the flimsy drainage pipe and planned to make my way down from the first floor.'

The mood is sombre in the room now as they wait for the climax.

'You could imagine my situation. I was cautious, scared, and alert, putting all my energy and concentration in trying to get down, and as I got out of the exhaust hole and was hugging the pipe for my life, cursing myself for being in this situation, you know what she said to me?'

The question jogs the men out of their trance. On drawing blank expression from his audience, he makes a coy face enacting the girl, 'So when will you come again?'

The room reverberates with thunderous sounds of hilarity. Dar had done it again with one of his adventure stories.

'The nerve of that girl, in that situation she is asking me when I'll visit her again?' Dar cries animatedly. 'Madam, please forgive me, I said. I'll never set foot in your street again. Ignoring her pleas, I crept silently down the pipe, landed in the back garden, jumped off the fence, hitting some trash drum on the way, which created a clanking noise in the dead silence of the night, waking up the neighbourhood. To my horror, dogs started barking, and I saw some lights switching on with shouts of 'robber, robber' in the background and couple of gun shots resonating in the area. Not looking back, I ran from the street as fast as my legs could run . . . for as long as I could till I got hold of a bus on the main road and made my way back to base camp.'

By now, the officers are rolling around with peals of laughter, imagining the whole scenario of their favourite hero officer Major Dar and his great escape from a foiled romantic day out. Dar was the most popular officer in the unit for his comic nature and a simultaneous daring attitude. With a spirit of 'never say die' in both his personal and professional life, he was also a role model for the junior officers in the unit, who tried to emulate his lifestyle.

At this moment, Dhil enters the boisterous room, happy to see them relaxed, especially after last week's ordeal, he smiles at his unit officers. The officers stand up and quiet down upon observing their honourable commanding officer at the door. Not wanting to spoil the mood, Dhil joins the fun by sarcastically asking, 'So, Dar, how did your weekend go?'

Dar, having just finished his story and embarrassed to be asked this question again responds dejectedly, 'Just great, sir.'

At this, the silent room again breaks into a chuckle, as the men know where this question came from.

Dhil also smirks, enjoying the atmosphere and then, as the tea break concludes, asks Rathore, Dar, the adjutant officer, and a couple of the senior officers to join him in a meeting.

*   *   *

The pin-drop silence continues in the courtroom, where the fate of Baaz hangs in balance. With bated breath, all eyes stare at the elderly Afghan judge whose wrinkled face and sunken eyes reveal the turmoil going on in his mind.

'Your Honour,' the controller speaks softly breaking the silence in the room, 'we all await your judgment, on which will depend the fate of this accused,' pointing at Baaz who stares blankly at the ground in front of him.

His face suddenly turning haggard and his physique now weak, the judge's lack of strength betray him, revealing years spent in turbulent and stressful conditions. There is tremendous burden on his shoulders to keep the boat from rocking. He clears his throat and gathers the strength to speak out loud.

'Mullah Baaz Jan, you have presented us with a unique situation here,' the judge shares his dilemma. 'On the one hand, you are a man of repute and honour, known for your bravery, sacrifice, and dedication to our cause. Having earned the title of "Mullah", you have fought countless battles, losing your family in the process and yet maintaining unflinching loyalty to our spiritual leader and his struggle for freedom from Occupation forces.' He feels it important to highlight the achievements of Baaz for the record before justifying his verdict to his Alqaeda comrades. 'On the other hand, it has been ascertained beyond doubt that in this critical battle, you left the area without giving it your best, something which was expected of a commander of your calibre.' He is now reaching the verdict. 'You ran from that fight and under such circumstances the ideal punishment for cowardice is death.'

'Allah O Akbar!' interrupts the bigger of the two Arab guards with jubilation, thinking that the verdict has been given for death, two to one.

'However', the elderly judge raises his voice to silence the others before they could follow the guard who also quietens down, embarrassed at jumping the gun, 'considering your background, I'll make an exception for you and would pronounce for you exile with disgrace out of Afghanistan.'

This time again a sigh of relief erupts in the room, and before it converts into a murmur, the elderly Afghan judge continues in an amplified voice, 'Till such time you do not prove without doubt that you are a true warrior of Islam and a Mujahid[63] of Afghanistan, you are stripped of your title of "Mullah" and banished from your motherland.'

This sentence was a first of its kind. Attendants in the room are unable to control their emotions and start whispering. Against this background noise, the judge concludes his sentence on the note, 'So as per the majority vote of the Shura, you live, but for now, you live the life of a disgraced, banished coward in a foreign land.'

With this sentence, he orders the Alqaeda guards to march Baaz out of the caves, out of the province, out of the country, and ensure that he does not come back again.

Baaz is aghast at the sentence. He is confused whether to cheer for his spared life or die out of shame and disgust. All his life's efforts, achievements, and accolades were snatched away on an assumption he considered wrong.

---

[63] Muslim Warrior.

What do these judges know — he thinks, a rebellious streak passing through his battered spine. *Have they ever been in real battle?* Staring blankly at the elderly judge, the chain of thoughts running through his head is broken by the strong tug from his captors who hold him by his arms and drag him out of the cage.

'Wallah,[64] if I did not respect the judgment, I would kill you right here right now,' the bigger of the two captors growls into Baaz's ear. Baaz doesn't pay much heed to this threat, knowing that in a free environment, he could tackle such goons on his own. Right now, his main concern is where he will be taken.

The other captor continues, 'You are our prisoner till we kick you out of Afghanistan, and that'll be very soon.'

This gives Baaz the idea. He knows that the border between Afghanistan and Pakistan's tribal area is porous and not under the control of the Pakistani State. In all probability, he could be taken to Waziristan or some other semi-autonomous tribal territory in Pakistan.

Seething with rage against his fate, he resolves to gain his lost respect and title and again stand tall in the eyes of his compatriots, since he feels it is his right to live in his motherland, in his village, with dignity and honour. How he achieves this under such challenging circumstances becomes his life's biggest priority.

But for now, his immediate concern is to gain acceptability from the remaining members of the Lashkar al-Mujahideen, who would have questions of their own to ask of him.

---

[64]   Swear by Allah.

Chapter 4

ACCLIMATISATION PAKISTAN

Please . . . don't go!

Don't be sad, my cherry pie, your daddy's always gonna be with you.

No! You're leaving me . . . Alex! Please stop Dad.

Hehehe . . . Sis, you can't come here.

Alex . . . Alex! Where are you going . . . stop!

Bye, hun, you know we love you . . .

Yeah, fatso! We'll be with you . . . always.

Stop, both of you, stop . . . don't leave me, pleeeeeease!

'Ma'am, ma'am? Are you okay?'

'Ladies and Gentlemen, InshAllah, we'll soon be landing at Islamabad International Airport . . .'

'Huh?'

'Where the temperature outside is 16 degrees Celsius and the local time is 7.37 a.m.'

Where am I?

'May we please request you to fasten your seat belts, fold back your meal trays, and bring your seat to an upright position? We hope you had a pleasant flight and will travel with us again. Thank you for flying Pakistan International Airlines.'

'I'm fine, I'm fine . . . thank you,' Samantha struggles to get back to reality, her mind preoccupied with the dream she just had, her head heavy from the long flight from New York.

Body fatigued and longing for more sleep, wanting to see her father and brother again.

Goodbye my child, remember I'll be waiting for you here.

Sam, you were not meant to sit behind a desk pushing papers throughout your life. Go out there and explore the real world yourself.

You're doing a great job, kid, and Jacksonville is proud of its daughter.

The voices of Catherine, James, and Forrester resonate in her mind as she goes in and out of sleep.

The Boeing 777ER of Pakistan International Airlines touches down with a slight bump at Islamabad International Airport, finally shaking Sam out of her lethargic dream state.

As the plane taxis towards the tarmac for a halt, Samantha peers out of the window. *Pakistan at last* — she thinks to herself.

It is a bright November morning with the sun shining in a clear blue sky, trying to disperse the morning haze enveloping the ground. Far away in the north, she sees the Margalla Hills stretched across from west to east rising higher as they spread across the eastern front into the Karakorum mountain range. Morning dew, settled on the grass on both sides of the taxi track, reflecting the bright sunlight on the surface, dazzles the eye. Samantha reaches for her shades to cover her haggard eyes. With a flight of twenty hours from New York to Islamabad and a time difference of nine hours, Samantha was jet lagged.

'Is this your first time?' she hears the shy reluctant voice of the geek, who sat next to her during the long flight. He had tried to start a conversation but was stopped in his tracks by Sam's cold vibes every time he made the effort.

'Excuse me?' Sam stares back, disliking the dual meaning of the question.

'Sorry, I mean, is it your first time in Pakistan?' struggles the geek, cursing himself for having asked this question.

'Yes,' comes the cold reply from Sam.

'I work in Microsoft and have come on a two weeks' vacation to visit my parents in Islamabad.' The geek tries to make one last effort. 'I'd love to show you . . .' he attempts to make an offer to Sam, who turns her face away staring outside the window again, 'around . . .

Well, anyway, have a nice stay in Islamabad.' The geek, embarrassed to the core at seeing the disinterest from the white woman, straightens his round, thick-rimmed specs as the plane stops, gets up to retrieve his bag, and leaves, while Sam continues to look outside the window, staring at the C130 Hercules military cargo planes of the Pakistan Air Force parked at a distance; the voices of her guides and instructors in Langley echo in her brain, advising her of some last-minute instructions:

> *Do not talk to strangers.*
> *Do not eat outside.*
> *Do not drink outside.*
> *Do not take anything from anyone.*
> *Do not accept any kind of offer.*
> *Do not let two or more people come close to you at the same time.*
> *Be wary of bearded men.*
> *Be wary of veiled women, they could be men with guns inside their cloak.*
> *Only go out in groups in a bulletproof vehicle.*
> *Do not stop for long in one place.*
> *If you need to go to the market, only visit during the daytime.*
> *Do not wander off alone.*
> *Do not go even in a group to a desolate place.*
> *Do not go outside the confines of the Green Zone in Islamabad.*
> *Always carry your service-issued weapon for self-protection.*

As advised, Sam continues to remain seated in the plane as all other passengers disembark one by one. Not wanting to engage in pleasantries with anyone, including the flight attendants, she continues to look outside for the vehicle she was briefed about. Once the buses carrying other passengers have sped away, she espies a black GMC Suburban with dark tinted windows, from a distance, slowly heading towards the plane.

Sam relaxes at the sight of two tall well-built Caucasian men in black suits and black sunglasses emerge from the Suburban, buttoning their jackets to stop them from flapping in the wind. While the younger-looking blond man stops at the stairs, the senior one, with grey locks, walks up the stairs nodding at the staff, enters the plane and heads straight for Sam, who was by now the only passenger left inside.

'Special Agent Samantha Albright?' he asks politely but sternly, to which she nods in the affirmative.

'Can I see some ID please?' the man in black requests. Samantha takes out her ID card, feeling odd at the way she was so far being treated. This never happened to her back home. She hands it over to the man who scrutinises it thoroughly before handing it back to Samantha.

'Well, Ma'am, welcome to Pakistan,' he finally smiles. The sudden softening of his attitude surprises Sam.

'I'm Agent Jim Dalton and outside is my colleague, Agent Dick Cage,' the grey-haired man makes the introductions. 'We just call him Dee,' he grins lightening the tone.

Sam also heaves a sigh of relief and relaxes, extending her hand to greet her compatriot. She was advised of these two men and shown their photographs for identification. Likewise, the case with the agents, but they had to follow this protocol. Getting up, she retrieves her bag from the luggage compartment and follows Jim off the plane and into the cold, damp winter wind of Islamabad. A welcome change from the stuffy cabin, she takes deep breath inhaling extra oxygen. Suddenly awakened and alert, she steps down the stairs to meet the blond Agent Dick, who offers a welcoming smile and a firm handshake. They then all settle themselves into the armoured GMC to make their way off the tarmac, heading for the VIP lounge of the airport to formally stamp her arrival and collect her luggage.

Once out of the lounge, the GMC crawls towards the airport gate. Sam fixes her gaze out of the window as a school child does on her first trip to Disneyland. This seemed like a strange new world to her, very different from whence she came. People of different shades of brown, some fair others darker skinned, were all over the place at the airport. Local cabbies with their small yellow hatchbacks and loaders, mostly with unkempt beards, dressed shabbily in their long shirts and baggy trousers ran after passengers to carry their luggage for a tip. Relatively smarter looking men attired in the local dress or even Western clothes made their way towards small Japanese sedans or older SUVs parked haphazardly in the open car park. Other men haggled with cabbies over fares, while their women dutifully stood behind, wearing bright printed local dresses with the additional 'dupatta'[65] mostly covering their heads. Families huddled together as they reached their transports, mothers making sure no child is left behind.

Sam notices personnel of the Law Enforcement Agencies, conspicuous among the crowd by their uniforms and weapons, patrolling the area in pairs, keeping a strong vigil for any unruly incident. A policeman at the gate smartly dressed in his sky blue shirt, dark blue trousers, and military boots gestures the traffic from the general car park to stop, much to their disdain, and signals the American black tinted GMC to make its way out of the airport.

Sam is surprised to see so many men with guns patrolling the airport. She is especially astonished to see, at the exit and entry gates of the airport, covered check posts complete with walls made up of sand bags and machine guns perched over the posts with gunners stationed on them.

'Are we in a battle zone already?' she inquires of Jim, who laughs at her innocent question.

'I've seen a dozen uniformed guys with their LMGs[66] and Subs[67] at this small airport and now these posts?'

'Ma'am, this is Islamabad for you, and this is just the beginning,' he sneers as Dick gets the GMC out of airport gate and accelerates it on to the Islamabad Highway leading towards the city from the airport. Sam is amazed to see the traffic as they drive up the ten-lane highway to the city. Old Bedford trucks and buses, brightly decorated with scenery and abstract images; small Japanese Sedans with a one odd larger SUV among them, all make room for themselves as they drive at breathtaking speeds in close proximity to each other. Meanwhile, people on both sides attempt death-defying stunts to cross this highway. They dodge the speeding vehicles as they disregard the overhead crossing bridges placed after every mile. Sam is especially amused by the way the small motorbikes are driven at equally high speeds by men whose long baggy shirts and pants flap in the wind as they ride past. Sam smiles at one particularly serious-looking rider

---

[65] A thin piece of cloth spread across the women's upper body doubly used to cover their heads as well. Part of women's traditional dress in South Asia.

[66] Light-machine guns.

[67] Sub-machine guns.

clad in the local dress, flapping away along with his Santa-size beard, also flowing back from both sides of his face.

As they drive past a small hill, Sam sees the picture of the founding father of Pakistan, Mohammad Ali Jinnah, made out of neon-lights. Along with his picture, fixed on the hill also in neon-lights, are three of his famous principles: Unity, Faith, Discipline. She scoffs at the image.

The current state of affairs in Pakistan does not reflect any unity among them — she thinks. *Faith . . . yeah maybe . . . but discipline?* She looks at the rowdy jay-walkers; vehicles indifferent to lanes, overtaking from the wrong sides; abrupt entrance of vehicles on the highway from side roads; and a general disregard for traffic rules. Dick also joining the party and driving like a carefree maniac just to keep pace with the traffic; *Naa . . . I don't think so* — she concludes her thoughts about these principles.

'Jim, how long have you been here now?' inquires Sam after having had enough of the view outside.

'It's my second year now, ma'am.'

'And you, Dick . . . I mean, Dee?' quickly correcting herself.

Dick looks back at Sam and smiles, 'I stopped counting after six months.' Seeing no pleasant response coming from Sam, he promptly corrects himself,

'Thirty months . . . ma'am.'

As they enter the periphery of Islamabad City, the vehicles slow down, eventually coming to a halt. Dick follows suit.

'Why are we stopping?' Sam questions, alarm evident in her tone. She had been strictly advised of not stopping anywhere and here she found herself surrounded by other cars, all now creeping forward at a snail's pace.

Seeing the concern on her face, Jim comforts her, 'It's all right. We are entering the city, and there is a check post in front. It'll take us not more than three minutes to cross this.' He looks back at her and says, 'Such check posts are all over the city from threat of terrorists.'

A sign of city under siege indeed — thinks Sam. On seeing the relaxed attitude of her fellow colleagues as they crawl forward, Sam tries to assert herself, 'Should we not be vigilant and be on a lookout for any suicide bomber or bomb-laden car? I mean, look at us, we are the only Black American GMC here . . . we are sitting ducks,' Sam's voice rise with concern.

The two men exchange a funny glance before Jim responds, 'Relax, ma'am, we are in an armoured vehicle. Besides, we cannot run over these cars.'

Dick, funnier of the two, tries injecting humour into the situation, 'Ma'am, you're new here. Wait till you get a little more acquainted with the place.'

'It's not a question of new or old, Agent Dick,' Sam angrily interrupts, 'it's a question of taking safety precautions. If this is your attitude, then you're lucky to be alive so far.' By this time, they cross the check post, where three cops armed with Kalashnikov machine guns gesture them to move on. Dick again steps on the gas, quickly accelerating forward, reflecting his reaction from the way he jerks the GMC.

Jim and Dick look at each other with disappointment and prefer to remain silent for the rest of the trip to the US embassy. Sam also, tired from the journey and having had enough from the two honchos, prefers to stay quiet and just looks outside the window.

It takes them another ten minutes on the winding highway before they reach another check post. By the time they arrive at this point, the traffic has thinned out, but again, Sam notices LMGs perched on the top of the posts and sand bags similar to the ones at the airport guarding the gunners inside. Unable to quell her curiosity, she asks Jim, 'Where are we now?'

'We are entering the diplomatic enclave of Islamabad. Embassies and High Commissions of many countries are in this area. It's a highly restricted area, where only embassy staff and authorised personnel are allowed in the so-called green zone.'

'What about the general public?' she asks.

'Well, they cannot come here on their own,' continues Jim, '"cause of the terror threats. They are supposed to park their cars outside this area and take shuttle coaches that take them to different embassies.'

Dick lowers his tinted window and shows his ID to the guard, who carefully examines the card, while his partner runs a bomb detector around their vehicle. Meanwhile, Sam notices, in the distance, an area where hundreds of people, struggling to find a space for themselves, clamour into shuttle buses parked in a line. Seeing the disorganised atmosphere, Sam thinks to herself, *What an inconvenient mess!*

Jim, who is also staring in that direction, looks back and notices the expression on Sam's face. As if reading her mind, he concludes, 'That's the price they have to pay for creating terror threats for us.'

Dick, who had remained quiet after his last failed attempt at humour, prefers to maintain his dignity and once again accelerates till they reach the compound, which looks familiar to Sam. In Langley, while being briefed on her next assignment, she was shown slides of the US embassy in Islamabad. As they start driving adjacent to the 5-metre high wall, with barbed wires on the top and observation posts every twenty metres, she knows they have reached their destination. Excitement running down her spine, she waits for Dick to turn the next corner towards the heavily fortified gate of the embassy. This time, she sees the familiar sight of smart young US Marines in their battle fatigues, guarding the entrance posts. One of them walks up to their vehicle as Dick lowers the tinted window again. On recognising Dick, he greets all of them and signals them to go inside the gate.

'Home away from home,' sighs Sam, excitement getting the better of her fatigue, she now looks forward to meeting her station chief and colleagues.

Her new assignment had just begun.

*   *   *

The first sign of a severe winter was evident in the rocky mountains of Waziristan. It is more than a month since Baaz was thrown out of Afghanistan back into the semi-autonomous Pakistani district of Waziristan. With Maulvi Najeeb killed and his Lashkar all but neutralised, Baaz had set about reorganising this outfit to resume the objective from the point it left off.

Maulvi Najeeb was a prodigy of Afghan jihad of the 1980s, having been trained by the US and Pakistan's intelligence agencies to fight the Soviets. Subsequently, he felt humiliated by the Americans who ignored Afghanistan after meeting their objective of disintegrating the Soviet Union. After the withdrawal of Soviet forces from Afghanistan in 1989, he turned his attention and resources to aid the Kashmiri freedom fighters in their fight for self-determination against Indian forces based in Indian-administered Kashmir.

He avoided merging his group with any other similar organisation, preferring to maintain his individuality and obtained aid from benefactors from across the world sympathetic to the Kashmiri cause. Throughout the nineties, he kept the Indians engaged, and the Pakistanis disengaged.

However, things changed after 9/11. The Pakistan government allied itself with the USA and declared a number of such outfits as 'terrorists' and pressurised them to stop their operations completely. Once again, Najeeb felt betrayed, this time by the Pakistanis. Years of financial aid and supply of armaments had enabled him to establish a lethal private army of his own operating out of Waziristan, with hundreds of foot soldiers and others in reserve. He declared alliance with the Taliban of Afghanistan when Coalition Forces led by the US attacked that country. In the process, he waged war against the US, and when Pakistan tried to forcefully stop him, he also declared war against the Pakistani forces, executing terror attacks on them, hence becoming a wanted criminal in Pakistan as well.

It was in the Afghan War just after 9/11 when Baaz, an Afghan Taliban, having lost his family, fled to Waziristan where Najeeb gave him refuge in his Lashkar.[68] Here, Baaz rose through the cadre to eventually become Maulvi Najeeb's chief security officer, until that fateful night.

Now, with no apparent heir to Najeeb's throne, the next people in line having been incinerated in the same missile strike, Baaz reorganises the Lashkar, finding little opposition in his becoming the next chief, ready to take on the mantle of his predecessor for the reborn Lashkar al-Mujahideen.

Baaz vowes to keep the objectives of Lashkar the same. He promises to continue their fight against US Forces until Afghanistan is rid of them and against the Pakistani military until they stop supporting the Americans.

While he projects these objectives to gather the support and loyalty of his fellow militants, he also yearns to regain his lost pride and reputation in the eyes of his Afghan compatriots and Alqaeda, who had evicted him from Afghanistan in disgrace. His hatred for his American and Pakistani enemies reinforced by an unfair and disrespectful exile, he resolves to leave no stone unturned in gaining back his repute.

---

[68]   Army.

                        *   *   *

25 December—Morning time at the Auditorium of the Army
Cantonment School in Attock

The hall is filled with parents of children who are excitedly
showing different skits and variety shows prepared to celebrate the
anniversary of the birth of Pakistan's creator Muhammad Ali Jinnah.
In the middle of the background is a huge portrait of Jinnah. On one
side is a large map of Pakistan distinctly showing the four provinces
Punjab, Sindh, Khyber Pakhtoonkhwa, and Baluchistan along with
other administrative areas of Pakistan, including Azad Kashmir,[69]
Gilgit Baltistan,[70] and FATA.[71] On the other side of the portrait is a
large flag of Pakistan tacked to the background curtain.

Parents, mostly officers and soldiers are delighted to see their
small children performing well. Dhil is seated smartly in the front
row courtesy of Rania. Dressed in dark grey trousers with a white
shirt and a blue blazer, his neck scarf proudly showing the emblem
of his unit, Dhil catches the eye of Rania who admires her man from
backstage.

Meanwhile, Dhil enjoys the show and is particularly overjoyed
to see his three children perform in the last tableau whose theme is
'Peace and Unity'.

> *You are Pakistani, I am Pakistani*
> *All else becomes secondary*
> *All the killing, all the bombing*
> *In return it gives us nothing*
> *Live with Peace, Live with Unity*
> *And enjoy the fruits of Harmony*

As the song resounds in the background, children dressed up in
various regional dresses, urban Western attires and military uniforms

---

[69] Pakistan-administered Kashmir.

[70] Northern Areas historically part of Jammu and Kashmir Province.

[71] Federally Administered Tribal Area—an assortment of seven territories
      bordering Afghanistan, one of which is Waziristan.

depicting different segments of the nation, come on the stage in a sequence, holding hands and occasionally waving to the audience. Taimur, Dhil's elder son is dressed in an Army commando uniform similar to that of his father. Dhil proudly looks at him and can't help but share his excitement with Mrs Hafeez sitting next to him.

'That's my boy!' he points out Taimur who's trying to concentrate on his actions. Mrs Hafeez looks a little surprised that Dhil would think she doesn't know whose son he is, but then smiles, seeing the excited and innocent look on this gentle giants face.

Not wanting to discourage him she responds, 'He fancies his father a lot,' correcting herself she continues, 'in fact all three of them do.'

Dhil, while looking at the children thanks Mrs Hafeez and says, 'My family is everything to me.'

By this time his daughter Ayesha comes up on the stage dressed in a white doctor's robe complete with stethoscope and specs on her nose, she acts as if attending to the injured in the play.

> *You are Pakistani, I'm Pakistani*
> *All else becomes secondary*
> *All the killing, all the bombing*
> *In return it gives us nothing*
> *Live with Peace, Live with Unity*
> *And enjoy the fruits of Harmony*
> *Long live Pakistan*
> *Our great Pakistan!*

As the song reaches its climax, a queue of little kids walk up to the stage and take their place in front of the older children. Dhil's little devil Hamza is one of them. Cutely dressed in brightly coloured local clothes complete with darker waistcoats and mirror tapestry on them, the children stand on the dais waving the flags of Pakistan.

Dhil, overcome with emotion feels a tear trickle from his eye. Quickly wiping it off, he heaves a deep sigh and wishes, *'If only things were this simple'*.

The show concludes on a boisterous note. The audience gets up on their feet clapping energetically until their claps resound in unity before tapering down. Children bow to their audience's applause with the fall of the curtains, signalling the end of the show.

On the way back in Dhil's Toyota Corolla the children briskly chatter their roles and how they felt doing the show. Taimur, in particular showing off his uniform asks his mother to take his picture on reaching home. Meanwhile, Ayesha floats the idea of going for a picnic for the rest of the day to the River Kabul flowing close to the Attock Cantonment and have tea, cake and sandwiches; food is always on her mind. With the prattle of kids in the background Dhil lovingly looks at Rania, holding her hand.

'That was a wonderfully arranged show, love,' he compliments her.

'Thanks dear, I guess all the time and effort paid off in the end,' Rania responds accepting his compliments. 'Thank you for your support and understanding for not spending enough time with you, as much as I would've wanted, in the last few weeks.'

'You will need to compensate me for that,' Dhil smiles mischievously at Rania kissing her hand and not realising that at that moment the children had stopped talking and were attentively listening to their parent's romantic exchange.

There is an embarrassing silence in the car as Rania signals Dhil to stop the talk as the children were listening. At this Ayesha gives out a giggle which is followed by Taimur's hearty guffaw. Hamza's 'me too' laughter joins the chorus. The whole family bursts into laughter at this scene, by which time they reach home.

Dhil carefully parks his sparkling clean Toyota Corolla under the porch as the children jump out of it enthusiastically discussing the picnic plan for the day.

'Kids wash the makeup off your faces and change first!' Rania cheerily instructs before they dash to the kitchen.

'But take my pic first, Ma,' protests Taimur.

'Mine too!' yells Ayesha.

'Me, me, me!' jumps Hamza not wanting to be left out.

Dhil leaves this commotion for Rania to handle and walks into the lounge to switch on the television. To his shock he sees the footage of another bomb blast and shouts from the lounge to quiet down. As the children fall silent and walk into the room, the news on TV continues.

   '. . . the suicide bomber forced his bomb laden truck
  through the guarded entry barriers of the park where different
  festivities arranged by Pak Army in collaboration with local
  civil administration, were in full swing to celebrate the birth

anniversary of Quaid-e-Azam.[72] *He is reported to have blown himself up in the middle of the crowd. Sixty-two fatalities including that of women and children are confirmed so far. The head of the suicide bomber has been found and he seems to be a young boy with scanty beard not more than sixteen years of age . . .'*

As the news reporter goes through the news, gory footage of the explosion site is aired again and again. People shouting for help, others injured and in pain, rescue workers trying to give first aid to the injured, people running around looking for their loved ones, ambulances rushing in and out of the spot, stalls blown apart, debris scattered like paper, chairs littered all over the place, blood, smoke and some body parts.

There is a pin-drop silence in the room as Rania covers the eyes of Hamza in an attempt to prevent him from seeing such horrible scenes. 'Why do they have to show such pictures on TV?' she complains about the media.

Ayesha starts sobbing and Taimur screams with anger. Dhil, disgusted and anguished to see this, hugs his two elder children and comforts them. He agrees with Rania that such gory footage should not be shown on television, as it is harmful especially to the young viewers.

'When will all this stop?' Rania protests helplessly, 'when will these terrorists see sense?'

But suddenly the TV reporter again claims the attention of Dhilawar.

'Lashkar al Mujahideen has claimed responsibility for this heinous act. Their spokesman Maulvi Abdul Jabbar has stated that this is in response to the CIA drone attacks on their innocent civilians including women and children and unless Pakistan de-link themselves from the US War on Terror and pressurize the US to stop these drone attacks, we will continue to wreak havoc inside Pakistan.'

---

[72] Founder of the nation — Mohammad Ali Jinnah.

Dhil is furious to hear this report. He is shocked to see how this organisation has regrouped so soon to execute such an atrocious attack. How come our intelligence did not report this regrouping? Who is their new leader? Questions crop up in Dhil's mind as he tries to connect the loose ends leading to this event.

The more we kill them, the more they spring up; a frustrated Dhil wonders how will this end.

*   *   *

25 December, in Islamabad

Sam is attending the Christmas Mass in the Church constructed inside the confines of the US embassy. It is her first Christmas out of the US, and she dearly misses her mother and Lia—her pet. As her fellow Christians, mostly Americans, sing Christmas Carols, her mind goes back to all the Christmases she spent with her family. It was their tradition that Christmas and Thanksgiving would always be spent together as a family; but this Christmas, it was different. She was in a foreign land and yearned to be with Catherine. She plans to call her in the evening; since Jacksonville was ten hours behind the time in Islamabad, Catherine must be sleeping right now.

The past month had been very busy for Sam, taking over charge from her predecessor; familiarising herself with her role, her contacts, and her overall job; finding a place to stay, furnishing it; making new friends and acquaintances; and getting to understand her logistics. While settling down in a new place had kept her very busy, she had found life in general to be restricted. Personnel were kept under high security. Local staff was always viewed with suspicion. Then there was George Yeats, a senior liaison officer in the US embassy, who always scared the young staff members, exhorting them not to wander off alone or mingle with the local crowd. However, his advice was often ignored by the youngsters, who found urban locals to be friendly and in awe of the American way of life.

Sam also found Islamabad and the twin city of Rawalpindi fairly peaceful, where life continued normally. Her few visits during the day, out in the city, remained uneventful and mundane. This was quite a contrast to what she was led to believe in the US.

On her job front, she had noticed that field reports were not very forthcoming. Their human Intel was weak, and they mostly had to rely on elements of local intelligence agencies for getting information, and this at times was not accurate. Her first priority thus became to improve this situation.

In her efforts to keep her professional life separate from her personal life, Sam made concerted attempts not to socialise with her colleagues from the Agency beyond the requirement of her job. In the first month, however, she befriended Rebecca Barney, thirty-two, an Afro-American from Queens, New York. A junior associate in the High Commission for two years now, Becy, as she preferred to be called, lived in a rented apartment inside the diplomatic enclave. The building was mostly rented out to foreign nationals working in the various Western embassies. This area had been cleared by their security agencies and was considered a safe zone for foreign nationals. The daughter of a stage-actor father and a hairdresser mother, Becy had worked hard to make it to the Foreign Service.

Becy had found her job in Islamabad very exciting. She had lots of stories to tell Sam about her social exploits with the local young upwardly mobile trendy crowd of Islamabad. Often meeting over the weekends with her group, she partied all night long with them. Their parties with song and dance, booze and fun on the poolside of big bungalows and farmhouses of the rich were comparable to the parties of Hollywood and New York's rich and famous. Although Sam was not yet interested in such adventures, she developed a liking for Becy for her friendly and jovial nature. Incidentally, Sam also found an apartment in the same building where Rebecca lived, thus further enhancing their friendship.

As they finish their Mass, the people in the church greet and wish each other Merry Christmas. On one side Santa, in his typical style, distributes gifts among the children of the staff who had preferred to keep their families in Islamabad. Sam also follows the ritual, greeting her colleagues before walking out of the church with Rebecca. Since Christmas Day is a holiday in Pakistan, as this date coincidentally is also the birth anniversary of Pakistan's founding father, Christians get to celebrate their Christmas in the traditional way as well.

It rained the previous night. So the weather is cold, and chilly wind runs through their hair. All of them are clad in overcoats and jackets. The sky is overcast with forecast of more rain later in the day.

Rebecca invites Sam over to a Christmas party being held by one of her Pakistani friends. 'Hey, Sam, come over, girl! It'll be fun,' she implores.

Sam smiles and shakes her head in the negative.

'Girl, you got some serious issues here. Hey, I go every other weekend out of this green zone,' she gestures at the area around, 'nothing's dangerous out there,' she shrieks. 'You're in Islamabad, not in some Goddamned Ban[73] land.'

'You go on, have fun, Becy,' Sam smiles, 'I've got other plans.'

'Yeah, I know your plans,' retorts Rebecca, 'Go to your damn office and look for America's most beloved, OBL!'

Both laugh off the sarcasm as they walk casually up to the main building, Rebecca still trying to entice Sam into coming with her. As they enter the corridor, they see Agent Jim walking towards them with concern on his face.

Sam holds Rebecca's arm to quiet her down as she nonchalantly continues telling Sam one of her stories without noticing Jim.

'News just came in,' he begins, 'a massive suicide attack in Bannu about 160 miles south-west of here.'

Both the ladies silently look at him, Rebecca now a little embarrassed about her enthusiastic rendition of the Christmas festivities.

As if reading Sam's mind, Jim continues, 'It happened in a funfair, a bomb-laden truck driven by a teenager forced itself in before blowing up. Till now death toll is reported at sixty-two and possibilities of more dead, mostly women and children.'

'Oh God!' cries Rebecca while Sam looks away.

Jim continues, 'Worst part is that LaM, the terrorist outfit which we thought was finished with the death of its leader last fall, has claimed responsibility for this attack, blaming our drone attacks for this retaliation.'

Sam gets concerned. She knows the background and remembers the mission she undertook in October from Nevada.

'Problem is these Pak officials will go on air again, protesting against us, and we can't even share the truth with their public,' he continues.

---

73   Ban—short for Taliban.

Sam is not worried about what the Pakistanis may or may not do. To her surprise, she finds herself less disconcerted by the loss of lives at the moment and more upset by the idea of a possible intelligence lapse at their end. Her only concern now is figuring out who has taken over this outfit. She feels their Intel is wanting. *How did they not know of this? Who has taken over this outfit? How did it get reorganised so quickly? Where's our mole on this?* Various queries going through her mind, her Christmas all but over, she excuses herself from Rebecca, who is still stunned by this news, and decides to go to her office.

Miles to go before I sleep, miles to go before I sleep—words from a poem resonating in Sam's mind as she briskly makes her way to her office in the compound, Jim following closely on her heels.

*   *   *

25 December, afternoon—in the freezing, dry snow-covered rocky hills of Waziristan

An elaborate network of dungeons, tunnels, and caves has been dug over the years where LaM houses its headquarters around the village of Bastikhel. Similar to the ones in Paktita Province of Afghanistan, the entrance to this network is through some huts clustered together in the small village spread across quarter of a square mile. This cluster of huts is zealously guarded by an inner ring of diehard militants surrounded by an intermediate ring of foot soldiers. Spies and supporters from the village also constitute Lashkar's first line of defence.

It is through one of these huts, a young man, with unkempt hair and a small beard, dressed in a white local dress now discoloured with dirt, expeditiously makes his way down a dark shaft. A lantern in his hand providing the only light and his back bent almost to his waist, he pants while making his way forward before the shaft leads into a larger opening, where he is able to stand properly. This cave, deep inside the ground, leads to a modestly lit room, where Baaz is seated on the ground with his close aids.

Hair spread over his face, a new eye patch firmly back on his dead eye, beads in his hand, and reciting verses, he looks inquiringly at the young man. His comrades huddled around him also look up at the youngster who tries to catch his breath.

Finding his voice, the youngster exclaims, 'Allah o Akbar! Allah o Akbar!'

'Is it done?' Baaz's lieutenant sounds irritated at the youngsters excitement.

'Yes!' comes the reply, 'Our fidayeen[74] have done it, congratulations.'

'Alhamdolillah,'[75] all four comrades exclaim before they shake hands with each other; all except Baaz, who remains silent staring straight at the wall in front with intensity, continuing to read his verses.

One of his lieutenants carefully addresses Baaz, 'Chief?' he speaks softly, 'Congratulations.'

'Don't congratulate me now, Abu Hamza,' Baaz snarls in a low tone at which all fall silent, 'congratulate me when Pakistan Army runs from here like headless chickens, congratulate me when Americans stop their devil attacks on us, congratulate me when we defeat the infidels,' his voice rising with every sentence, 'then I'll accept your congratulations.' He looks back at his lieutenants who are dumbfounded by now.

Looking at the other subordinate, Baaz asks authoritatively, 'How many more fidayeen can you provide me?'

'Our local khateeb[76] has prepared some boys to become suicide bombers. They can be bought whenever you desire,' he says, looking at others with pride. Then trying to gain points in front of his leader, he explains, 'Besides, there is no dearth of suicide bombers in this region since most madrassas[77] have a select number of boys brainwashed from childhood into laying down their lives for the cause of Islam. But they are available for a price. It's only a matter of how many we can afford to acquire.'

In the past two months, Baaz had gathered his intelligence to confirm that the attack launched on them in October was by the Pakistan Army Commando Unit based in Attock Cantonment. From

---

[74]   Historically 'fidayeen' were the diehard highly motivated warriors of Islam who preferred to die fighting in the name of God, rather than come back from a battlefront. Presently, the militants have controversially termed their suicide bombers as 'Fidayeen'

[75]   Thanks to God.

[76]   Islamic priest.

[77]   Religious schools.

the events of that night, he presumed that this was a coordinated strike between the Pakistan Army and the CIA, launching a two-pronged attack ensuring that no one survived the assault.

Baaz gives his subordinate a long and intense look and then peers straight at the blank wall, once again blood soaking into his eye with anger, 'I want to blow up Pakistan Army, I want to kill the people who killed our leader, I want to kill the families of those who killed ours.'

He then looks at his subordinate, holds his shoulder and firmly gripping it, declares, 'For now, get me enough to blow apart Attock.'

To break the tension in the room, one of his comrades yells nervously, 'Allah o Akbar!' at which all follow suit before Baaz stands up and wraps his shawl around his upper body, hair still unkempt and scattered across his disfigured face; he nods at his subordinates and, in the same dark mood, walks out of the underground room, the thump of his heavy 'Peshawari' sandals audible as he strides away into the darkness of the cave to the relief of his lieutenants.

Their next mission — Attock Cantonment.

Chapter 5

STATE HITS BACK

It is 31 December, in Attock Cantonment, just five days after the deadly suicide bomber struck in Bannu, killing seventy-eight men, women, and children.

The shadow of the off-white building with a red-tiled roof, where Dhilawar's unit is nestled, gradually stretches towards the green garden across the dirt track, separating the building from the garden. American grass, more popular for its hardy nature and lower maintenance need, is immaculately cultivated across the garden surrounded only by a flowerbed, housing a variety of colourful roses and jasmines. A solid oak tree, reflecting decades of sagacity stands at one corner, its shade stretching out across the garden. Next to this tree, four contemporary wooden armchairs are placed neatly, facing each other with a wooden centre table in the middle, a favourite spot for the senior unit officers for their tea breaks during the day. This serene environment is supplemented in the background by the chirping of sparrows, call of the crows, and an odd song of the cuckoo, all beckoning their mates home for the evening as the afternoon sun makes way for dusk.

Dhil is in the garden resting after a hard day's work, conducting assault drills with his fellow commandos, on simulated terrorist camps especially constructed inside the wide span of Attock Cantonment. His pleasant gaze is fixed on some birds in their nests, built at the end of the rainwater drainpipe attached alongside the slanting tiled roof of his unit building. Dhil is seated under the tree across from the building on one of four chairs, enjoying hot tea from a cup placed on the wooden table in front, steam escaping in the cold winter dusk. He mulls over the intelligence briefing given the day before to him and his fellow senior officers of other units in Attock Cantonment.

'Gentlemen, we have received Intel that Lashkar al-Mujahideen has regrouped in Waziristan under a new leader who is originally an Afghan. His name is Baaz Jan, and our Intel has advised that he is much more ruthless and cunning than his predecessor. Fear is his main weapon and hatred is his ammunition. He has no love lost for Pakistan or Pakistani military, and what is of concern is that he has made plans to bring this war into our military cantonments. While other militant outfits fight us out in the open, he feels that by hitting the military's soft underbelly, he will be able to demotivate our men from fighting them altogether, thus fending the military off their back. This way he feels that they'll be able to concentrate more on waging their war in Afghanistan. But we are cognizant of his tactics now and are taking utmost precautionary measures to ensure no such act of terror takes place within the military cantonments.'

Dhil recalls the serious atmosphere then prevailing over the briefing room and remembers the various safety and precautionary measures advised to them by the chief security officer of Military Police for the cantonment.

Dhil and his fellow officers had their doubts about these foolproof security arrangements.

'When you are willing to die for whatever reason and take along many with you, no degree of security measures can stop you from doing that,' he remembers one officer sharing his concern in private after the meeting, 'you always have a way out.'

'These bloody chaps are so motivated to kill themselves that if stopped from doing that, they break down and cry like kids on not being able to go to heaven,' had laughed another CO of an infantry battalion based over there.

'Well, how many can there be?' Lt. Col. Ikram Bajwa, a highly charged commanding officer, 23rd Punjab Battalion of Infantry Division had scoffed, 'How many? They cannot destroy the whole of Pakistan,' determination written all over his face.

'They don't need to, partner.' Dhil remembers the response of one of his senior comrades, Colonel Ramzan. A superseded colonel in administration, who was due to retire in a year had also been posted in Military Intelligence in his earlier days and was well aware of the psyche of these militants, said, 'All they need to do is make a few strikes inside the cantonments on the families of our soldiers, and you'll see how the motivation plummets. As it is, it has taken us years to realign our men's thoughts from perceiving not just the Indians as our enemy but also these bloody militants. And now when we are getting our desired results, a few such incidents are all it will take to send them back into their shells.'

Dhil remembers Bajwa countering Ramzan, 'Sir, I beg to differ. In fact, on the contrary, if they come here and cause destruction, it will motivate our soldiers more out of vengeance to go out there and eliminate them completely. This war will become personal to them and any such strategy of the militants will backfire.'

'But you are missing the point, Bajwa,' Ramzan had countered, 'Why attack them, then lose your family and then kill the bad guys with vengeance when by not fighting them you can avoid the possibility of losing your family in the first place.' There was silence in the group as Colonel Ramzan had lit up his cigarette, 'That's the predicament we may face if such incidents commence.'

Bajwa, not willing to back down, had taken one more shot at Ramzan. 'We put our lives in danger the day we signed up in the army.'

'Yes, we offered our lives when we signed up for this,' Ramzan agreed, 'but we didn't offer our beloved wives and children up for this. When you joined the army, your enemy was another professional army, whom you could look in the eye! You were at the borders where you knew that your loved ones were safe back home, but now you have enemies within you. You have their sympathisers, their financiers, and their complete bloody support structure within our society who don't give a damn about others. How are you going to eliminate these fanatics among us? Here no one is safe, not you, not your wife, children, parents, no one, and this is what these bastards are relying on . . . fear.' After another uneasy pause, he had concluded, 'Anyway, gentlemen, let me not demotivate you here. I've played my inning and will be on my way out in a year's time. But you guys have a long way to go yet. So do what you think is best for the country.'

With these parting words, the elderly colonel had excused himself and walked away, puffing on his cigarette.

'What a pessimist!' Bajwa had said scornfully once Ramzan was at a safe distance.

He was countered by another fellow officer, 'Rather, what a realist!'

Dhil then remembers breaking this deadlock. 'Well, gentlemen, let's stay vigilant in our units and also believe in ourselves. I'm sure Colonel Adnan will implement foolproof safety precautions, and our families can sleep in peace. It's not easy for these suicide bombers to just walk into our bases and blow themselves up. After all, we are the Pak Army.' At this, the group had shared faint laughter and dispersed.

Dhil's chain of thoughts is broken by the pleasing call to prayers emitting out of the mosque situated some distance down the road from his unit. He decides to offer his Maghrib[78] prayers before going home, and just when he gets up for ablution, he sees Maj. Saifullah Dar walking up to him with a box of sweets in his hand.

Dar was on a short leave and had just come back. Dressed in civvies,[79] he comes up to Dhil, stands at attention, and still holding the box in one of his hands, he greets his commanding officer.

Dhil smiles and, being in uniform, responds with a casual salute, asking him to ease off and walk with him up to the mosque that lay about 200 metres down the road.

'Welcome back, Dar, how was your leave?'

'Fine, sir, thank you, spent some quality time with my parents back in Lahore,' and without wasting any more time on pleasantries, Dar blurts out, 'Sir, I got engaged,' excitement etched all over his face.

Dhil, unable to understand Dar's words, looks perplexed. 'Come again . . . ?'

'Sir, my parents got me engaged this time when I went to see them, and I thought I'll share this good news first of all with you.' Dar's response is more settled and slow this time.

Dhil gives out a laugh, 'Well, I'll be damned . . . Did you know the girl from before?'

'No, sir! My mother saw her at a marriage party recently, liked her, took the initiative and sent my proposal after consulting my dad. They had not kept me in the loop but had my general consent. So when I went this time, she advised me of it minutes before the function she had arranged between our two families and got me engaged,' he pauses, 'more of a surprise party for me, I guess.'

Dhil, astonished at this story, lets out another laugh. The concern about suicide bombers, terror threats, and other dangers take a back seat. 'And you expect me to believe this story of 'Saif—the Playboy',

---

[78] Dusk.
[79] Military term for civilian dress.

who a couple of months back had another close encounter in one of his escapades, agreed to an "arranged" marriage?'

A little embarrassed from the jovial taunts of his commanding officer, Dar replies, 'Sir, in fact, those hours I spent cocooned in that steel trunk under the blankets made me realise it was time to move on. Sir, I'm thirty-three now, a Major in the army and way past the stage of engaging in such fun and frolic. I decided that day that it's high time I get settled and what's better than getting married to a girl of my parents' choice? Maybe God likes this gesture of mine and forgives me for my sins. I know I've not been up to the mark by His standards, but He knows I never meant ill towards anyone,' remorse is plainly written all over his face.

Dhil, realising the topic is serious and that Dar is sincerely engaged, changes his tone as well, 'Well, Dar, we always knew that the brave soldier that you are, you were also a good person, and the girl who would eventually get married to you would be a lucky girl.'

He pauses, then concludes, 'Congratulations, son. May you have a long happy married life and God bless you,' elderly grace written all over his statement, he shakes Dar's hand firmly. 'Now will you continue feeling all melodramatic or offer me some sweets from the box you're holding?'

Dar gives an embarrassed smile and offers the sweets to his revered commanding officer.

'So how is she and when's the marriage planned?' Dhil continues with his questions, trying to be part of his junior officer's happiness as they walk together up to the mosque to offer their Maghrib prayers, thanking God for another day well spent.

*   *   *

31 December, New Year's Eve in Islamabad

Sam sits in her barely furnished two-bedroom apartment. One room still empty, the other only had a queen-size bed with a wardrobe, dressing table, and side tables, completing the set. Her living room was also sparsely furnished with just an ethnic sofa set along with an ethnic rug, placed in the middle, which she had bought from one of Islamabad's antique shops. Plain dark-red curtains hung in front of glass windows opening on to the balcony. Sam had made it a point to bring her family pictures, and these along with her clothes were about the only things she brought from home. Even in Islamabad, pictures of her father in Vietnam, brother, and other family members adorned the white walls of her living room. A pleasant addition to this picture gallery was that of her dog Lia, whom she left back with her neighbours in Nevada.

The television is on in the background but Sam is oblivious of the happenings on the TV screen. She is seated at the kitchen counter sipping a hot mug of coffee to beat the winter cold. Having collected information on the latest suicide bombing on 25 December in Bannu, she is now going through the file of their latest casualty Hamidullah Mehsud, a young man in his late twenties and son of a shopkeeper, who was also a supplier of foodstuff to LaM. Hamid was a local of Bastikhel Village in Waziristan, who regularly visited Peshawar to buy goods for his father's shop. Semi-literate, he was very fond of Hollywood and was fascinated with the American way of life. On observing his frequency of visits to cinemas showing old Hollywood movies in Peshawar, he had been identified by CIA as a prospective informer for them. Once having confirmed his potential, another one of their Caucasian American woman agents in Peshawar was given the assignment of befriending him and starting an intimate relationship with him. Out of his love for the girl and in an endeavour to impress her and to be taken to America with her, Hamid had started providing her with accurate information on the movements of the Lashkar in Bastikhel Village. It was eventually on his firm information and assistance that Sam from Nevada was able to successfully command the drone strike.

Hamid's American dream had come to an abrupt end when he was traced and identified by Baaz's men once the Lashkar regrouped. By then, abandoned by his perceived girlfriend and the Agency, he was abducted in November, weeks before the Lashkar was to re-emerge. After the suicide attack of Bannu on 25 December, the battered and headless corpse of Hamid was found in front of his father's shop in Bastikhel with the usual warning note attached to it.

The note, as in all such cases, read: *Hamid was an American spy and was responsible for aiding our infidel enemy in killing our Mujahideen. Let it be known that we would do the same thing to any traitor caught spying for America or its allies, including Pakistan. There will be no heaven for his headless corpse.*

Sam feels sorry for Hamid, a regular guy longing for a better life. Could he have imagined how he would meet this tragic end? Her chain of thought is broken by a loud knock on her door.

'Sam!' comes a familiar voice, 'Hey, Sam, ma' girl . . . open up.'

Sam knows its Rebecca and her reason for coming to her flat. She shakes her head with a smile, walks up to the door, and opens it up.

'Becy, I'm not going anywhere,' Sam starts before Rebecca could even begin; 'I'm working on something.'

By this time Rebecca has walked up to the kitchen counter, and seeing Sam's hot mug of coffee and an open file, she responds, 'Yeah, reading another sob story of a dead village spy.' She protests, 'There are hundreds of those out there, and all have the same story. They get lured in with women, money, or something. We get help from them, they get caught. We look the other way, and they get killed. The lucky ones at least have their heads on,' she pauses before complaining again in her high-pitch tone, 'You can't go around crying at their fates, you'll be a mental wreck.'

'Nobody is crying here, Becy. I just feel concerned that with this attitude of ours, we'll lose out on our support base once the locals realise we're not there for them when they get caught. No wonder the info from our local assets is reducing with time, and even when we get it, most of it is inaccurate. We are forced to rely on Paks to get our Intel, and that is my other concern,' Sam explains seriously.

'I've a perfect answer for your concern, girl,' she says, mischief written all over Rebecca's face. 'Come with me.'

'Where?'

'Well, there is this good friend of mine, Fred.'

'Fred?'

'Yeah, Fred, short for Fareed.'

'Oh, I see,' Sam is amused by the Western translation of his Pakistani name.

'And who is this Mr Fred?' she asks sarcastically.

'Well, he calls himself an agriculturist who studied in America and liked it there. His friends call him a feudal lord, but the hell I care.' Rebecca continues, 'What I care about is that he's a good laugh, throws great parties, and has booze flowing all over the place. He has some real hot-looking guys there, you're gonna like it.'

Rebecca tries to lure Sam in.

'What's our Intel on him?'

'Here we go again, Special Agent Scully,' jokingly referring to Gillian Anderson's character in *X-Files*, 'the detective in you is always alert,' laughs Rebecca. 'He's clear. Even Barney and John visit him often,' referring to two Marines posted in Islamabad, 'I'll pick you at 10.30 tonight; the party begins at 11.'

Rebecca waves as she quickly leaves Sam's apartment before Sam can cook up another excuse.

*   *   *

Sam, finally convinced by Rebecca, decides to attend Fred's party. She thinks some time-out would refresh her. It is a cold damp winter's night in Islamabad as they drive outside the confines of the diplomatic enclave. The temperature is down to almost zero degrees Celsius. Although New Year's Eve is not generally celebrated among the masses in Pakistan, with 1 January being a working day, the urban youth and high society of the large cities throw New Year parties celebrating with booze and fervour.

The traffic volume in Islamabad is still high as people drive to different parties and restaurants, celebrating the New Year. There is no sign of a country fighting terror as young men party on the streets to loud Western and Indian dance music blaring from their car stereos.

The police are also on patrol, and Sam notices pickup trucks and cars, with their police lights on, slowly prowling the city streets with their armed contingent of men sitting inside. Rebecca drives her little Suzuki Swift hatchback out of Islamabad City. On the inbound road, in the opposite direction, Sam notices the usual traffic jam at the check post entering Islamabad.

'Where are we going?' She asks Rebecca, a little alarmed.

'Take it easy, sister! I ain't kidnapping you!'

'But where is this place we're going to?' Sam persists as they speed up on the highway leading to the hill station of Murree, thirty miles from Islamabad.

'It's a farmhouse ten miles out of the city on the way to Murree. Don't worry, the area is A-okay.'

Street lights all but gone, they get off the winding highway as it starts snaking its way up the hill, leading to Murree. On a small metal track leading to some farmhouses outside of Islamabad, they are soon joined by some other cars all making their way in the darkness with only their headlights for illumination. Another seven minutes before they reach a huge Victorian-style gate, the entrance brightly lit up in this wilderness, they see spotlights throwing beams of light across a 50-metre circumference of the gate and its adjacent high-rise boundary wall. Looking at the area, Sam feels that she has reached some up market suburb of Los Angeles or even Beverly Hills itself.

'What is this place?' she asks Rebecca, this time sounding more amazed than alarmed.

'Didn't I tell you, you'll like it here,' replies Rebecca with a smile.'They call it Bara Khu, and this is Fred's weekend resort.'

On seeing four vehicles standing in a queue at the gate, one guard walks up to Rebecca, while the other one holds his position with his pump-action shotgun ready. The guard asks for ID, but seeing two foreign-looking ladies, he eases off and lets them in before checking the other cars for their ID.

As they drive up to the single-storey farm house, 200 metres down the winding paved path, Sam is astounded at the show of wealth around her. Victorian-style fountains running alongside them with statues of cupids and half-naked women spurting water from their mouths; lush green gardens on both sides; two tennis courts in the background; flower beds spread around the gardens. As they park their car in the parking lot, Sam checks out the expensive European cars and a few pricey SUVs also parked alongside. This parking lot seemed a far cry from what she generally saw on the roads of the city.

Already late for the party, she follows Rebecca into the house like a faithful puppy towing her mistress's heel where they are received by loud rap and dance music from the latest Western singers blaring in the hallway. Disco lights adorning the walls and ceiling give the ambiance of a top-class discotheque. She is stunned to see men and women attired in Western designer outfits thronging the interior. It is the first time in her month's stay in Islamabad that Sam has noticed such skimpy clothes on Pakistani women in this warm indoor environment, who otherwise would be covered from head to toe in public places. Most people are dancing their hearts out while others sit in groups; some couples even enjoy intimate moments together.

People can be seen all across the hallway, disco hall, and even the rooms adjacent to the hallway. *Who are these folks?* she wonders as a big fat guy with his arms stretched open makes his way towards Rebecca, hugging her in the process and kissing both her cheeks.

'Fred, I'd like you to meet my good friend Samantha. Sam, meet Fred.'

Sam is not impressed with Fareed's demeanour. A aged man in his fifties with a pot belly, trying to act as if he is still thirty something, he is dressed in a two-piece designer blue suit with red-and-white striped shirt. With shirt buttons opened down to his waist, revealing his hairy chest, he has his hair dyed jet-black and gelled back. But wrinkles on the face and the white hair on his chest betray his real age. Breathing liquor through his nostrils, Fareed is already drunk and in a party mood. He lunges towards Samantha to greet her wholeheartedly.

'So you are Samantha,' he tries to hug her, 'Becy has told me so much about you,' referring to Rebecca.

Seeing his drunken condition, Sam avoids the bear hug coming her way, and with equal speed just extends her hand across, taking one step back in the process. Her intent all too obvious, Fareed holds himself back and sheepishly shakes Samantha's hand, welcoming her to the party.

'Well, you girls make yourselves comfortable. Sak must be around,' referring to his wife Sakina, who is busy chatting away with her group of friends in the smaller room adjacent to the main disco hall. A heated pool emits steam creating a special ambiance in this room.

Sakina is wary of her husband's company of friends. Lady friends of Fareed are not Sakina's friends, and male friends of Sakina are not Fareed's pals either. But Rebecca does not care. She is here to have a good time with her group, comprising both locals and foreigners who also just want to party. In return, Fareed is happy that his parties are a roaring hit with international guests and are always the talk of the town.

Soon Barney and John, the two marines from the US embassy, also join the fun, and Sam watches them all having a rollicking good time after the clock strikes midnight and the New Year begins.

Sam has already had enough of this. She had never felt comfortable even back home attending such wild parties. Getting hold of a glass of wine, she prefers to sit down in one corner of the warm pool room, graciously declining the advances of a couple of hunks seeking her company.

By about 0130 hrs in the morning, bored to the hilt, she decides to ask Rebecca to leave this place. As she gets up, she notices through the steam, sitting in the other corner of the room, a man dressed in a white baggy shirt and black pants, like a character straight out of *Zorro*, looking outside the foggy window at the dimly lit far end of the manicured garden. Sporting a well-built physique, straight black hair reaching down the neck and chiseled features with a sombre look; Sam finds herself walking up to this man to discover the source of his predicament. She thought she was the only one bored by the boisterous partiers, but suddenly she has found someone she actually felt curious about. She feels herself being pulled towards this person even though her instinct dissuades her.

What the heck? she scoffs at her fears and slowly walks up to him.

'Hi,' she softly greets.

The person opposite her, so far deep in his thoughts, looks around in this dimly lit room and finds Sam standing behind him. He stands up quickly, sounding a little alarmed at this sudden greeting.

'Hey,' he says in a husky voice.

'Sorry, I didn't mean to startle you,' Sam tries to explain, feeling foolish about the whole situation. There is silence between them as both of them gawk at each other, expecting the other one to break the ice. 'It's just that you are the only person sitting with a Coke in your hand, gazing out there, whereas all the others are having fun in the hall celebrating the night away . . . with booze and dance. I just felt a little curious and walked up to you. Sorry about that,' she apologises, and just when she begins to leave, this handsome person responds.

'I'm Khattak . . .' he clears his throat and hesitatingly adds, 'I mean, Bilal Khattak.'

*   *   *

1 January, 0630 hrs at Bastikhel Village in Waziristan

Comprising a cluster of about fifty mud huts and a core population of around 500, Bastikhel was a small village spread over an area roughly the size of six football pitches, located a few miles on the other side of the hill range from the site where the Union Mosque was destroyed the previous October. Its locals were economically poor. Mostly small time farmers, they sold their produce in the towns of Khyber Province. It also had a few poor traders trading basic goods and necessities from across the border. Some of the locals who had earlier joined the government-sponsored levy forces later joined the Taliban mostly out of fear of retribution to their families and to at least earn a decent living. However, most of the villagers were uneducated daily wage labourers who wandered to distant urban centres looking for work. At times, a few of them would be also used by State intelligence forces to assist them in targeting militants from the air.

It is through a few of these huts in the periphery that an elaborate network of tunnels had been dug leading to larger underground rooms and caves in the adjacent hills surrounding the village. This was historically Lashkar's base camp deep inside the militant-controlled hinterland near the border of Afghanistan, where the writ of Pakistani State never got established. As in other militant-occupied areas in the territory, a strict code of Shariah[80] was implemented to maintain law and order in Bastikhel. This village and the main accesses to the underground complex were fiercely guarded by diehard fanatics of the Lashkar. Even the village locals, who had initially invited the militants from across the border to support them in their livelihood, were afraid of these foreign elements that had taken the villagers hostage. Anyone who dared to raise his voice met a fate similar to that of Hamidullah Mehsud. Each family was forced to give up one of their young sons to the Lashkar to fight in the name of Jihad.[81]

Today is a cold winter's morning, and the rays of the sun are yet to spread across the eastern horizon. The temperature is below freezing point, and the small enclave of huts is dimly illuminated with portable lanterns giving out faint light peeping through the cracks between the small window covers.

In the distance from these huts but within the enclave, the shrill voice of a child yet to reach adolescence is heard giving out 'Fajr Adhan'.[82] Slowly, but surely, men from the huts close by start coming out making their way to the mosque to offer their pre-dawn prayers.

---

[80] Islamic code of conduct.
[81] War to protect Islam from non-Muslims and, in the case of these fanatics, even Muslims, whom they perceive as supporter of non-Muslims.
[82] Pre-dawn call to prayers

In twenty minutes, there is a gathering of approximately forty men, some militants, others civilians, some locals, and other ethnic Pashtuns, Chechens, and Arabs, young and old, with different shades and sizes of beards, wearing white prayer caps and covering themselves with thick dark shawls over their local dresses, brave the winter cold to make it to the mosque — most of them, more out of fear of being reprimanded by the militants than by God Himself.

The mosque's imam[83] leads the morning prayers for the congregation and then sits down to give them a sermon on a religious topic as the faint rays of sun gradually light the sky on the eastern hills, signalling the break of dawn.

Most seek permission to leave while children of the local madrassa and the militants prefer to stay back and hear what the imam has to preach today, their assault rifles and rocket launchers kept close to them. They treasure these weapons much like women treasure their jewellery.

'In the name of God, the most Beneficent the most Merciful,' the imam begins his sermon.

*   *   *

1 January, 0715 hrs — Pakistan Air Force Base at an undisclosed location deep inside the plains of Pakistan's Punjab Province

Each loaded with 1,000 — pound 'laser guided' bombs and two AIM-9L Sidewinder air-to-air missiles at their wing tips, two US made Lockheed Martin F-16As of the Pakistan Air Force are lined up on the runway at idle engine thrust, awaiting clearance for takeoff. They are on a 'silent' operational mission and their target, a certain militant training camp deep inside Waziristan.

'Tower, this is lead Auqab.[84] Lead and number two, ready for lineup,' the lead F-16 pilot gives a call on his RT[85] as the two combat jets wait for instructions from control tower to take off; the growl of their engine's resembling to that of the tigers before their impending assault on an unsuspecting prey.

---

[83]   Muslim priest.

[84]   'Falcon' in Urdu language.

[85]   Short for radio transmitter.

'Clear line up and wait,' comes the calm response from the Tower.

*   *   *

'When you get killed fighting in the name of God, you actually don't die,' the imam is well into his sermon, 'you simply change your shape and you live for eternity in heavens where seventy-two hoors[86] take care of you and provide you with all kinds of pleasures you could not even imagine on this dastardly earth!'

The imam's audience is enamoured by his speech and already drooling over the prospects.

'Our infidel enemy says that we are terrorists, they say we are ruthless killers, they say we'll go to hell as we kill fellow Muslims too,' the imam continues with anger in his tone and fists waving in the air.

'I want to tell them. It is not us but they who are terrorists, they are the ones who have come to our lands, they are the ones who are killing our innocent people, and they and all of their partners, be they the devilish Muslims, Mushriq[87] or infidels, are worth killing.' Voice raised, he continues animatedly, 'If anyone of you has any doubt, let the ruins of our Masjid Al-Itihad[88] remind you of their cruelty towards us and their apathy for our places of worship.'

The room again reverberates with the chants of 'Allah o Akbar'[89] and 'There is but one God and Mohammed[90] is his Messenger.'

And then the imam gives his punch line. Fist raised in the air, shouting at the top of his hoarse voice, he thunders, 'So go out there and defend your religion, defend your home, and do not feel any remorse when you kill your enemy because it is not us, it is they who are wrong, and hell awaits not us but all of them.'

The scene is electrifying inside the small mosque. The imam has given a highly charged sermon, referring to religious doctrines for their cause; emotions now run high and all start shouting in unison

---

[86]   Angelic clean women of the heavens.

[87]   The ones who share God in his Sovereignty — reference to Christians and Jews.

[88]   Union Mosque.

[89]   God is Great.

[90]   Prophet Mohamed (peace be upon him).

repeatedly 'Allah hu,[91] Allah hu, Allah hu . . . ,' as their collective roar shatters the silence of the quiet village.

*   *   *

1 January, 0720 hrs

The lead pilot gets impatient with the delay as he sees the first ray of light dawning on the plain farmlands of Punjab.

'Tower!' he again addresses, 'We are clear for takeoff,' impatience reflecting in his voice.

Before he can say anything else, both pilots hear the calm voice from the control tower on their earphones.

'Auqab 1 and 2, you are now clear for takeoff, proceed to runway one three.' There is a pause before the controller adds, 'God Speed and Allah o Akbar.'

The fighter jets make their way to the designated runway for their take-off run. On reaching the spot, both the pilots park their aircrafts next to each other and open the full power of their engines finally engaging afterburners while still applying the brakes. With 23,000 pounds of enormous thrust coming from the back of the engines, the jammed tires of the jets plead to be let loose.

'Stand for roll . . . roll . . . roll . . . now,' the lead pilot releases the brakes of his 'Fighting Falcon'[92] as it lunges forward for takeoff with a deafening roar, wiping out the prevalent calm of the dawn. His number two punches his clock to begin the ten-second countdown. His F-16 is also at full afterburner. Brakes applied, holding the bird back, 'Ten, Nine, Eight . . . Three, Two, One — releasing brakes.'

The second Falcon also thunders down the runway for its take-off run, shattering the morning calm as it accelerates to maintain its distance in 'stream take off' formation with his leader, who is already airborne.

Initial vector pre-defined and number two Falcon joining the left wing of his leader in 'shooter formation', the lead pilot disengages his

---

[91]   'O God,' stated in reverence.
[92]   'Fighting Falcon' — F-16A Aircraft.

afterburners and, ten miles out of airbase, gives his final call before observing radio silence.

'Bearing two eight zero, climbing to 20,000 feet, ATLIS beam liaise,' referring to the beam activator which points the laser at the target for the LGB[93] to follow, 'TOT.[94] one three minutes, standby for PIP.'

As the two fighters zoom to 20,000 feet, the lead pilot goes through their standard procedures as he activates his avionics to initiate the bombing run on his target, which according to his calculation will commence in about thirteen minutes.

* * *

0730 hrs — in Bastikhel Village

The sun has now crept out from behind the eastern hill range. Morning dew reflects the rays of the sun, giving a fine gloss across the rocky hillside in front. There is a blue sky with combination of grey white clouds flying in the cold gentle wind like cotton fluff.

The imam completes his short and fiery sermon as the militants holding their weapons walk out of the small mosque and children scamper to the adjacent religious school for their daily classes. As they get together for their morning routine, these men are completely oblivious to the two birds of prey heading in their direction; their target, the training camp adjacent to the 'madrassa'[95] situated behind the Bastikhel Mosque.

* * *

0733 hrs — 20,000 feet over Bastikhel Village

Flying over the patchy clouds, the lead Falcon pilot activates the laser beam and searches for the madrassa building situated in-between the mosque and the training camp, which is nothing more than two small mud huts and an open firing range. Being a

---

[93] Laser-guided bomb.

[94] Time on target.

[95] Religious school.

silent mission, the pilot then identifies the target on his radar screen, fixes the beam on to it, and releases his payload of two bombs of 500 pounds, each containing highly explosive TNT enough to wipe out the whole complex.

After releasing the payload, the pilot gives a short call, 'Target identified, payload released, awaiting impact confirmation,' referring to confirmed hit as he guides the bombs on to their 'painted' targets. His number two follows suit and releases his two 500 pounders as well, his bombs gliding towards the adjacent building, which incidentally is the Bastikhel Mosque.

*   *   *

On the ground, while the men are chatting away, they hear the yell of one of the boys screaming as he looks up.

'Bomb!'

But before anyone could react, the bombs drop on them, exploding with deafening sound blowing the whole complex to smithereens; the bodies of men and boys, militants and bystanders, foreigners and locals, all blow apart like rag dolls.

The lead Falcon pilot flying over the area at 20,000 ft observes the impact on his radar screen and finally calls back to his base, 'Hits confirmed, target destroyed, Allah o Akbar!'

His number two follows through with a similar message on his RT as both head back to base after a victorious bombing run, with different thoughts going through their minds. The lead pilot thinks—*I hope this teaches them a lesson of not messing with the State*—while his number two's mind is occupied with—*I wish they learn their lesson now and stop terrorising us*.

On the ground, the mosque, the school, and the whole compound that once was the pride of LaM are now a destroyed wreck. The thunderous boom of the explosion whose shockwave shatters the windows of huts in the valley gives way to an eerie silence as the villagers gather their nerves to come to the site where once stood the complex in Bastikhel; the possibility of their children having perished in this attack numbs their minds.

Baaz also makes his way out of his cave on hearing these thunderous explosions. Aware of the location where the noise originated from, he also makes his way to the rubble, trying to rescue any survivors. The chances of his comrades surviving this bombing are bleak, but he does not want to let go until all bodies or their parts have been accounted for.

He had lost track of the number of times he entered into such salvage exercises. Exhausted and disgusted, he sits down remembering the October incident. Temper rising and nostrils flaring with rage, he yells at the thought of losing his 'fidayeens'[96] in this raid, and just as he stands up to go back to his caves to re-evaluate his assets, two teenage boys with torn clothes and dust all over them walk up to him.

Tears run down one's cheeks while anger is written on the face of the elder of the two, who says, 'Bhai Jan![97] We want to be your fidayeen.' Baaz brushes them aside, taking them to be regular village boys presently disturbed by this attack. As he ignores them and walks away, the elder of the two shouts as the younger continues to sob, 'We lost our father and little brother in this blast. Our mother is already dead, we have nowhere to go!'

Baaz stops in his tracks on hearing this, *These could be ideal fodder for my mission,* he thinks.

He turns back and addresses the boys, 'Are you willing to avenge your family's murder?'

'Yes,' comes the determined response.

'Are you willing to give your life to safeguard your religion?'

'Yes!' comes the answer, this time with even greater determination.

'Do you want to go to heaven for your feat?'

'Yes, we do,' the boys yell back in unison, vengeance running high in their blood.

'Then welcome to Lashkar al-Mujahideen, my fidayeen brothers.' Baaz goes up to the boys and embraces both of them to give them comfort and motivate them to meet their explosive end.

His plan back on track!

---

[96] Dedicated religious warriors sworn not to return alive from a battlefront.

[97] Dear Brother.

Chapter 6

WHEN ENEMY RESPONDS

As the freezing cold and gloomy winters give way to a bright and delightful spring, the capital city, known to Pakistan as 'Islamabad the Beautiful' awakens to live up to its reputation.

Millions of trees in the parks and gardens all over the city and the adjoining hills spring out fresh leaves signalling the arrival of the new season. Grass, both domesticated and in the wild, turns to different shades of green from the barren rust facade during winter; brightly coloured flowers blossom in this season completing this picturesque scenery. Complementing this ambiance is the chirping of birds and calling of the cuckoos inviting other mortals to enjoy nature in its full bloom. Squirrels dash up the tree trunks with their corn as they avoid the prying eyes of the lonely fox, happy to see its prey wake up from hibernation.

Awaiting the serene environment of this scenic city are the citizens who yearn to shed off their warm clothes, inhale the fresh air, and enjoy the bright sunny days with pleasant winds blowing across their faces. They like to visit various public parks and hiking trails going up the magnificent 'Margalla Hills' situated on the northern front of the city. Parks, gardens, and open-air eateries being their common hangouts, people heave a sigh of relief at the current lull in terrorist activities, praying that these do not come back to destroy the peace in their city.

23 March[98] is also nearing, and this year the government and the military have decided to undertake the 'Pakistan National Day'

---

[98] 23 March 1940 — a resolution to create an independent homeland for Muslims in South Asia was passed by All India Muslim League (political

parade with full zeal and vigour in front of the presidency. For the past few years, this anniversary had not been traditionally celebrated due to the terror threats; however, this year, to pep up the morale of the nation, the State had decided to conduct a 'show of force' declaring victory over the militants. Contingents of Pakistan's defence including the military, paramilitary, and civil defence forces had arrived along with their military equipment. Dress rehearsals complete with battlefield tanks, self-propelled artillery guns, armoured personnel carriers, strategic missiles, and other such equipment along with 'floats' depicting the culture of the different regions of the country were being conducted every alternate day in the morning. The star attractions of the ceremony were the formation fly past of Air Force's combat jets followed by low pass of the Army's AH-1 'Cobra' attack helicopters. With respite from suicide terror attacks in the country, the general mood of the nation was upbeat and belligerent. They felt their defence forces had won, and the days of living in terror were gone. But the sceptical few were not so optimistic. They knew that winters in tribal areas brought life to a standstill over there, and though violent incidents may have stopped for the time being, they had not yet ceased to exist.

Sam had been in Islamabad for four months now, and this was her first springtime in this city. She also belonged to the sceptic minority who felt that this was just the lull before the storm. Her days were so far spent reorganising the CIA's intelligence, gathering capabilities for their drone operations from the local assets based in Pakistan. Her biggest challenge so far was to promote a sense of loyalty and support for their 'Humints'[99] who felt unprotected and exposed while working in their areas. Especially in cases where someone was caught, the indifference of the Agency towards the ensuing fate of that individual had caused them to lose many spies. Sometimes, they turned double agents too, or even triple agents working for the militants, local intelligence agencies and the CIA, all at the same time.

Sam also devised the methodology of 'Matrix', where each hired 'local informer' was to be monitored by two other informers who in

---

party representing the majority of Muslims of India). This homeland was to be called 'Pakistan'.

[99] Human intelligence assets.

turn were monitored by two others, without any of them knowing who was watching who. While on the one hand, this strategy gave the individuals a sense of hope that they were always under protection and their employers would not leave them in tough times, this had also instilled fear in them of getting eliminated by the very same employer if they were discovered double crossing the Agency. This strategy was still at its nascent stage, but initial tests proved to be highly satisfactory.

Sam is busy in her cubicle at the CIA centre in the US embassy. Her mind is occupied with aligning different assets under the Matrix scheme, when her chain of thought is disrupted by the thundering roar of the fighter jets overhead, flying in low level formation. Irritated, she puts her pencil down on the desk.

'Show offs!' she mumbles, 'they are the same everywhere,' remembering her own jet jockeys in USAF Air Base in Nevada.

As the roar of the jets recedes in the distance, her mobile phone rings. Her frown turns into a pleasant smile as she sees the name blinking on the display screen.

'Hey!' Sam answers the phone with a smile, happiness on receiving this call written all over her face. 'Where've you been?' She asks letting her guard down for a moment.

'Hi, Sam,' comes the husky voice from the other end. 'Why? Did you miss me?' followed by slight laughter.

Sam gushes over the tease. She does not want to reveal her growing fondness towards Bilal just yet.

Sam had found in Bilal a sensitive and caring man who, despite having a very masculine facade, was devoid of any chauvinism. Over the past three months, their friendship had blossomed beyond their expectations, and for the first time since her days at Harvard, Sam had found in Bilal a male friend in whose company she felt comfortable. But, because of the nature of her work, she had not revealed her true identity to him. He still thought of her as a normal staff member in one of the departments in US embassy.

Not one to take any chances, she had run a complete background check on Bilal and found him to be sparkling clean. Bilal Khattak, thirty-five, belonged to an ethnic 'Pathan' family from Kohat. The son of a retired professor of 'Political Science' from Peshawar University,

Bilal studied for his MBA[100] in the US, where he married a Pakistani American citizen living in the States since childhood. Following the situation in America post 9/11, Bilal preferred to return to Pakistan, where he joined a multinational telecom company. Making his way up the corporate ladder, he held a senior position in its marketing division.

Father to a lovely daughter and living close to his ailing parents, he thought he had a perfect life with his wife in Islamabad. But his marriage did not weather the test of time when his wife realised that Bilal would never settle down with her in America. Although initially she had come to Pakistan with Bilal, it was on one of her trips with their little daughter back to America that she sought a divorce from Bilal on the pretext that he belonged to a conservative 'Pathan' family, who did not like the American way of life, an accusation Bilal could not fend off even though he considered it far from reality. This experience was a great shock to Bilal. Unable to get a US Visa to meet his daughter, he had become a lonely person at heart.

More than two years out of this turbulent marriage now, he had lost the meaning of a cheerful life. His friends tried to revive him by taking him along to wild parties and weekend getaways, but he would end up confined to a corner by himself missing his daughter and the lovely days he spent with his ex-wife. It was at one such party on 31 December that he and Sam had met. Each with their unique backgrounds found comfort in the other's company and did not look back from then on. Another aspect of particular interest to Sam was the 'Pathan' background of Bilal. She felt that through him, she would be able to get first-hand insight into the psyche of these fiercely independent people who now fought the US and its allies both in Afghanistan and Pakistan. Bilal also had his own reasons for befriending Sam. He felt that through her influence, he might one day get a US Visa and at least get to see his daughter again, after having craved to meet her for the past two years.

There is a silence while Sam, feeling exposed at Bilal's query, takes time to find the right words. 'Well, I didn't see you at Kitch's party last weekend even though you said you'd come,' she struggles,

---

[100]   Masters in Business Administration.

'even Becy asked about you,' she adds not wanting to be the only one appearing to miss him.

'I was visiting my parents in Kohat, In fact, this time I mentioned you to them, and they said they wanted to meet you too.'

Sam again goes in a tizzy. *Where are we heading with this? Why does he want me to meet his parents? He thinks I am an innocent associate in the US embassy? This is going too far?* With these questions arising in her mind, she tries to buy some time. 'That's nice of them,' she pauses, 'hey, listen, why don't we meet up this Friday night at 'PappaSallis[101] 'and talk it over?'

'Sure thing! Does eight o'clock sound fine?'

'Yeah, perfect, I'll come by myself since I have to go somewhere before that,' she says, deftly discouraging him from coming up to her apartment. In the past three months, Sam had kept their meetings restricted to various parties or restaurants and did not yet take him to her place. Thus far, Bilal had also not made any advancement on their budding friendship, something that Sam also appreciated.

'That's correct,' Bilal is quick to agree, not wanting to sound imposing, 'so I'll see you at eight in PappaSallis.'

'Yeah! Bye and take care.'

'Yup, you too,' and they hang up. Sam, both excited and apprehensive at the same time, is unsure where this relationship is heading. On the one hand were her personal emotions which after a very long time found a man in whom she could confide, could be comfortable with, and with whom she could enter into a long-term relationship, but on the other hand, her professional obligations forced her to think objectively. Bilal was not an American, was not from her background, and did not even know who the real Sam was. In fact, to him, Sam was an ordinary employee of the US embassy. Whereas to Sam, he was to be just a source through whom she could better understand her enemy.

With such a torrent of emotion running through her mind, she decides to take a short break to make some sense of this situation. An opportunity to informally visit Kohat overshadow all her other thoughts for now.

---

[101]   An upscale Italian restaurant in a quiet neighbourhood of Islamabad.

*   *   *

It is March in Waziristan. Activity in Bastikhel Village again commences as the snow starts to melt from the passes ushering in a new season of action. The ruins of the destroyed mosque, the 'madrassa' and their training camp are left there as a testament to the apathy and brutality of the State towards the tribal people of this region.

The resolve of Baaz and his Lashkar is firm. After the destruction of their infrastructure, he had stated resolutely to his supporters and villagers,

'How much more can they destroy? If they destroy our camps, we'll operate from our mosques; if they destroy our mosques, we'll operate from our madrassas; if they destroy our madrassas, we'll operate from our homes; and if they destroy our homes, then by God we'll operate from caves.'

Encouraged by their energetic response, he had continued, knowing full well how to play with the emotions of his followers, and bringing in Islam was an ideal recipe for motivation:

'Our enemies think that by killing us they can silence us. How many more of our people can they kill? Well, I want to tell them that you better kill all of us 'cause if you kill our men, our boys will fight; if you kill our boys, our women will fight; and if you kill our women, our children will fight; but fight we will for our religion and our way of life.'

This hi-octane speech had again won him the support of the locals as well as the loyalty of his comrades based in the village and around. However, following the strategy of other militant organisations operating in the tribal areas, Baaz had decided to lie low for the winter and prepare to take the war to the cities of Pakistan with the arrival of the spring season and opening up of the hilly terrains.

With the devastating strike in Bannu last Christmas, Baaz had again won the recognition of other similar outfits in the region. Once back in their fold, logistic support did not remain a problem. He did not need to worry about his supply lines. His aim now was to execute what he had planned last year.

Holding a lantern in his hand, he slowly makes his way through a tunnel, opening into the interior of a camouflaged mud hut, placed in the periphery of the assortment of huts in Bastikhel Village. Blowing out the lantern, he hangs it on a latch in the wall. Creeping out, he makes his way through the narrow gully towards another small hut not more than twelve square metres in area. As he nears the hut, he hears the sermon of his spiritual cleric, the Khateeb, responsible for brainwashing young minds into becoming suicide bombers:

'And as you call the name of Allah and press the button, everything turns white. Your ears hear nothing but calmness around you and then you see in front of you a door that beckons you towards it. Your body feels no pain of death. In fact, you feel the pleasure of becoming a martyr for your beloved religion, Islam.'

His audience is made up of nine teenage boys between the ages of fourteen and eighteen, selected after the previous lot was killed in the air attack. They appear mesmerised by the sermon of their cleric. The scenes of heaven already circling in their minds, each itches to become the next suicide bomber for the Lashkar.

'As you open this door, you see seventy-two beautiful 'Hoors'[102] waiting just for you on both sides of the pathway, welcoming you in their lovely embrace and ready to serve you with all the pleasures you could not even dream of in this dark and miserable world.'

Since their adolescence, these boys were kept in an extremely restricted environment in the village. Just the idea of these angelic women and the promise of heavenly pleasures motivate them to do whatever it takes to reach their embrace.

Ensuring that the trance of the boys is not broken, Baaz silently makes his way to one side of the hut. There he sits down, not wanting to disturb the trip into fantasia being created for his would-be weapons.

'But before you begin your afterlives with your wives, you are given the honour of having a feast with our respected Shuhada[103] who welcome you to heaven as real martyrs of Islam. So, my sons, prepare yourselves for your final journey to the heavens and have no remorse when you press that button. 'Cause you will not kill the innocent and

---

[102] Beautiful angelic women of the heavens.
[103] Rightful martyrs who fought legitimate battles in history.

the pure but would be doing service to your religion by cleansing this world of munkirs,[104] munafiqs,[105] mushriqs,[106] and their kith and kin.'

Adil and Amir are also in this group of boys. They were the ones who had volunteered to join Baaz's cause after losing their father and little brother in the January air strike over their mosque in the village. With their mother already dead many years ago, these two boys could find no meaning in their lives in this world and thus were destined to meet their family in the afterlife. To reach that life, they were being prepared for their mission.

Baaz watches them intently listening to the sermon. On seeing their innocent eyes and open mouths drooling, he experiences a fleeting moment of regret. His heart questions the whole logic of such missions, where teenage boys are cannon fodder and their targets fellow Muslims, but he quickly shakes the feeling off on the pretext that they are in a state of war, where the cause is greater than the lives of a few downtrodden souls who would be better off in their afterlife than what they have now.

*   *   *

23 March — Pakistan National Day, Capital city of Islamabad

Fajr[107] prayers in the city have been attended to, and the first ray of sunlight gradually creeps from behind the hills of Islamabad, stretched across north-easterly direction towards the hill resort of Murree before reaching their final destination — the Karakorum Mountain range in the north.

The central grounds of the capital are already abuzz with activity of men and women in uniform preparing themselves for the Pakistan

---

[104] The ones who turn against their faith and become atheist.

[105] Hypocrites, usually referred towards fellow Muslims, who, in the extremists views, are not following the true tenets of Islam.

[106] Referred towards Christians and Jews who claim Christ and David to be sons of God, thus diluting His sovereignty.

[107] Pre-dawn prayer. One of the five mandatory prayers of the day for a Muslim. Others being Zohr (midday), Asr (afternoon), Maghrib (dusk), and Isha (nightfall).

Day Parade due to commence at 0900 hrs. Uniforms crisp and boots polished, hearty looking soldiers belonging to different battalions possessively guard their ceremonial weapons as they congregate at their designated places, ready to take this parade forward.

Behind the formations are lined up columns of shining military hardware to be rolled proudly across the presidential dais in the hours to come. Not wanting to lower their guard on this commemorative day, a few thousand personnel of the secret police, intelligence agencies, and other security apparatus are busy guarding the area, scavenging for any intruder or terrorist trying to infiltrate the high-security zone drawn around the parade area. German Shepherds and Labrador dogs dutifully sniff for bombs and other explosives in the seating enclosures. Overall security is at high alert, and the State is not in the mood to let anyone spoil their festivities.

Sam also has an invitation to this ceremony along with other prominent personnel from the US embassy. It is now 0630 hrs in the city when Sam's alarm clock starts to ring. Deep in her morning snooze, Sam throws her hand at the clock to shut it down before realising what day it is. She gets up with a jerk from her bed to get ready and meet her escort for the occasion—Mr George Yeats, senior liaison officer of the US embassy. He is scheduled to pick her up at 0730 hrs to reach the parade square well in time for the ceremony scheduled to start at 0900 hrs.

*   *   *

23 March—Morning time at Attock Cantonment in the Dhilawar house

'Wake up, kids, it's 6.30 a.m. already,' echoes the sweet voice of Rania as the children struggle to get some more minutes of sleep. 'Wakee wakee,' Rania pulls the blanket off Taimur as he crouches in the bed. Ayesha is the first one to wake up in her room on hearing her mother's pleas. She dashes to the toilet to get ready, as today was a big day for all of them.

'You don't want to miss the function at school, do you?' Rania refers to the 23 March function that her 'Army Cantonment School' arranged for today. One prime feature in the function was the award distribution ceremony where Taimur was to be presented with the 'Best Horse Rider' of the year award among the boys category.

'Doesn't matter, Ma,' giggles Ayesha from her room, 'if he won't come, I'll go up to the stage and receive it for him.'

This is enough to wake up Taimur from his slumber by which time it is already seven.

'Hey!' he shouts promptly jumping up from the bed, 'it's my award and I'll receive it myself, thank you!'

Listening to the morning banter, Dhil walks into the dining room where Rania is giving the final touches to the breakfast. Dressed in his khaki ceremonial uniform with the commando's insignia of a 'dagger with wings' firmly perched on the right and shining medals hanging on the left side of his muscular chest, he readies himself for the flag-hoisting ceremony to commemorate 'Pakistan National Day' in Attock Cantonment.

'My knight in shining armour,' compliments Rania as Dhil gently kisses his adoring wife in return as they sit down for breakfast.

'Colonel Saheb,' lovingly addressing Dhil, 'even now my heart skips a beat when I see you in this ceremonial uniform,' she continues with her adulation.

Dhil stretches his arm to hold Rania's hand and rubs it affectionately. 'And my heart skips a beat every time I see you, my love.' Eyes staring intently into hers, Dhil reveals the tender heart buried under this manly facade. 'You can't imagine how much I adore you. You and the kids are everything to me.' Having lost his parents early in life and raised by his only elder sister, Dhil's world now revolved around his wife and children. He had seen enough death and destruction in his professional life and the thought of seeing his family in harms way now haunted his subconscious.

Rania, seeing her husband's emotional outburst, gets up from her seat and hugs her 'gentle giant' from behind while he is still seated, gently placing a kiss on Dhil's cheek who softly pats her hand.

By this time, Ayesha and Taimur enter the dining room discussing the function to be held at their school. Seeing their parents in an emotional embrace, they quiet down as they take their chairs. There is a moment of silence as Rania goes back to her seat, and Dhil makes an effort to extricate himself from the troublesome thoughts plaguing his mind.

He then asks cheerily from Taimur, 'So, my knight, all excited to receive your 'Best Rider' award?'

The tension eases as Taimur responds excitedly, 'Yes, Baba, but will you be coming to our school after your ceremony?'

'Affirmative!' replies Dhil. 'How can I miss the award distribution ceremony of my son?'

'Baba, the ceremony will start at ten o'clock. Please be there,' requests Taimur.

As Dhil nods with a smile, Ayesha suggests, 'And then we can go out for a picnic to our favourite spot for lunch,' referring to the banks of river Kabul flowing close to Attock, 'and have our yummy cakes and sandwiches with coffee,' her chubby figure revealing her passion for tasty food.

All laugh at the sight of her salivating at the very thought, and as Rania sees the situation settling back to normal, she leaves behind the lively chit-chat in the dining room. Dhil finishes his breakfast and leaves for his unit. Rania bids him farewell at the door, then retreats to her room where she bursts into tears at having seen her husband's state earlier. But strong willed as she is, she composes herself quickly before getting herself and little Hamza ready for the function; her mood made sombre by the morning incident.

*   *   *

23 March, 0800 hrs — Islamabad

George Yeats had arrived on schedule to pick Sam up from her apartment. Another ten minutes, and they reach the parade square. They make their way to their designated seats in the VIP enclosure, where Agent Dick Cage, assigned for the protection of his US embassy colleagues, is already present.

'Hey, Dee,' greets Sam.

'Ma'am!' Dick nods at Samantha.

'What's the security situation so far, agent?' asks George, his tone nervous and hands sweaty. George Yeats, fifty-three, had spent most part of his career posted in the USA, Europe, and Japan. Starting his career in journalism, he made the switch to the US Foreign Service about a quarter of a century back, with the aim of roaming around the world on government expense and enjoying the goodies that came with it. Little did he know then how this world would evolve in the twenty-first century. Having so far avoided the hard area postings in his career, his stint in Pakistan was the one tenure he could not avoid.

This was his third—and last year running in Pakistan, and he yearned to go back to the States in one piece. Challenged with a receding hairline, overweight, and always dressed in a three-piece suit with a chequered waist coat and a polka-dotted bow tie, George, with his spectacles parked on the tip of his nose, was the epitome of aristocratic bureaucrats that once roamed the earth throughout the twentieth century and before.

His fear of a terror bomb attack was known to all who would take a crack at him, from time to time, just for the fun of it.

Dick, on seeing George's nervous state, takes a shot at him. 'Well, the Paks have intercepted three truckloads of bombs coming to Islamabad from different routes, but our Intel says there's one more, still out there.'

'Then we should get out of here!' comes the panicked response as George turns around, struggling to find strength in his legs to take him back.

Dick holds him by the shoulder, 'Sir, don't go back to your car, for all we know the truck might've reached there already,' winking at Sam who reckons, from Dick's carefully made up tone, that he is pulling a fast one.

'Oh my God, what do we do?' George raises his voice in panic, attracting the attention of other foreign dignitaries sitting in the enclosure.

'Okay, that's enough,' asserts Sam, seeing the situation may spring out of control anytime soon.

George looks at Sam with bewildered eyes. 'George, you know, Dee,' she tries to calm him down, 'he's kidding.'

'You should be ashamed of yourself, young man,' George protests as Dick smirks at the situation.

'Sorry, sir! Just couldn't help lightening the situation seeing you so nervous,' Dick laughingly apologises.

'At my expense?' retorts George.

Sam is quick to intervene and ease the situation. 'Stop it, Dee, you would give George a heart attack one of these days, and we don't want that happening, do we, George?'

'Certainly not!' agrees George as he straightens his jacket and bow tie to seat himself at his designated place.

Sam also shakes her head negatively at Dick, who tries to control his laughter and assures Sam that the security over here is in good hands.

*   *   *

23 March, 0800 hrs — Attock Cantonment

Dhil had reached the sprawling gardens of the old Corps Headquarters building where officers and soldiers from different units stationed in the cantonment had gathered for the flag-hoisting ceremony in commemoration of the National Day. Since the relocation of Corps Headquarter away from this double-storeyed building, it housed administration and public relation offices only. However due to its Georgian architecture — a legacy of British rule, all major events of the cantonment were still held in its sprawling lawns, and today's ceremony was one such event.

This ceremony was organised in such a way that approximately eighty officers from different units and Corps HQ and about 200 selected junior commissioned officers and soldiers from various outfits had been invited. Today, the flag of Pakistan was to be hoisted by the seniormost officer of the cantonment, a three-star Lieutenant General and also a corps commander who would then follow it up with an 'Order of the Day' address to the congregation. The meeting was scheduled to commence at 0900 hrs and conclude by 1000 hrs. Dhil then planned to join his family at the Cantonment School Auditorium, like many of the other officers, and enjoy the function arranged over there.

Col. Adnan Aslam, the chief of security for the cantonment was also among the officers gathered here. Speaking on his cell phone and looking concerned, he catches the attention of Dhil who walks up to him.

'Assalam u Aliekum, sir,' Dhil greets Adnan with a salute.

'Walekum-us-salaam, Dhilawar . . . How are you?'

'Fine, sir, thanks. Is everything okay? You seem very concerned?'

'Yeah, everything is fine so far,' Adnan tries to dispel Dhil's anxiety. 'The problem is that this cantonment is a small city in itself. Milkmen, shopkeepers, hairdressers, teachers, contractors, and many civilians . . . you name it, either live within our area or commute in and out on a daily basis. Their numbers run into thousands. The flow in and out of traffic is so much that it's very difficult to keep tabs on all of them. How many can you check thoroughly? How many?' Adnan asks in frustration. 'If you start doing that, it would create a huge traffic jam at all entry and exit points.'

'So what's the answer to this, sir?' Dhil asks politely.

'Well, partner, we rely on our local intelligence to the best of our abilities. So far, it has worked for us, let's pray to God it continues like this.'

Dhil's unit was part of the counter terrorism team, so he was aware of the challenges faced by their security apparatus and acknowledged the work being done by Adnan and his Military Police in maintaining peace in the cantonment.

He excuses himself as Adnan's cell phone starts to ring again. By now, it's 0830 hrs as Dhil decides to meet a couple of other officers before seating himself in time for the 0900 hrs ceremony to begin.

* * *

23 March, 0830 hrs — Attock Cantonment School

Rania had reached the school along with Ayesha, Taimur, and Hamza. She took Hamza to the school nursery situated inside the school building. After making him comfortable with other children of his age, she went to the auditorium located outside the school building but within the same education block. This auditorium was a large complex having a seating capacity of 300 people distributed between the ground floor and the mezzanine floor. Ayesha and Taimur were led to their designated seats, where they settled themselves with their friends. All were excited about the variety show and chattered excitedly about the ensuing trip down the history lane of Pakistan and the award distribution ceremony that was to follow at about 1000 hrs. Once free from her children, Rania makes her way to the front of the hall where she greets Ismat, who was already there.

'Hi, Rania!' responds Ismat. 'What does it feel like, not being part of the organising committee, for a change?'

'Relaaaaaxed,' comes the response, 'I can now sit back and enjoy the show . . . for a change,' quips Rania in the same manner. 'I guess we both needed a break from the organising committee.'

'Yeah,' agrees Ismat, 'Asim had started taunting me now for not giving him and the kids enough time at home. I guess he ran out of patience,' referring to her husband.

'Not my Dhil,' replies Rania, the smile on her face reflecting the affectionate feelings she had in her heart, 'He never gave me that impression, but I myself felt that I need to give him more time and curtail my extracurricular activities for the school.'

'You guys are just out of this world,' Ismat raises her hands in exasperation. 'You and Dhilawar bhai[108] are one of a kind, I tell you,' she smiles, 'I've yet to see a more loving couple than you guys, in fact you are quite the talk of the town.'

'Thanks for your compliment, deary,' Rania pats Ismat on her arm. 'Now stop flattering me and let's take our seats. The show is about to begin, and for once, I just want to take a deep breath, chill, and relish this moment,' referring to not having to monitor and manage this function.

'But before that, let's meet Mrs Hafeez. I've noticed her conspicuously eyeing us from her seat,' jokes Ismat as they both decide to greet Mrs Hafeez, the school principal; before taking their seats in time for the show to begin.

*   *   *

0845 hrs — Outskirts of Attock City

A 2-ton 'catering truck' of the Iqbalia Restaurants & Caterers makes its way towards its destination — the Army Cantonment School inside Attock Cantt.[109]

In a bid to outdo the previous organising committee in every aspect, the new organising committee at the school had given the catering order to the city's famous Iqbalia Restaurants & Caterers, instead of having the refreshments prepared by the Corps Mess inside the cantonment.

Cantt. security was advised of this order, and the trucks were to be allowed entry into the cantonment. The company in question was a popular name in the area, and they had also catered for some private functions held previously inside the cantonment.

---

108   Brother — a term used by wives of army officers when referring to other officers. A tradition of the Pakistan Army.

109   Short for cantonment.

After driving along a narrow winding side road, the truck enters the adjoining village that had sprung up on the periphery of the cantonment. This village was separated from the cantonment only by way of a tall wall with barbed wire running along the top and watchtowers every 300 metres. Its inhabitants had mostly taken up menial jobs inside the cantonment where they shuttled in and out daily through the gate under the watchful eye of the army and its intelligence units.

On reaching the gate, this truck slowly brakes to a halt. Its driver is a young man, clean-shaven with sunglasses, dressed smartly in a white local dress. Accompanying him is another person in his early twenties, dressed equally smartly in a waiter's uniform, with a small beard, a common feature among the people of this area.

'Salam, saheb,'[110] the waiter inside the truck greets the guard on duty, who carefully walks up to the truck with his semi-automatic machine gun loaded and finger on the trigger.

'Salam . . . come out with your hands, where I can see them and show me your identifications,' commands the soldier as his comrades watch intently from the gate. There is another soldier perched on the watchtower with his LMG[111] pointing at the truck in case of any untoward incident.

There is silence in the area as an old car and two motorcycles come and park themselves behind the truck, patiently waiting for their turn to enter.

By then, the time is 0900 hrs.

---

[110] Sir — used as a sign of respect in Urdu Language.
[111] Light machine gun.

Chapter 7

TERROR STRIKES

23 March, 0900 hrs — in Islamabad

Sam, George, and Dick are all seated now along with other dignitaries from various countries, ready for the ceremony to begin.

'Ladies and Gentlemen,' echoes the voice of the convener from the public address system, 'Welcome to the Pakistan National Day parade at the Presidency, Islamabad.' As she begins the ceremony, all three smartly attired contingents of men from the three main arms of Pakistan's defence forces Army, Navy, and Air Force stand to attention in neat columns, in front of the presidential dais waiting for the President to arrive.

Within minutes, the four horse-drawn open-air carriage of the President, a replica of one of the Queen's carriages in Buckingham Palace, is seen coming from the side of the Presidential House, duly escorted by a strong colourful batch of 'Presidential Guards' of the Pakistan Army — men dressed in their ceremonial uniforms comprising traditional pugrhees[112] on their heads, dark-red long tops and off-white trousers tucked into long black riding boots, a relic of the British Raj.[113] A dozen handsome men bedecked with medals and ranks astride tall

---

[112] Traditional headgear worn on ceremonial occasions in Pakistan. Starched thin cloth wrapped around a similar coloured cap worn by the rider. One end of the cloth is starched up spread like a hand-held fan, whereas the other end of the cloth is allowed to fall at the back of its wearer.

[113] British Raj is the time referred when the Indian subcontinent was under the direct control of the Great Britain and constituted part of the British Empire.

muscular horses; half of them leading the carriage in two parallel lines and the remainder following behind. Holding the reins of the horses in their left hand and presidential flags in their right, they gracefully escort the carriage trotting up to the dais amidst the resounding applause of the audience. The President of Pakistan gracefully waves at the people, acknowledging their cheers and jubilation before disembarking from the carriage in front of the dais. Here he is greeted by the Prime Minister, the Joint Chief of Staff, and service chiefs of the Pakistan Army and the Navy, along with the Vice-Chief of the Air Force, all smartly attired for the occasion. While the Prime Minister and the President are dressed in black sherwanis,[114] the Joint Chief of Staff and Army Chief wear their ceremonial uniforms in khaki, and the Naval Chief wears his sparkling white uniform. As for the Vice-Chief of the Air Force representing his boss, he is attired in his dark blue ceremonial uniform. All uniformed gentlemen, wearing their side caps respectively to complete their uniforms.

Seeing the men make their way to the platform for the proceedings to begin, Sam gets amused at all the pomp and show projected in this ceremony. As she turns around and sees the smartly dressed people in the stands, ardently watching their armed forces in all their splendour, she smiles at the presented glory and reminisces about her first thoughts regarding Pakistan when she was advised of her assignment in Nevada. *A poor war-torn country with gun-toting militants roaming around freely, and bombs exploding all the time.* This here was a far cry from the impression she had in her mind then.

This place is quite a surprise — she thinks to herself as she waits for the President to begin his address of the day.

*   *   *

0900 hrs — in Attock Cantonment

After the customary greetings with their colleagues and friends, Dhil and Rania find their seats and wait for their respective functions to begin.

---

[114] Pakistan's formal dress, resembling a long cloak up to knee length, worn over a long shirt and a baggy white trouser.

Meanwhile, at the guardroom, the waiter gets out of the Iqbalia Restaurant's truck on the command of the soldier.

'Saheb, what is there to see?' the waiter implores as he shows his identification card to the soldier. 'We are already late for the function.'

'Open the back of this truck now!' the soldier commands, ignoring the plea of the waiter.

As the waiter takes the soldier to the back of the truck, the soldier calls on his comrade to join him with the bomb detector sensor but finds he has gone to the toilet.

Seeing all this delay and traffic queuing up behind him, one of the motorcyclists standing behind the truck waves at the soldier guarding the gate.

'Salam, saheb, can I pass through? I'm Rashid, the tailor in 39 FF Unit . . . I pass through this gate every day, you know me,' pleads the motorcyclist as he shows his official ID.

The soldier looks towards his sergeant sitting in the guard room next to the gate, who signals him to let the traffic roll while the truck is inspected on the side. Rashid brings his motorbike slowly to the gate. He has a young teenage boy sitting behind him. He smiles at the guard and takes out his ID card.

'Who's this boy behind you?' asks the soldier looking at the boy.

'He's my nephew, saheb,' comes the uneasy response, 'he'll be helping me out in my work. Here is his ID.' He hands over the card to the soldier and explains his reason to be here on a holiday as the soldier asks more questions from Rashid about his nephew, simultaneously scrutinising the card for authenticity.

As the conversation ensues, other people in the queue start imploring them to hurry up. A little disturbed by the noise, the soldier gives a final look at both of them, changes his mind on seeing the innocent looks on the boy's face, and hands him back the ID card, gesturing at Rashid to move on as he asks the next motorcyclist to come over. By this time, the waiter of the Iqbalia Restaurant's truck, after having failed in his negotiation with the adamant soldier, opens the rear door to let the soldier enter inside for inspection. He climbs up into the rear of the truck to see neatly stacked trays of snacks and drinks covered with plastic sheets on shelves running on both sides of the cabin. He carefully and slowly inspects the cabin, munching on a sandwich, as he hits the butt of his rifle against the steel floor and the walls to check the hollowness of the area. He concludes the inspection inside, sandwich in hand, then jumps out to take a tour of the truck from the outside, again looking at the driver in the process, who offers a nervous smile.

Reluctant to let them go, he commands, 'Wait for the bomb detector before you go inside.'

Just then, they see the soldier with the bomb-detector device coming towards them from the nearby toilet. This development is enough to trigger panic in the waiter who was uneasily waiting for clearance from the gate. On seeing the guard come closer, he shouts at the top of his voice.

'Adil!'

Adil was the driver of the truck, one of the two brothers prepared for this suicide mission and now nervously waiting for the truck to pass to reach their eventual target. Reading through his verses, he does not flinch for a moment and before the solider manning the LMG can fire a volley of bullets at him, he shuts his eyes tight while pressing the dreaded button.

A thunderous blast resonates across the area as a 500 kg bomb, comprising a mixture of urea, nitrate, and C4 explosives, fitted inside the middle of the truck, blows up incinerating the guard room, the watch tower, the tall boundary wall, and the surrounding area, destroying men, machines, and buildings within a 20-metre radius before the shockwave shatters the glass windows and panes of buildings, ripping leaves off the trees, bending the street lights and other hoardings cruelly in a 150-metre radius, also damaging the cars in that area while shaking people off their feet. A fire erupts that rages through buildings, consuming any trees still standings around the area of the blast.

*   *   *

Rania, Ismat, and other wives and children of the officers are intently listening to the welcome speech of Mrs Hafeez when they hear the thunderous boom of the suicide bomber blowing up his truck at the gates of the cantonment. The whole building vibrates violently as they hear windows outside shattering from the shockwave followed by large secondary explosions coming from detonating ammunition and gunshots from exploding bullets. Within seconds, they hear the noise of sirens and alarms surround the area, giving the impression to all that they are under attack.

The auditorium building, being a strong structure and out of the destruction parameter, survives the initial blast, but not before the electricity shuts down putting the whole hall into darkness. It does not have any windows, and only a few red-coloured emergency lights at the emergency exits are switched on, and these are not enough to illuminate the large hall. A haunting silence prevails for a moment inside the hall, before the women and children gather their nerves. Some, in a state of panic, from all the noise outside, start screaming of suicide bombers in their midst at the top of their voices, despite appeals of calm from the organisers. But their appeals fall on deaf ears as others follow suit and soon, the whole auditorium reverberates with screeching mothers clamouring over each other, trying to get to their screaming and crying children seated at the rear and on the first floor of the hall.

Rania and Ismat, seeing the confusion in the large auditorium, also spring up to get hold of their children. There is complete chaos in the dark hall as about 250 frightened women and children create pandemonium, struggling over each other to get to their loved ones.

Attock Cantonment is under horrendous attack.

*   *   *

0925 hrs—National Day Parade in Islamabad

The President is in the midst of his annual address to the nation:

'We are not fighting this war for any other country,' making an obvious reference to the US War on terror. 'This became our war the day the writ of the State was challenged and the disillusioned few among us rejected our democratic constitution and tried to impose their skewed version of our great religion[115] upon us. This became our war the day the first terror attack took place within our boundaries. This became our war the day Pakistanis started getting killed by these ghastly attacks. I want to take this opportunity once again to make it clear to these self-proclaimed 'Mujahids'. The Pakistani

---

[115]   Islam.

nation is resilient, valiant, and strong enough to withstand the terror onslaught and will not be subjugated to the few extremists hell-bent on spreading an environment of terror and darkness.'

He continues, 'Our armed forces, with the support of the peace-loving masses, will thwart the nefarious designs of these terrorists and will not leave any stone unturned in eliminating such threats from the face of this country.'

Enough of the hi-octane speech, the President lowers his tone, 'One more time we offer them a hand of friendship, a hand of peace, a hand of unity. Let's think again about what we are doing, sit down and talk our differences over. Pakistan is ours and is large enough to accommodate all of us.'

The President continues with his speech as Sam's cell phone, kept on silent due to the requirement of the function, starts blinking, the SMS[116] text reads: *Large bomb blast heard in Attock, many feared killed . . . details still coming in.*

Sam reads the message, a feeling of despair goes through her mind, as she looks up towards the President busy making his passionate speech. *This is not going to be easy* — she thinks and shakes her head in the negative — *this is not going to be easy*; her mind repeats these thoughts again.

* * *

0915 hrs — in Attock Cantonment

The 'Order of the Day' commences in the sprawling gardens of the old building. Lt. Gen. Tariq Hashmi, corps commander, has just begun his speech with the customary greetings to the officers and soldiers on this auspicious occasion. As he starts enumerating on measures taken by the Pak Army in defeating the enemies of the State, both from within and outside its boundaries, they are all shaken by the loud blast of the bomb exploding in the truck at the cantonment gate, within an 80-metre straight line from their venue.

Within seconds, the shockwave reaches them, bringing with it flying debris destroying property and maiming all those unfortunate

---

[116] Short message service.

enough to be in its way. While the sturdy white building withstands the shockwave, all its glass windows shatter into pieces. Shards of glass pierces into the men in close proximity, injuring them, but not before the accompanying gust of wind sweeps them off their feet, as they fall or bend down to avoid flying debris and splinters.

Lieutenant Colonel Dhilawar is one of those men feeling the heat of this situation. He ducks for cover as soon as he hears the primary blast, aware of what will follow. As the secondary explosions of vehicles and ammunition surround the area, Dhil takes a minute to come to his full senses. He shakes his head while getting up on his feet and bangs his hand on his ears to rid himself of the muted sensation to get his hearing back. Head still a little dizzy, he hears the wails and groans of the injured men, seated closest to the building, who had not been lucky enough to escape the flying metal debris or shards of broken glass that accompanied the blast.

The corp commander was among those standing at the dais close to the building and was the first one to have flying sharp glass pierce him from behind before making its way towards the officers facing the building. Injured and bleeding with a torn uniform, he put on a brave face and got up on his feet to assess the situation around him and ensure there were no fatalities.

Dhil looks around at all the mayhem in the area. This place, that minutes earlier housed a clean white building facing green sprawling grounds encircled by grey tarmac separating it from the building, now depicted a war zone. The same premises where manicured gardens accommodated the flag post, with a small dais and hundreds of seats facing the dais, set up neatly for the occasion, were all now covered in brown dust, including the white building and lush green lawns. Moreover, the building was badly damaged with all windows shattered and doors pulled away from their hinges. Some men lying on the ground, others, struggling to regain their senses, and a few more, preparing themselves to take action against an impending threat. However, the flag of Pakistan, hoisted at the beginning of the ceremony, still fluttered. Although tattered and torn, this flag symbolically echoed hope for the people there, that all was not lost yet.

Rania . . . I hope they are safe—the thought of his family hits Dhil's recovering mind like another shockwave. He quickly pulls out his cell phone from his pocket and dials Rania's cell phone number as he looks around for the other men of his unit who were also invited to the ceremony. With several thoughts going through his mind at the same time, he itches to hear the familiar ring-tone but finds only the recorded message calmly stating, 'The number you have dialled is not responding at the moment, please dial again later.'

'Damn it!' Dhil shoves the phone back into his pocket, presuming that the signal tower must also be destroyed. He sees Major Rathore, also injured with facial wounds from flying glass, struggling to find his strength to get up.

'Rathore!' shouts Dhil as he leaps towards his deputy, 'You okay?'

'Yes, sir.' Rathore tries to compose himself, 'Where the hell did that come from?'

'Shockwave came from that direction,' Dhil signals beyond their building in the direction of the cantonment gate, 'seems like those fuckers were trying to enter the guardroom and got challenged.'

'Bloody bastards!' responds Rathore now back to his senses and nursing his facial wounds.

Rania . . . the thought of his family again reverberates in his mind as he sees Colonel Adnan frantically yelling on his wireless set, 'Close all gates, close all gates, over.'

'Roger that, sir, over,' comes the response from the other end.

'Engage Operation Charlie Alpha,' shouts back Adnan in the wireless set. Operation Charlie Alpha was the codename for calling in the 'Quick Reaction Forces' to their designated areas to quell any follow-up action carried out by the terrorists, in case they were to infiltrate the premises.

On hearing this, Dhil goes into a frenzy. He dreads the thought of infiltrating terrorists and his mind again goes towards his wife and children. He looks at Rathore who, as if reading Dhil's mind, implores, 'Sir, you rush to your family, I'll take care of our men here.'

Dhil knew that Rathore's family had gone to Islamabad on this long weekend. He was also confident that his unit's QRF,[117] trained by him and under the command of Maj. Saifullah Dar, was already on their way.

His primary attention now focuses on reaching Rania and the kids. He looks around for his driver[118] only to find him injured too.

---

[117] Quick reaction force.

[118] In Pakistan Army, it is a norm for the commanding officers to reach for official functions in their 'staff vehicles' driven by the unit's driver/

Feeling that the driver would be slow, he snatches the keys from him and rushes towards his Land Rover Defender SUV parked in the car parking area behind the building and in direct proximity of the cantonment gate. To his horror, he finds his SUV damaged and blocked by other vehicles. Some have been overturned and others now wrecked; these cars also block the exit/entry gates of the car park. There is no way to quickly get out of here in the SUV, Dhil grudgingly realises as he sees some other men running out of the premises on foot, including Lieutenant Colonel Asim, his course-mate and Ismat's husband.

'Asim?' Dhil shouts at him to inquire about his plans.

'Gotta get to Ismat and the kids!' comes the hurried response as Asim continues to run down the road in the direction of the auditorium about two miles away from their area. Seeing no other option and desperation overcoming his composure, Dhil joins the officers running towards the auditorium, as others try to move those vehicles blocking the gates. All visibly shaken from the event and concerned for the safety of their loved ones, the whole atmosphere reflects an aura of fear and panic as the fire rages in some bushes and trees and smaller explosions erupt all around them. This war had finally reached the army's soft underbelly.

*   *   *

Over at the auditorium, as the women clamour over seats and other women to get closer to their screaming children, Rania and Ismat also struggle through the terrified crowd to reach their own children. Rania's mind also goes to Hamza and Dhil. She tries to call Dhil whilst searching for Ayesha and Taimur but cannot seem to pick up a mobile signal inside the auditorium.

'Ayesha! Ayesha! Taimur! Taimur!' her yells finally reach Ayesha and Taimur who were equally scared and confused by the situation. While Ayesha simply crouched in her seat hearing people talking about the suicide bomber, Taimur had stood up yelling for his mother.

'Mama! Mama!'

---

chauffeur.

Taimur yells back as he hears his mother's faint calls in the midst of all the chaos and noise in the dark hall. Within another couple of minutes, Rania reaches the back of the hall where she finally sees Taimur standing, struggling to keep his balance on the chair, while dodging other people around him, and waving in the direction of his mother — all at the same time.

'Taimur!' yells Rania as she finally jumps over the seats nearest to Taimur who hugs his mother with a mix of relief and panic on seeing her. She hugs him back for a second before searching around for Ayesha, who by now had crouched in the leg space between two rows of seats, upon hearing of a suicide bomber in the hall.

'Ayesha, my jan,[119] you okay?' Rania reaches her trembling daughter, who hugs her mother back hysterically.

'Mama!' Ayesha finally belts out on realising that her mother is here and so is her brother standing next to her.

'It's okay, it's okay. We are fine, see?' Rania comforts her two elder children while thinking of Hamza and Dhil. Forgetting in the panic, about the safety precautions recently introduced by the school, she yearns to rush out to her little baby, Hamza, whose condition she is unaware of. She also prays to God at the same time to keep Dhil safe, wondering where he would be right now.

It takes Rania a few minutes to comfort Ayesha who would not leave her side.

'Mama, I'll go get Hamza,' suggests Taimur on seeing Ayesha's hysterical condition.

'No, Taimur, you will not leave this hall,' orders Rania before Taimur could rush outside.

Her mind confounded by the situation, she does not let Taimur leave the auditorium hall. She knows that if there was a suicide bomber inside, he would have blown himself up by now. So the chances of survival inside the hall are better than being outside, where they could still hear explosions, sirens, firing, and general chaos.

'You stay inside and protect your sister, and I'll go for Hamza,' she commands Taimur, knowing well that a less authoritative tone

---

[119] Life. Used in Urdu when showing love for any one. Similar to 'my life' in English.

will be ignored by her brave son who wanted to go out to protect his little brother.

'Ayesha, my jan, don't be afraid, you're okay, you're okay. Now pull yourself together and stay here with Taimur. He'll take care of you.' Rania hurriedly gets up to get to her baby. She makes her way to the nearest emergency exit and finds to her horror, the door locked.

'What the hell!' she yells in frustration, as she checks the next door, which is also locked. She makes her way down to the main exit door, where she finds a crowd trying to get out. They are being stopped by yet another locked exit door.

'Let us out, let us out!'

'Why have you locked the doors?'

'We'll die of suffocation inside!'

'Are you guys mad?'

Rania hears the pleas of different women trying to get out of the door.

'We have been advised to remain inside as we don't know what may happen outside.' The big burly spokesman of the organising committee tries to explain. 'We can't let anyone come in, neither will we allow anyone to go out while uncertainty prevails. This is our standard operating procedure, and we request you all to remain calm and get back to your seats until advised further . . . This is for your own good,' he pleads vociferously with all the women and their children clamouring to get out.

Rania elbows herself to the front of this crowd. Acknowledging the point of the spokesman, she still yearns to reach for her Hamza. Her motherly instinct would not let her settle down till she has her baby in her arms.

'Listen, mister,' she addresses the big guy authoritatively, 'my baby is out there in the Montessori, and I want to get to him, you open this door right now!'

'Ma'am we don't have orders,' comes the curt response, 'I'm sure he's fine.'

Seeing that this ploy has not worked, she struggles to make her way out of the crowd and rushes straight to Mrs Hafeez, whom she spots seated in the front row, her demeanour dishevelled and her face buried in her hands.

'Ma'am please help me, I need to get to Hamza,' Rania pleads to Mrs Hafeez and is joined by more hapless mothers, all wanting to reach their small children in the adjoining Montessori, uncertain of their conditions.

Finally, Mrs Hafeez raises her head, looks in the direction of the main organiser, and thinks about the safety of the little children in the Montessori; then she nods at the organiser to let the big guy open one of the doors to let these pleading women out.

As the man opens the main door, he is almost trampled by fifty odd panic-stricken women and children as all try to get out of the door at the same time, trying either to escape the dark, suffocating, uncertain atmosphere inside or simply to get to their loved ones outside. Rania also rushes out with this crowd and heads straight in the direction of Hamza's Montessori. Heart pounding, legs trembling, and mind fearful of the unknown, she prays to God for the safety of her family. At the other end of the cantonment, Dhil runs towards their location as fast as his legs can carry him. Similar thoughts rushing through his mind that this is not what they had wanted in their lives.

*　　*　　*

Earlier, at the guardroom, as Rashid the tailor was allowed to pass through the gate, he accelerated his motorcycle to get as far away from the truck as quickly as possible. He had been aware of the contents of this particular truck and was part of the terror plan devised by Baaz Jan for this occasion.

Behind him was not his nephew, or even his relative, but Amir, the younger of the two brothers who had volunteered to become a suicide bomber after the death of their father and younger brother, Adil being the one in the truck. Amir's mission was to infiltrate the cantonment lines and blow himself up in the auditorium once Adil had exploded his truck, causing the primary destruction. Once the rescue staff and uniformed personnel were gathered for salvaging, Amir was instructed to blow his bomb in that mayhem, to bring more death and devastation to the cantonment. However, in case Adil's truck got intercepted midway, if Amir succeeded in infiltrating inside the cantonment, then he was to carry out the mission on his own. Coerced into being part of this operation partly by death threats to his kidnapped family and partly by financial reward on its successful completion, Rashid, the tailor was tasked with stitching up the bomb-laden suicide belt, to keep it ready for Amir and also to help him with the back-up plan.

That back-up plan now in force, Rashid knew that he had a short window of not more than fifteen minutes to take Amir to his tailor shop nearby and then on to the auditorium for him to carry out his mission. It does not take him more than two minutes after leaving the gate, when he hears the thunderous boom of the bomb exploding in the truck.

'Allah o Akbar!' [120] yells Amir in a trembling voice, trying to get the nervous feelings out of his mind. He holds Rashid tightly from behind like a child clings to his mother, as Rashid ducks and weaves on his speeding motorbike struggling to maintain his balance. Within seconds, the gust of wind hits them hard from behind, just as they are within ten metres of Rashid's shop. The gust is so hard that Rashid almost loses his balance on the motorbike but not before braking to a screeching halt in front of the shop.

Rashid's tailor shop was one of a dozen small retail outlets in a modest shopping centre purpose-built in the middle of the cantonment. Shops pertaining to grocery, butchery, tailors, barbers, hardware, video rental, and others catered to the personnel living inside the cantonment. Today being a holiday, during the morning time, these shops were closed, and the civilians running them were not present.

As the mayhem begins inside the cantonment, Rashid unlocks the door and quickly goes to the storeroom at the back of the shop, where he opens a large steel trunk and takes out clothing material from inside to reach the base of the trunk. He then inserts a screwdriver at one end of the floor to actually take this false floor out. Underneath the false floor, hidden from all in the shop, he finds the dreaded thick cloth suicide belt he had been working on for many days. Now completed with explosive gunpowder pouches, metal slugs, nails, the bomb fuse, and initiator—all neatly stitched together for today, he carefully takes the belt out and shows it to Amir who had been following him obediently so far.

On seeing the belt, Amir gives out a beaming smile. A boy of not more than fifteen years of age, with brown facial hair barely

---

[120]   God is Great.

struggling to come out of his fair-skinned face, he was brainwashed to such an extent that he had started waiting impatiently for this moment. Having lost Adil, the last of his relatives, minutes earlier, Amir was now anxiously waiting for his turn to reach his family in the life hereafter and to make his comrades proud of him in this world too. Such were the feelings bouncing in his dazed mind, which was stunned an hour before from special drugs to ensure that he did not chicken out at the last moment. This was a standard procedure carried out by the militants before setting these teenagers off on their suicide missions.

'La Ilaha Ill Allah[121] . . . ,' he recites his verse as he takes off his loose long shirt slowly extending his arms in front gesturing at Rashid to help him wear the belt. There is uneasy silence inside the storeroom as the outside resonates with secondary explosions, wailing of sirens, and a rat-a-tat of exploding munitions in the armoury near the site of the explosion.

'Congratulations, my brother, your day of reckoning has come,' Rashid taunts Amir, who, dazed as he is, takes these as words of comfort coming from a comrade as he assists him in wearing the belt. 'You can now go and meet your loved ones in the life hereafter after being received by the angelic women in heavens.' A pinch of sarcasm is evident in Rashid's tone.

Amir looks at Rashid and gives him a feeble smile, sweat pouring out of all of his pores. 'I'm not nervous, Brother Rashid, I'm in fact anxious to complete my holy mission.'

Rashid marvelled at the expertise of Amir's teacher in convincing him so comprehensively of this action that Amir did not have one iota of remorse for the act he was to commit. Rashid himself was afraid of Amir and his backers and wanted to finish off his part in this mission as soon as possible and get on with his life with his family, held captive for now and to be released on completion of this task along with a reward from Baaz. He could not take chances with anything foiling this mission, as he did not know who else would be watching him.

It takes them about eight minutes to get ready and get out of the shop unnoticed by the panic-stricken people around them.

---

[121]   There is no creator but God.

'My mission ends here,' Rashid hurriedly tells Amir as Amir carefully gets on the motorbike to reach his final destination—the auditorium building which was about two minutes' drive from here.

'Thank you, Brother Rashid, see you in heaven,' Amir calmly bids farewell to a nervous Rashid as he speeds off towards the target.

'You guys are crazy!' shouts Rashid towards Amir but not before Amir had left him a fair distance behind.

Another couple of minutes and Amir would be in front of the auditorium.

*   *   *

A few minutes earlier, Dhil had started running on the road going towards the cantonment auditorium and school. Each minute seemed to him like an hour as he mustered up all his commando strength and stamina to sprint faster than the other officers and men, who were running out of breath and lagging behind in the process. *Oh God, please keep Rania and the kids in your safety*—the same prayer repeated in his mind as he got closer and closer to his destination.

At about the same time, Rania had succeeded in getting out of the auditorium with the other terrified women and children. She dashed towards the Montessori School, which, to her horror she found to be empty.

'Hamza! Hamza!' she yells at the top of her voice in the corridors as she looks in the school block. Some other mothers yell for their little ones as well as they catch up with Rania. She also yells for the staff, but there is no response. What Rania had forgotten in her panic was the recently introduced safety measures in the school that within five minutes of the blast, all the twenty odd children, along with their four staff members, were advised to lock themselves up in a soundproof bomb shelter adjacent to the Montessori. From there, the only connection with the outside world was to be through a telephone landline. Their orders were not to get out until they were advised of the same by way of a coded message via this telephone link. This measure was to save their lives in case of such an attack, and today it had come to good use. The memory of these precautions strikes Rania while frantically looking for Hamza and now knowing of her helplessness in this situation, she hopes to God that Hamza along with the other children must have been taken to that strong room.

Adrenaline settling down for a moment, she tries to catch her breath as she looks around at the situation.

'They are in the strong room, and there's nothing we can do,' she tries to comfort fifteen other mothers who had followed Rania to get to their little ones in the Montessori.

'How do you know that?' one of them retorts.

Before she can respond, another one replies, 'Obviously, they are not here, so they have to be somewhere safe.'

'How do you know they are safe?' wails the first woman as she collapses on the ground.

'I just remembered the safety measures designed in case of this eventuality, and since there is no sign of destruction or explosion here, the kids must have been taken to that room, and they will not be allowed out on our calls,' Rania explains to her.

'Let's get out of here and get back to the auditorium,' another mother hurriedly suggests as they continue to hear sirens blaring and small secondary explosions in the background.

'No!' wails the first mother, sobbing on the ground, 'Let's just stay here in one of the rooms and wait for this hell to end. It's dangerous out there.' She points in the direction of the school gate from where all the commotion could be heard.

As other women reluctantly agree with her, Rania shakes her head in the negative. With Hamza presumably safe in the room here, and Taimur and Ayesha risk-free with Ismat inside the auditorium, her mind dashes towards Dhil and his safety. Unaware of the bombsite and fearing that it might have exploded at Dhil's function itself, she quickly decides to rush to her car and drive straight towards her beloved husband whose situation was unknown to her. Her car was parked in the parking area outside the school block and adjacent to the auditorium about 300 metres from her current position. Once out of the car park, she could drive straight on to the ring road of the cantonment to Dhil's place within minutes.

She bids the other women goodbye and rushes out of the school block. At about the same time, Amir reaches the ring road from an inner street. He sees two ambulances crossing him. With sirens wailing, they seem to be heading in the direction of the blast site. As he reaches about fifty metres from the gates of the auditorium, he sees two armed guards supported by an armoured SUV with a gunner atop manning a machine gun. These soldiers stood at the gates of the auditorium, protecting the premises, which housed some desperate women and children of soldiers, haplessly wandering around, struggling to make sense of this situation. The doors of the auditorium building were again locked from the inside once the wave of panicky people had left. While fifteen of them went with Rania to get their kids inside the school block, some others had rushed straight to their cars to get out of the area and were gone by now.

Seeing little chance of entering the building and having already mentally prepared to kill himself for his cause, Amir makes one last attempt to enter the gates. He waves his hand at the guards as he closes in on them shouting, 'I've come to take my mother and sister from here!'

'You can't go inside. Now stop where you are, stop!' yells back one of the soldiers. Amir closes in on the gate to about thirty metres, but slows down his motorbike in the process, so as not to prompt the gunner into firing at him, as the gunner aims the machine gun his way.

'But please let me in!' yells back Amir, pretending to show his desperation and slowly creeping forward.

All this happens in seconds as Dhil runs out of breath and stamina, finally closing in on the car park area. Forty metres in front of him, he sees Amir pleading with the soldiers to let him in. They are about sixty metres further down the road in front of the auditorium gates. Cognizant of the danger of getting shot by his own soldiers in the heat of things, and fearing Amir to be a suicide bomber, he stops in his tracks to see the drama unfold and raises his hand signalling other men following him to stop as well.

At that very moment, Dhil sees, to his horror, his own wife running out of the school gate, further down from the auditorium, in the direction of the car park, crossing the armoured SUV in the process. As one soldier guarding the rear of the SUV tries to stop her from crossing it to reach the car park where Amir has reached by now, Dhil, with all the strength his voice could muster, yells at Rania and frantically waves his hands in the process.

'Rania! Go back! Go back!' Presuming by now that Amir may not be who he is posing as, and with the likely danger of him actually being a suicide bomber becoming imminent, Dhil instinctively dashes towards the suicide bomber, not caring for his own life but wanting to save that of wife.

Dhil's reaction distracts the engagement for a second and is enough for Amir to realise that his cover is blown, and before the guards are able to take any further action, he looks up as if telling the heavens of his arrival and presses the dreaded button. By this time, he is within seven metres of the soldiers' manning the gate, while Dhil is within thirty metres of him.

BOOM!

The bomb strapped to Amir's body explodes tearing him into several pieces as his head detaches from his body and lands several metres away in the direction of Dhil.

Metal slugs and nails attached with the bomb, to make it more lethal in a crowd of people, spread all around with great velocity penetrating and piercing the bodies of all within a twenty-five metres distance. The accompanying shockwave also sweeps Dhil and his fellow comrades off their feet, and they fall to the ground.

Dhil, once again facing a bomb blast, struggles to get up. Uniform torned and hands and face cut from the striking debris, he again hits his ears with the palm of his hand, trying to regain his hearing as he forces his lungs to breathe air back in.

Other men behind him also try to get their bearing as they see in front to their horror the plume of dust and smoke dissipating, and emerging from within, the burning wreck of Amir's motorbike and the SUV along with the gory scattered remains of the poor soldiers guarding the auditorium gates.

'Oh God! Rania . . . Oh my God, no!' tired of the ordeal and battered from the blast, Dhil struggles to walk towards the ruins, which were once the gates of the auditorium. Fear of uncertainty and not wanting to think about losing his beloved life partner, Dhil's mind goes numb as his heart bears the rush of tumultuous feelings.

Legs barely having the strength to walk up to the site, Dhil had never felt this way in his life even when facing great odds at the battlefronts. But this was a different situation for him. The fear of losing the person he loved the most had sucked the strength out of his body.

It takes him a couple of minutes as he struggles forward, oblivious of the crying and wailing of women from inside the destroyed wall of the auditorium, the blaring of ambulances sirens coming in their direction and other commotion around him. Dust still in the air, as he crosses the wreckage of the SUV to his right, he sees a familiar body lying face down, motionless, on the ground. Clothes tattered, body ruptured from the pierced nails and metal slugs from the bomb and flesh protruding from the broken skin with blood trickling out from all over the body, here lies, to Dhil's horror, the motionless body of Rania.

He reaches Rania and gets down on his knees, hoping against hope that his wife would get up. He gathers the strength in his arms to reach for Rania and slowly picks her up and turns her around to see the battered face of his once beautiful wife, blood oozing out of her bruised mouth and nostrils. She had turned around in the nick of time to run back after hearing her husband shouting. While this saved her face from the direct impact of the bomb, it did not save her completely. The bomb blast had ripped her body from behind, mortally wounding her.

'Rania . . . Rania, please get up. See, I'm here,' a ray of hope runs through Dhil as he feels a faint pulse in Rania's neck.

'You'll be fine, everything's gonna be fine,' he emphatically pleads with the love of his life to open her eyes, but there lay Rania, showing no response.

Minutes tick by as Dhil tries to revive her. His course mate, Lieutenant Colonel Asim finally comes up to him.

'Partner, pull yourself together. The ambulance is here, let's take bhabi[122] to the hospital?' he asks Dhil who looks at him inquiringly.

'Kids are fine, thanks to Allah . . . They are with Ismat,' Asim assures a bewildered Dhil. 'For now, we must take bhabi to the hospital, and you need attention too,' observing Dhil's face and hands also badly cut and bleeding.

'We'll take your children home, they shouldn't be seeing this,' concludes Asim as he gestures the paramedics to bring the stretcher and take Rania and Dhilawar to the Cantonment Hospital.

In his twenty-two years of service, this was the first time that Dhil was not sure of what just happened. While his mind advised him to come to terms with the facts, his heart persuaded him to live in denial.

This cannot be happening to me. Rania and the kids are at home. This is not Rania. What am I doing here? Who is this woman? What is happening to me? Am I going mad? Dhilawar get a hold of yourself! A plethora of

---

[122]　A term used out of courtesy for wives of fellow officers, friends, and colleagues in Pakistan.

turbulent thoughts run in his mind as his eardrums ache from the blaring siren of the ambulance racing towards the hospital at the same time as paramedics struggle to plug the wounds of a motionless Rania.

Lt. Col. Dhilawar Jahangiri was hit for the first time in his life.

* * *

1000 hrs — National Day Parade, in Islamabad

The President's address to the nation ends. Sam sees the Joint Chief of Staff saying something in the President's ear as he walks back to his place on the dais after delivering his speech. Sam infers, from the concerned look on their faces, the topic of discussion. The news of the terrorist attack at Attock had reached them, but the parade was to continue. No act of the militants could stop the State now from showing their resolve against the enemies of the State.

The brigadier leading the main contingent of the parade smartly marches up to the presidential dais.

'Sir! With your permission, may we begin the National Day Parade?' he authoritatively seeks the customary permission from the President to begin the day's proceedings.

As the President consents, the Chief of Air Staff gives his air salute in the solitary F-16C Fighting Falcon; flying fast and low at 150 metres, he comes in from the left side of the dais, flying over the army's hardware and contingent of men neatly standing in parade formation, ready to begin their march towards the presidential dais. Streaking towards the presidential dais, the Air Chief pulls up the fighter jet in a ninety-degree climb right in front of the dais, rolling and drawing applause from the general public and dignitaries attending the ceremony. Thirty seconds later, he is followed by formations of Air Force's F-16s, Mirage IIIs, JF-17 Thunders, and F-7PG Skybolts combat aircrafts showing off the Air Force in all its glory at just about the time when Amir is blowing himself up in front of the auditorium gate, causing mayhem and horror to people there.

As the air formations pass away and the ground contingents begin, their march to the beat of the military drums, Sam's cell phone starts blinking once again. She takes her eyes off the glorious spectacle and looks at the phone.

Another bomb blast at Attock Cantonment a while back. Casualties feared in this one too . . . further news coming in.

She reads the message coming from her loyal deputy agent Jim in the US embassy. As she looks up, she sees around her other dignitaries looking at their cell phones. There is a buzz in the seating area from discussions between people concerning this matter.

Sam sees, in front of her, columns and columns of men, in different military uniforms representing their Arms and Units, in all their magnificence, proudly marching in perfect synchronisation with the military bands, who are belting out the tunes of patriotic songs of the country. The same thoughts again resonate in her mind, *This is not gonna be easy, this is not gonna be easy.* She shakes her head in despair.

Chapter 8

PAKISTAN'S WILD WILD WEST

Midnight at Bastikhel village. It is thirty-nine hours since the day Attock Cantonment suffered its terror attack orchestrated by Baaz Jan. Since then, the periphery of Bastikhel Village, being the stronghold of the Lashkar,[123] has been relentlessly bombarded from the air by the combat jets of the Air Force in response to Lashkar's public claim of being behind this terror attack. These strikes are being carried out by the State to warn villagers of the dire consequences if they do not hand over the anti-state elements or continued to harbour them in their village. Moreover, signals were also being sent to the Lashkar, affirming that the State would not be subjugated to any kind of terror attack; rather, the State will continue to strive to rid its territory of all terrorists.

While the news of this attack was received with extreme distress and anguish in the country, it was appreciated by all the militant organisations operating in the border area. Baaz received a message from across the border too, applauding him on this mission and returning to him his title of 'Mullah', but he was still not allowed to enter Afghanistan.

Baaz sat in his dark, damp room deep inside the cave network, safe from the bombing outside, which had started coming closer to the village, putting villagers' lives in imminent danger.

The frustrated look on Baaz's face reflected his unhappiness with the outcome. He had wanted to kill the families of officers and soldiers gathered at the auditorium but was unable to do so. The collateral damage was restricted to twelve civilian men killed around

---

[123] Baaz's organisation.

the guardroom; ten soldiers stationed at the guardroom and outside the gate of the auditorium were also killed. While the injured were aplenty, there was no report so far of women or children of the men in uniform having been killed.

It had been extremely difficult for him to acquire a truck and convert it into an Iqbalia Restaurant's carrier, arrange for the large bomb, and also infiltrate a suicide jacket and bombers inside the cantonment.

Replaying the scene of the attack as planned in his mind, the young faces of his 'fidayeen', Hashim, Amir, and Adil, flashed past him as he felt that all their efforts went to waste.

As he hears the thunderous explosions of more bombs landing around the poor villagers of Bastikhel, showing him that his enemy is angry, he gives out a roar of anguish on missing his planned objective.

'Well, at least they'll fear me now!' he finally tries to console himself, punching his fist into the hardened ground, devoid of any sorrow at losing innocent villagers from the retaliatory bombing.

As Baaz is busy contemplating his next move, he hears familiar voices hurriedly coming towards him. From the tone, it appears as if an argument has broken out between them.

'Qasim!' he yells out the name of his deputy Qasim Afridi, whose voice he recognises. The voices stop.

'Assalam u aliekum, Chief!' his deputy greets him softly.

'Yes! What is it?' shouts back Baaz.

'I have Gulab Mehsud with me,' Qasim refers to the chief of the village who has come to see Baaz in his cave network. Baaz signals both of them to come inside his dark dingy room.

Baaz's room was not more than three meters by four meters in size. A lantern was the only thing that provided illumination. Some books mainly on religion and history were kept at one end and two sets of clothes hung from a hook on the mud-hardened brown wall at the other end. A rug doubled as his sleeping as well as seating area. Not to forget his personal weapon collection—a Russian AK-47 Kalashnikov assault rifle, with two magazines of bullets taped together, another belt full of bullets hung from the wall—a .30 bore 'Magnum' hand gun taken as a bounty from a dead American soldier in Afghanistan, and a 'Rambo' style multipurpose dagger brought especially from Darra near Peshawar completed his armoury. Lastly, a satellite phone was also kept with a UPS Battery used for charging it from time to time.

He seldom allowed anyone to come to his room, as a bigger cave at the other end of this tunnel network served as their usual meeting place, but on this occasion, there was no time to go there given the urgency written all over his visitors' faces.

'Baaz Jan,' the village chieftain nods at Baaz, his wrinkled old face displays signs of fatigue and concern.

'We have received warning from the Pakistan Army,' he continues, trying to avoid the stern stare of Baaz by looking down. 'They have warned that unless we help them in . . . ,' he stops, unable to gather the courage to complete his sentence.

Baaz looks at Qasim, who figures that Baaz wants him to continue instead.

'Chief, he wants to say . . . ,' as Qasim begins, Baaz raises his hand abruptly signalling him to stop.

'Let Gulab Mehsud complete his sentence,' he orders Qasim as he stares again at the village chieftain.

'What I mean, Mullah Baaz Jan, is that . . . the military is warning that . . . they will destroy the whole of Bastikhel Village, if . . .'

There is again a pause.

'If?' asks Baaz.

'We don't stop supporting you guys and help them in finishing off your organisation . . . they will destroy the whole Bastikhel Village . . .'

'As a punishment for not helping the State,' completes Qasim softly.

'Yes, I know, Qasim!' yells back Baaz. 'Do not talk when the village chief is talking.'

Baaz then tones down his anger, looks towards Gulab and asks, 'And what is your response to this warning?'

There is a minute of silence in the room as the elderly chieftain gathers the nerve to respond to the most feared person in the valley.

'Mullah Baaz Jan,' he struggles for breath, bitterly repenting his decision of coming to the caves of 'Lashkar' rather than discussing this issue in the friendlier surroundings of the village. But unable to hide his true emotions and hoping for sanity from Baaz, he continues, 'People respect you in the village; they support your cause and are

willing to die fighting for you as long as you wage Jihad[124] against the
Western occupation forces in Afghanistan and their allies in Pakistan.'
The chieftain tries to explain his position, 'But when they have come
to know that your plan is to kill innocent women and children inside
Pakistan, for whatever justification, and is bringing on them the wrath
of the State, they are getting afraid.'

'Are they getting afraid or are you getting afraid, old man?' Baaz
tries to control his temper, as his face turns red with rage.

'Please understand, Baaz Jan,' the chieftain pleads, 'taking on the
full fury of the State is too much for them to handle . . . Besides, our
religion also does not allow us to kill innocent women and children or
elderly, who are not part of the battle,' hoping that Baaz takes the hint
and spares him for now.

'Hah!' Baaz scoffs, 'now you will teach me what Islam says?
Haven't you heard what our revered 'Muallims'[125] say about it?'
referring to the fiery edicts declared by various religious clerics in the
area.

Before the elderly chieftain can explain his point of view further,
Baaz, in a fit of rage, reaches for his Magnum and fires a volley of
bullets into the chest of the surprised chieftain, who hits the ground
on his back, his eyes intently stare at Baaz emitting surprise as he
breathes his last, signalling the exit of life from the aged body of the
elderly chief of the village, Bastikhel.

There is silence in the room as Qasim, stunned from this outburst,
stares at the limp body of Gulab Mehsud.

'Now I am the chief of Bastikhel Village,' claims Baaz
authoritatively as he tries to control his temper.

'Let it be known to all in the village that if anyone talks of defeat or
collaborates with the enemy, he will also meet the same fate,' he looks
at Qasim and concludes in a low tone, 'besides, when the State comes
to know that the village chief was killed by us as he tried to side with
them, they will spare the village and concentrate on us only.'

There is again silence in the room as Qasim, still too stunned to
say anything, struggles to carry the dead body of the village chieftain
for a decent Islamic burial.

---

[124] Holy war.
[125] Priests.

*   *   *

It is Saturday morning in Attock Cantonment, two days after the terror incident took place on the National Day Anniversary.

On that fateful day in Attock Cantonment, Rania had gotten badly injured in the second bomb attack as shrapnel and metal slugs from the bomb hit her body from the rear, one penetrating into the back of her skull, thus badly damaging her brain and spinal cord. She was operated on and was now in a deep coma from her wounds, currently placed in the Intensive Care Unit under the strict watch of medical staff in the 'Combined Military Hospital' in Attock.

The cantonment still reeled from the devastating terror attack. The terrible experience of that day had created fear in the hearts and minds of the people. With such brazen tactics of the militants, nothing seemed safe to them; however, they knew that they must move on in life, whilst taking protective measures to safeguard themselves. Life was to go on.

The military police had arrested Rashid — the tailor, and he was under the custody of the 'intelligence services', extracting information from him.

Meanwhile, back at the CMH, Dhil attended to streams of friends and extended family who came from far and wide to see Rania and offer their sympathies and support to a beleaguered man. For Dhil, the past two evenings had been very taxing, both mentally and physically. Rania's parents had since joined them from Karachi where they resided. The children, traumatised from this experience, were for now in the loving care of their maternal grandparents, who doted on the children of their only daughter, now fighting between life and death.

Dhil, nursing wounds of his own, was given a few days sick leave that also gave him the chance to be with his beloved wife all day long. While hoping and praying for her recovery, he became increasingly confused and angry. Reputed to be the man in control of any situation and a pillar of support for others, he hid his torrent of emotions from his children and the visiting guests but felt the need to share them with his only confidant, Rania, and not being in a position to do that made him feel sad, lonely, and frustrated.

He now sat next to Rania's bed in the ICU. The room was moderately lit. Different gadgets attached to her motionless body monitored her heartbeat, pulse, blood pressure, and other vital signs. Her heartbeat was faint and blood pressure low. Her head was wrapped up in bandages, and she was placed on her side since her back was all burnt and wounded.

Just then the doctor on his morning round walks into the room, and Dhil immediately gets up from his seat. After the complimentary greetings, Dhil asks the doctor about Rania's situation, hoping to hear some positive news.

'Colonel Dhilawar, it's too early to say anything,' the doctor informs him soberly, 'surviving a bomb blast from such close proximity is a miracle in itself.'

Unsatisfied with this noncommittal answer, Dhil asserts himself, 'But, Doctor, how long will this uncertainty continue? Can't you guys do anything to bring her back?' referring to Rania's coma. 'This situation of hers is killing me from inside, my kids are also in a terrible state!'

The doctor, while maintaining his composure, understood the situation of a frustrated man deeply in love with the person whose recovery was by no means assured. After two days, this situation had not eased, making Dhil more impatient as time passed.

'Sir, I understand your situation. But we have done the best we can. The shrapnel had pierced through her skull and gone into the rear of her brain just above where the brain connects with the spinal cord. Please understand that our neurosurgeon did a great job in taking the shrapnel and its splinters out of her brain, repairing the damaged area and, in layman's terms, then joining up her skull. But the damage is deep and intense, and while we have done the best we can, we can never be certain of the outcome. Not to forget the burns on her body and other wounds. We can only pray to Allah now for her full recovery.'

Before Dhil could respond, the senior doctor pats him reassuringly on his arm and leaves him still dumbfounded. Once again, finding himself alone in the room with Rania, he looks towards her with inquiring eyes.

'Rania!' he drags his chair next to her motionless body and sits down holding her limp bandaged hand in his own injured one. Slowly rubbing it for warmth, he pleads, 'Rania, please get up,' his voice trembles. 'Your parents are here, and they want to meet you. Kids are worried about you, Hamza thinks you are sleeping and doesn't want to disturb you. All he asks me is when will Mama wake up . . . What do I tell him, huh?'

Dhil pauses to see any response from her, but nothing is forthcoming. He continues, 'You know on that day when I heard that you were coming looking for me whereas all others had taken shelter in the school and auditorium, I felt so proud of you. I told them that's my Rania, all right,' continuing to rub her hand as he struggled to speak, 'brave, caring, and a wee bit foolish,' giving out a small laugh to stop his voice from cracking as his eyes well up.

Dhil remembers the first day he ever saw Rania. It was about fifteen years back when he was posted to Karachi in his unit. Then a young captain, Dhil was the epitome of a 'Gentleman Officer'. Tall and handsome, with a stately presence, he was known for his reserved demeanour towards the fairer sex; that was more an outcome of his shy nature towards them rather than any attitude problem. Having lost his parents in his childhood, he was raised by his elderly sister, the only person he was close to and who at the time resided up north in the country's picturesque valley city of Abbottabad. So in the port city of Karachi, the only family he had were his army buddies.

It was at one of his friend's marriage that he met Rania, who was then in her final year of graduation. Finding her nature bubbly and vivacious, his heart was smitten by this charming girl with a tall shapely figure and long wavy brunette hair falling casually on her back and shoulders. Feeling the urge to spend the rest of his life with her, he had sought the assistance of his sister to formally propose to Rania's parents seeking her hand in marriage. Once proposed to, Rania had also found it difficult to spurn the advances of a charming young Captain Dhilawar, and with her parents' approval, their courtship began with their engagement ceremony.

He remembers when they were married thirteen years ago, the simple ceremony, which seemed the happiest moment of their lives. The blissful occasions that followed and the postings to different locations from the mountains in the north to the small towns across Pakistan. How they spent the tough times loving and caring for each other. Then the birth of their firstborn; how happy they were when Ayesha opened her eyes to see her parents looking ardently at her. Her first smile, her first walk in the park, and soon the arrival of Taimur. They were elated at having a son to complete their family, and their pleasant surprise and shy excitement on welcoming the arrival of little Hamza into their lives, whom they termed an additional gift from God.

Being the daughter of a naval officer herself and sister to two younger brothers, Rania complemented Dhil in both his personal and professional lives. Married for thirteen years, she gave Dhil the comfort of a home and warmth of a family that he always aspired for. While he would be more involved in his professional tasks, he knew for sure that his 'heaven of a home' was in the capable hands of his wife. Over the years, he had become so dependent on her that a life without her became inconceivable to him. But today, he felt alone and helpless, desperate to wake his soulmate and take her home in his loving embrace.

There is silence in the room as only the beep of the monitors betrays the stillness around him. 'Okay, this is enough now. You win, you win!' he whines again, pleading with her to wake up, 'I'm nothing without you, you hear that? Ayesha has not eaten anything for two days, and Taimur is also praying to Allah continuously for your return. You can't do this to us. I'll do anything you say, you just say it, love, just say it, but please don't leave me?' his voice trembles again as he utters his pleas.

Watching this from the glass window in the door is Brig. Haider Khan. Haider had been out of the station and returned last night. Saddened at hearing Dhil's outburst clearly audible outside the door, he feels for Dhil in his time of despair. Just as he gathers enough courage to knock at the door, inside the room, Dhil notices a tear trickling out of Rania's closed eye as the heartbeat monitor beeps an increase in activity. He gets ecstatic and rushes out of the room. Haider clears the way for this giant of a man to pass through as Dhil, in his excitement, does not even notice his boss.

Dhil yells for the doctor to come and see Rania as the nursing staff rushes to the room to check on her. As one opens Rania's closed eyes to check movement of the pupils, the other records the readings on the various monitors. The doctor on duty also briskly walks into the room with the usual stethoscope hanging across his shoulders. Just then, Dhil notices Haider standing in the hall, waiting to greet him.

'Sir, you saw that! . . . She can listen to me!'

Haider prefers to remain quiet and just nods back with a conciliatory smile.

As both men stand quietly outside the room, with Dhil anxiously praying to hear some good news, out walks the doctor without exhibiting any joyous emotions.

'Sorry, Colonel Saheb, she is still the same,' shaking his head in the negative, he looks at Dhil who stares back with inquiring eyes.

'But I just saw the tear dropping out of her eye and the bleeps getting faster,' Dhil angrily responds.

'That was just a random action in the body,' comes the soft response.

As he walks away from the two men, Haider tries to comfort his distressed comrade. He pats Dhil's back and tells him to gather the strength to face this situation for the sake of his sanity and his children.

'I'm fine, sir, I'm fine, it's Rania . . .' Dhil gestures at her while trying to again put on a brave face in front of his boss.

'We'll get the culprits who did this, don't you worry on that front, brother,' Haider tries to assure Dhil who looks back at Haider with inquiring eyes.

'Pardon me, sir, but who's the culprit here?' Dhil asks sarcastically.

Haider is taken aback at this unexpected query and just gives a confused look, noting the question and devil-may-care attitude currently in Dhil's tone.

'Sir, who do we blame for this situation? Should I blame those fucking terrorists who think they are doing Jihad for Islam, or should I blame the arrogant Americans whose presence in this region has led to all this in our country?'

There is silence in the hall as Haider tries to grapple with this unusual situation.

'Do more, do more . . . What more do they want us to do, what more?'

Dhil directs another questioning look at Haider. Haider, however, chooses to remain silent and let Dhil relieve his burdened heart.

'Our loved ones are not safe, our homes are not safe, bloody hell any place in Pakistan is not safe any more, and you want to know why, sir?'

There is a pause before Dhil answers his own question, 'Because we look the other way when Americans strike with their drones, killing our villagers who are not all terrorists. And what does that do in return?'

Haider gives a feeble smile and lets him continue. 'It turns the fundo[126] lunatics in them against us . . . against their own State, whom we then fight off to keep them subjugated.'

---

[126] Slang for 'Islamic fanatics' also referred as fundamentalist.

There is silence in the hallway before Dhil concludes his grievance, 'This is America's war, sir, and we are paying a heavy price for siding with them.'

'Get a hold on yourself, Dhilawar,' Haider puts his hand on Dhil's shoulder reassuringly and tries to comfort him. 'A lot of people depend on you, starting from your kids and then, of course, your unit men. We'll pray for Rania Bhabi, she'll be fine, but you must take rest to get in shape first.'

'I'm done, sir,' Dhil shakes his head in despair, 'this is not my war any more.' His mind still stuck on his earlier thoughts, a frown comes on his face as he looks intently towards Rania, lying motionless on her bed.

'Please count me out . . . I've played my part.'

Haider looks at Dhil with disappointment. In front of him was a soldier whose name in the Army was synonymous with various feats of valour spread over years, but this soldier was now hit and did not know how to respond to this challenge.

Assessing that this is not the right time to discuss this matter, Haider prefers to maintain silence as he excuses himself to leave a distressed Dhilawar by the side of his wife, still struggling for her life.

*   *   *

It is Saturday afternoon in Islamabad, two days after the glorious National Day's parade was held here. While the troops, military hardware, and civilian floats, depicting cultures of various areas of Pakistan, had all since left the city, the news of the twin bombings in Attock Cantonment reminded the nation that the worst was still not over. However, the festivities of that day also sent a ray of hope across the country, assuring the people that the government and the armed forces will continue their resolve to annihilate the militant network in this country that wanted to extend its reign of terror under the pretext of spreading their version of Islam.

As if waiting for the National Day parade to conclude under a sunny sky, the weather had since turned cold and cloudy, and intermittent rain showers cleared the dusty atmosphere of the city, giving it a sparkling clean look. The green Margalla Hills, against the backdrop of grey cloudy skies, invited city dwellers to leave their homes, and come trekking and driving up the various trails, to restaurants and picnic spots spread across the hillside.

Not wanting to be left behind, Rebecca had pulled Sam out of her warm blanket in the morning. The two had then gone for hiking on one of the mud tracks on the green Margalla Hills. Sam enjoyed the hour and a half of walk up the trail through natural forests with thick foliage running along the track and, in the process, made acquaintances with a large family of monkeys who were friendly enough to walk next to the hikers, expecting to get food from them in return. She laughed as she threw bread at the monkeys, especially brought by Rebecca for this purpose. These monkeys happily accepted the donations as they patiently followed the two ladies up the track. Feeding monkeys, although prohibited, was a common feature in this area, as other people too enjoyed the hike and pranced around with these primates on the trail. Sam had thrown her caution to the winds, and for the first time, she also shared pleasantries and smiles with other local people walking around.

Rebecca noticed this change in Sam's attitude from how she was on the first day she met her in the US embassy. She liked what she saw and hoped that with time Sam would become more at ease with her surroundings. As for Sam, she had acclimatised well as the days had passed, and her earlier apprehension towards Pakistan and its common people seemed to decrease, in spite of the various warnings and 'be cautious' notifications being received by her from time to time. Today they happily talked about their relationships and memorable experiences as they walked up to Daman-e-Koh from the base of the hills.

Sam was fascinated to see the breathtaking view of the city from this spot nestled about 600 metres in the hills above Islamabad. Complete with painted maps of the city on billboards, binoculars perched on stands, souvenir shops, parks, and open air restaurants, this place had developed into a popular tourist attraction, which foreigners also frequented to enjoy the panoramic view of the sprawling city set out in front of them.

Today was no different from any other weekend. Groups of people, young and old, families, both Pakistanis and some foreign, enjoyed the weather at this serene spot. Witnessing such harmony all around them, the two ladies also felt relaxed. Soon they felt pangs of hunger and decided to check out one of the open-air restaurants neatly situated another ten metres higher up the hill. They had heard about the delicious barbecues at this place, and today seemed like a good day to taste it.

As they find a suitable table with a good view and make themselves comfortable, Rebecca places their order for an assortment of barbecued pieces of mutton and chicken along with a variety of bread rolls and green salad. She then turns to Sam who is busy looking at the Presidential Avenue.

A twelve-lane avenue, stretching about three miles from end to end, with the beautiful buildings of State—Senate, National Assembly, President House, and Prime Minister Secretariat accompanied by Supreme Court, all were situated in a row on one side, whereas the State's Islamabad Television Station and various ministries stood on the other. Each building unique and more beautiful than the other, some were built on modern Western designs, while others depicted the more traditional and historic 'Mughal'[127] architecture of the region. Sam was particularly intrigued to see limited traffic movement on this gargantuan road due to barricades and check posts now placed at either end and at all entry points joining with the Presidential Avenue. This clearly showed that these were not normal times, and a high level of security was a standard requirement to safeguard the symbols of the State.

As Rebecca finishes, with the excited waiter, eager to promote all of their dishes to the two foreign ladies, she looks towards Sam. 'So ma' girl, what you thinking now?'

Sam takes a long breath. She has a thoughtful expression. 'I don't know, I feel sorry for this place now.'

Seeing the curious look on Rebecca's face, Sam continues, 'Look at these people around you . . . men, women, kids, young and old, families, couples.'

Rebecca, trying to find some humour in such a philosophical response replies, 'Duh! Yeah, what's there to see?'

Sam, ignoring Rebecca's light tone, continues, 'Becy, don't you feel they deserve a better life? I mean, look at them. These are ordinary friendly people and even though they're trying to chill out, they're still cautious of their surroundings, looking over their shoulders, uncertain of who's sitting next to them, wondering if that person

---

[127]   Time reminiscent of Mughal Empire from 16th Century to 19th Century AD in Indian Subcontinent where Islamic architecture and culture were at its prime.

walking in their direction is a suicide bomber?' She pauses for a while and concludes, 'They live a life in perpetual fear.'

Not wanting to spoil her high mood, Rebecca responds, 'Ma' girl, I ain't seeing no such shit. All I'm seeing are people enjoying their stuff and having a good time. You think too much Albright, you gotta chill out.'

Sam smiles back at Rebecca; seeing no hope of having a philosophical discussion with her, she responds, 'You won't understand,' to which Rebecca quickly replies, 'Hey, I don't wanna understand. I wanna take life as it is. Just live for the day, and here we are today, enjoying the walk, the weather, the freedom . . . and now the food.' Her eyes widen with delight, and she rubs her hands with glee as the waiter places an assortment of well done barbecued food in front of them, complemented with sodas and salad — the aroma of the cooked food floating past her nostrils opens up her appetite.

As they dig into the delicious meat, Rebecca continues, 'Hey, how did your date go last night?' referring to her meeting with Bilal Khattak at PappaSallis.

'That wasn't a date, that was just two friends having dinner together,' retorted Sam.

'He he he, I know "just friends" when I see them, and you ma' girl certainly ain't one of them,' Rebecca smiles back mischievously at Sam.

'Well, we belong to different backgrounds. He doesn't even know who I really am, and I can't afford to bust my cover.'

'Well, that's a shame, 'cause he is a real nice guy for you and someone who I thought you liked too?' responds Rebecca as she continues chomping on the meat.

'But he has invited me over to his ancestral town of Kohat, and I might take him up on that offer,' Sam shares her feelings with Rebecca with a twinkle in her eye.

As if stunned by lightning, Rebecca stops chomping on her food and looks up at Sam, who is now busy tackling her own piece.

'You crazy? Woman?' Rebecca lets it out in a high shrill voice as the people around stop and look at them.

Embarrassed by the situation, Sam signals Rebecca to quiet down. Rebecca, seeing the eyes all around composes herself before continuing, 'Islamabad is okay, but Kohat? Do you even know where that place is?'

'Yeah, I know. It's about three hours drive from here towards the west.'

'Yeah and very close to that dreaded place Waziristan, where even Paks are afraid to go . . . We all know that, don't we?' Rebecca whines as she suddenly starts to lose her appetite. 'I thought you were the careful kind, but now you're going to the other extreme.' She pauses for a while before exclaiming, 'Going with a man whom you've met only a couple of months back—for all you know he could be a Taliban! Didn't you tell me his wife had taken that plea for getting a divorce?'

'Three months,' comes the quick correction from Sam, trying to hopelessly pep up a sullen Rebecca. 'And besides, I've run my checks on him. He's as clean as a whistle, in fact, his whole family is clean.'

'Whatever.'

'Okay, okay, take it easy, dear. I had just thought that I'd go there myself to take a first-hand account of the situation on the ground, you know, get to meet some people there, understand their points of view, and maybe try to make a difference in their thinking or you know . . . just to understand the situation better,' Sam attempts to make Rebecca understand her position.

But not ready to be convinced so easily, Rebecca responds in one breath, 'What you're trying to do is go looking for trouble . . . I'm sure you have people to do what you are planning to do, and over one weekend, you can't possibly do all that you're telling me you'll do . . . and Kohat . . .' as she pauses to take a breath, Sam interjects.

'Kohat is not a dangerous place. It's still under State control. For crying out loud, it's a garrison town itself. What can go wrong over there?' Sam tries to make her argument as she finishes her food.

Rebecca retorts, 'My dear, we are Americans working for our government, and we have been clearly instructed not to go beyond the boundaries of Islamabad without formal protocol, and you know that better than me,' hinting at her position in the agency. 'For your own good, if I even suspect that you are planning to go, I'll be forced to report this matter.'

There is an uneasy pause between the two of them before Rebecca starts again, 'Besides, do you even know this Bill guy that well to trust your life with him?'

Sam does not take this discussion well. She considered Rebecca to be her confidant, but the thought of her spilling the beans makes Sam take some evasive manoeuvres. She lightens the mood, 'Okay, okay, take it easy, I ain't going nowhere ma' girl. I was just thinking aloud,' mimicking Rebecca as she concludes.

Rebecca, seeing the humorous side of the situation, eases off and gives a slight laugh.

'You spoilt my food, girl,' she responds.

To which Sam quickly replies, 'And you spoilt my plan.'

They both laugh out loud with Rebecca thinking the matter is concluded.

'When I used to force you out with me, I never thought you'd become this reckless,' Rebecca remarks as an afterthought.

Sam smiles back as she winks, 'Being reckless is my hobby, Becy.'

Rebecca fears the look in Sam's eyes. She cannot fathom the real meaning behind Sam's response but prefers to stay quiet as they get up from the table and start their descent back to the base camp to reach Rebecca's hatchback standing in the parking lot.

While Sam tries to ease the tension between them, Rebecca mostly remains silent, unable to decipher the conversation they just had and deeply concerned about the direction Sam was planning to take. She remembers her first encounter with Sam: reserved, cautious, and an introvert. Reluctant to roam around the city or meet people for that matter, and just five months later, she was ready to venture into Pakistan's forbidden territories on her own. She prays that Sam does not proceed with her dangerous plan.

Sam believes there is nothing stopping her. She had taken her time to adjust to her surroundings, to better understand her work and obligations. Her confidence was in overdrive now turning her back into the 'Ball Buster' she was known to be back home. She had made up her mind to visit Kohat with Bilal and to get to see that area and the people herself. She felt that the risk was acceptable, and no amount of warnings was going to stop her.

Pakistan's Wild Wild West awaited her audience, and her audience is what she was going to give them — and this would happen the very next day.

Chapter 9

HELP FROM UNEXPECTED QUARTERS

It was Saturday afternoon at Bastikhel Village. The weather was cold and cloudy here too as intermittent showers made the otherwise dry rocky hillside wet and muddy. There was an uneasy calm in the village for two reasons. Firstly, the State suspended its activities after two days of relentless air bombing around the village; and secondly, in the early morning hours of the day, the dead body of the revered village chieftain, Gulab Khan Mehsud, was found outside the village imam's[128] small mosque, with a note on it saying:

> To all the villagers,
> For the sake of some money, your village chief was about to sell your 'Mujahideen'[129] brothers to the enemies of Islam. We came to know about it through our reliable sources and took action against him after finding him guilty. Let it be known to all that any person found colluding with our American enemy or the Pakistani forces will meet the same fate. There will be no heaven for Gulab Mehsud. May Allah be your Protector.

This news of last night's killing of the revered village chief, Gulab Khan Mehsud, had spread out to the other villages in the area and, without paying any heed to the weather conditions or State bombing, a large congregation of about a thousand men gathered to attend his funeral. The State also ceased its operation for the time being to avoid

---

[128] Muslim priest.

[129] Muslim warriors. A term used by the militants for themselves.

the risk of killing civilians unnecessarily. Baaz Jan's gamble had paid off. He had rightly calculated that the moment the people of the area would come to know about the death of their respected chief, they would come in droves to attend his funeral, and when the State would learn about this development, it will cease bombing the area to avoid the risk of creating enmity among the common villagers towards itself.

These men waited for the Zohr[130] prayers to conclude before they could bury Gulab Mehsud's body and thereafter hold a jirga[131] to decide the future course of action.

This jirga consisted of four judicial council members, whose verdict on any matter brought in the jirga was to be considered final. Heading the jirga were two elderly men from the village Bastikhel. One of them was Arbaz Khan Mehsud, younger brother of Gulab Khan and a retired teacher now in his early sixties, who was next of kin to Gulab Khan and who now, by virtue of this position, took the seat of his deceased brother. About twenty years earlier, his secondary school in the village was forcibly converted into a 'madrassa' upon the arrival of Maulvi Najeeb Mohammad to the area. Although this was a consensus decision taken by the jirga at the time, the underlying reason for this step was a deep-rooted fear of God and His perceived wrath for promoting conventional forms of education rather than the religious form. The fury of the militants was also a factor, since they considered it their divine duty to eradicate all practices that seemed contrary to their vision of Islam. From that time onwards, Arbaz Khan had opted to stay mostly retired and only taught mathematics from his home since that did not contradict the militants' doctrines. So far, he was spared the wrath of the militants as he kept himself neutral in terms of the conflict around him.

The second member was Asmatullah Mehsud, a retired 'mujahid', now in his late sixties, who fought the Soviet Army in Afghanistan in

---

[130] 'Midday' prayers. One among the five mandatory daily prayers stipulated in Islam.

[131] Court in which the select few elders of the village constitute the judiciary and decide on the case at hand. An informal, albeit arguably effective, way of dispensing law in these semi-autonomous territories where State laws are inapplicable.

the 1980s and now managed a small orphanage close to the village, an activity appreciated and respected by the people in the area. Asmat sympathised with the militants as he considered them an extension of his own being and what he stood for in his younger days. His orphanage imparted religious training to the orphans and then encouraged them to join the militants in their fight against the US and their allies. Poor people from the area, who could not financially support their own children or orphaned nephews, left them to be raised in Asmat's orphanage. Donations came from local welfare organisations, as well as from militant organisations in the region, since he provided them with the necessary manpower for their cause.

The third member of the judicial council was the local imam,[132] who survived the earlier bombings by the State. In his midforties, he was the successor to the earlier firebrand imam, who had died in the January bombing. This new imam held a more balanced view of Islam. While he too was famous for making fiery speeches projecting the fight against American forces and their Muslim military allies as 'Jihad', he also refrained from promoting killing of ordinary people in the name of Islam.

Last on this panel and youngest of them all was Mullah Baaz Jan. He was part of the judicial council by virtue of being the commander of LaM; since the time of his predecessor Maulvi Najeeb Mohammad, the commander of this organisation was designated a seat in the judicial council of this jirga. All these men were viewed as reputable individuals due to their services to the village and its surrounding areas.

By afternoon, the clouds showed signs of dissipating in the blue sky as the spring sunrays made their way to the ground, bringing with them a bright clear sunshine, only occasionally blocked by a passing cloud. This beautiful weather was of least importance to the people in the village. Their attention was towards the jirga that was being held at the village square to discuss the tragic event of last night and to appoint the new chief of the village. The four men were seated next to each other on chairs and a crowd of approximately a thousand men, young and old, and from different walks of life, had gathered in a large circle in front of them. There were some other village elders

---

[132] Religious priest.

and notables too who were provided with chairs, whereas the masses squatted on the ground.

Baaz Jan was not concerned about his safety from the villagers since, for about every ten villagers, there was one fully armed and locally feared militant spread throughout the village square. He was also not concerned about their safety from an air attack from Pakistan Forces since he knew the State would not risk collateral damage. His concern was only from a possible missile strike from a US drone lurking on the western horizon. As of late, such missile strikes had become more frequent, and his comrades from other villages were fatally hit from such strikes. He had been out on the ground during most of the day. Wary of this danger, he now wished to conclude this jirga and return to his cave network; but asking to expedite proceedings would make him sound like a coward, and today was not the day for him to give such an impression to anyone, at least just as yet. He felt he had a chance for the coveted position of village chief and to aggressively fight for it became his immediate objective.

At about two o'clock, the convener, observing the strength of the crowd, felt it right to begin the proceedings. This convener was Hidayatullah Mehsud, an ex-sergeant of 5th FF[133] Infantry Battalion of the Pakistan Army, who opted for retirement after completing his twenty-two years of service in the force. Now in his late forties, he had resorted to farming his fields on the outskirts of the village and making a living from selling his agricultural produce. His administrative and crowd management capabilities, acquired during his stint with the Army, gave him the coveted post of a convener at such jirgas in the area. He was wary of the ruthless capabilities of these foreign militants who had made their way into his village with the aid and assistance of his fellow villagers and the Maulvis.[134] Although he never really accepted them in his heart, he preferred to maintain neutrality to avoid getting slaughtered at their hands. He had also pulled out his two sons, now in their early twenties, from

---

[133] Frontier Force. Infantry Battalions of Pak Army are named after the four provinces of Pakistan, namely Punjab, Sind, Baluch, Frontier and the Pakistan-administered area of Kashmir called Azad 'Free' Kashmir.

[134] Religious leaders.

the local 'levy forces' of the State, and all three of them resorted to tending to their fields.

Baaz Jan always remained suspicious of Hidayat, even suspecting him of aiding the January bombing. Knowing his military background, he regarded him as a threat, keeping him and his family under surveillance from time to time.

Hidayat was in a very sombre mood today. His beloved and respected elderly chieftain, whom he also advised against welcoming these foreigners into their fold as 'guests', was no more. Cognizant of their guests' intents and capabilities, he was always afraid of the day when these guests would turn against their hosts at the slightest possibility of their weakening towards the State. And that dreaded day arrived yesterday.

'Assalam u aliekum!' Hidayat yells authoritatively as the crowd quiets down. Hidayat continues, 'We have gathered here today on the sad demise of our chief, Gulab Khan Mehsud, who was respected and loved by all in the village.' He looks at the crowd who look back with sad expressions on their faces. 'May Allah All Mighty rest Gulab Khan's soul in Jannah[135] as he was a good man.' As Hidayat prays for his dead chief, he looks at Baaz, who glares back at Hidayat with his one eye; no sign of remorse or fear is visible.

Hidayat continues with his speech, 'Under normal circumstances, we would be looking for the murderers of our chief and bringing them to justice, but the current circumstances inhibit us from taking such action.' Clearly hinting at the militants but succumbing to their pressure as they had warned earlier in the day that any action taken against them for this act would result in a bloodbath in the village, where no one, not even the women or children, would be spared. Under such threats, it was deemed prudent by the village elders, including the judicial council members, to avoid such a ghastly scenario and only convene the Jirga to appoint the new chieftain of the village.

'Hence, this Jirga is being held to appoint our new chief,' concludes Hidayat.

There is pin-drop silence in the crowd as the militants, armed with their guns and rocket launchers, patrol the periphery, eyeing each

---

[135]   Heavens.

villager squatting on the ground and huddled together like sheep, all looking at Hidayat and the judicial council with expectations and anxious to see who will be their new leader.

*   *   *

0215 hrs—Nevada Desert, USA

Deep inside the grounds in the CIA operation room, a mission is in progress. The mission commander, a colleague of Samantha Albright from the CIA, is busy looking for 'targets of opportunity'. Any congregation of people where militants can be identified, carrying weapons like machine guns, rocket launchers, or mortars is a target for them. Trucks and vehicles, where weapons can be seen installed, are also termed as 'hostiles'.

Over the past few months, the CIA increased their operations in the Af-Pak border area, which was considered as a staging point for attacks on coalition forces inside Afghanistan. Missions of pilotless Predator Drones were flown on a daily basis from classified airbases in the region to identify targets of opportunity and destroy them with missile strikes. While this strategy had political and ethical implications, these were considered to be a success by the military commanders and the CIA since it put the operations of the militants in disarray. With enhanced capabilities of these drones, neither day nor night was safe for them any more. Mullah Baaz Jan had so far escaped the wrath of the CIA since, due to his ruthless reputation in the village, very few dared to collude with the US forces to share the dreaded commander's whereabouts, and with no tangible information on Baaz, he and his men continued to remain unscathed in their cave network.

But today was different. Mullah Baaz has been out for most of the day as the Predators lurk on the western horizon, looking for targets of opportunity. All is quiet in the cold and dark mission control room in Nevada as the mission commander and his crew fix their gaze on the large television screens relaying real time imagery from the powerful cameras on-board the drone. Suddenly, the camera operator shouts in excitement.

'Large gathering of people on the ground . . . thirty-two point five four degree lat and sixty-nine point three five degree long,' referring to the latitudinal and longitudinal coordinates of the area.

'English?' taunts the mission commander sombrely asking for the name of this spot.

'Seems like village Bastikhel, sir,' comes the sheepish response of the drone camera operator—a young man in his early twenties and eager to make his mark in such missions.

On hearing the name, one of the team members specialising in that area blurts out, 'Affirmative. This is the den of LaM, which is currently being headed by Baaz Jan, an Afghan.'

'Yeah, I know about him, they are not prime on our list of enemies but a nuisance, nonetheless,' the commander responds.

Historically speaking, from the time of Maulvi Najeeb, LaM was never amalgamated with others to be part of the larger AIA—Army for Independence of Afghanistan. While Najeeb used to send his men to fight alongside the larger AIA, this clever ploy of his put them down the priority list of the Coalition Forces in Afghanistan, whose Predator onslaughts primarily concentrated on AIA. On the contrary, due to LaM's destructive role inside Pakistan, they were high on the Pakistan Army's list of 'hostiles', especially after the ghastly attacks on Attock.

'Check for weapon details in the congregation,' the commander orders his specialist. As an afterthought, he concludes, 'If there are weapons in the crowd, then they are hostiles.'

People in the dimly lit room concentrate on the large television screens on the walls, as the drone's cameras zoom in closer on the people on the ground, depicted as bright grey silhouettes against a dark background on screen, enabling the team to make out whether they are carrying weapons.

'Weapons . . . identified,' comes the excited response as the drone pilot hovers in a circuit pattern, enabling the camera operator to zoom in on the congregation.

'What's the Intel on this gathering?' the commander asks his intelligence specialist just to be doubly sure of the situation.

'We have no Intel on this gathering . . . We have no local mole in this area,' disappointment evident in his tone since they were unable to buy a local, following the murder of Hamidullah Mehsud at the hands of Baaz's men after he was identified as the spy responsible for killing off their leader last fall.

Also, since the murder of the village chief took place only a few hours beforehand, the news had not yet reached the Americans from other sources.

Meanwhile, the camera zooms in on the four council members seated and facing the congregation. Their bright silhouettes complete with turbans[136] or caps and long shirts with waist coats over baggy trousers reassure the drone team that they are some sort of leaders of the 'hostiles'.

As if to close the discussion, the commander concludes, 'Village Bastikhel is a hostile village . . . There is a large gathering of men carrying weapons . . . which obviously makes them enemy combatants . . . but we have no Intel on this gathering so far.'

The pilot, while remotely flying his drone thousands of miles on the other side of the earth at 20,000 ft above sea level, paints the area where these gents are seated, readies his weapons, switching the safety button to off. The camera operator keeps zooming in on men carrying weapons on the ground, ensuring that all of his team members see these men clearly. They know that any decision to fire the missiles into this congregation will result in a large number of fatalities, an action that would have repercussions if these are non-combatants. But there is no doubt in their mind that they have to follow the orders of their commander. There is silence in the room as all wait with bated breath for the final order.

*   *   *

1415 hrs — Bastikhel Village, Waziristan

The crowd is still silent as Hidayatullah concludes his introductory speech and then throws down the gauntlet in front of the four council members. The rule of selection was that no council member could nominate himself as the chief. He had to nominate someone else. The person among the four who got the highest vote was then appointed as the chief. Although Baaz aspired to this position, the others did not consider him a likely candidate for the slot because he was not a son of the soil, a sentiment Baaz was well aware of and a position he loathed. Under such rules of the village, the four men look at each other as about 2,000 eyes stare at them. The members, having been

---

[136]   Head gear — long cloth wrapped around their heads. Bigger the turban, higher the stature.

nominated by the villagers over other village nominees due to their reputation and services to the area, knew that the fate of this village and its periphery depended on any decision taken now towards the appointment of the new chief.

Arbaz Khan Mehsud, the younger brother of the slain chieftain doesn't like his other two fellow villagers due to their radical philosophies and militant backgrounds, but he has to nominate one of them. Meanwhile, the other three also have to nominate someone else; they all feel that they are the best for this job, including Baaz. Silence prevails as the four of them gather the courage to discuss the situation.

Baaz then starts to get uneasy. Having been exposed on the ground for such a long time in the day makes him extremely uncomfortable. His instinct tells him that they are under surveillance by now, and he is not wrong.

*   *   *

0230 hrs — CIA Operation room, Nevada Desert

The cold dimly lit room is illuminated from the lights of the large television screens relaying the situation in the village of Bastikhel. Grey silhouettes of people against the black backdrop give them all a sinister look.

Silence prevails in the room as the commander contemplates his next move. Second thoughts creep into his mind whether these are actually hostiles or could they be 'friendlies'[137] that have raised arms against their militant guests, since such incidents of villagers turning against their militant guests and driving them out of their villages had occurred in that region. This commander's predicament is whether, by undertaking the missile strikes, he might be destroying his allies, thus aiding his enemy.

'What are my orders, sir?' comes a soft reminder from the drone pilot as he sees the fuel gauge of the drone showing just about enough fuel for them to loiter for another ten minutes before heading back to base.

---

[137]   Villagers who are pro-Pakistan and US and raise their village armies to fight off the militants.

'Hold circuit pattern,' comes the stern response from the commander as he continues to fix his sight on the screens, suppressing the temptation to fire to grant benefit of the doubt to the designated target.

*   *   *

1435 hrs — Bastikhel Village, Waziristan

Baaz cannot take this suspense any more. He notices a familiar hut nearby, about fourteen metres to his right and just behind the chairs of the other local dignitaries attending this meeting. He remembers one tunnel goes through this hut down to the network of caves and tunnels that spread across the village. Having spent enough time on the ground, and the fear of being attacked by a drone overriding all his other emotions, he makes a forceful suggestion to the rest of the members who are silent and still coming to terms with the unfortunate development of last night and the consequences of their future decisions.

'If you don't want to talk here, let's go to that hut over there and discuss the matter in privacy between the four of us,' Baaz points in the direction of the small hut.

Arbaz Khan, apprehensive of meeting the same fate as his elder brother, asks Baaz, 'Baaz Jan, what's wrong over here? Any decision we make here in front of the whole village would be considered fair.'

'It will be considered fair if there was to be a decision,' Baaz snaps, losing his cool but trying to maintain his composure. Seeing blank looks from the others, he continues, irritated, 'We are sitting ducks here for a drone attack . . . This large congregation . . . since morning . . . and now us, sitting as inviting targets . . . the Americans must be watching us.'

At this, the local cleric gets up, sounding visibly shaken. 'Let's go,' and, without waiting for others to follow, starts walking towards the hut.

Asmatullah, the elderly militant, doesn't like this conversation or the running off of the local cleric in front of the whole gathering, questions Baaz assertively, 'And what makes you think that we'll be safe from this . . . a . . . missile strike inside that mud hut?' He looks disapprovingly at the hut.

'Sir, there is a tunnel dug from that hut, which will take us to a shelter where we'll be safe,' replies Baaz, controlling his temper but showing respect for the elder. Baaz does not like being questioned, and his patience with all this conversation is wearing thin.

Asmat looks towards Arbaz inquiringly at which Baaz bursts out, 'Either we stay here and get toasted, or we do as I tell you to do!' This time his voice is audible enough for the people in the vicinity to hear.

Not wanting to create a scene here and lose their honour in front of the villagers, Arbaz nods at Asmat to get up and follow Baaz Jan, hoping that he will not meet the same fate as that of his elder brother, Gulab Khan.

The two elderly men get up from their chairs and gesture at a confused Hidayatullah of their plan to go to the nearby hut for discussion. The three men then start walking towards the hut, where the village cleric has already reached by now. On the way, they advise the dignitaries that the decision will be made soon after they discuss the matter in the privacy of that hut.

*   *   *

0240 hrs—CIA Operation room, Nevada Desert

On seeing the objects standing up, the camera operator screams, 'Targets are moving, targets are moving!'

'Zoom out,' the commander calmly responds as they see the men walking in the direction of the hut.

Still not sure of the situation, he looks towards his intelligence specialist for advice, 'Could these be friendlies . . . what's the Intel on the villagers?'

'Hell, no, sir!' comes the quick answer, 'Large congregation at a designated enemy village with men carrying weapons surrounding the congregation makes the target hostile. If it was a village army, most of the men in the crowd would be carrying weapons instead of some surrounding them,' the intel specialist gives his logic, 'I suggest we take them out since they look like HVTs.'[138]

The commander nods at his intel officer as the drone pilot looks inquiringly at his commander for the order. He has only a couple of

---

[138]   High value targets.

minutes of fuel left before the drone has to start heading back home. Meanwhile, they see on the screen the four men going into the hut.

'Bingo,' the commander smiles at what he sees, 'the rats are going home.' As if injected with a high dose of energy, the commander states for the record, 'Based on the situation at hand and the advice of my intel specialist, I feel that the designated targets in Bastikhel are "hostiles" and good for elimination. As targets are now enclosed in a hut and the chances of collateral damage is minimised, we can proceed with the kill.' He then looks towards the drone pilot and orders authoritatively, 'You may fire at will at the hut.'

*   *   *

1442 hrs — Bastikhel Village, Waziristan

As soon as the three men join the fourth member already in the hut, Baaz springs into action. Fear overcoming his composure, he quickly reaches for the steel trunk placed next to a wall and flings it on one side throwing the rug underneath it as well in the process. Grabbing the battery-powered torch hanging on the wall above, he quickly opens the lid on the floor and jumps inside the tunnel on to softened ground eight feet underneath. 'Jump if you want to stay alive!' he yells at the others still perplexed by Baaz's actions.

Meanwhile, on the other side of the world, inside another room, underneath the ground, a pilot operating his drone over the Af-Pak border responds excitedly to his commander's orders.

'Yes, sir,' he targets the hut and fires his Hellfire missile. 'Fox one!' he exclaims anxiously pressing the trigger on his control column. The missile leaps laconically forward from the wing of the drone screaming towards its target. 'Eighteen, Seventeen, Sixteen . . . ,' the pilot begins his countdown; placing his aim reticle firmly on the small window of the hut, he steers the missile towards its intended target, a measly mud hut where the four HVTs are busy making their escape.

In the hut, the local cleric jumps after Baaz without giving it a second thought, leaving behind the two elderly men.

'Eleven, Ten, Nine, Eight . . . ,' the drone pilot continues with his countdown as the people in the operation room concentrate on two screens: one relaying the images from the missile camera itself, showing its intended path heading towards the 'painted' hut and the other showing the trajectory of the missile from the camera on the drone towards its intended target.

'Hurry up!' yells Baaz at which Asmatullah, being the eldest of them all and reluctant to jump due to his old age, gestures at Arbaz Mehsud to jump in first.

'I'll go down and catch you, don't worry,' Arbaz calmly suggests to Asmat, still oblivious of the javelin of doom seconds away from them. Arbaz jumps inside the tunnel and takes a few seconds to get on his feet and look up through the dark tunnel at the opening into the hut. Through the light from the window illuminating Asmat's face, Arbaz sees his elderly friend's wrinkled and haggard face smiling at the window as if welcoming his angel of death. Asmat had just heard the commotion outside as the crowd, in the last few seconds, saw the missile nearing the hut. Feeling his death pouncing towards him, there is nothing he can do in those last few moments but stare his death in the eye.

'Three, Two, One . . . Bull's-eye!' the pilot at the operations room in Nevada concludes his loud and excited countdown as he sees his missile on his screen making its way through the open window and then suddenly the screen relaying images from the missile camera goes blank.

'We have confirmed impact,' the camera operator verifies the pilot's claim as they, on the other screen, see the missile exploding inside the hut, blowing the whole place apart, including the elderly militant.

'Noooo!' screams Arbaz as he sees the detonation in the hut. Deafened from the loud explosion and the shockwave, Arbaz loses his consciousness as the opening above him caves in burying him under the mud and debris fallen from above.

Meanwhile, in the CIA Operation room, the drone commander, content with the outcome of his mission, orders the drone to return to base while he leaves the operation room to debrief his station chief on another mission well done.

*   *   *

The missile strike is a precision strike, and while the destruction is limited to the hut only, the shockwave from the explosion sweeps the people close by off their feet, showering them with debris and damaging the nearby surroundings too. There is silence in Bastikhel after the thundering explosion as people around the site struggle to regain their bearings.

People are horrified to see the mangled wreck of the hut as a small fire still burns within. Fearing the loss of their leader, some of the militants slowly tread towards the remains, hoping against hope that men inside would have escaped through the tunnel in time to avoid this destruction.

Baaz and the village cleric narrowly escaped from the caving mud. They had run down the dark earth tunnel for about ten metres before stopping, and looking back, by which time the entrance from the hut was blocked, with no sign of Asmat and Arbaz.

Baaz looks at the cleric, and says, 'They're gone, let's go,' and starts walking inside the tunnel towards his hideout with the torch firmly held in his hand.

However, the cleric, already ashamed of his cowardly action earlier in the day, thinks otherwise, and with no light in hand, he rushes back towards the blocked entrance and frantically tries to dig through the caved-in mud with his bare hands. A product of Asmat's orphanage and student of Arbaz, he held both these men in high esteem, and the fear of losing them was too much for him to bear.

Baaz walks a few feet before he realises that the cleric is missing. For a moment, a sense of regret flows through his heart. He stops and points the torch in the direction of the caved-in entrance, where he sees the cleric vigorously shovelling away the mud with his hands, desperately trying to dig through. Shaking his head, he walks back to the cleric and asks him again to come with him since the other two are surely dead.

'No!' screams back the cleric. 'I will not leave unless I see them with my own eyes.' He breaks down on the floor of the tunnel, suddenly feeling the strength rushing out of his body as his adrenalin settles down. 'Islam does not teach us to leave our dead and wounded behind,' sobs the cleric. 'What good are we if we cannot help other humans in distress.'

Baaz, speechless at this outburst and not wanting to challenge religious teachings of the cleric, agrees to dig a little to see if anyone is alive. He is not concerned for now about his own safety since he knows his people will come to him through this network of caves to rescue them.

As they dig for a few minutes, they feel a head. Excited at the outcome of their efforts, both dig more vigorously until they dig out the whole head of Arbaz, who is still unconscious and barely alive. A little more digging through the falling mud enables them to reach for his underarms from where both the men pull out Arbaz from underneath the caved-in entrance.

'Sir! Sir!' yells the cleric, slapping Arbaz's face in the attempt to wake him. Meanwhile, Baaz continues to dig for Asmat, expecting him to have jumped at the last moment but finds no one.

A few more minutes go by when Baaz hears the shouts of his comrades making their way towards them.

'Chief! Chief! Are you there?'

'Yes, comrades!' yells back Baaz on hearing the familiar voice of his deputy. Soon he sees lights coming from the corner of this small two-metre high tunnel. Complete with shovels, lights, and oxygen cylinder and masks, the rescue party reaches them within minutes.

Within no time, they set about attending to Arbaz Khan Mehsud by giving him oxygen and reviving his lungs. Suddenly Arbaz wakes up with a loud cough as he tries to inhale oxygen but feels restriction inside his lungs from the inhaled mud. Although breathing slowly whilst unconscious had limited the damage to his lungs, he remains stunned even after gaining consciousness, due to the apparent damage to his brain from lack of oxygen.

'Any news on Asmatullah?' Baaz asks his deputy, who shakes his head in the negative.

With Asmat obliterated and Arbaz incapacitated, the village will have to select new council members to go through the nomination process and, until such time, Baaz sees for himself a bright chance of becoming the de-facto village chieftain. He smirks at the thought as he glances towards the shaken cleric, who appears no match for Baaz's position. Confident that he will get away with his plan, he orders all the men to move out of the tunnel. His chance of directly ruling the people of the village is now written on the wall.

*   *   *

Sunday: 0600 hrs — Islamabad, Diplomatic Enclave

It is early morning in the city where all is quiet on this holiday. Sam's building is situated in the residential block inside the diplomatic enclave. The block housing Sam's apartment is a cluster of six, three-storey buildings in two rows of three, having twenty-four apartments each. In the middle is a small fountain encircled by a car-parking area, where mostly locally manufactured Japanese sedans and SUVs belonging to the occupants of the buildings are neatly parked. This March morning is still cold and cloudy, giving a gloomy, grey aura to the surroundings. Augmenting this gloomy aura is the deserted look of the area as its residents, mostly foreign nationals and employees of embassies or multinational agencies, are still asleep from their late-night revelries over the weekend. In this deserted environment, a lonely dog is scavenging through a litterbag carelessly thrown next to the litter drum, since on Sunday, even the city's municipal waste-disposal staff takes a day off. His quest to find some worthy food is disturbed by a couple of early-morning joggers who, clad in their warm sport suits and covering their heads with hoods from the morning cold, jog past the dog on the adjacent footpath. These three are the only life forms in the area at this early hour. Apart from them a police truck, with a crew of eight armed policemen patrols the area, slowly passing the apartment block carefully looking out for any suspicious activity. They notice only one illuminated window among the hundreds in the block. This window belongs to Sam's apartment, and she is busy getting ready to head outside the city of Islamabad and into the unknown.

Excited, and anxious at the same time, she keeps one eye on the wall clock. After getting her bag ready with the essentials for a day's outing, she sits on the counter with her hot mug of coffee to write down a note to her one best friend in Islamabad—Rebecca.

> *Dear Becy,*
>
> *If you have picked up this letter from my apartment's counter after 1800 hrs and are reading it, then obviously I have not yet returned from my day trip to Kohat with Bilal.*
>
> *I know you must be mad at me by now and getting all frantic but just to let you know, I thought hard about it and presumed that this trip would be safe since I'd be visiting only a garrison town with a person I trust. However, it seems like it has not worked out as planned.*
>
> *Now please take this letter to my station chief and tell him that I left Islamabad at 0630 hrs Sunday morning for a day trip to Kohat with Bilal Khattak, who works as a senior executive, marketing, in Instaphone Ltd. Just in case you*

*don't have his cell phone number, it's 0777 1234567 and
his house address in Islamabad is H 34, St 9, Sector F 8/5,
Islamabad.*

*You can get further details on his background in the
attached paper. Please hurry up since my life, if not already
ended, could be in danger by the time you read this.*

If alive, I'll make it up to you when we meet. :-)

Luv,
Sam.

Sam reads the note carefully once more before placing it on the
kitchen counter. In the full-length mirror hanging atop the side board
in her drawing room, she looks at her freshly dyed wavy hair, now
a dark shade of brunette to give herself a more local look, she thinks
again to herself whether she should go ahead with this trip.

*Why am I getting all this nervous? This is unlike me. Kohat is a safe
place and only about three hours journey from here . . . It may be bordering
on the Wild, Wild West, but it's a garrison town under State control. Besides,
I'll not be conspicuous with a local like Bilal* — she comforts herself.

She looks at the clock that now reads 0625 hrs. A shiver runs down
her spine out of anxiety, and she thinks to herself again, *Maybe I should
take my gun, but what if I get caught with it at the check point. I might be
asked questions. My American identity will get revealed.* She looks around.
*Maybe I should just abort this plan altogether. I'm not authorized anyways
to leave Islamabad. Becy was right; there are protocols for going outside
Islamabad.*

As she gets up from her stool to call Bilal, expecting him to reach
her any minute now to pick her up, her vision alights on the pictures
of her deceased father and brother, and she stops abruptly. *I am the
daughter of a heroic soldier and sister of a brave war journalist* — she thinks
again — *valour runs in my blood. I cannot freak out at the last moment.* She
takes a deep breath and stiffens her posture — *everything is fine, and
I'm not gonna let some Pakistani think of an American as a coward . . . It is
either Kohat or bust.*

Her plethora of thoughts is abruptly disturbed by the ringing of
her cell phone. She reaches for it and sees the name 'Bilal' blinking
on the screen. As planned at 0630 hrs sharp, Bilal has arrived at her

apartment complex to pick her up for their day trip to his hometown of Kohat.

Sam picks up the phone. 'I'll be out in a minute.'

No longer pondering over her decision, she wraps her shawl[139] round her long shirt, covering part of her head as well in the process, picks up her bag, and gives a last look in her living room before closing the door behind her. Excitement now running in her stride, she reaches the entrance of the building and flings the glass door open. The sudden exposure into openness with cold wind blowing in her face and the sight of a tall broad Bilal leaning against his Honda Civic VTi sports sedan smiling at her evaporates her fears. Hanging her bag on her shoulder, she returns a beaming smile to Bilal. Confidence now creeping back into her, she looks forward to her first outing into the Wild Wild West of Pakistan.

---

[139] A long piece of warm cloth to wrap around a dress as a means of covering the body from cold or simply for modesty.

Chapter 10

A TRIP TOO FAR

'Good Morning!' greets Bilal.

'Hey!' responds Sam.

'All geared up for the day?' Bilal notices her dyed hair and the shawl wrapped around her head as he takes the bag from Sam to put it in the rear seat.

'Yeah! Hope it's safe?' Sam shivers a little from cold and excitement.

'Well, I often go there on weekends. It's pretty safe from here to there. I thought you were fine with it, but if you have any second thoughts, we can always cancel it,' replies Bilal as he sits down in his Honda.

'No, it's okay . . . Let's go. I'd like to meet your family and see that place. I've only heard about Kohat so far. That area has always intrigued me, you know?' Sam sits down next to Bilal in his Honda.

'As you wish . . . You'll like meeting my father. In fact, my elder brother would also be there with his wife and kids. He's on vacations and visiting family and friends back home.' Bilal starts the engine.

'Wasn't he in the Air Force?' Sam asks as she buckles herself up.

'Yes, but now, he's an airline pilot, flying Boeings around the region. Here we go.'

Bilal puts his car into gear, and they set off on their journey to the small garrison city in the west of Pakistan. He looks at her changed appearance and cannot resist but compliment, 'I notice you've changed hair colour!'

'Yeah,' Sam grins, 'I thought it would give me a more, kinda ethnic look.' After a moment's silence, she asks coyly, 'You like it?'

Bilal smiles at her and, after a short pause, comments, 'You look pretty in dark brown hair with a shawl wrapped around your head . . . You look like a nice Pathan girl.'

200

Sam exchanges a smiling glance with Bilal as she blushes at the compliment. Both then look to the front, trying to pass over this romantic lapse before Sam clears her throat to respond to Bilal's compliment, 'Gee, thanks. Well, the idea was to, you know . . . blend into the crowd . . .'

Before she can complete her sentence, Bilal interjects softly, 'And it's worked.'

By this time, the sun has risen fairly above the horizon and out of the morning smog. As the sunshine becomes brighter, Bilal's sporty Honda makes its way on the circular highway of Islamabad, leading towards the Intercity Motorway from Islamabad to the frontier city of Peshawar.

Upon reaching the motorway, Sam notices at three places along the way on the opposite side, police security barriers stopping and checking any car entering into different areas of Islamabad. Since it is Sunday morning, the traffic is far less, with only a very few cars getting due attention at the posts.

After seeing three such barriers, she asks Bilal, 'It must be a nightmare on weekdays for people to enter Islamabad?'

'Yeah, it is. My colleagues living in Pindi and other adjacent towns, commuting in and out of Islamabad for work, sometimes have to wait for up to an hour to get through these check posts into Islamabad.' He stops as if thinking about something and then as an afterthought, adds, 'I guess this is the price normal Pakistanis have to pay for being a front-line State in US War on Terror.'

Sam is taken aback by this comment, as if this gibe is directed at her. 'Well, I guess we all are facing hardships in our countries due to enhanced security checks. It's not the same any more even at US Airports with all those random spot checks, pat downs, and now the new screening system, which sees through your clothes. It's become difficult over there too.'

Bilal suddenly realises that his guest has taken it personally, so he tries to clarify his stance. 'Yes, I guess this cleaning that our forces are doing in Af-Pak is necessary for a brighter future of both our countries, free of intimidation and terror. We should not mind the little inconvenience we face while the fight is on. After all, these safety measures are for our own good.' Continuing in the same breath, Bilal then changes the topic, 'So where did you say you did your graduation?'

Glad that the atmosphere in the car has become warm again, both friends chat away in a lighter mood. Talking about their lives and various funny experiences, they speed away on the six-lane motorway before reaching an exit leading to Kohat. Sam, while talking with Bilal, also keeps an eye on the changing topography. As they exit Islamabad, they leave behind the towering Margalla Hills on their rear north side and enter the plains of Punjab. Exiting the motorway puts them on a dual-carriage metal road with sprawling farmlands on both sides. Apart from the usual mode of transport plying this road, Sam is particularly amused to see the 'tractor trolleys', a farm tractor tugging an open-air container on wheels, having either farm produce or villagers inside it; men clad in their traditional long shirts and a cloth wrapped around their legs and women dressed in a similarly colourful ladies version.

These tractors, apart from its driver seated on the only seat available, would often have two passengers precariously perched on the fenders of the large rear wheels balancing themselves marvellously as the tractor trudged along with its trolley dutifully in tow. Bouncing inside the trolleys on a bumpy road, its passengers made an amusing sight for Sam, who couldn't resist smiling at them every time her car overtook one such contraption lumbering along the road.

As if reading her thoughts on seeing these tractor trolleys, Bilal asks Sam if she finds them amusing. As she looks at him, he smiles back. 'This is the normal mode of transport in our villages, comes in real handy for our farmers who are too naive to understand the international safety standards for themselves. To them, anything with wheels that moves can carry people.'

Bilal laughs as they cross a lone donkey cart, a flat-bed, two-wheeled, joined by an axle contraption tied to a small donkey, galloping on the road. Its occupants, a teenage boy in rags as the driver and a young woman, draped in a shawl trying simultaneously to keep it on her head and holding her infant in her lap, with a small child seated next to her on the flat bed, both tightly holding on to the only rod sticking from one side of the platform.

'Look at that,' Bilal points at them, laughing at the galloping contraption with its passengers jumping up and down.

But this time, Sam doesn't find any humour in that. She retorts, 'Hey, that could be very dangerous. That kid can fall off or what if the rod comes out or something happens, they'll be flung off the cart.'

As if struck by an afterthought, she asks impulsively, 'Why don't we give them a ride?' Impressed by the good heart of his lady friend, Bilal obliges and pulls over to offer them a lift to their destination, but to Sam's surprise, the woman declines the offer, fearing criticism from her family. She prefers to ride along on the dangerous donkey cart rather than reach her destination in the comfort of a secure automobile.

'Our rural women are not that open to outside help, they need to take permission from their family men before doing anything, even if it's for their own good,' Bilal explains to a stunned Sam as she sees the woman speeding off on their donkey cart, holding on to her children, while Bilal decides to get tea from a ramshackle roadside cafeteria nearby.

Since morning, in the last two hours, Sam had seen some extraordinary things for the first time in her life, and she did not find some of them to her liking. After taking a short break midway, they again start off for Kohat, expecting to reach Bilal's parents by ten in the morning.

On the way, Sam notices the scenery changing from the green farm lands of Punjab stretched across miles and miles of plains to the arid desolate hills of the western province of Khyber, as they cross the provincial boundary at Khushalgarh on an old iron-girdled bridge atop the huge river Indus, running from the Tibetan plateaus in the north of the Himalayan Mountains all the way down to the Arabian sea near the port city of Karachi in the south.

Bilal explains the stark difference in the topography, 'The general temperament of the people is also different and defined by their habitats. You'll find Punjabis living on the plains to be different in their attitude from the Pathans living in tougher environment of the hills of Khyber.'

Seeing the inquiring look on Sam's face, Bilal elaborates — 'Well, no offense meant to anyone, but as a Pathan, we find Punjabis to be more docile and fun-loving, with their culture also more open to festivities. They readily adopt people from other parts of the region welcoming their culture too, whereas we, Pathans, are more conservative and possessive about our ways of life. We don't particularly like foreign intervention or influence in our traditions, which are centuries old. Our customs, rituals, and civilisation is zealously guarded, and as you can see from our tough environment, it makes us tougher and hardier than people from other parts of Pakistan.'

Sam had been advised well about Pakistan and its people from the different areas and could relate to what Bilal was saying, but acting aloof, she innocently asks Bilal, 'Are you praising your kind over other Pakistanis?' Bilal laughs at this seemingly naïve question, 'Well, Pathans are a real proud nation. I guess I am praising my kind over others.' Not wanting to stop, he continues, 'But we are also very hospitable people, and once someone seeks our shelter, he becomes our guest for whose security we will even offer our lives.'

Sam naughtily replies, 'Well, is that restricted to only he's?'

Bilal gives out another guffaw, 'Well, he or she, it doesn't matter.'

Seeing the deeper meaning of this hint, Sam inquires, 'This means my being your guest for the day, you'll protect me with your life, if need be?'

At this, Bilal looks into Sam's eyes, pauses for a moment, and with a deep intense look in his eyes, he responds, 'Is there a doubt in your heart about that?'

Again, the two fall silent as the car stereo plays the love songs of Bryan Adams. Soon they reach the outskirts of the small valley of Kohat at the first check post before the entrance to the city. In front of them are a few buses, trucks, and cars. They see the guards entering into each bus inspecting each of them while the trucks and cars are also stopped and identifications checked. Seeing this, Sam gets nervous and fears being detected by anyone here. Although as an American working in the US embassy, Sam was legally allowed to travel around Pakistan, but she didn't want to unnecessarily blow her cover and attract unwarranted attention. She knew that no one could prevent the Pakistanis from stopping her or asking her to turn back to Islamabad since she was very close to the wild west of Pakistan. Moreover, even Bilal did not know her real identity, and if caught here, her real self would eventually be exposed, which wouldn't go down well with Bilal.

'I hope they don't ask me for my ID . . . What if they don't let me enter Kohat?'

'It shouldn't be a problem,' comes the cool response from her host.

Soon they make their way to the check post, and the police guards standing at the post glance at them and gesture them to move on. Sam, feeling tense for a moment, relaxes on seeing that they were allowed to pass and breathes a sigh of relief. 'Well, that wasn't too hard, they just let us pass?'

'Yeah, they usually don't stop cars with women and children, and look at us, do we look like terrorists?' He gestures at their Western dressing and clean looks, 'And as for you, like I said, in your new disguise, you don't even look like a foreigner to them. For all you know, he might have thought of us as a married couple visiting Kohat on the weekend.'

Sam, feeling a little embarrassed at the last conclusion, blushes, 'Okay, I get the idea, thank you.' As an afterthought, she continues, 'But you know what, with this kind of lax security, terrorists posing as couples can enter a city without getting checked.'

'Yeah, Sam, but then if they start stopping each and every car with women, they'll be facing trouble from the possessive men folks for whom security is secondary to family honour when it comes to women of their household. Besides, traffic would come to a standstill if each vehicle is stopped for a thorough check.'

'It's a tough choice . . . very tough, indeed,' Sam concludes shaking her head as she sees a convoy of military SUVs and trucks crossing before them on the road. Inside the open trucks, she sees the tired faces of soldiers holding their weapons and clad in full worn-down battle fatigues seemingly returning from a battle front.

Bilal, on entering the small city of Kohat, passes through the dusty and crowded downtown area where Sam is fascinated to see, in this small garrison city of Pakistan, anything and everything with wheels moving on the roads—from trucks and buses, to sedans and wagons. Even the horse-driven carriages and donkey carts carrying cargo are plying on the road. The traffic is at its worst, with everyone struggling for space to move forward. Vehicles parked randomly on the side of the roads and even blocking one lane at times, the hapless traffic police constable desperately whistles away, endeavouring to bring order to the traffic, but his efforts are all in vain. Bilal also jumps into the traffic mess and slowly inches his way forward to cross this congested area, where business is going on as usual in small shops in the market blocks selling all kind of things from groceries, clothes, and shoes to music CDs and foreign movie DVDs, household electronics, and even hardware. Indian Bollywood[140] and Pushto music blaring out

---

[140]   Hollywood of India—Indian movies and songs are very popular across Pakistan.

at the same time from different shops mixes with the honks of vehicles and the sales pitches of people selling their produce, to the people in vehicles crawling on the roads; all combine to create complete chaos on the roads.

Sam suddenly finds two gruff Pathan boys in their late teens with unkempt beards, woolly hats, and untidy dress, carrying on their shoulders a large carpet carelessly rolled, knocking at her car window. She jumps back in alarm. She sees these boys trying to say something to her pointing at their carpet and looks inquiringly at Bilal, who, reading her mind, replies calmly, 'They are trying to sell their carpet to you. Take it easy, this is a normal sight here; just don't put down your window.'

Trying hard but in vain for a few minutes to get the lady's attention, these boys finally give up and decide to move on to their next target. Sam notices other young men roaming on the roads with their products in hand, desperately trying to make a sale. The diversity of products from Persian carpets to designer sunglasses, and from US Army boots to hosiery, all is for sale in the shops and on the roads. Some men even attempt to sell fruits to passengers of stationary buses and cars.

Bilal carries on, 'Most of the goods you see are smuggled from Afghan transit trade. You'll find original designer stuff here at a fraction of a price since it would either be stolen off from consignments going to Afghanistan via Pakistan or sold back from Afghanistan to traders in Pakistan.'

'But I thought this was a garrison town under State control?' asks Sam.

'Yeah, but the local administration or the military cannot stop this kind of business which has become a way of life here. The scale is too large. Go further west towards Afghanistan border, and you'll also find weapons and drugs. At least, Kohat is safe from such goods.'

Seeing the hustle and bustle in the market, Bilal also explains to Sam the logic behind keeping the market open on Sunday. He explains that the conservative Muslim clerics of the area had branded Sunday to be a Christian holiday and preferred to maintain the weekly holiday on Friday. So irrespective of what the official holiday was in Pakistan, Kohat and most of the commercial areas in Khyber Province took Friday as their day off and remained open on Sundays. He adds as an afterthought that this works to the advantage of people at large since on their weekends, they find the commercial areas open.

Sam is flabbergasted to see Kohat. She finds this small city in complete contrast with the more clean, developed, and modern environment of Islamabad. But this is what she wanted to see and has got an eyeful of it on this trip so far. She heaves a sigh as they leave the congested commercial downtown of Kohat for the more harmonious environs of the cantonment area, where they follow a narrow four-lane highway running through the cantonment, with different army units situated on both sides of the road. Their unique emblem on each of the gates identifies each unit. Sam notices walls of up to about two metres high with barbed wire stretching on top. Soon the couple reaches the Kohat Development Authority, where Bilal's parents live.

This housing society was considered the most up-market residential area in the city. Nice-looking houses neatly constructed in rows, each one designed differently from the other and separated from each other by tall boundary walls. The peace of the area only occasionally broken by a braying donkey of a cart whose owner is called to deliver something to the resident of this area. After about five minutes' drive on the narrow metal roads, Bilal stops his car in front of the black gate of a modest looking white coloured, double-storeyed house constructed on a plot of land not more than 500 sq. metres in area.

'Welcome home,' Bilal smiles at a tired looking Sam, as he honks for the servant to open the gate from inside for them to enter. Sam heaves another sigh of relief at finally concluding their seemingly unending journey. She looks forward to meeting Bilal's folks and to get to know from his sagacious father everything that she had been unable to gather about the psyche of Pathans and their motivation to continue fighting against heavy odds, that is, the Coalition Forces in this region. Tired after the journey but also excited, she finally gets out of the car and stretches herself after Bilal parks his Honda at the entrance porch of the house.

*   *   *

It is Sunday morning in Attock Cantonment, about 10.30 a.m. Dhil's house is abuzz with activity. In the living area of the large hall are seated the elderly parents of Rania who were joined by Dhil's elder sister Zainab, a little while back. Zainab has arrived from Abbottabad with her youngest son Babar, who is in his final year of college over there. Meanwhile, Dhil's kids sit in the dining area struggling to eat their breakfast, as the atmosphere in the hall is full of gloom.

Babar, being in his early twenties, doted on his little cousins who also enjoyed a good rapport with him. While the elders sit in the living area silently sipping on their morning tea, Babar prefers to spend time with his little cousins to pep them up, which he finds difficult under the current circumstances.

'When will mummy wake up?' Hamza abruptly asks his big cousin, who is desperately trying to tell him a story about Iron Man, Hamza's favourite super hero.

There is stunned silence in the room as all try to grapple with the answer. Before anyone can respond, Taimur yells back, 'How many times have we told you, she will wake up when she feels like . . . Don't you understand?'

The little four-year-old cannot understand and starts weeping, 'But she told me she will take me out for picnic that day, and she isn't waking up,' his little mind unable to comprehend the seriousness of the situation they are in. His mummy had never left him alone for this long. His mother was always there for him by his side, and he could not come to terms with the situation. Missing the warmth of his mummy's presence, Hamza cannot put on a brave face any longer and breaks down, tears rolling down his plum-red cheeks.

Seeing her little brother cry, Ayesha goes in a fit of rage and shouts at Taimur, 'Why did you yell at Hamza? See what you have done!'

Unable to control her emotions, she gets up from her dining chair and goes towards Hamza, hugs him, and while trying to pacify her little brother, also starts weeping profusely. Missing the presence of her loving mother and her inability of comforting her kid brother, she herself begins to cry. Seeing his siblings crying, Taimur also gets up and hugs his sister and little brother, while trying to hold back his tears.

'I'm sorry,' he struggles for words, 'I also miss her.' Taimur also breaks down as Babar helplessly looks at the elders sitting across the hall in the living area, lost in their own thoughts.

As the situation unfolds, Dhil, who had been in the hospital since dawn, enters the house to the crying of his children huddled together looking for comfort. He looks at them and feels frustrated by his inability to provide any solace. Gathering all his courage to deal with this new challenge, he takes a deep breath, nods at his in-laws and his elder sister; on the way, giving a courteous hug to his nephew Babar, who had walked up to him at the door, he then goes up to his weeping children.

'Baba?'[141] Taimur cries out inquiringly as he sees his father walking towards them. Dhil reaches for Taimur and gives him a hug before Ayesha reaches up for him, while Hamza stays seated on the chair covering his sobbing face with his little hands.

'Heyyyyy, why are my kiddos crying?' Dhil tries to cheer up his children as he sits down and holds little Hamza in his lap. Cursing himself in his heart for not being there for the children for the past three days and desperately trying to cheer them up, he now cooks up a story. 'The doctor just told me that your mama is going to be okay.' All in the room look at him believing what he is saying. Dhil continues with his story, 'She is resting for now . . . You know it was very tough surviving the bomb attack . . . so let's act brave and pray to our Allah that she wakes up soon and comes back home.'

'When will she come home?' Hamza innocently inquires while trying to control his sobs.

'Very soon, my darling . . . very soon.' Dhil hugs his little devil to share his warmth, as his voice also chokes with emotions, conscious of Ayesha and Taimur standing at his side, wanting to believe every word of their dad.

There is a minute of silence as all grapple with the depressed environment at home before Dhilawar's voice breaks the silence. 'Hey, why don't you kids take Babar Bhai[142] out and show him around the cantonment?' Looking at his nephew, Dhil asks, 'Babar, have you tasted the chocolate chip ice cream at the Cantt's ice-cream parlour?'

Babar, realising the real intent behind this plan, shakes his head in negative. 'No, but I'm hungry and would love to have it . . . so who wants to take me?' He tries to raise the spirits in the room.

Dhil then asks his elder two to take Hamza with them and show Babar around the cantonment. This would provide some temporary relief at least. Later, in the day, they could go to see their

---

[141]   Father in Urdu.

[142]   Brother — term used in Urdu Language for elders out of respect.

mother during visiting hours. The elder two silently oblige, and the three dutifully leave the house with Babar, who relentlessly tries to somehow cheer up his kid cousins.

As Dhil sees them leaving the gate, he comes inside the living area and greets his elderly sister with an intense hug, trying to find reassurance in the embrace of his only sibling who raised him after the death of their parents, early on in Dhil's life. As if sent back in time, Dhil experiences the same emotions that he did thirty years back when he lost his parents and his ten-year-older sister had come to his rescue.

'Apa,'[143] he struggles for words trying to maintain a bold face.

'What you said just now about Rania, is it true?' Rania's mother anxiously asks Dhil as her father, who had since folded the morning paper, closely looks at Dhil.

Dhil drops down on the couch next to Zainab. There is pin-drop silence in the room again as all eyes are fixed on Dhil. He looks at his elder sister and then towards his parents-in-law, seated across him in the room. Disappointment now written on his face, he shakes his head in the negative.

'Oh my God, please help us!' wails Rania's mother on seeing Dhil's response. Her sobs now disturbing the silence of the room, they all feel the utter helplessness of their situation.

This once blissful abode is engulfed in total despair.

*   *   *

Earlier in the day, Bilal's parents, his brother, and his brother's family welcomed Sam wholeheartedly. Even the servants of the house — the maid, a young girl in her late teens, and the elderly cook showed their excitement at meeting, for the first time in their lives, a Caucasian American; the kind they had so far only seen in Hollywood movies which had found their way to the cinemas of Khyber Province. This maid even went to the extent of seeing a resemblance between Sam and Angelina Jolie, who had often visited Pakistan as a UN Goodwill ambassador and was well known to the masses. Despite the advice of Bilal's mother to keep this visit hush-hush so as to avoid drawing

---

[143] Big sister — used in Urdu Language, out of respect, for an elder sister.

unnecessary attention, this maid had not been able to control her excitement and had called her family back in the village situated in the outskirts of Kohat, advising them of the arrival of an Angelina Jolie look-alike in the home of her master. Soon this rumour had spread across her village like wild fire that Angelina Jolie was actually visiting her master's house in Kohat.

Back at the Khattak house, Sam was treated to a sumptuous meal of chappal kebab,[144] sweet yoghurt, naan, and green salad topped up with Cola soft drinks. This cuisine was considered an ethnic delicacy, and revered guests were treated to this wholesome food. Sam was no exception. She thoroughly enjoys the hospitality of her hosts and the food at hand after an exciting journey from Islamabad.

After the main course, Sam is treated to some locally made sweets that are also to her liking. As they conclude their lunch, Professor Afnan, an elderly gentleman with a clean-shaven but wrinkled fair-complexioned face and neatly oiled and combed back long grey hair, invites Sam for a cup of green tea in the veranda. They seat themselves on comfortable cane chairs overlooking the nice green manicured garden not more than ten metres by twelve metres in dimension, surrounded by flower beds housing beautiful flowers of different kinds, reflecting the essence of the spring season. Chirping birds sitting on the mango tree add allure to the cool ambiance of the place.

Before lunch was served, the ice-breaking session with Bilal's family had concluded successfully. Although careful to avoid details of her father and brother's death, Sam had introduced her family back home and had also got to know more about Bilal and his background. His childhood days were reminisced upon, and he was the butt of many light-hearted jokes made by his elder brother Khalid Khattak and his wife. Sam felt that Bilal, being the youngest in the family, was the most beloved, and his divorce had not gone down well with his relatives. Hence, they would look for ways to cheer him up from time to time. She had also found these folks to be at peace with themselves and their surroundings, and what she felt good about them was their resilience and determination to make their lives happy despite the danger of militancy lurking in their neighbourhood. On the concept

---

[144] Beef flat patties grilled essentially in animal fat—similar to a well-done rib-eye steak.

of terror and fear, Afnan had very eloquently put across his beliefs. 'Samantha, as Muslims, it is our faith that the time and date of death of each person is predetermined by fate, and it cannot be changed. If my death has to come, it can come in the comfort of my room, and if it's not due, then I can even be saved from the mouth of a dragon. So why fret about it?'

On Sam's query whether this means that a person can jump into fire and expect to be saved if it is not his day, Afnan had coolly replied, 'I'm not saying that you go deliberately looking for trouble, but if it comes to you, don't panic, and if despite your trying, the angel of death prevails, then you simply have to accept it as the Will of God.'

Difficult as it was to comprehend this logic, Sam still envied the inner harmony Afnan shared with his surroundings but then she preferred to change the topic.

As they seat themselves on the cosy armchairs in the open veranda, they are joined by Bilal and Khalid. Khalid, thirty-eight, was the larger of the two in size. Fair-complexioned with light brown eyes and straight pointed features, he also sported a beard a little more in size than a stubble. Sam noticed that Khalid drew his resemblance from his mother, whereas Bilal took after his father who actually looked like an older version of Bilal in his late sixties. The four make themselves comfortable as Bilal's mother, a pleasant-looking lady, aging gracefully into early sixties, dressed modestly in a long shirt and shalwar[145] with a black shawl wrapped around her plump body and head, goes about directing the servants on their next chores. Not very conversant in English, she preferred to remain silent listening intently to the conversation. Despite not talking, she had made sure that Sam felt welcomed in their house and enjoyed her day with the family. Meanwhile, Mehreen, Khalid's wife, another pleasant-looking lady about Sam's age, with nice shoulder-length wavy brown hair casually falling on her shoulders and clean fair skin with grey eyes, tended to their three children aged eleven, nine, and seven. Originally from Peshawar and a paediatric doctor from its Khyber Medical College, Mehreen, dressed in a loose long top and jeans, with a beige shawl

---

[145] Baggy pants worn below the loose long shirt, part of the two-piece ethnic dress worn in Pakistan.

draped around her, was now based in Karachi, where she and her husband resided with their three children. She and Sam had a good talking session in the morning, but seeing Sam's interest lay more towards discussing geopolitics and international relations, Mehreen had found their mutual topics of interests soon exhausted.

Sam now feels the time is right to get the elderly professor's perspective on the current situation prevailing in his country. She puts the question across abruptly.

'So what is your view on this War on Terror our countries are fighting together?'

There is a pause in the veranda as the men grapple with this direct question. The elderly Khattak smiles, his wrinkled shining eyes recessed in his red cheeks, as he decides to respond whereas his sons prefer to maintain their silence, not wanting to say anything which might offend their valued guest.

'My dear, what is there to say about this war?' he tries to ignore the question, but seeing the fixed expression on Sam's face, he decides to air his feelings, 'I think this is an exercise in futility.'

Sam did not expect this answer, as her first impression of the professor, with his modern outlook on life, his knowledge of science and technology, and an overall contemporary lifestyle, made her think of him as a pro 'War on Terror' person from whom she could expect to get insights on how to defeat their common enemy, that is, the religious radicals. But his opinion of this war being futile came as a surprise to her. Not wanting to offend her host or discourage them from airing their opinion, she changes her tack. After all, her mission of today was to get proper insights on her perceived foes.

'That's a very interesting comment, sir,' she responds diplomatically, 'quite contrary to what we hear from our governments or even from some sections of the media.' She pauses for a while as if trying to ensure that the right words come out and then puts another question across, 'You know, speaking as someone working for the US government, we want to believe that we are succeeding. However, I'm also keen to know other perspectives on this issue . . . so why do you think this is an exercise in futility?'

The professor casts a look at his grown-up sons. Khalid smiles back and advises his father to let Sam know what he feels.

'See, my child,' Professor Afnan addresses Sam affectionately much to her pleasant surprise, 'first, you need to define what is it that you mean by — winning this war.'

There is silence in the veranda as Sam tries to think of an answer. The professor, seeing the confused look on his guest's face, prefers to answer his own question.

'If you mean killing your enemy soldiers, destroying their weapons and ammunition, disrupting their lines of communications, and over all, eliminating their war machinery, then maybe with some assumptions we may say that the US and Pakistan are winning this long-drawn war.'

Sam smiles back as if this is exactly what she wanted to hear from a source locally embedded in this region. But before she can respond, the professor continues.

'However, if by winning you mean killing your enemy's spirit to fight, destroying their support base, and eliminating their cause to fight, then my dear . . . we are certainly losing out in this war.'

Silence follows as all try to come to terms with the professor's explanation. Sam then musters strength to respond to the respected professor's logic.

'But these terrorists have no cause or agenda. All they want to do is spread terror in the region and beyond in the name of Islam. How can we even succumb to their ambition, which is to one day make the world a more dangerous place to live where only their extreme interpretation of Islam prevails?'

Bilal gets uneasy as he feels this discussion may become sour. He attempts to change the topic but is stopped by Khalid, who smiles and shakes his head in the negative, gesturing at them to continue with this interesting debate.

'It's all right, Bilal,' Sam looks at Bilal's uneasy antics, 'I value your father's opinion and want to know his point of view. After all, we also need to know the mindset of people at large over here who are not even involved in this war.' She then looks at the professor and requests, 'Sir, it's all right, please continue as I would really like to understand their cause and will to fight. You know, maybe I can go back and advise my superiors of what I learnt from this discussion?'

In fact, she is keener to know the inner motivations of her enemies so that she could kill that.

The professor takes a deep breath before he begins his explanation, trying to ensure that his valued guest can relate to it.

'Samantha, let's take the example of USA and Canada. Just for the sake of this discussion, let's assume that Canada is invaded by Russia on the pretext that some Irish living in Canada destroyed the Red Square in Moscow, for whatever ideological reason. Now tell me, what would be the reaction of the Americans towards this invasion?'

Sam thinks for a moment. 'Well, the Americans will not like that. Why penalise the Canadians for an act committed by a bunch of Irish?'

'Exactly! Now let's take it a little further — Russia tells the US government, "Either you are with us or against us. Either you help us get these Irish from Canada, or we will bomb you back to the Stone Age." Now considering your relationship with the Canadians and the Irish, would the Americans want to help the Russians under fear of this threat?'

Sam can now make out where this discussion is going and tries to give a logical reply, 'Sir, Canada has an established judicial system, and their stand should be to try these Irish under their court of law, especially when no extradition treaty exists between Canada and Russia, and as for the Americans, we are strong enough to defend ourselves and will not take dictation from any other country.'

The professor smiles back. 'My dear, now you are thinking like a Superpower. For a moment, think that the US government, afraid of getting nuked by Russia, succumbs and allows the Russian forces to use bases in the USA to strike your fellow Canadians. As a regular American, what would be your reaction?'

Sam is speechless; she feels she has been checkmated. The professor, seeing the look of frustration on Sam's face, decides to conclude his argument. 'Now put Pakistan in place of the US, Afghanistan in place of Canada, these foreign terrorists we call Alqaeda in place of the Irish, and America in place of Russia and see how would an average Pakistani and especially the Pashtuns living on both sides of the Durand Line[146] feel?'

'In your fight to bring some alleged terrorists to task,' he continues, 'you guys have taken on the resentment of Pashtun nation, who now consider you as an occupation force in their country Afghanistan.

---

[146] 1,500-mile-long porous Afghanistan-Pakistan border.

Furthermore, their cousins living in Pakistan feel morally obliged to sympathise with them,' before Sam could assume anything the professor continues, 'now I'm not saying that all Pashtuns are your enemies and will fight you, all I'm saying is that you have given a sizeable part of this nation a reason to dislike you, and unless you attend to this reason, people from this nation and their sympathisers in the region will continue to resist the foreign forces here and their perceived partners, essentially the Afghan and Pakistani States, no matter what logic we give them. And in this messy . . . chaotic situation, the alleged terrorists will successfully promote their agenda among the gullible few who then become their weapon of destruction. Till such time foreign forces are here, this area will continue to be unstable and dangerous; where a small, vocal but fierce minority will fight all who are perceived as their enemies, including the silent indifferent majority of Pakistanis.'

Sam is intrigued to hear this logic. In her endeavour to defeat her enemies—the religious extremists in this region, she had overlooked the psychological aspect of this war altogether.

'I respect your point of view, sir,' she pauses for a moment, as if thinking for her answer. 'It may seem like we are going in circles, but the bottom line is that we need to remain in this region to help the moderate majority and their representatives in governments, root out the menace of religious fanatics who are hell-bent on taking over control of the Af-Pak region with nukes. Besides, we need to arrest OBL and his bunch of cohorts, who are the root cause of this situation. They need to be brought to justice, and anyone who stops us from doing that is perceived as our foe. After all,' Sam concludes, 'it was they who conducted the biggest terrorist act in our country, bringing down the twin towers and killing thousands of innocent people.'

At this point, Khalid, who had been listening attentively to this whole debate, interjects, 'Sam, I agree with what you're saying about the concept of bringing perpetrators to justice. They should be apprehended and given the worst kind of punishment for others to fear, but tell me one thing . . . those bunch of rookies who you say were from OBLs organisation and who, we are told, hijacked the aeroplanes and then commandeered their way stealthily towards their targets and flew them into the World Trade Center Twin Towers and The Pentagon with pinpoint accuracy . . . Do you actually believe they were capable of doing that?'

Sam is stunned to hear this question. She cannot believe a progressive-looking ex-officer of Pakistan Air Force, now flying passenger jets, would doubt the facts relayed by her country. She begins her response in defence of this theory, 'Well, we are made to believe . . .'

'Exactly my point . . . made to believe!' blurts out Khalid.

Sam doesn't like being interrupted and continues, giving Khalid a stern look, '. . . made to believe, from facts on the ground, that those terrorists had taken flying lessons and had hours of simulated flying experience on those types, sufficient enough to fly those birds into their intended target buildings without getting detected. They had done their homework.'

As she gasps for breath trying to lower her temper, Khalid pauses for a while and then softly responds,

'Sam, I've been a combat pilot myself, having flown thousands of hours on fighter bombers in which I've made countless bombing runs as part of my training. I'm also now an airline pilot flying the same Boeings that were flown into those Twin Towers. You ask any pilot, and he'll tell you that it takes hours and hours of actual flying and formal conversion courses to successfully fly those planes and then hours and hours of training to successfully take those planes into their intended targets. The margin of error is so little at that high speed and low altitude that I feel it could not have been done by some rookies who were also busy hijacking the planes at the same time.'

Sam cannot believe what she is hearing. An attempt to completely deny the facts that she had been told repeatedly, she scoffs at Khalid, 'So you mean to say that those planes were remote controlled or something?'

At which, Khalid responds, desperately trying to control his voice, 'Yes, indeed, I mean to say that, Sam. To me, there is something much more than meets the eye. Time will tell that this was the biggest conspiracy hatched in the world to bring the two great civilisations at war with each other! Both our people are dying for the benefit of somebody else, and you guys are just too naïve to understand this conspiracy!'

Seeing tempers flaring, Bilal interjects helplessly trying to ease down the situation, 'Okay, Okay, time out please. Take it easy guys, what's wrong?'

Professor Afnan also tries to bring down the simmering heat of the argument, 'Hey children! Take it easy . . . let's just keep it as a healthy debate.' He then looks at Sam, 'Samantha, would you like to have some more green tea?'

Sam understands the efforts being made to placate her and nods back, 'That'll be nice, thank you.'

Meanwhile, Khalid excuses himself from this discussion on the pretext of attending to his wife and kids, who had preferred to remain out of harm's way at seeing this heated discussion in the veranda. The elderly professor also gets up, 'I need to offer my Zohr[147] prayers before the time lapses.'

Getting up he looks at Sam, 'I hope you found the discussion fruitful and might have understood the other side of the story for which you came here,' he winks at her, and Sam feels like a child who has been caught with her hand in the candy jar.

'My dear, we as normal Pakistanis like and respect American people, you can see that around you too. It is only your government's policies towards this area that very few of the rigid among us have a problem with . . . and I'm sure that will also go away if these policies change. Now if you'll excuse me?' Bilal's father gives a considerate smile and leaves them to each other.

Sam smiles back faintly and nods preferring to remain silent this time. She certainly got more than what she came here looking for.

As the professor departs, Bilal looks at Sam apologetically. 'Sam, I'm really sorry if you've felt bad. It's just that these are very sentimental topics, and emotions run high when these topics are discussed here.'

'It's perfectly fine, Bilal. Everyone is entitled to his opinion, and I respect that. In fact, Khalid has a very strong opinion about the current war on terror, but I'm fine with that too.'

'Yeah he has. In fact, you know he left the Air Force because he could not bomb those villages harbouring "terrorists" on the Af-Pak border. He used to say that he didn't join the air force to bomb his own people.'

Sam is confused by this statement and asks Bilal, 'But don't you guys bomb the terrorists on confirmed Intel and in designated areas?'

---

[147] Midday prayers — one of the five mandatory prayers of the day.

'Well, Khalid compared this retaliation to killing a fly with a sledgehammer. He said that when we react to their acts of terrorism by dropping a large bomb in their areas, that bomb doesn't distinguish between a terrorist and innocent civilians standing in the proximity. He used to say that he could not live with the guilt of killing innocent countrymen who just happen to be in that vicinity at the wrong time . . . Anyway, he is happy now being out of that situation.'

Sam tries to digest this logic. Since morning, she has learnt many things about this region and its people. She now plans to write a report on her discussions here and see how this information can be used in furthering her cause, which can eventually bring victory for her country and restore peace in this area.

She takes her cup of tea from the excited maid who had by then brought two cups of steaming green tea for Bilal and Sam. Brushing aside Bilal's concerns and showing keen interest in him, she asks, 'So what's the plan now?'

'Well, it's about two now. We have three more hours of good light before it starts fading away. My plan is to take you around Kohat and show you the serene outskirts. There is a scenic large water reservoir twelve miles further west. It's called Tanda Dam. I'd like to take you there too. By about five, we'll come back here, make a pit stop, before setting course before six to safely reach Islamabad by nine.'

'Sounds good,' Sam again thinks about the safety of going further west towards the tribal areas of Pakistan but then prefers to remain quiet not wanting to offend the sentiments of her sensitive host. 'Let's go, I do need some fresh air after this discussion we've had,' she smiles as Bilal takes his last few sips.

Thoughts of Rebecca come into Sam's mind. She knew that Rebecca had gone on a day trip to Fareed's farmhouse and won't miss Sam during the day. However, she decides to call Rebecca just to update her on the situation at 6 p.m. when they return from this sightseeing trip. Little does Sam realise that this time she might have taken a trip too far.

Chapter 11

INVITING THE UNWANTED

It is Sunday morning in the small village of Lodhi Khel situated in another small scenic valley one-hour drive west of Kohat and north-east of Hangu—the last of the cities bordering Pakistan's semi-autonomous tribal region, dubbed as the Wild Wild West of Pakistan. Cold wind blows through the village with white patches of clouds floating aimlessly like candy floss in the blue sky. The small farmlands are spread across the valley on the banks of the river 'Khanki' winding its way through the valley providing much-needed water to the farmlands. The contrast between the dry desolate mountains and the green valleys below them is spectacular, thanks to the fertile mud brought down by Khanki River from the Hindukush Mountain ranges in the north, which has made the land fertile for farming different fruits and vegetables all year long.

In one cluster of brick huts is the small house of Zaman Khan, a local farmer and father of six boys and girls. Zaman, a sturdy man in his midfifties has been a farmer throughout his life. A dropout from school while still a junior, he learnt from his father the ways of farming and had since maintained his small farmland, cultivating apples, wheat, and corn during the different seasons of the year. Finding it difficult to make ends meet and responsible for supporting a large family, he had ensured that his children find employment once they obtained a basic education up to junior high and to then contribute to the family's modest income. He had come to know of Professor Afnan through one of his elder sons who became Afnan's chauffeur in Peshawar University. Knowing the benevolent nature of the professor and his educational background, Zaman had requested Afnan to keep one of his daughters as a domestic help and also educate her in the process, partly due to an unfortunate incident that

220

happened with her back home. A task graciously agreed to by Afnan after consulting his wife, and hence this girl had started living with the Khattaks.

Today, the seventeen-year-old Sadia is very excited to see a beautiful foreign lady in the house, who looks like a character right out of a Hollywood movie and who even talks in an English accent she has only ever heard on television.

After exchanging her own pleasantries with the foreign 'Maim,'[148] in the morning, she was unable to control her excitement and called her mother back in Lodhi Khel village, sharing with her this news of hosting a foreign lady who looked like Angelina Jolie. Angelina, due to her frequent visits to Pakistan as a UN Goodwill ambassador, was a household name among the people who all liked her for her humility and benevolence. To compare someone to 'Angie' was considered a big honour for that person. And today, Sadia bestowed that honour on Sam.

Her mother, unable to contain her excitement at hearing this incredible bit of news, told Sadia's younger siblings about their sister's meeting with an Angie look-alike. This gave her younger brother, a budding teenager of fourteen years of age with testosterone running high, an opportunity to show off with his village friends that his elder sister was hosting none other than Angie herself at Professor Afnan's home. These boys, bubbling with excitement, shared this news with their households.

Soon the news spread throughout the small assortment of village huts of Lodhi Khel where women and children gathered at Zaman's home to get first-hand information from Sadia's mother, who, in her innocence, narrated all the details, adding whatever spice she could to make the story exciting and colourful. She was oblivious of the fact that one of the younger men in the village was an informer to the militants based in the neighbouring tribal lands and who at once notified their commander of the possibility of an American celebrity out on a personal visit to Kohat. This commander was none other than Mullah Baaz Jan who got ecstatic at hearing this news. He alerted his men, seconded to a sister 'organisation' in the neighbouring agency,

---

[148] Term referring to a Caucasian lady in Pakistan. A derivative of English word 'madam'.

and sent instructions for this informer to be double sure about their target's movements. Better still was for this informer to himself reach the outskirts of Afnan's home on his motorbike, about an hour's drive from his village, to provide them with a first-hand account of the American's movements. With the possibility of failure, and well aware that time was of the essence here, Baaz at once got down to hatching a plan to somehow get hold of this American celebrity who had wandered too far west to her own detriment. How to get his militants inside Kohat became Baaz's next challenge.

*   *   *

Back at the house of Professor Afnan, Bilal and Sam decide to take a drive around Kohat. They invite Khalid and Mehreen to join in the drive, but Khalid politely declines the invitation on the pretext of letting Bilal and Sam have their own privacy. Before they are about to leave, Bilal's mother calls him in to her room for a minute. As Bilal enters, she closes the door behind him and, with concern in her eyes for the first time since morning, addresses her favourite younger son.

'My dear, why exactly did you bring this girl here to us? Are you getting serious with her or something?'

Bilal, seemingly a little surprised at this question, tries to reassure his mother, 'Ma, I said it before as well. She is just a friend I made in Islamabad and, as your son who is very hospitable at heart, I invited her to my hometown, which she agreed to. You know these Americans, they are simple, straightforward people and love to meet new people and visit new places. I also told her that my parents wanted to meet her.' He concludes with a twinkle in his eye.

His mother, still concerned, responds, 'As your friend, she is most welcome, Son, but I don't have a good feeling about this . . . Are you sure she is what she claims to be, an employee of the US government,' referring to the US embassy, 'and not some spy . . . Didn't you notice how she was getting worked up when talking to Khalid?'

Bilal laughs at this assumption, 'Ma, you are always the suspicious kind! For God's sake, for once, take someone at face value.'

Before he can continue, his mother interjects, 'My son, all I want is your safety even before your happiness. I haven't shared my concern with your father, as I know he would laugh at me like you, but I urge you to please be careful and take her back as soon as possible. You know taking her around could be dangerous for you too since things are not as safe as they are made out to be even in Kohat.'

Bilal, on hearing his mother's voice, shake with emotion, gives her a loving hug, kisses her on her wrinkled forehead, and tries to cheer her, 'Take it easy, Ma. It's all right here.' The elderly lady tries to control her emotions as she speaks, 'Son, she is a big responsibility on you, and your safety is my concern too. So please take her back safely since it's your prime obligation. After all, she is your guest.'

Bilal, looking at the wall clock and realising that there is not much time left, tries to conclude this discussion 'Okay, Ma, as you wish. I'll give her a small, round tour of the city since I've said it already and then leave for Islamabad well before sunset.'

His mother kisses Bilal on his forehead and gives him a warm hug. 'You were always my obedient little boy as Khalid was always the rebel kind.' She affectionately looks into her handsome son's eyes and prays, 'May Allah grant you a long healthy life.'

Bilal smiles, looks back at his mother while still holding her in his embrace, gives the customary reply to her perpetual prayers, '. . . and a meaningful death.'

'Stop saying that!' comes the usual response from his mother as she lovingly admonishes her son who then laughs out loud as he walks up to the door to open it.

Seeing the others waiting anxiously for them to come out, Bilal excuses himself and bids his family goodbye for now. Sam and Bilal settle down in his Honda to take a drive around Kohat and the nearby Tanda Dam. The time by then is around quarter to three in the afternoon; inhaling the cool and clean wind that blows into their faces energises the couple's spirits on this picturesque drive around the city.

* * *

Gul Khan was a young man, barely a couple of years out of his teens. Semi-literate and the youngest in his family of four brothers and two sisters of aging parents, two of his older brothers were employed in the oil-rich Gulf States, whereas the third was employed as a driver for a multinational firm in the port city of Karachi. By sending a decent monthly allowance to Gul's elderly father, a retired government employee of lower cadre, these brothers had made the life of Gul's family economically comfortable.

With his sisters married off and brothers employed elsewhere, Gul was the epitome of the youngest spoilt brat of the family, who was not allowed to leave his parents due to their overwhelming love for him. However, having ambitions of his own, he found this love frustrating and suffocating, turning him into a rebel without a cause. Refusing to study any further after middle school or work on his small piece of farmland in the village, thereafter rented out to tenant farmers, he gradually formed a liaison with the village militants whose way of life and reported heroics against the government forces made them a kind of 'ideal' in Gul's impressionable mind. Scared of his father and the dangerous repercussions of leading such a life, he had, so far avoided becoming a full-time militant warrior since he would then have to leave his family and move to the militant stronghold across the border into tribal territory. But because he wanted to be among the militants, he agreed to keep them advised of any worthwhile development that took place in his village and beyond. Today was his day to be counted as one of them.

Interestingly, he had also secretly courted Sadia two years back when she was still a naïve teenager in the village. To impress her, he used to show off his imported watches, sunglasses, music system, and other such possessions sent to him by his elder brothers from the Arab Gulf States. It was when Sadia's mother noticed the foreign branded perfume and a cosmetic set given to Sadia as gifts by Gul that the courtship was finally exposed to Sadia's parents. Zaman Khan, her father, deemed it prudent to let Gul's parents know of this association. They could then formally seek Zaman's daughter's hand in marriage for Gul, since in a deeply conservative society, any kind of relationship other than marriage between a girl and boy, not otherwise from immediate family, was always frowned upon bringing shame, especially to the family of the girl. Ironically, Gul's father, with his apparently more educated and established background and affluence due to his sons having good jobs, did not view this situation positively. He accused Zaman Khan of encouraging his daughter and enticing Gul in order to climb up the social strata through this relationship. This led to an estrangement between the two fathers, who did not approve of their children's courtship. While Gul was severely reprimanded for his actions, Sadia's father sent her to Professor Afnan's house on the pretext of getting a better life. But this had not deterred the two lovebirds from talking to each other off and on, thus keeping alive the possibility of a life together in the future when Gul becomes twenty-one and Sadia reaches her legally mature age of eighteen.

Today was the day when Gul could not believe his luck. His girlfriend, although completely oblivious of the repercussions of her actions, had provided him with an ideal opportunity to gain the respect of those he idealised.

Now, with a task at hand, he surreptitiously calls his girlfriend on her mobile phone, something now as common among the masses in Pakistan as their toiletries.

Sadia is alone in the kitchen, washing the dishes when she hears the ring tone specific to the number of her paramour. Excited by the day's events, she quickly shuts the tap, dries her hands, and picks up her phone, exiting the house from the back door of the kitchen towards her residence quarter at the back of the house.

'Salam, Gul Khana!' she whispers, her smile beaming across her face as she tries to hide the joy in her tone.

'Walekum Salam, dear,' she hears Gul's voice from the other side, 'You didn't tell me you had special guests today at home.' Gul tries lovingly to tease his beloved.

Sadia, embarrassed to hide this event from a person whom she considered to be her future husband, responds, 'I would have told you afterwards. It's just 'Begum Sahib'[149] had strictly told me to keep this visit of hers a secret.'

'So you thought you can share it with your mother but keep it as a secret from me?'

'Sorry, Gul Khan, I didn't have the time . . . but how did you know?'

'I'm very close to your little brother . . . my future brother-in-law.' Gul tries to lower the alarm levels he notices in Sadia's voice.

'That brat Yasin, I'll get him when I come back,' Sadia airs her frustration towards her younger brother.

'Hey, it's okay, don't you trust me?' Gul tries to lower his girlfriend's guard, 'Listen, so what's their plan for the day?' He tries to seek information on the couple's movements so as to report the same to his militant friends.

---

[149] 'Madam' in Urdu.

Sadia, in all her innocence, spills the beans. 'I don't know, when I went to them to serve tea, Bilal Bhai was saying something about showing her around Kohat in the afternoon. He was talking about the lake,' referring to the Tanda Dam West of Kohat City parameters. 'But why are you asking?' she asks sounding a little curious.

'Well, I was just wondering if you could come with them, then maybe we could meet too? You know, I can come there within an hour on my motorbike from here,' Gul makes a convincing story as Sadia is not aware of his liaison with the militants built up after she was sent off to Professor Afnan's house about a year back. He had preferred not to share this development with her so as not to scare her off or to invite more trouble just in case this news leaked to Gul's parents, who were still not privy to their son's ambitions.

'No, Gul Khan. I cannot come at all even if they are going to the lake . . . They did not ask me, and I cannot request them to take me too.'

Gul notices disappointment in her tone but disregards it since he has obtained the information he wants and also he sure as hell does not want her to be with the couple in case the militants reach there to conduct their operation.

'It's okay, my dear, we'll make our own plan, and I'll take you to the lake . . . just the two of us.' Gul pacifies her, thanking his lucky stars that she has bought his story and seems not to be suspicious at all.

After exchanging a few more pleasantries, they hang up, and Gul sets about providing this information to his heroes; the trip of his prey to the Tanda Dam all but imminent within the next two hours.

*   *   *

It is late in the afternoon as Bilal drives Sam around the scenic surroundings of Kohat. They leave his father's house in KDA and take the northern bypass road to reach Tor Speen Ziarat—the shrine of an old Muslim saint, located atop a hill overlooking the green valley town of Kohat. In response to her query about Tanda Dam, Sam is advised of its location beyond the hills south-east of their position. These hills completely hide the lake from where they are now, which Sam finds very peculiar, considering the close proximity of a few miles between their current location and the lake. Shaking off the feeling, Sam takes some photographs of her host Bilal with Kohat in the backdrop, for her mission. Bilal reluctantly obliges his valued guest, completely oblivious of the real Sam and her motives for being here. Although Sam justifies this act for her cause and on behalf of her country, she cannot help but feel an attraction towards Bilal for his sincere nature and strong manly demeanour. Bilal also cannot resist the feeling of affinity towards Sam as she casually laughs and jokes with him, taking his photos all along the way. Their easy laughter and casual jokes help to lower their inhibitions and create a friendly cordiality as their sentiments for each other start becoming more pronounced.

After taking enough photos of the area, they drive south of the city, towards the archaeological remains of an old Hindu temple destroyed and replaced by a mosque constructed by the invading Muslims of Afghanistan into India, back in the fifteenth century. Sam is quite impressed with the serene environment, her first impression of downtown Kohat being anything but calm. Taking snaps here too, she now recognises why Bilal loves his hometown and likes coming regularly to stay in touch with his roots. She also understands why his ex-wife could not continue with Bilal, as his ancestral side obviously connected back to a conservative background. But Bilal himself is different as he maintains a balance between his modern and progressive outlook on the one hand and his conservative traditions on the other, and hospitality is one of them.

Wary of time, they finally make their way towards the beautiful Tanda Lake as they have about one hour of good light left before the sun starts to make its way down the hilly horizon. Bilal drives his Honda as he explains to Sam the origin of this magnificent lake in a beautiful green valley, with a dam built on its south-eastern side. They first go north on a winding road up a small hill, and as they reach the top, Sam sees on the other side one of the most beautiful sights of her life: a sprawling reservoir of fresh water gleaming against the afternoon sun, bouncing its rays off the white patches of clouds on to the surface of the lake and water entering from Khanki River coming from the west end. Momentarily stunned by the breath-taking beauty of the place, the company of Bilal and the soft romantic ballads of Bryan Adams dutifully crooning in the background, Sam experiences a whole new level of mental peace. She feels the urge to forget her present self, forget that she was actually working for the CIA, forget that she was on a mission here, forget that she was a Christian American and Bilal, a Muslim Pakistani and just fall into the loving embrace of a man she had begun to feel for tremendously in the past few hours. These feelings take her to a state of trance as she silently looks out of the window, hating what she is and desperately feeling the need to change her identity. But how to reveal her true self and her feelings towards Bilal becomes her biggest predicament for now.

'Sam, are you okay?' Bilal, seeing her all quiet, softly calls out as he holds her cold hand placed on her thigh. He then turns right, eastbound, after driving down the small slope towards the lake.

'Huh?' As if shaken out of her trance, she looks at Bilal and smiles. 'This is just awesome . . . How beautiful and serene!'

They notice theirs is the only car on that road now crossing over the dam next to the lake and leading eastward towards a solitary restaurant.

'There is a nice restaurant at the edge of the lake close by, let's have a nice warm cup of coffee there?' Bilal invites Sam. As they reach the restaurant, they see a couple of Kohat University buses parked outside along with a few cars. The restaurant is a large double-storeyed circular-shaped building built on a terrace overlooking the lake. Glass windows make up the walls joining the red-tiled slanting roof at the top. Upon inquiry, they are informed by the guard that students from the university have come on an excursion trip to the Lake valley and are now culminating their day trip over a boisterous eat-out at the restaurant.

With no possibility of getting a peaceful cup of coffee in this area, Sam asks Bilal whether they can drive on the beautiful narrow tarmac road going along the lake and find a nice place where they could sit alone and enjoy the scenery. Having seen no signs of militants or peculiar-looking people in trucks with beards and guns in the city since morning, Sam had become very comfortable with her surroundings and wanted to spend some more time in the open before returning to her confines in Islamabad. The open spaces reminded her of her hometown back in the US. Bilal looks at the time now nearing his five-o'clock deadline before the sun would start to set for the day. He realises the need to go back, but the thought of spending some more time with his beautiful guest under the idyllic backdrop of the lake and setting sun gets the better of his rational self. He feels that another half an hour would not hurt. He accedes to her request as they take hold of their hot coffees and make their way to the car under the naughty prying eyes of a hundred youngsters, mostly boys, looking for any reason to have some fun.

Once in the privacy of their car, Bilal turns back westward on this side road, driving along the Tanda Lake. A few minutes out, after crossing the dam, they reach the end of the lake from where onward the road would lead all the way to Hangu, the last bastion of the State before the tribal areas and beyond. Just as Bilal decides to turn back, Sam notices a nice flat spot atop a hillock with a track leading towards it from the road. She just wants to open her arms and take deep breaths of fresh air to remember the lovely smell and landscape before commencing their return journey. Bilal obliges and parks his car on the side, and before he can say anything, he sees Sam getting out of the car and walking up the track to the high point.

He sees her walking up swiftly. Irresistible feelings of affection begin floating through his heart; he thinks, *If I could only tell her how much she has started meaning to me.* He thinks about what to say to her, doubting whether she would take him positively or otherwise. He tries to muster up the courage while still seated in the car.

She is my guest and to honour her is my first priority — he tells himself. *If I say anything right now, she might take my words of love for some derogatory harassment while she is alone and dependent on me and that may spoil my impression on her, our friendship . . . everything. Damn it, I don't even know how she feels about me.*

He finally thinks that this is not the right time to reveal his growing feelings towards her and decides rather to do this when the right time comes in Islamabad. He smiles to himself as he tries to shake off his romantic feelings and then gets out of the car to join his guest, who, by now, has reached the spot overlooking the sprawling lake in front as the sun starts to reach the western horizon behind her.

As Bilal reaches Sam from behind, she cannot resist and turns around to give him a warm affectionate hug. There is a moment of silence as the rustling wind is the only sound in the area. Bilal grapples with the situation. Still in their embrace, Sam whispers softly into Bilal's ear, 'Thanks a lot, dear, this is just about the best time I've had in years.'

Bilal, feeling the touch of her warm body in contact with his, also gets comfortable and puts his arms firmly around her. Unable to control himself any further, he blubbers softly, 'Thanks to you, Sam. I've also not felt so happy for a very long time.'

And before he can say anything further, he feels Sam's tender lips kissing him on his rugged cheek as a gesture of fondness and thanks.

He softly responds too while keeping Sam in his embrace, forgetting about the surroundings for a moment and just feeling the warmth of each other.

Bilal finally releases the pressure off Sam as he notices her eyes still closed and with her arms around his strong body, in a state of pleasant trance. He plants another kiss on her forehead and rubs her back with his hand as he softly signals her to come out of her intense mood. Suddenly Sam also realises what has just happened and lowers her head shyly. Happy to have Bilal's secure arms still around her, she decides to explore with Bilal, the possibility of having a serious relationship together on their return journey to Islamabad. She feels tonight may be a special night for her after sharing these intimate moments with him. She giggles as they loosen their arms around each other. Bilal also smiles back confidently, a feeling of relief and achievement running through his heart. They both decide to sit down next to each other for a while, whispering silly nothings to cool themselves off for now as they face the beautiful lake from this high point. Sam lets her guard down and leans against Bilal, placing her head against the side of his broad shoulder; Bilal puts his arm around her to give her the warmth of his body and deriving mental peace out of that as well, the feeling of urgency all but gone from him for now.

Before they realise, Bilal's mobile phone rings. The time is 5.30 p.m. and about half an hour from dusk.

'Yes, Maa,' responds Bilal with an embarrassed smile, as if caught doing something naughty. 'Yeah, I know, Ma, we'll be home within half an hour . . . Just starting off from the lake now . . . Yes, all's well, Mama . . . Allah Hafiz,' he completes his sentence in Urdu.

'What happened?' asks Sam, straightening up from Bilal's shoulder.

'That was my mother,' he smiles, 'she's getting worried for us, as we were supposed to be home by 5 p.m. and it's half an hour late already.'

'Mothers,' Sam concurs missing hers back in Jacksonville, 'they are the most wonderful relation you can have . . . loving and caring.'

'Gosh, how I wish the time would just stand still,' Bilal speaks softly, intently looking into Sam's eyes, who gives back a beautiful smile revealing the inner peace and bliss of her heart, '. . . but I guess we should make a move,' suggests Bilal, breaking the romantic silence as he gets up after another pleasant exchange of looks.

'We should reach home a little after six, and from there, set course for Islamabad around half past six max.' Standing up, he extends his hand to help Sam up to her feet. She smiles, takes his hand, and gets up with a jerk. Head no longer covered by the shawl, with face exposed, she continues to hold on to Bilal's hand. As both of them start walking down the track towards the car parked about twenty-five metres from their position, they see a double-cabin pickup truck slowly coming towards them from the Hangu side and heading in the direction of the dam. Inside, they notice four rough-looking big-bearded men with huge turbans wrapped around their heads staring at them as the truck crawls past them.

Bilal hushes Sam up. She is also alerted on seeing the suspiciously slow speed of the truck and the obvious interest of its occupants in them. As the truck passes by, they quicken their pace — the car now about twelve metres away. Suddenly they notice the truck, now about fifteen metres away, turning back in their direction.

'I don't like this . . . Let's hurry to the car!' Bilal anxiously tells Sam as both hasten their steps to reach the car and quickly get in. Sam curses herself for inviting trouble on her and her host and asks Bilal if he is carrying a weapon, repenting her decision not to bring her service-issued handgun with her on the trip. But before he can respond or even move the car, the pickup truck quickly parks itself in front of them and out jump two turban-clad militants wearing the traditional thick-cloth shalwar kameez, carrying assault rifles and running towards them, while a third points his semi-automatic gun from the rear door window of the truck straight at Bilal and yells at him to put his hands up.

Disregarding his command, Bilal, who by now has started the engine, puts the car in reverse gear and accelerates away from the truck as the two men try to open Sam's door. The roar of their engines, the screech of their tyres, and yelling of militants shatter the tranquillity of the area as the two vehicles speed off — one in pursuit of the other.

'Gimme your gun!' Sam screams, hoping against hope that Bilal is armed, but to her horror, he shakes his head in the negative, just when she hears the most terrible noise she could think of. The truck driver, on seeing Bilal accelerating in reverse, has moved his truck and is chasing Bilal as he speeds backwards. The militant sitting in the back of the truck then fires a volley of bullets at Bilal, who puts his hand on Sam to push her down so as to save her from the hail of bullets hitting the car. By now, the truck is gaining on the car, and Sam yells out in horror as she sees another volley of bullets hit the car, this time making their way inside the cabin and penetrating Bilal's chest in the process. All this happens within seconds.

'Aaahh!' Bilal grimaces with pain as the 7.62 mm bullets from the 'semi-automatic' pierce through his upper chest and collarbone spewing out fragments on a screaming Sam stooped under the dashboard, praying to somehow get out of this situation unscathed. As Bilal loses the struggle to maintain consciousness, the reversing car veers off the road and, with a big bang, hits the embankment of the lake, coming to a halt with a jerk, which sends Sam hurtling against the front passenger seat from the footwell, where Bilal had pushed her down to save her from the bullets. Bilal, now bleeding profusely from his punctured chest and shoulder, tries to hold on to Sam with his functioning left hand as he also rolls sideways towards her, succumbing to his injuries.

'Bilal! Bilal! Look at me, look at me man!' Sam yells at Bilal slapping his cheeks, but the bullet wounds are too deep.

'Here . . . here . . . Bilal, stay with me, stay with me, don't leave me!' Sam cannot help but utter these words as Bilal looks at her and tries to give a feeble smile struggling to stay conscious.

Just then, the unthinkable happens. The largest of all the militants, at two metres height, with a heavy build, and who had gotten off the truck earlier, reaches them and shatters the glass window of Sam's door with the butt of his rifle. Unlocking the car from inside, he pulls the door open and gets hold of Sam by her hair roughly dragging her out of the car. Sam yells and screams as a badly injured Bilal, using all his remaining strength despite his semi-conscious state of mind, tries to hold on to her from the other side struggling to keep Sam in the car. But his efforts are short lived as the second militant, smaller in stature but more hideous looking, without giving it another thought comes close to the car at the side of Bilal and fires one shot straight into his head thus bringing Bilal's life to an instant end. Sam yells hysterically at seeing her dear friend getting ruthlessly murdered in cold blood, as part of his brain splatters in her direction and his body slouches to the side in the car, motionless.

'Butchers! Butchers!' she yells at her burly kidnappers, whilst throwing her punches around, as she also winces with pain at being pulled away from the car by her hair, with the blood of Bilal splattered all over her. This militant is strong, and Sam, with all her strength, cannot get him to loosen his grip on her. Even her judo techniques taught at the CIA Academy are of no use against this goon. Just when she throws another volley of punches at her kidnapper, she feels a strong butt of the gun hitting her just below the back of her head as she struggles to stay conscious. She feels one arm taking hold of her from behind, while one hand places a cloth smelling of chlorine on her nose and mouth. Her cries of enragement, her attempts to break free from the strong grip, and the cloth on her face are the last things she remembers.

'Stay awake . . . stay awake . . . Bilal! Bilal! I'm awake . . . I'm awake . . . I'm . . . I'm,' words swirl before she loses consciousness, despite making all efforts to stay awake. The larger of the militants, a man with the strength of an ox, lifts the limp body of Sam on his shoulder like a feather and dumps her with a thud on a rug placed in the back of the truck.

'You didn't have to kill him like that,' he growls at his hideous compatriot who had fired the fatal bullet into Bilal's head, and was now sitting at the back waiting for their victim.

This second militant, viciously smiles back, showing his two golden teeth, as he flings his weapon on the side, 'Any friend of our enemy is our enemy too. That traitor deserved to have his head blown off,' he barks as he brutally gags an unconscious Sam's mouth with a dirty rag and wraps the rug around her, making it look like a rolled carpet, tying it up with ropes after rolling.

The entire gory episode does not take more than ten minutes from start to end, as this militant settles next to his prey while banging on the roof of the truck signalling the driver to move on. The two militants guarding them, upon receiving the signal, quickly sit inside the truck, without looking for their prisoner's belongings in the car, as the driver accelerates along the tarmac road on to the dirt track bypassing Hangu and leading in the direction of Orakzai Agency.[150] A couple of minutes after they disappear from the crime scene, leaving behind a deathly silence in the air with only the soft sound of the small waves of the lake lapping against the embankment, Sam's cell

---

[150] One of the seven federally administered semi autonomous tribal areas (FATA) dubbed as Pakistan's Wild West.

phone starts to ring; its shrill tone breaking the silence but with no one left alive to attend to it. The time is six o'clock. A terrified Rebecca is at the other end of the line, desperately trying to contact her good friend. As if synchronised, soon Bilal's mobile phone also starts ringing; this time, his worried brother is on the other end of the line.

Rebecca had made it back home just before six from a whole day's outing at Fred's farm house and straight away gone looking for Sam at her apartment. On not getting any response, Rebecca used her spare key to open Sam's apartment and, to her horror, had found the note left for her in case of extreme emergency. An extreme event had indeed occurred a little while back, and now was the time for Rebecca to inform the authorities. Hands shaking with fear and anxiety, Rebecca finally calls the CIA Station Chief in Islamabad to advise him of the dreadful possibility of Sam being in trouble.

*　　*　　*

It is past 6 p.m. and the sun finally makes its way down the hilly horizon in Kohat, leaving behind its dark yellow litmus on the western horizon. Khalid has been frantically trying to call on Bilal's mobile phone but hasn't gotten any response. The family is worried. This is unlike Bilal. He should have been home more than half an hour back or at least, he should have called. That he is not even attending to his phone starts sending alarm signals to his family. Khalid calls his friend in Kohat Police to assist as he and Professor Afnan leave the house, in search of Bilal and Sam.

'O God, please take care of my Bilal,' his worried mother pleads as she sees her elder son and husband drive out of the gate looking for Bilal in the setting evening. Trying to brush aside from her mind thoughts of any tragedy, she still wishes to see her son safe and sound back in her embrace; little does she know that her beloved son is no more with them, having sacrificed his life trying to protect his beloved guest and thus embracing the meaningful death, he so ardently desired.

*　　*　　*

Monday: 1030 hrs—Helipad of the Corps Headquarter, Attock

Lt. Col. Dhilawar Jahangiri slowly drives his Toyota Corolla into the parking area of the old corps headquarter building that bore the brunt of last week's terror attack. Whereas the area has been cleared of the wreckage of vehicles, shattered glass from the broken windows, and other debris, the building is still under repair and being renovated. The resilience of the Engineering Corp is admirable as they intend to put the building back into operation within a month to show their resolve at not succumbing to terror, come what may.

Dhil was summoned from his sick leave for an emergency meeting at Army General Headquarters based in Rawalpindi—the twin city of Islamabad. He was not aware of the reason and wondered what could be so important that he was made to leave his wife behind in a coma and children struggling to cope with a very difficult situation. He was not fully battle worthy himself after facing last week's double bomb blasts. Although he had satisfied himself by sending his children to school in the morning with the intention of getting their minds off the tension at home, he hoped to be back before evening and be with his family in their time of need. As a back-up support, his parents-in-law were asked to stay with them until Rania's situation improved, and they had willingly acceded to his request.

Dhil, dressed in his beige-green camouflage working uniform, parks his car and makes his way towards the Mi 8, a medium-sized transport helicopter, used for airlift operations in Pakistan Army. The engines are already on, and the huge blades atop the helicopter are rotating fast, throwing up dust into the air around the large craft as Dhil presses down his beret on his head with his left hand so as to stop it from flying off. Bending a little out of instinct, to avoid the fiercely rotating blades of the heli above, he briskly makes his way to its door where the Master Chief awaits his entrance. Being the last one to board, the Master Chief salutes the colonel as he enters the helicopter and quickly closes the door behind him, blocking out the dust and noise.

'We lift off in a minute, sir, please buckle up,' he quickly advises Dhil, who nods back in acknowledgment.

Just then, Dhil looks inside the dark cabin and is surprised to find Lt. Gen. Tariq Hashmi seated next to Dhil's boss, Brig. Haider Khan. The General had borne the brunt of the flying shattered window glasses in last week's bomb attack and was badly cut from behind. He was given sick leave and was not supposed to be on duty for at least three weeks to allow his wounds to heal. But here he was, albeit dressed in civvies, but nevertheless going with them to GHQ. Dhil nods at both men as he sits across from them and fastens his seat belt giving thumbs up to the Master Chief, who by then has reached the front of the cabin, just outside the cockpit. On seeing the final person buckle up, he gestures to the pilot who increases the rpm[151] of the engines, finally enabling the big lumbering bird to lift off from the ground, but not before the officers inside feel the creaks and groans of the hull as if cursing the pilot for stressing it yet one more time.

'Assalam u aliekum!' Dhil shouts out at his superiors over the noise of the engine and huge blades rotating outside. His superiors smile back at him as all of them hold on to the harness to avoid getting bounced around during the thirty-five minutes buffeting air journey to GHQ, Rawalpindi.

'How is Bhabi, Dhilawar?' the General inquires about Rania to which Dhil shakes his head in the negative. 'Sorry to hear about her. Samina and I, both are praying for her.' Dhil nods in thanks at his General's concern.

'How are you feeling, sir? I thought you were also on sick leave after what you faced last week?' Dhil speaks loudly, trying to make himself audible over the noise of the heli.

The tough-looking fifty-two-year-old General, with dark patches under his eyes, a receding hairline with a bald top and thick moustache, smiles back, 'In our jobs, our own lives and its comforts are secondary.'

Dhil prefers not to continue this topic. He has gotten the hint from his superior. He had felt frustrated at being summoned by GHQ despite his wife's precarious condition, and here was his General who, despite being badly injured, had disregarded the doctor's advice of bed rest and volunteered to accompany his junior officers to GHQ for something very important. Dhil feels a little embarrassed at his earlier frustration and tries now to concentrate on the job at hand.

Fifteen minutes into the flight, as the helicopter passes over the Gandhara ruins of Taxila, Dhil tries to make conversation with his quiet superiors to get his mind off home.

'Sir, any idea why we are being called in such emergency to GHQ?'

Brigadier Haider looks at General Tariq who smiles back at him as he rests the back of his head against the cabin wall, finally closing his

---

[151] Revolutions per minute.

eyes. Haider, understanding the signal of his superior, looks at Dhil, smiles at him, and pauses for a minute before speaking, 'We don't know yet other than the fact that the Americans have requested us to meet them in GHQ asap, and the higher command has summoned us immediately.'

Haider's voice, barely audible above all the noise in the cabin, reaches Dhil who cannot understand what all the suspense is about.

'Any idea why, sir?'

'We are not sure yet, and it's better to keep the speculations under check,' replies Haider, looking all the while at Dhil, who gets more and more inquisitive on receiving such a response.

Dhil nods back with a concerned look on his face. *What could it be?* He wonders, but before speculating any further, he prefers to hear it from his superiors. At this time, he feels the lumbering giant slowing down and then turns around to see from the small circular window, the familiar sight of the helipad at GHQ, where, within the next five minutes, the pilot lands his bird with a thud and shuts down the engines. As the noise of the engine and rotating blades begin to recede, the Master Chief flings open the door of the heli to let the important gentlemen carry on with their assignment at hand.

Perplexed by the secrecy, but with steely emotions, Dhil follows his superior officers out of the helicopter, anxious to hear the story lying ahead for them.

Chapter 12

CLASH OF PERCEPTIONS

Monday: 1000 hrs — Bastikhel Village, Waziristan

Mullah Baaz Jan is ecstatic about his catch. Sitting in his small underground bunker of a room, there is an arrogant smile on his scarred face as he stares at a battered old English dictionary with his one eye.

After the withdrawal of Soviets from Afghanistan in 1989, many young Mujahideen[152] like Baaz Jan found themselves unemployed. While most of them, being from villages, had come back to their family tradition of farming, agriculture, and small time trade, some youngsters made efforts to get menial jobs with the Western oil, gas, and other exploration companies who had come to Afghanistan, looking for opportunities in her mineral-rich terrain. Since the money was good, Baaz also tried to adopt a more civilised life. Freshly out of his teens and then fascinated with the Americans, he made efforts to learn basic English and to drive vehicles and get a job in a multinational firm. Finally, he found a job as a chauffeur for a Western mining company working out of Kabul. A village boy from Khost, with his orientation more towards his religion, he soon got branded an Islamic fundamentalist by other local colleagues from Kabul and northern areas, much to his frustration. This discrimination became more obvious with the developing civil war in the country in the early 1990s between the majority Pathans of the south and east on one side and the minority Uzbeks, Tajiks, and Hazaras based in the north and the west of the country. His Western employers, wary of

---

[152] Holy warrior then fighting the Soviet occupation.

238

his religious inclination, finally fired Baaz from his job when he beat to pulp a fellow Uzbek colleague who had earlier incited Baaz. The year was 1994, and Baaz did not take this termination well. Accusing his Western employers of being in bed with his colleagues from the north, he then decided to go back to his village in Khost and join the ranks of the Taliban, a rising force from the south ready to take over Kabul within next couple of years.

His trip down memory lane is abruptly interrupted when his lieutenant Hazaar Khan walks up to the entrance of his room.

Hazaar Khan was a college dropout from the neighbouring Orakzai Agency in Pakistan, with basic English-speaking skills; a person of medium height, lean built, and a crackling voice, he was in his early twenties. Having become enamoured by the speeches of Mullah Baaz Jan's predecessor, he joined the Lashkar about two years back. Still not a very tough militant, Baaz had preferred to keep Hazaar for his administrative and accounting work. Today his English-speaking abilities were to be brought to good use while communicating with their captive.

'Lala[153] Baaz Jan?' Hazaar politely calls his commander.

'Yes!?' comes the gruff reply.

'She has woken up and is asking questions.'

At the time of her kidnapping, Sam's abductors had given her a very strong doze of sedatives that kept her unconscious for hours. Rolled in a carpet covered by two cotton sacks at each end, she remained limp in the open back of the truck for the most part of last night, without making any movement. This gave her abductors enough time to proceed undetected through the rough hilly tracks within small ravines going in a westerly direction towards the inhospitable terrain of Waziristan. Once crossing Hangu, the last bastion of the State, to their north, and out of the government-controlled area, the abductors had sped across the non-metal tracks winding through the bantam valleys and dried-up water streams towards Bastikhel Village; praying along the way not to be detected and blown up by a CIA Predator Drone, lurking at night, and with its infra red capabilities, looking for targets of opportunity along the Af-Pak border. Last night, they felt that lady luck smiled on

---

[153] Big brother in Pashtu Language.

them since they were not at the receiving end of any Hellfire missile. Little did they know that the sole reason for not getting devoured by a Predator was not their expertise in the art of evasion, but rather the reluctance of the Americans to destroy any moving object in the area for fear of killing their kidnapped comrade, whom they did not want to lose just yet—not before assessing her fate.

It had been well after two in the morning; the whole village was asleep and not a leaf stirred. In the dead of the night, the rumbling noise of a Toyota Hilux's diesel engine and the rolling of its tires on the dirt track cracking any small stone underneath disturbed the stillness. Slowly creeping forward, with its lights switched off, the driver had made his way through the difficult terrain, with the help of night-vision goggles taken a few weeks back from an intercepted 'container' meant for American Forces in Afghanistan.

The creaking of the truck's chassis revealing its gruelling life, the truck finally braked to a halt as its occupants disembarked, thanking their lucky stars to have safely concluded yet another of their trips, and this time, with the mission accomplished.

As the driver had gotten off to check the situation of his truck, the biggest of the four thugs had pulled the rolled bundle towards him, dropping it with a thud on the ground. Sam, who was semi-conscious by now and trying to get her bearings, had shrieked in pain, but her voice was muffled by the dirty rag shoved in her mouth. The rolled carpet around her had also acted as a scream absorber. She had felt herself falling on to the ground with a jerk, but not before feeling her bladder finally giving up as she wet herself, much to her frustration. Tears welled up in Sam's eyes on seeing her utter helplessness, just as she had felt herself being raised up by two of her abductors, who unfolded her from the carpet, while a third one viciously smiling down on her had tugged the dirty rag out of her mouth. She had never felt so anguished in her life, at the thought of losing Bilal and now finding herself in this situation. But quickly, her training had taken over her emotions, as her mind had begun to run countless checks and procedures taught to her in case she ever found herself in such a situation despite thinking that no such event would ever arise.

Suddenly free from her binding and out in the dark open surroundings, with only a little glow of a lantern providing limited illumination, she had quickly assessed that she was far away from help and actually could be deep inside Pakistan's Wild Wild West.

Pulling together all her strength from her weakened body, Sam had managed to stand up, with legs shaking from the effort. Seeing the rough-looking goons around her, dressed in traditional shalwar kameez with weapons in their hands, she had assessed that trying to run away from here would not only be futile but also reveal her weakness. She was certainly not the meek American cry-baby type of woman her abductors might have expected her to be, and she did not want to give them that satisfaction. Angry from her ordeal, she had held her ground. She had stared at her captors, who had looked back at her. The viciousness in their smiles had turned to confusion. They had thought that this American woman would cry, scream, run, or simply fall at their feet, begging to be set free, but there she was standing firm and looking them in the eye with stern determination.

'Who is your commander?' Sam had inquired in a firm, raised English voice.

While these guys, ignorant of the English language had remained silent, she had heard a voice from behind in the darkness of the surroundings saying, 'He will meet you in the morning, now for your own good, don't try to run away or scream since you are not in Pakistan. You will be taken to a hut nearby where you will remain as our guest. Any attempt to run would result in painful death and unless you want to die needlessly, you do as we tell you to do.'

This person had then directed two other comrades, standing behind him, in Pushto,[154] 'Take her to Mehsud's hut, chain up her hands in front, and lock the door from outside. Baaz Jan will meet her in the morning.'

At that time the most vicious of them all, the killer of Bilal, had given out a mischievous smile, clearly revealing his intentions for the night, but on seeing that look, the voice had sternly reprimanded him, 'Ajab Khan, any attempt to misbehave with our guest will be severely dealt with.'

After bringing the abductors back to their senses, the voice had said, 'Baaz Jan will commend you all in the morning. Now all of you go and take rest while we will take it from here . . . and remember . . . don't you dare come close to her, and that goes for all of you,' the

---

[154] Local language of Pathan Talibans.

sternness behind the command clearly conveyed that they were not to take any liberties.

Pin-drop silence had prevailed thereafter since the name of Baaz Jan was good enough to send terror through his men. Sam, fatigued from the ordeal, and feeling filthy in her clothes, had also decided to recoup herself. She had bravely followed her new team of abductors to the small mud hut, with only a door and a small caged window covered with a rag for ventilation and had preferred to get her bearings before taking any other step. She had realised that panicking at this stage would only deteriorate her mentally and physically, and that was not the right thing to do under these circumstances. Exhausted from her ordeal, and feeling deeply saddened for Bilal, she had soon dozed off under the residual effect of the strong sedatives given to her last evening.

Baaz, standing in the dark, had seen all this activity from a distance and felt his entire being thrilled with a sense of victory. Unnoticed by the others, he had preferred to meet his victim in the morning under more composed circumstances.

That morning finally arrives as Hazaar Khan stands at the door of Baaz's underground room, advising him of Sam's awakening. Baaz lifts his glance from the English dictionary as he sets his eyes on his able lieutenant. He nods back at Hazaar Khan and gives out a contented smile. 'Give her some breakfast and a new set of clothes from the village women. Tell her to freshen up, and I'll meet her during the day.'

As Hazaar turns around to adhere to his commander's wish, Baaz advises with a concerned voice, 'Remember, she may be from enemy country but still she is a woman, so don't treat her harshly . . . unless she tries to flee or act hostile.'

Hazaar, with his hands held in front with respect for his commander, nods back in agreement and makes his way out of the dungeon. Baaz again looks back towards the worn-out English dictionary as he decides on how to address his American captive. After succeeding in the first phase of his mission, and discounting the immediate possibility of rescue by her allies, to know more about her and bring this abduction to good use becomes his next objective.

*   *   *

Monday: 1100 hrs — Army General Headquarter Building, Rawalpindi

Dhil makes his way, with his superiors, into the main building of Army General Headquarters, popularly called GHQ. Based in Islamabad's twin city of Rawalpindi and spread across acres of land, this was a highly guarded complex of various single-storeyed buildings neatly painted in off-white, each with red-tiled roof, constructed around a larger double-storeyed building, housing the important offices of the Chief of Army Staff and his support team. In recent years, this complex was further secured by the construction of high-security guardrooms at the gates, a high rise cemented wall around its perimeter with soldiers manning the watchtowers and barbed wire running across the top of the boundary wall. Care was taken to not tamper with the aesthetics. Adding to the grandeur of the complex between the perimeter wall and each building were neatly manicured lawns and flower beds. Small pavements adjoined the entrances of the buildings to the tarmac road running throughout the complex. On one side was housed the car-parking shed, where the black shining staff sedans of the senior officials were parked, each car proudly carrying the flag and emblem of its commander. Along with various offices, the main building also housed meeting rooms and a larger conference room, where most of the scheduled meetings were held between the Chief of Army Staff with his corps commanders and other senior military and civil officials.

But today's meeting is unscheduled. While General Tariq and Brigadier Haider are summoned inside the conference room, Dhil is asked to sit in the adjoining waiting room where he finds, to his surprise, his colleague and fellow commanding officer, Lt. Col. Ehsan Rabbani. Two courses junior to Dhil, Rabbani, thirty-nine, recently took command of the 2nd Pak Commando Battalion, based in Tarbela. Six feet tall, muscular with a thick black cropped beard covering his whitish-complexioned face, this officer was a hardened third-generation soldier, whose stories of bravery on the Siachin Glacier[155] battling the Indians and the recent Swat front eliminating

---

[155] A strategically placed highest battleground on earth, where Pakistani and Indian forces, at more than 20,000 ft, are locked in a low-key battles all year long.

the militants, were known across the Army. A local of the southern dry and hot city of Bahawalpur, he never hid his feelings towards the militants, whom he considered traitors, who had turned their guns against their own mentors, the Pakistan Army.

'Sir, did you notice the American embassy SUVs parked outside?' Rabbani asks Dhil as the two of them settle down after exchanging initial pleasantries where Rania's situation was also discussed.

Dhil nods, not wanting to speculate with his excited junior officer.

'I think we are up to something interesting again,' Rabbani answers his own question with a hint of curiosity in his voice.

Dhil, least bothered at this time about what they are up to with the Americans, prefers to maintain his silence as his mind again drifts back to Rania and his children. Seeing no reaction coming out of his senior colleague, Rabbani also tries to control his excitement while looking around for some magazine to read. The silence in the room is broken when they hear the heavy mahogany wooden door of the conference room being flung open and the voice of their Chief of Army Staff talking to someone in English.

'Don't worry, Mr Ambassador, we'll have our best men put on this job.'

Dhil and Rabbani overhear the low baritone voice of their chief as he crosses the door of their waiting room with a concerned-looking US ambassador to Pakistan beside him, followed by their close aide. Both of them stand up in respect just in case these people walk into their room, but that doesn't happen, and the two tough-looking officers look at each other inquiringly. As this group of men moves on, the entire room again falls silent for the next few minutes before a smartly dressed non-commissioned officer comes into the room and requests them to follow him.

Rabbani, out of respect for Dhil, gestures at him to lead the way, and as they enter the room, they find themselves in the presence of their Army Chief along with Lt. Gen. Tariq Hashmi, Brig. Haider Khan, and a few other high-ranking officers—all of them seated. The American delegation had left by then, and now the time has come for the 'Men in Khaki'[156] to get into action.

---

[156] Term used for men of Pak Army due to the beige color of their uniform called khaki in Urdu.

Dhil and Rabbani stand at attention and smartly salute their chief.

'At ease, gentlemen,' Gen. Afrasiab Malik, Chief of Army Staff, responds in his low-pitched voice as he nods back at his commandos' salutation. Looking at Dhil, the General continues, 'I heard about your wife, Dhilawar. Very sorry to hear about her . . . We are both praying for her recovery.' The General refers to himself and his wife.

Without wasting any more time, the graceful General, with streaks of grey running across his immaculately combed back black hair and wrinkles stretched across his serious-looking face, continues, 'Gentlemen, we have a situation where our friend and ally needs our help, and our government wants to stand up to their expectations.'

Dhil wants to scoff at these terms but prefers to maintain a straight face so as not to embarrass his top brass. However, his facial expressions are not lost on the astute General.

'I've tasked Brigadier Haider with this mission, and he'll take it from here,' with these crisp words, the General gets up from his chair as all rise with him out of respect. He walks up to these two men standing near the entrance of the room and shakes the hand of Dhilawar, 'Wish you all the very best.'

Dhilawar nods back at his chief as he moves on to Rabbani to wish him the same, but before leaving the room with his entourage, the General directs his parting words at these two officers. 'Remember, as officers of the Pakistan Army, we expect nothing but the best from you . . . so make us proud of yourselves once again.'

Soon Dhil finds only himself and Rabbani inquiringly looking at the third person in the room, their reporting officer Brigadier Haider.

Seeing the curious looks on the faces of his commandos, Haider decides to come straight to the point. 'We have been advised that last evening one of their embassy staff was kidnapped from Kohat. While we do not have a fix on that US National, our initial Intel suggests that the kidnappers could've taken their booty across the border into the militant area, and since those areas fall under your jurisdiction, your units have been selected to conduct the rescue mission if the need arise.'

There is silence in the room as both the commandos grapple with the idea of what is coming next. Dhil clears his throat to speak. 'That's fine, sir, but have we taken into account the probability of rescuing alive this American from deep inside enemy territory? I mean, for all we know, he might be dead already or even if he's alive, what is the possibility that he may not be killed or moved away the moment the militants get to know about our presence in their area?'

Rabbani nods in agreement as both men again look towards their boss.

'First of all, he is not a he, but actually a she,' Haider struggles for some humour in this tense situation, 'and secondly, we need to make the rescue party as small, stealthy, and efficient so that when we infiltrate the designated area, we don't give a chance to our enemies to do anything unfavourable to the woman or even to us.'

Rabbani, responding to his boss's humour, also tries to lighten the mood. 'Aha! So we need to save a damsel in distress,' he laughs, but Dhil does not find it funny.

Giving Rabbani a stern look, Dhil inquires of Haider, 'Permission to speak freely, sir?'

'Go ahead,' comes the short reply.

'So Miss Lara Croft goes looking for trouble, and when she finds it, we are asked to risk our lives to save her?'

Haider does not like Dhil's insinuating tone. 'Although it is of no concern to you, but just to let you know, the girl was a 'friendly', who had gone to Kohat on a personal trip with a local guy, without informing her people, such was her desire to meet his family. This poor guy was found dead last night near Tanda Dam, brutally shot by the militants—so, all the more reason for us to save her and also avenge the death of our compatriot.'

Seeing the situation getting tense between his two senior officers, Rabbani tries to ease the situation. 'Sir, happy to be of service in saving Miss America,' he smiles, 'what are my orders?'

'Well, for now, you need to be on standby and prepare yourselves for a rescue mission. Our Intel is working on it, and in the next couple of days, we should know of her whereabouts. Depending on whose area she is in, one of your units will then need to go in and get her out.'

'Sir!' Rabbani acknowledges the order of his superior. Fresh in his command and wanting to prove his capabilities, he stands at attention and smartly salutes Brigadier Haider as he seeks permission to leave the room. 'Looking forward to doing my duty for my country and nation, sir!'

Haider also gets up and shakes the hand of Rabbani, wishing him all the best, as he exits the room, leaving behind a concerned-looking Dhil.

Haider then sits down next to Dhil, who is looking at the floor, not at all happy with the situation.

'Dhilawar, what's your problem, brother . . . talk to me?' he softly asks Dhil, whom he wanted to speak to, especially after Dhil's outburst in the hospital.

Dhil struggles for words, as the room is quiet. Haider tries to make Dhil talk, 'I've known you from the time you were a cadet. You have been an exemplary officer all along. I have never doubted your conviction and your loyalty towards the Army and your country. We know your feats of valour in Siachin and Kashmir. You have been entrusted with the command of one of our finest units, and up until now, you have not let your men down. But over the last few months, I'm seeing a change in you. Earlier, I tried to ignore that, but now it's becoming a matter of concern to me. Do you want to run away in the face of adversity?'

The last question shakes Dhil out of his silence, 'Of course not, sir!'

'Well, it looks like this to me: a couple of bomb blasts and Colonel Dhilawar fizzles out!'

There is again silence in the room as Haider tries to comfort Dhil, 'I'm indeed sorry for what has happened to Rania Bhabi, but she is not, God forbid . . . dead. But by acting all low and demoralised, you are actually playing into the hands of the militants who want to take the will out of our army men to defend our motherland . . . Do you want them to succeed?' Haider's voice rises in frustration.

'Certainly not, sir!' Dhil tries to respond to his commander's query in the same manner.

'Well, then, get up, soldier, pull yourself together and get a fix on your real enemy, who is trying his utmost to destroy the fabric of our society while we sit here trying to fight our demons.'

'Just one question, sir, if I may?' Dhilawar abruptly puts it across to Haider, who had thought this pep talk was over. 'Why so much favour for the Americans? Why risk Pakistani lives to save one American life? Haven't we done enough for them already?'

Haider stares blankly at Dhil while trying to find the right words to answer him, giving Dhil enough time to clarify his question.

'I mean, sir, look at us . . . We have succumbed to their demands and started killing our own people who resist the US occupation in Afghanistan. Those Mujahideen whom we considered our allies till yesterday have become our biggest foes. This 'War on Terror' has divided us as a nation, and when America leaves this region tomorrow, we'll be left alone to fend for ourselves from these extremists whose radical ideology is seeping into our masses.'

'You think I don't know that?' Haider blurts out, showing his frustration for the first time in all these months. 'First of all, since when did we start thinking about nationalities? To us, she is just a victim, a woman who needs to be rescued. Period.' He pauses before continuing, 'And if we don't do this, the Americans will come from across the border into our territory and do this for us . . . rubbing dirt in our face, which is just not acceptable to us.'

Silence prevails in the room as Haider tries to compose himself.

'Our job is not to question the orders of our government,' he continues in a lower tone, 'Foreign policies are made in the greater interest of the country, and not on what people of a certain area think. Earlier, our interest was in fostering and cultivating these bands of Jihadists[157] to promote our interest in the region. But things changed after 9/11. Now our interest lies in joining the mainstream opinion of the world. We had to change ourselves according to the new realities of the world, and these militants also needed to change with us. Despite being our protégé, they refused to budge, which has caused all this turmoil now in our country.'

Haider pauses for a while then continues,

'We are a professional army, and our job is to enforce the policies of our democratic government. Besides, our higher command is in hundred per cent agreement with our political leadership on this issue, and as for you and I . . . our motto is very clear . . . do or die, never ask why,' he pauses to let his words seep into Dhil's perplexed mind, then concludes,

'Am I clear on this now? Are there any more questions?' Dhil, understanding his boss's point of view, decides to stand down, 'No, sir,' he replies quickly.

Haider then gets up from his chair as Dhil also follows suit out of respect for his senior. 'Considering your immaculate career and with our friendship in mind, I want you to make the decision for yourself. If you still want out, tell me now, and I'll get you posted to some measly staff job. Otherwise, make your peace with your tumultuous

---

[157] Militants following the principles of Jihad (Holy War).

feelings and get back to what you were before; the brave and gutsy Dhilawar Hussain Jahangiri, because this is not the Dhilawar I want to remember.'

Dhilawar nods in the affirmative, looking straight at the wall as Haider shakes his hand and also rubs Dhil's arm with his left hand reassuringly that all will be fine. He then asks Dhilawar to check on the helicopter for the flight back as he leaves for the Army Chief's office. Struggling with his thoughts and praying for his beloved wife's recovery, Dhil firms up his stature as he walks out of the building towards the heliport, looking forward to taking on his next assignment if and when it comes to him.

* * *

Monday: 1130 hrs — Intercity Highway, Islamabad

The US ambassador to Pakistan, Mr Daniel Redford, is sitting with a tense look on his face as his bulletproof black GMC Suburban makes its way back from GHQ in Rawalpindi to the diplomatic enclave in Islamabad — a good forty minutes drive through the suburbs of the two cities. He stares outside his tinted window on the intercity highway joining Rawalpindi with its twin city of Islamabad. It is business as usual for the normal Pakistanis as he sees the traditional multicoloured buses and smaller wagons bedecked with silver ornaments hanging around them, picking up passengers from the bus stops located at the side of the roads. His attention goes to bus 'conductors', young men in their early twenties, shabbily dressed in the traditional shalwar kameez, with windblown hair, yelling for passengers to come to their buses, eagerly wanting to fill their contraptions and move on. Daniel smiles at them.

Daniel, fifty-three, was a career diplomat with the US Foreign Service. Originally from Washington State, this tall and lean ambassador had his straight blond hair neatly parted from the side and combed back. His deep blue eyes and pointed nose suited his well-defined jawbone and thin lips, adding an aristocratic touch to his personality. Smartly attired in a dark blue pin-stripe working suit, white shirt, and dark-red tie, Daniel made quite an impression wherever he went. His demeanour complemented his calm personality, which often came into conflict with the hawks present in his team. But Washington liked the problem-solving skills of Daniel, and as a reward, he was given important assignments throughout his career—South America, Middle East, and now Pakistan. This was his first ambassadorial duty, which he found challenging. Affable and approachable, he liked to build consensus among his team rather than steam down his orders. He felt this was the only way to get the job done, with the loyalty and support of his junior colleagues: a strategy that worked so far in his favour.

Sitting beside him is assistant director CIA, Richard Knox, forty-seven, a bald, barrel-chested ex-Marine of medium height. Richard joined the CIA after taking premature retirement from the US Marines. A diehard patriot from Arizona State, following the philosophy of doing anything to keep America safe, he was considered a hawk in the establishment. He had been especially appointed as CIA Station Chief in Pakistan for his effective and, at times, brutally direct methods of getting the job done, a fact also disliked by his counterparts in the Pakistan Intelligence outfits. Today, Agent Dick is driving their GMC Suburban while Agent Jim sits in the passenger seat next to him. Both are equally concerned for their immediate boss, Samantha Albright's fate.

Accompanying them in the other GMC Suburban, as a safety precaution of not keeping all the senior personnel in one vehicle, is the US Military Attaché to Pakistan, Col. Raymond Gaunt, forty-five. Gaunt, from the US Army, was considered a friend of Pakistan due to the close working relations enjoyed between the military of the two countries. His presence in today's meeting was especially requested by Richard, who was wary of the level of cooperation coming from the Pakistan Army. The presence of Col. Gaunt and the ambassador gave him an audience with the Chief of the Pakistan Army himself at such a short notice and their willingness to assist Richard.

Noticing the concern on his ambassador's face turning into a smile, Richard cannot help but ask His Excellency what thoughts are going through his mind.

Daniel turns his attention from the window to look at his CIA Station Chief, takes a deep breath, and shares his feelings, 'I envy the jobs of these . . . what do you call them . . . bus conductors?' pointing in the direction of some parked buses as they pass by. 'Their only objective is to fill up their own bus with as many passengers as they can to appease their boss, the driver . . . just living for the day and not caring the hell about what's going on in this world.' He admires all the wind blowing through their hair and faces as they precariously hang from the rear doors of the moving buses, jumping off as the bus slows down to pick up more passengers, and jumping back on again once their bus starts to accelerate after the pickup. Their carefree and simple lifestyle reflected in their actions.

Richard, not agreeing with this philosophy, tries to motivate his ambassador.

'And, sir, I envy your job, which is so important for the relations between us and Pakistan.'

Daniel looks at him and smiles as Richard continues, 'Sir, I consider you a lynchpin between two uneasy allies who blame each other for the mess they have found themselves in trying to win a war over phantoms.'

'Well, that's quite a compliment coming from you, considering your reputation,' Daniel returns the compliment.

'Sir, don't get me wrong. I'll still do anything to keep my country secure from terrorists, but I feel that our enemy is becoming more elusive as time passes, and we may need to change our strategy in tackling them sooner rather than later . . . This overt confrontation is not getting us anywhere.'

There is silence in the vehicle as Richard goes over the content of their meeting with the Pak Army Chief. 'Do you think they'll buy our story?' he abruptly puts the question across to his CIA Station Chief.

'Well, sir, what choice do we have? Hopefully Sam will not have revealed to her abductors who she really is, and if we tell the Paks that one of our CIA officials has been taken, they might covertly take her into their custody. Worse yet . . . what if there is a terrorist's mole in among them, and they get to know of Sam's real identity . . . They'll tear her apart until she breaks down.'

Daniel nods, the sombre look back on his face. 'But what if they get to know from their Intel about her real identity? That'll be even worse since their distrust of us, which is already high, would rise by another notch.'

Without showing his frustration at restarting the topic again, Richard tries to bring the discussion to a close, 'Sir, as you recall, we had a detailed discussion on this earlier, and our consensus decision is what we are following. Sir, I suggest we don't change our version now since it'll only be detrimental to our efforts to get Sam back.'

There is again silence in the car as Richard notices his ambassador's face turning red with rage for the first time since he knew him.

'Bloody hell, what the fuck was she thinking!?' Daniel yells, startling the others present in the vehicle, who maintain a prudent silence at his outburst, not wanting to invite the wrath of their ambassador. 'It's a fine mess she's gotten us into!' he says.

Richard, feeling uncomfortable at putting his ambassador in such a difficult situation created by one of his staff, curses Sam in his heart. He also curses himself for blindly trusting his subordinate. Wishing he had put more tabs on her, he hopes to get her back so that he could personally make an example of her. He feels that, by being so reckless, she has put the US into a weaker position vis-à-vis Pakistan. At this time, he can only pray to God that the militants don't get to know of her real identity because that may put their drone operations in this region in jeopardy.

The rest of the journey is spent in silence as the GMC makes its way back to the US embassy, each occupant thinking of his role in getting Sam back safely from the clutches of her kidnappers.

*   *   *

Monday: 1700 hrs — Bastikhel Village, Waziristan

The whole day passes by as Sam struggles to make sense of time and her location. Imprisoned in this small hut, left vacant after the death of its former occupant, Sam was given a clean set of clothes in the morning — a set of shalwar kameez worn by the local women of the area. Despite protesting to Hazaar Khan, her only point of contact and the only person who seemed to know some English, she was provided with a barrel full of water and was asked to refresh herself on one side in the room itself, which Sam found very disgusting. With her hands chained in front, she had only managed to change her dirty jeans with the shalwar given to her after she made for herself a makeshift toilet in one corner of the small hut from some cloth available inside and the charpoy.[158] In the afternoon, she was given one meal for the day made of spicy lentils and naan.[159] Tired from her ordeal, chained,

---

[158]   Local bed made of straws.
[159]   Local peta bread made of flour.

and hungry, Sam tried to gulp it down with some water, hoping to God that her stomach wouldn't give up on her. She had not liked the frequent intrusions of her captors into her hut. They had looked at her with lustful eyes speaking to her in Pushto—a language unknown to her, but not daring to come close to her: the fear of their commander's wrath effectively instilled in them by Hazaar Khan. They would then leave her hut, locking it from the outside. By evening, her frustration level peaked, and she started to yell for Hazaar Khan.

As Baaz hears the shrieks and yells of Sam from a distance, he feels that the time is now right to meet his prisoner.

He walks up to her hut with Hazaar obediently in tow. The gruff-looking guards, on seeing their commander briskly coming towards their hysterical prisoner, quickly unlock the hut from outside and spring open the door. Baaz walks inside the small hut, where he is greeted by damp and musty air with its accompanying unpleasant smells. His facial expression clearly reveals his disgust on entering the one-room hut. Sam quiets down on seeing this rough-looking, broad-shouldered, one-eyed monster with unkempt hair flowing down his stout neck and head covered in a black turban. He is clad in a thick brown-coloured shalwar kameez with a grey woollen shawl wrapped around one shoulder and chest, freeing his right arm, whereas his left hand is visible from under the shawl. His long, black beard covering the lower half of his face and upper neck, and black patch covering one eye, he gives his prey an intense look with his other blood red eye. Showing no sign of any remorse, Baaz holds his 'Magnum' handgun in his left hand as he points the index finger of his right hand at Sam, signalling her to shut up.

He struggles for words in English, 'You shout again, and I will kill you!'

There is silence in the room as Baaz again looks around, seeing the squalid situation in the room. As he turns around to leave, Sam scoffs. 'Well, what else can a terrorist like you do . . . kill?'

Baaz understands her and turns back in rage as he rushes towards a chained and seated Sam, who puts her arms around her head to protect herself from this tough-looking goon. Baaz raises his right hand to slap Sam but stops himself at the last moment.

'Who you call terrorist!?' his native Pushto dialect obvious in his English.

Choosing discretion over valour, Sam prefers to stay quiet.

'You come to my Afghanistan, you kill my people, you destroy my country, your army take my land, and when I fight back, you call me terrorist!?' he screams, comparing his struggle against US forces as a war for liberation.

Not willing to stay subdued for long, Sam tries to argue, 'When you support terrorists who want to kill Americans, what do you expect from us . . . flowers?' alluding to Osama Bin Laden and Alqaeda.

'Shut up!' Baaz roars back. Never in his life did he get himself into an argument with a woman. He could not think of any way to handle this American firebrand. Although he didn't seem to hit her into subjugation, he also did not want to skittle out from this argument, which was obviously being overheard by his men outside.

Baaz composes himself before replying to Sam's accusation, 'I am no politician,' he struggles with a logical answer since he is not used to explaining and that also in a foreign language. 'But I know one thing, fighting does not solve your problem . . . Now you say the terrorists are in Pakistan, but you don't attack Pakistan . . . Why!?'

'Well, because they are our allies, and they are helping us eliminate terrorists,' comes the curt response from Sam.

Baaz disagrees. 'No, because they have atom bomb, they have big army, and they are stronger than us, that is why. So you talk to them and don't bomb them . . . For us, you think we are weak and poor and will not fight you back. So you come with your soldiers and bombs to kill us . . . to scare us?'

Sam understands the elementary English of Baaz and answers with silence as Baaz lets out his fury.

'You are mistaking . . . We are Pashtun of Afghanistan. We not scared, we will die, but we will not scare. We fight English, we fight back Russians, and now we fight Americans until you leave Afghanistan . . . You will see.'

Seeing the steely determination in Baaz's eye, Sam silently puffs out of anger. Baaz also feels lighter by venting out his frustration. Trying to control his temper, he asks Sam in a lowered tone, 'Who are you?'

Upon receiving no answer, Baaz tries again. 'You, American actress?' still thinking that maybe he has caught Angelina Jolie.

On hearing this ridiculous question, Sam frowns back at Baaz, 'No! I'm no American actress.'

'But you are American, I know,' comes the quick response from Baaz.

'Well, I'm not even American. You've caught the wrong person,' Sam tries the deception tactic of confusing her abductors.

Baaz thinks for a moment, trying to make sense of what his prisoner has just claimed. His information was that they will be having an American celebrity as prisoner, and here was this woman denying being an American altogether. He thinks again of the possibility of her lying to him, but before her identity can be confirmed, he decides to throw the ball back at Sam.

'You are white woman, so you are friend of America, and that is good for me,' Baaz, in his myopic thinking presumes all Westerners to be the same. 'Don't worry, as long as you be good and do what I say, you will be okay,' he smiles viciously, revealing his big yellow teeth from underneath his black bearded mouth.

'And what if I don't act good?'

Trying to control his mercurial temper, Baaz, this time, responds with action. He quickly points his Magnum at her temple and cocks it; the click of the pistol making his intentions obvious, Sam prefers to withdraw, to let the argument rest for the time being.

There is silence in the room for a moment as both of them try to compose themselves. Baaz, seeing his victory in their first meeting, decides to leave her alone. He comes out and looks at Hazaar, 'Keep the keys with you and let her rot in this dump till she comes to her senses,' he orders in Pushto.

'And, yes,' he turns back to Hazaar as if struck by an afterthought. 'Tell Masood Khan to prepare speech for her to read in front of camera.' Hazaar Khan knows what his master is talking about as Baaz continues in his native Pushto language. 'We will make her plead to her people to stop the drone attacks on us and leave Afghanistan. We will also tell the Americans that this white woman is anywhere and everywhere in this area, and if they conduct drone attacks in our territory, then they'll be responsible for any harm that is brought to her,' he gives these instructions for his group's media spokesman. 'Now let's see how much they value one Westerner's life?'

He pauses for a moment, giving out a rare victory smile before walking towards his underground bunker as his subordinates marvel at the ingenuity of their leader — their respect for him increasing manifold in their impressionable minds.

Chapter 13

MISSION 'DAMSEL'

Monday: 1930 hrs — Bastikhel Village, Waziristan

The sun has settled down over the western hills, snaking towards Afghanistan, giving way to evening stars. The men of the village have concluded their day's chores with their offering of the Maghrib[160] prayers in the makeshift mosque prepared after the main mosque of the small village was destroyed in the winter air strike. The tiny assortment of huts in the small valley is dimly lit from inside with lanterns as the women of the house set about preparing a dinner of naan and pulses for their male relatives to eat, only to later content themselves with the leftovers.

There is unease among the people of the area as the village is abuzz with news of the kidnapped white woman brought in last night and now held captive in a hut on the outer periphery of their neighbourhood.

Mullah Baaz, after his meeting with Sam, has retreated back to his underground room at the other end of the village from her hut. He had deliberately not brought his captive close to his cave network so as not to let her have a view of his stronghold. Moreover, wary of his own men, he cared for her well-being for now, fearing that if she is brought in his nest with sexually frustrated men all around her, they might pounce on her as bees on honey, and a situation may arise where even his own authority would be challenged. Furthermore, he did not want to put himself to the test as admonished by the village cleric. Hence, to avoid any such tricky situation and also to keep her

---

[160] Dusk prayers.

from harm's way, he had preferred to keep her chained in a hut at the other end of the village and have a few trusted men only guard her from outside, led by his able lieutenant Hazaar Khan.

Over the past few months, the general sentiments of 500 odd villagers of Bastikhel were gradually changing. The foreign militants whom their village elders had invited in the past, encouraging them to make a strong base to fight the infidels and their Muslim allies, seemed to have become a threat to the villagers themselves. On the one hand, the regular killing of their young men at the hand of militants, on the pretext of them being spies, and on the other hand, the destruction of their livelihoods and property by the State for aiding and abetting these 'terrorist' elements, instilled in them a miserable feeling of getting stuck between a rock and a hard place. Furthermore, the forceful indoctrination of boys from each family to convert them into fighters, or even suicide bombers, was now the norm and any dissent towards this was adjudged as cowardice, an act punishable by death.

Despite the changing feelings, the villagers at large preferred to remain silent attributing their plight to God's will. The disadvantage of not being accessible to the State, being outgunned against their militant guests, the death of their village elders, Gulab Khan and Asmatullah, the incapacitation of Arbaz Khan, and finally, the self-elevation of Baaz Jan as the de facto village chief had made them further resigned to their fate.

Sitting outside his small four-room house was Hidayatullah Mehsud, the ex-sergeant from the Pakistan Army. His house was near the south-eastern exit of Bastikhel Village and about 800 metres south of the hut where Sam was held captive. It was also 1,100 metres diagonally across from Baaz's cave, located at the north-western end of the village facing towards Afghanistan.

He also felt for the plight of his innocent villagers and the crossfire they had found themselves in. He could see the situation deteriorating for his village if they continued to remain subservient to the militant's philosophies and doctrines. He too sensed the need to get out of this bondage. He resented Baaz's self-appointment as village chief after the drone attack in his village. But to confront Baaz Jan and his men without support from the State would have meant suicide for him and his family. With direct confrontation unfeasible and aware of the prying eyes of Baaz's men upon him, he had earlier decided to remain neutral in this conflict. However, for him the final nail in the coffin became the kidnapping of the 'poor' white woman. Hence, after giving it long and careful thought, Hidayatullah finally resolves to take action against Baaz.

Fixing his gaze on Sam's hut from his house, built strategically on higher ground overlooking the assortment of huts in the village, he looks for ways to secretly revive his contacts with his old institution and then effectively rid his village of these foreign elements. But how to inform them of this situation without getting detected by Baaz or his spies becomes his biggest challenge for now.

*   *   *

Tuesday: 1800 hrs — Rania's room
Combined Military Hospital, Attock Cantonment

Dhilawar, dressed in his working uniform comprising of green camouflaged Bushirt and trouser with DMS,[161] has just reached the hospital where his parents-in-law are sitting beside an unconscious Rania. The room is lit with the fluorescent tube lights, and the only sound in the room is the beep of a monitor reading her steady heartbeat as she lies in a coma, covered with a white blanket. A slight clanking of the ceiling fan adds background noise as it rotates slowly and gently blowing air around the room, thus pushing away the few odd mosquitoes which have found their way in with the arrival of the evening cold. Rania's parents are seated on the two armchairs in the room. Her mother, with a dark brown shawl draped around her shalwar kameez and also covering her head is busy reading the Quran;[162] her father dressed in a grey safari suit is busy reading a historic book on Admiral Nelson's 'Battle of Trafalgar' as he sips his hot cup of tea.

'Assalam u alikeum,' Dhil greets them as he enters the room, stopping first to knock at the door.

'Walekum salam, Dhilawar,' replies his father-in-law, 'How was your day at work?'

---

[161] Service-issued army boots.
[162] Islam's holy book.

The previous night, Dhil had shared with his family, the news of his trip to the GHQ and what could ensue in the coming days. He felt it better to mentally prepare all, especially his children, about what their daddy could be embarking on. It was also essential to know about the plans of Rania's parents and whether they could take care of his children while he was gone. This her parents wholeheartedly agreed to, so Dhil was satisfied on his home front.

'Very busy,' comes the short response as Dhil settles down on a chair next to Rania's bed. Dhilawar had been occupied the whole day planning and preparing for the mission, in case his unit was ordered to go in.

'Any progress about Rania?' Dhil asks.

'Son, from the last time you asked . . . about two hours back . . . nothing,' the retired naval officer responds glancing at his watch, assessing the last time Dhilawar asked about Rania's progress. Dhil nods as he looks at his beloved wife sleeping peacefully as all around her continue to be tormented by her ordeal.

'Thank you very much for taking care of the kids during my absence.' Dhil tries to make conversation in this serious environment. 'It means a lot to me.'

'Son, you don't have to thank us,' comes the quick response from Dhil's father-in-law as his wife looks on in despair, 'we are one family, and I wish you a triumphant mission . . .'

'Thank you, Dad,' Dhil smiles back.

There is a pause in the room as the three of them go into their respective thoughts; then Rania's mother breaks this silence.

'You know, Son, you really don't have to go . . . I mean, look at your family situation?'

Dhil, not wanting to start this subject again looks towards his father-in-law for help.

'Shaista, stop it,' the retired admiral admonishes his emotional wife.

'Being the wife of a defence officer, I also know a thing or two about Military,' Shaista pleads, 'Dhilawar is the CO of his unit and can appoint another officer to lead his men into this mission . . . he doesn't have to go himself!'

'Well, being the wife of a defence officer, you should also know the military traditions; a brave commander always leads his men in battle, he doesn't hide behind his family problems to avoid danger. I thought this discussion was over last night,' Rania's father reprimands his wife at which her voice shakes with emotions.

'Seeing Rania and the children's situation, I just don't want Dhilawar to also get in danger.'

Wanting to put an end to this argument, Dhil gets up from his chair and walks up to his mother-in-law, embracing her in his arms, he kisses her forehead and tries to ease her mind.

'I'm sure if my mother was alive today, she would have the same feelings for me . . . but, Mom, if this responsibility is given to me, then I'll have to lead my men in battle as Dad rightly said, I can't hide behind my wife's dupatta.'[163]

Dhil continues to hold his mother-in-law in his embrace as she weeps out of feelings for her daughter and her family. 'You just pray that Rania recovers, and we can all revert back to our normal happy selves.'

'InshAllah,[164] all this will go away,' comes an assured response from the elderly admiral as his wife also controls her emotions.

There is another uneasy pause in the room before Shaista suggests as an afterthought, 'If only that girl wouldn't have gone on her own near that tribal territory . . .'

Dhil trying to change the topic asks about his children and his elder sister, Zainab.

'They just left a while back,' replies Rania's father. 'Your sister had brought them over after school, and they stayed here for most part of the afternoon . . . I think you should also go home and freshen up, see the kids as well. They need your comfort too.'

Dhil acknowledges the considerate advice of his father-in-law. He holds the cold limp hand of his beloved wife for a minute, before getting up to leave.

'I'll come back at around eight to take you back home for dinner . . . will see you in a couple of hours.'

As Dhil leaves the room after taking one last look at his wife, his cell phone starts to ring. He takes it out of his pocket to see a familiar name on the caller ID. A sarcastic smile comes on his face as he presses the green button to attend the call.

---

[163] Cloth used as scarf to wrap around the head and upper body.

[164] God willing.

'Dhilawar,' he takes his name out of habit in his usual low baritone, when attending a call.

'Salam, sir, I'm calling from Brigade HQ. Sir, you're requested to report at once at the HQ building in the operations room. Brigadier Haider and other staff officers will see you there by 1830 hrs.'

Dhilawar looks at his service issued Citizen Watch which shows the time to be 6.20 p.m. Only ten minutes before he is to meet his superiors. Dhil knows what's coming. He feels a moment of despair and disappointment knowing what lies ahead for him. His mind goes towards his hapless children waiting for him at home. At the same time, he is also pulled towards his men who have always looked up to their brave commander for leadership, motivation, and direction. The idea of leaving them on their own is also not acceptable to him. He shrugs away these thoughts so as not to weaken out of his love for his family. Mixed feelings running in his mind, he quickly walks over to his LR Defender and rushes towards Brigade HQ mentally strengthening himself to listen to whatever orders come his way. For him duty called first.

*   *   *

Tuesday: 1910 hrs—Operations Room, Brigade Headquarters, Attock Cantonment

Dhil had reached Brigade Headquarters within ten minutes of the telephone call, well in time for the briefing to begin. The operations room was more of a small hall with a four-metre square wooden table placed in the middle on which a large three-dimensional scaled model of the Af-Pak border area was fixed. A large spotlight suspended over the top illuminated the whole table. There were various tags pinned on different parts of the map denoting different forces operating in the region. The dark green tags pinned on the western and southern side of the map denoted various army posts from where their contingents surrounded the tribal area. The area under State control was also shaded in light green, whereas the blue tags on the Afghan side of the border depicted posts of the Coalition Forces and their Afghan Army partners. The mountainous area in the middle was shaded in red. This area was hilly in terrain with numerous dry rocky valleys winding through them and a few clusters of mud huts dotted throughout reflected the overall spread of small villages. The various tags in this section denoted the perceived dens of the militants from where they launched their cross-border attacks. These were also the places where the CIA drones were most active in their bombing campaigns.

The floor on three sides of this table was raised by about a metre in the style of a small auditorium. On two opposite sides of the room, three rows of armchairs were neatly placed on three-tiered landings. On two opposite walls behind these chairs hung various other maps of the region, whereas the dais across the entrance door housed a large rectangular table with four armchairs facing the modelled table in the centre. Behind these four chairs on the middle of the wall was a large rectangular white board and next to this hung a 65-inch LCD television screen. There was nothing on the other side of the white board as a rostrum was placed in front for people to address the congregation—but there was no congregation here tonight to listen to a war-game presentation. The only men present in the room tonight were those who were involved in the planning and execution of a 'hostage rescue mission'.

These men fix their gaze on the prospective combat zone lit up on the centre table from the only light in the room coming from that large suspended spotlight overhead.

'Our concern has always been the safety of the innocent villagers stuck in the crossfire; otherwise taking out the damn militants in these areas is not a problem for the Army. It's the collateral damage that we want to avoid at all cost, and this consideration has so far stopped the Army from physically entering into Waziristan territory.'

Brigadier Haider interrupts the Intelligence Officer out of frustration, who had earlier begun his presentation on the matter at hand, with the words—'Gentleman, we've located the woman.'

'Yes, sir, but our concern right now is also the recovery of this woman,' humbly suggests Maj. Suhail Khan.

Suhail, forty-three, was an undercover operative of the Army's premier Intelligence Agency. Originally from the old frontier city of Peshawar, he was stationed close to the tribal territory and, for years, had gained extensive contacts and knowledge of this area. Lean with medium height, this unassuming-looking officer was a career spy, whose objective now was to rid his province of the foreign elements carrying out acts of terrorism, killing thousands of innocent Pashtun people over the years. This bearded and moustachioed spy believed that a true Muslim and also a Pashtun would never kill fellow innocent Muslims and that these problems were being created by foreign enemies of his country. Such was his conviction for his cause that he had undertaken many dangerous infiltration missions to identify terrorist elements hiding within the masses that would then be picked up by the law-enforcement agencies. Operating from a location close to the border town of Sheranni, he kept tabs on all his sources operating in the area. Aware of the retired soldier's background, Suhail had also approached Hidayat during one of his trips to Sheranni, where he had come to sell his crop. At that time Hidayat preferred to remain neutral fearing for his and his family's life in case the news reached Maulvi Najeeb and his Lashkar, and after Baaz's takeover last autumn, he had become even more careful. However, after the various incidents that had followed, especially that of Baaz's self-proclamation, Hidayat was finally determined to break his shackles. Moreover, he had also felt now that after Arbaz and Asmat, he should have been the rightful village chief. Hence, this morning, and with great risk to their lives, he had secretly sent his younger son to Suhail with the news on Sam and also with the offer of assistance in case the Army decided to rescue her; but there was one condition, that the Army would ensure Baaz's elimination too in this operation. Otherwise, he and his family's survival would be at stake and his plans for chieftainship doomed.

'Besides being an American national, there must be something special about her. I wonder what it is,' asks Colonel Akram, another senior-ranking officer in Haider's staff in-charge of logistics.

Haider shakes his head as if he is disinterested due to its irrelevance, and sometimes too much information is also not good for a mission, but Suhail decides to respond. 'Off the record, but I did some background check on her. She is a CIA Agent sent to Pakistan on managing their assets in the tribal territory, and I presume she went to Kohat to get a first-hand account of the situation there.'

This news comes as a shock to all officers there as they were advised of her being simply an embassy staff. There is stunned silence in the room as all mentally curse the Americans for putting them into trouble.

'Was that Pakistani her accomplice?' finally asks Haider, trying to control his temper.

'No, sir, he was clean, probably he didn't even know of the woman's actual identity,' comes the response from Suhail, 'he leaves behind grieving parents and a brother.'

'Bloody idiot!' curses Haider. 'This is what happens when you act "Casanova".'

'But how was she kidnapped from the outskirts of a garrison town? We know there are lapses in security over there, but this is too much.' Once again, the colonel tries to show his importance.

Haider politely shuts him up by saying, 'Akram, you know that plugging of valleys and gorges from either side is an arduous task, which works to the benefit of these militants who find ways to move in and out of their area without getting detected from State forces. But I guess this matter is irrelevant for us as of now. I'm sure the concerned authorities are handling that.'

Bringing every one's attention back to the subject, Suhail continues, 'There is a strong possibility that this woman may be shifted from her current location. As we have seen in such cases, the victim is not kept for long at one location for fear of revealing her position. It's already been forty-eight hours since she was kidnapped, and my belief is that within the next thirty-six to forty-eight hours, she might be either sold off to the highest bidder or simply moved elsewhere.'

Haider looks towards his young assistant, Capt. Shahid Shirazi. Shahid, twenty-six, belonged to 22 FF Mechanised Infantry Unit. He was an energetic young officer detailed to Haider for the past year. Eager to make a mark in his boss's mind, he conducted a thorough study of all assignments given to him before he reverted to his superior with his findings.

'Shirazi, what's the news on the weather there?' Haider previously tasked him with checking on weather forecasts.

'Sir, we have reports of worsening weather in the next day and a half . . . a weather system is brewing over Azad Kashmir and is expected to increase into a hail storm, bringing with it high winds of up to 60 knots and tremendous hail as it travels south-westwards. This weather will persist for a day or so, sir.'

Haider encouraged his young officers to offer their suggestions thus grooming them for greater tasks at hand in their careers. Shirazi was no exception to that. 'So, what do you have to say about this mission, Shirazi?'

'Sir, the possibility of her kidnappers getting to know of her real identity can also not be discounted, and if they come to know of her real self, then anything can happen, hence whatever we do, we need to do it fast. So I concur with Sir Suhail. We need to go in quickly and rescue her, but, sir, our problem is this location. Bastikhel is close to the Afghan border and is surrounded by hilly territory hostile to us,' Shirazi points at the location, 'to reach the woman, we'll need to go across hostile land, essentially valleys with all guns blazing, and this could take days with a brigade strength force, and by the time we are able to reach our objective, the hostage may be simply taken out of Bastikhel and into Afghanistan, if not killed in the process already. Not to forget the collateral damage incurred in this mission.' He pauses for a moment, 'It's a difficult mission, sir.'

Dhil smiles at Shirazi and appreciates his concern.

There is a pause in the room, as Haider composes himself. He then continues in a sombre tone, 'Gentlemen, the situation is obvious now. Americans are seeking our help as a formality. They are expecting us to fail. Soon they will know the location of this woman as well, and when they do, they'll try to either rescue her or terminate her themselves since they would not want the terrorists to know her real identity. Judging from past record, they also don't care much for the villagers' lives too. What a shame it would be for us if we botch up this mission and they come into our territory and succeed in their designs!'

Again there is silence in the room when Dhil speaks up.

'Coordinates of Bastikhel are 32°54'08" long. and 69°30'40" lat. Drop us on the village from the air, we'll take out the militants, rescue the girl, and make our way out of that place up to a rendezvous point . . . say at village Dree Khazay,' he points at a small village of a few huts close to Sheranni as he summarises his mission in his usual low-pitch voice. All officers look towards him in stunned disbelief.

Then Colonel Akram asks Dhil in a sarcastic tone, 'Lt. Col. Dhilawar, isn't that highly ambitious? You plan to get heli-dropped into a beehive of terrorist, fight them out there, and make your way back with that woman, in whatever condition she is, across the rugged hostile valleys winding tens of treacherous miles before reaching State-controlled territory, and you expect to do all this in a hail storm?'

Haider signals his colonel to shut up. Being a commando himself and having respect for Dhil, he did not want a colonel from another branch ridiculing his fellow commando in front of others.

'Dhilawar, please tell us of your plan in detail. It seems like a good idea, provided we make it work.'

Dhil glares at the colonel airing his anger at his behaviour. Wanting to convert perceived weaknesses into strengths, and his mind made up to quickly complete his mission, he sets about sharing his plan in detail with the others.

Time to mission launch — thirty hours and counting down.

*   *   *

2130 hrs — Tuesday evening, Baaz's cave network Bastikhel Village

The end-of-the-day assembly concludes with an account of his men and material presented to Baaz as per standard procedure. This assembly is followed with Isha[165] prayers and a simple dinner of naan, chappal kebab,[166] and onions, which Baaz gulps down with water in the company of his lieutenant Hazaar Khan and four other trusted section commanders in the larger room dug out next to his underground room. Dimly lit with lanterns hung on the brown mud walls, the six metres by five metres in dimension room has a roof little more than two metres high supported by thick wooden planks running across the ceiling for support. This room was used as a meeting place with his section commanders and close aides, who could not be fitted into his tiny modest room. Today's count was 60 per cent of his force, about 120 fighters, at various battlefronts in Afghanistan while another fifty volunteers were dispatched to territories across the Af-Pak border fighting the Pakistani forces. His stronghold in the village was secure from both sides as his militant allies held firm the territories around the village, thus enabling him to have a smaller strength of around thirty men guarding the village, and also keeping a vigilant eye on the 500 odd locals. With some men and boys from the village itself indoctrinated into LaM's philosophy,

---

[165]   Night prayers. Last of the five mandatory prayers of the day.

[166]   Mutton steaks similar to kebabs.

keeping the village people subdued was not considered a problem for Baaz, whose mind for the past two days was preoccupied with his prisoner.

Despite resisting himself, his heart seemed attracted towards this fiery yet pretty white woman, who did not show any fear even when facing the barrel of a gun. After the death of his wife, with his children at the hands of the marauding army of the Northern Alliance in 2001, he had not been close to a woman, as he thereafter dedicated his life to the freedom of his country. Such was his fanaticism towards his goal that all else had become secondary to him. He intentionally had preferred to remain this way so as not to create any weakness in himself, which could be taken advantage of by his enemies lurking at every juncture. Following the principals of Islam, he had also refrained from committing illegitimate acts to fulfil his sexual desires; but it seemed that ten years was too long a time to remain emotionally celibate. He felt his heart softening for the first time, but his principles forced him to resist. He deliberately stayed away from his captive for the whole day, not wanting to weaken in front of her or show any such weakness to his subordinates, but the urge to meet his beautiful prisoner finally gets the better of him.

By now, all in the room have left except for Hazaar Khan, who is busy giving accounts of their finances, which is also an important part of running his organisation. '. . . Mullah Kareem Khan has confirmed that our share of rupees one million will be sent to us from Khyber Agency within the next week by . . .'

'Did she eat anything?' Baaz abruptly interrupts Hazaar Khan, the only other person in the room.

'No, Lala, as you had ordered, I also tried to make her read the message in front of the camera, but she refused and insisted on meeting you.'

There is silence in the room as Baaz tries to contemplate the situation. Hazaar, seeing no reaction from his boss, continues.

'We have tried to be reasonable with her, but she is stubborn. I think we'll need to be harsh with her, maybe beat her up or . . .'

'No!' comes the strict response. 'You will not touch her unless I say so.'

There is a sudden rush of blood in Baaz, and all other practicalities take a back seat. He quickly gets up and breathes heavily trying to control his excited state.

'I want to see her right now . . . Let's go!'

Hazaar finds this action of his commander very surprising. In his years of association with Baaz, he had never seen him this interested in a woman before. But without a word, he agrees as both men take a walk across the dark, silent village towards their prisoner's hut. It takes the two men about seven minutes to reach the other end of the village. Sam's small hut is all but dark from inside, as is obvious from the window. The two guards holding their AK-47 Kalashnikovs casually sit outside busy talking to each other to kill time, while their four other partners are huddled in a hut next to Sam's, sleeping soundly. Each pair of guards was to remain on watch for three hours before their shift changed. The six guards complete their night duty at the call of Fajr[167] prayers the next morning. Oblivious to their surroundings, they jump up with alarm as they see their commander and Hazaar standing close to them.

'Salam, Lala,' they hurriedly wish Baaz, who nods back with a frown on his face.

'You fools are chatting away while we sneak in close to you!' admonishes Hazaar as he was made the man in charge of the guards. 'What if someone comes for her?' he continues, 'You will not even know what hit you.'

'Hazaar Khana, who will come here to get her?' the older of the two tries to defend their laxness. 'We have friends all around us, and our enemy is too afraid to come to us,' he says, boasting about the tactical depth of their location.

'Besides, she says she is not even American,' the younger of the two guards tries to side with his comrade as both reflect on this guard duty as a futile exercise.

Baaz, disinterested in this argument, signals Hazaar to open the lock on the door whose keys are in his safe custody.

Sam is half asleep as she hears the opening of the lock followed by creaking of the door as Baaz enters the room with the lantern dimly lighting it up.

The sight of Baaz in the dim light of the lantern coming from below his face scares Sam. Clad in thick brown shalwar kameez, with dark grey shawl draped around his body and a huge black turban

---

[167] Pre-dawn prayers — first of the five mandatory prayers of the day in Islam.

wrapped around his head with his eye patch firmly on his scarred face, Baaz's stout physique and unkempt beard gives him a look of anything but handsome.

Seeing him already inside the hut, Sam quickly sits up and huddles in one corner. The presence of Baaz at night in her room all alone sends an eerie chill down her spine, but she quickly overcomes the feeling as her mind starts running checks on her training in self-defence. There is a pause in the room as Baaz looks down at the helpless foreign woman untidily dressed in the local attire, huddled in one corner of the small hut and trying to look the other way.

'Don't scare . . . I will not harm you,' Baaz breaks the silence as he conjures up his English again.

Sam prefers to remain quiet to avoid irking her unstable kidnapper. There is silence in the room as Baaz again tries to make a conversation.

'You don't want to save women and children here?' he asks Sam, who this time looks up at Baaz trying to understand the meaning of his question, her query written all over her face. 'Your drones kill less Mujahideen and more family, you know?'

Sam wants to respond but at once realises that this could be a ploy of this militant to suck her into this discussion and identify her real identity. She prefers to remain muted.

Baaz now starts getting impatient again at seeing no response coming from his captive.

'You think I'm bad man?' he pauses before recollecting his thoughts, 'I have wife, I have children . . . one, two, three . . . four children. One boy, three girl. I love my family, but they dead now, killed by my enemies . . . my wife . . . my children . . . all dead because I am Taliban?' Baaz struggles with his broken English.

In the diminished light of the hut, Sam notices, to her surprise, Baaz's eye welling up on remembering his family. This was a far cry from the man who had furiously entered her hut yesterday, yelling at her and pointing his gun twice in the process. She also feels a genuine intent in his conversation. Grabbing on to this moment to reason with her kidnapper, she abruptly blurts out, 'I'm sorry to hear about your family,' she responds softly, 'but by kidnapping me and threatening to kill me, you will not get your family back, will you?'

Baaz pulls himself out of his emotions.

'You have family?' he puts the question to Sam, who again prefers to remain quiet at this personal question.

'I keep you here and I protect families from your . . .' he points up in the direction of the sky and completes his sentence, '. . . drones,' he pauses for a moment before concluding his thoughts. 'You will help me, okay?'

Yeah, I know whom you wanna save—Sam thinks sarcastically as she believes Baaz is actually trying to save his fellow militants from US drone attacks. Like a few other Western hostages kidnapped over the years, Baaz wanted Sam to give a recorded message as well, denouncing the occupation of the US-led Coalition Forces in Afghanistan and also pleading to the US government to stop the drone attacks in this region. She decides to continue resisting this demand of her kidnapper and tries to distance herself from this conflict.

'But I'm not an American and my pleading to the West will not stop the military from doing what they are doing in this region . . . I'm telling you keeping me in confinement here would not be of any benefit to you.'

Baaz understands Sam's plea. He looks at her and smiles letting her know that he does not believe her.

'I will see,' he replies, 'good for you is, you do what I say and not make us be bad to you . . . You know I'm no bad man.'

Seeing the steely determination in his now-turned bloodshot eye, Sam becomes quiet, fearing that Baaz's presence in the hut at night alone with her might bring out the animal in him, a thought truly repulsive to her.

An uneasy silence prevails in the dimly lit room for a while as Baaz looks down at Sam who is in turn looking at the hardened ground. Smitten by his growing emotions towards his foreign prisoner, his heart fancies getting intimate with her. He starts walking slowly towards her with the urge to force himself on her. At this point, the silence in the room is only spoilt by the creaking noise of his thick leather sandals as he steps closer to Sam. Breathing heavily, Baaz slowly squats next to her, his piercing gaze at her beautiful face. Sam can smell the odour of his sweat on his woollen shawl mixed with the unpleasant stench of his breath from his slightly opened mouth. Sam gets uneasy, desperately thinking of yelling but who to call for help becomes her predicament. Just when he extends his hand to touch her soft cheek, she turns her face away from Baaz, trying to avoid his rough fingers. This second is enough to jolt Baaz's inner conscience, as he recollects the words of the local imam:[168]

One of the biggest sins in Islam is to commit adultery, and a sin bigger than that is to rape a helpless woman. Rapists are the worst kind of men in this world, and they will never go to heavens, as hell will await their torment. A Mujahid[169] can never be a rapist.

Baaz freezes in his track. Torn between his raging testosterone and the teachings of his imam, he curses himself for slithering down to this quandary. With great difficulty, he retracts his hand but stays frozen for a while, as Sam also tries to slowly drag herself away from him, not taking any abrupt action that may startle this unstable militant hence unleashing him on to her.

A couple of minutes seem like eternity to Sam as Baaz finally returns to his senses and abruptly gets up, moving away from Sam before his devil can get the better of him.

'You do as I tell you, and you will live,' he softly advises Sam as he wraps his shawl around his shoulders and opens the door of the hut with a jolt, only to find his three men bending close to the door with their ears intently trying to listen to the proceedings inside. Surprised, they jump out of Baaz's way on his sudden exit from the hut. He orders Hazaar to lock the door while beating a quick retreat to his cave. For once, Sam feels secure at being locked inside the dark hut, alone. She heaves a sigh of relief as she evaluates this incident seeing for the first time the humane side of a terrorist. She ponders over the life of Baaz Jan and his becoming a militant commander. An hour or so pass by as she reminisces over her life up to now, where she finds herself all alone in alien territory, having lost her good friend two days back, and with no sign of her rescue in sight. Finally, feeling zapped from this intense encounter, she slowly drifts into a deep sleep.

---

[168]   Muslim cleric.

[169]   Muslim warrior.

Chapter 14

OPERATION 'BRAVE HEART'

Wednesday morning: 1000 hrs
9 'Crack' Commando Unit, Commanding Officers Office
Time to Mission Launch 15 Hours and counting down

The night before, Dhil had been working on the planning of his mission down to the last detail. With the help of his support team comprising intelligence officers, logistic support, communication staff, and other senior officers, including Major Rathore, the second in command of his unit, Dhil had been finalising his mission. The final selection of men for his team was left for the following morning. Concluding the planning, he had arrived home late at night, after stopping over at the hospital; but by the time he reached home, the children had gone to bed. Slowly creeping into their room, he had given them a long loving look before kissing the three good night. Then he had proceeded to get his much-needed rest for the day ahead. Not wanting to disturb his children, he had decided not to share the details of his mission with his family members until the last moment. That moment could wait until night since Dhil still had to select and prepare his men for the job ahead, in the morning.

Today is a cloudy day with forecast of slight showers starting in a few hours. Dhil is sitting in his office with a detailed map of the 'action area' laid out in front of him on the wooden table. An old, traditionally designed black steel table lamp placed on the corner of the glass top table, angles light on to the map where Dhil has marked certain areas important to his mission.

Major Rathore is seated across the table on the other end. He ardently listens to his commander as Dhil once again goes through the planned stages of the mission and contingency plans.

'Partner, I'll be personally relying on you to get the chopper to the rendezvous points on the scheduled time even if we lose communication,' Dhil concludes as he looks towards his trustworthy second in command.

'Sir, leave that part to me. But I'm just concerned about the weather conditions. Although MET has told us that weather will become fly worthy by our planned time, but you never know,' replies Rathore. He pauses for a moment to think. He held great respect for Dhil and wanted to play his part in easing Dhil's torment. He felt that Dhil's preoccupation with Rania might impede his performance, thus risking the lives of his men and also jeopardising the mission itself. With the desire to help his commander in his time of need, he pleads again. 'Sir, I urge you to think again about leading this mission. Please, sir, with all due respect, and I'm not insinuating here, but your family situation . . . ?'

'Rathore,' Dhil interrupts as he raises his hand with open palm facing his 2nd in command, not wanting to discuss this topic again.

However, Rathore quickly concludes his thoughts, 'Sir, for the sake of your own safety, I'd like to volunteer again to lead this mission.'

Dhil smiles back as he reclines in his chair. He appreciates the concern of his junior officer but doesn't want to get soft in his demeanour.

'Partner, you'll have your chances, but this one is for me, and I want my best guy here covering my behind when I'm out there,' he leans forward putting both his hands on the table as he stares Rathore in the eye with steely determination, 'now have I made myself clear on this?'

'Yes, sir.'

'Thank you and yes . . .' Dhil pauses before smiling again at Rathore, 'I appreciate your concern.'

As the atmosphere in the room eases off again, they hear the customary knock at the door of Maj. Saifullah Dar, the flamboyant commando, who seeks permission to enter the room.

'Sir, I would like to volunteer for this mission.'

After sharing the mission details with some of his senior unit officers in the morning, Dhilawar had then tasked Dar with collecting the suitable men at 1030 hrs for the selection process. While Dar understood his own assignment, he too desired to participate with his respected leader in this mission, and before anyone else could be selected, he decided to offer his own services to Dhil.

'Good, we'll see about that . . . Are the men ready?'

'Yes, sir, they await your presence.'

Dhil and Rathore get up from their chairs putting their berets on as Dhil, with his towering stride, leads them out of the room to the congregation area, where the group of twenty select commandos anxiously awaits them.

*   *   *

Wednesday: 1400 hrs — Bastikhel Village

Baaz has guests today. A delegation representing the supreme council for the liberation of Afghanistan was visiting Bastikhel today from across the border. They were advised by Baaz Jan on his successful abduction of Sam from the outskirts of Kohat. The men had concluded their midday 'Zohr' prayers and now gathered in the underground room, where Baaz treated them to a sumptuous lunch of balti gosht,[170] lamb kebabs, and naan, along with soda.

The delegation comprised two men representing Alqaeda and Taliban Afghanistan joined by a senior member of the Taliban Movement, Pakistan. They were all respectable men in their fifties who had been veterans of the Afghan Jihad against Soviet forces in 1980s. They had come to Baaz today to buy from him the Western prisoner. The mood was boisterous as the three of them along with Baaz, Hazaar, and two of Baaz's senior team members talked about their tactical successes in pinning down the US and Pakistani forces and deflating the morale of their foot soldiers.

'The day is not far when the Christian crusaders will flee from our lands, and we'll have Shariah[171] in our countries,' declares the black turban-clad red-bearded Aurangzeb Khan, representative of Taliban Afghanistan as he munches on a lamb chop.

---

[170]   Mutton curry cooked in animal fat, a delicacy in Pashtun areas.
[171]   Islamic form of governance.

As they finish their lunch, Abu Abdul Rahman, the Arab representative of Alqaeda, steers the discussion towards Baaz's prize catch about which Baaz is reluctant to talk now.

'Mullah Baaz, you indeed have proven us all wrong about your loyalty towards our cause,' the Syrian militant talks in fluent 'Pushtu' language as he tries to make amends considering they were the ones who wanted Baaz hanged for leaving the battlefront last autumn, 'for that, we are indeed sorry.'

Baaz nods back with a smirk, preferring to remain quiet. Today is the day he felt vindicated.

'You can come back to your country, Afghanistan, anytime your heart desires,' says Aurangzeb Khan as he backs his colleague's stance.

Seeing the opportunity, Abu makes the offer, 'Our supreme commander is very happy with you on abducting this white woman, and we have come here to take her with us . . . Name your price?'

Baaz thinks hard as his heart does not allow him to part with Sam. Her beautiful helpless face in the dim light of the hut flashes in front of his eyes. He feels a pinch of remorse at the thought of selling her off to his comrades who may ill-treat her once she was in their possession. While his mind advises him to get rid of the woman and grow in stature, his heart pounds inside him to keep her for himself. The thought of his lost wife and the celibacy of ten years also flit through his mind. An uneasy silence prevails in the room as all wait with baited breaths for Baaz to name his price.

'The woman is not for sale,' blurts out Baaz to the astonishment of all, including himself.

Abu's face turns red with anger. His offer had never been rejected by anyone, and in fact, it was on Baaz's invitation that the delegation was invited. He looks towards Aurangzeb who then tries to convince Baaz.

'Mullah Baaz, maybe we can talk about it . . . ?'

'There is nothing to talk about!' Baaz rudely interrupts, as his men get uneasy on hearing the raised voice of their commander, 'that woman will stay with me,' his emotions towards her intensify as he fights to keep her.

Noticing the feelings oozing out of Baaz, the third member of the delegation, from Taliban Pakistan, softly asks, 'Are you falling in love with that Christian woman?'

'That is none of your business, sir,' Baaz deflects the answer as he tries to control his temper on being asked an embarrassing question, cursing himself in his mind for the stand his heart has forced him to take.

'This is preposterous!' yells Abu, getting up abruptly and losing his temper. 'Do you know what could be the repercussions for this blatant disobedience?' He quickly wraps his shawl around him and adjusts his white cap. Aurangzeb, however, being the eldest of them all, remains seated. He tries to lower the temper in the room, saying, 'Mullah Baaz, think about it . . . We are brothers in arms. You get your money and weapons from us, your men fight next to our men in Afghanistan and Pakistan, after giving you back your title, we have come here to take you back into our fold and invite you back to your country . . . whereas you are again taking on a confrontational path against us for a foreign woman who will not respond to your feelings towards her.'

He then gets up and moves towards Baaz, who had stood up earlier and was now looking towards the ground in deep tormented thought of his own. 'You know our might. If we wish, we can easily eliminate your organisation of what . . . about 200 men . . . scattered all over and take the girl away by force. But we don't want infighting among ourselves, which will only make our enemies strong.'

Baaz remains silent as he pants forcefully through his nostrils, trying not to retaliate to Aurangzeb's veiled threats, who then puts his hand softly on the shoulder of Baaz and suggests politely, 'On the one hand, you have all to gain, and on the other, all to lose for a woman who you would lose in the end yourself this way or that way. So think about it again rationally and let us know of your final decision in two days . . . a lot will depend on your decision.'

He then gestures at his comrades to follow him out of the room as they decide to move back to their base camp across the border, leaving behind a perplexed-looking Baaz.

'Aaaaaaaaagh!' Baaz, disgusted with himself on letting his emotions get the better of him, punches his fist on the mud-hardened wall of the room as his men scamper out to avoid the wrath of their commander.

*　　*　　*

Wednesday: 2130 hrs — Dhilawar's Home, Attock Cantonment
Time to Mission Launch three Hours thirty minutes and counting down

Dhil, dressed in his black battle fatigue and army boots is sitting in the living room with his children and parents-in-law. His elder sister Zainab had since gone back to Abbottabad with her son Babar with the promise to visit again next weekend. The mood is very sombre as Taimur and Ayesha both cling on to their daddy's arms as they sit on his two sides. They feel secure in the presence of their daddy, whose pleasant scent instills in their innocent minds a sense of security. The presence of Rania is greatly missed by all as this is the first time that Dhil is proceeding on a mission without Rania to bid him farewell, under the blanket of her prayers.

Earlier in the evening, they had all had a family dinner together after which Dhil personally took his baby son to bed. Hamza had innocently asked him, 'What toy will you get for me from there?' his young mind not going beyond the prospect of his toys.

'Whatever my little sonny wants,' Dhil had responded with a fatherly smile as he kissed his little bundle of joy on his cheek.

'I'll miss you, Baba, please come back soon,' were the parting words of little Hamza as he had slowly and gradually drifted into a deep sleep, finding warmth in the presence of his big daddy.

Back in the living room now, as he gets up to leave home, he walks up to his parents-in-law and hugs them both. 'Thank you once again for all your help . . . InshAllah, I will see you in a couple of days.'

Rania's parents wish him a safe return and reassure him of their support. Dhil then turns to his elder two children, giving them a warm hug one by one as he kisses them on their foreheads. Seeing tears in the eyes of his bubbly daughter, he tries to comfort her. 'Hey, my princess! Don't cry like this, you'll make me weak . . . Do you want your daddy to cry too?'

He makes a crying face to make his daughter laugh, who responds with a small laughing cough while controlling her hiccups as she wipes off her tears.

'That's like my princess,' Dhil hugs her again. 'You are the eldest of the three, and I would like you to give me a full report of your brothers when I return, okay?'

He tries to make her feel important. Seeing her under control, he turns to Taimur, who also controls his tears, acting brave in the process.

'As for you, my tiger . . . you know that you're the guardian of the house in my absence. I'll trust you to take care of your siblings and also your grandparents since they are staying here for all of you.'

Taimur, feeling important and manly at being given the coveted post of a guardian, controls his tears and nods vigorously at his hero dad. Dhil then gives them another hug before getting in his SUV for the trip to his unit.

'Please come back soon!' yells Ayesha, as his children wave their daddy goodbye.

Dhil looks at them out of the SUV's window. 'Before you kids will miss me . . . I'll be back,!' he comforts them, waving in the process as his driver slowly takes the SUV out of the gate and on to the road to his unit. On the way, he feels the urge to make a visit to his beloved wife in the hospital.

*   *   *

Wednesday: 2200 hrs — Bastikhel Village

Baaz was unable to control his passion towards Sam and had starting feeling the urge to spend time with her to at least gain her attention. However, he also felt constrained by his status among his subordinates and did not want to give them reason to undermine his authority. In this confused state of mind, he had visited Sam's hut once again after his meeting with the delegation, and this time asked his men to unchain her while she was inside and get a new set of clothes for her from the villagers. He had also directed Hazaar to let Sam have a place to bathe. Baaz felt that giving this reprieve to Sam from staying inside this squalid small hut may improve his stature in her mind.

Sam had jumped at the opportunity; while being taken to a villager's hut in the village maze about hundred metres South of her own hut, under the personal guard of Hazaar Khan, she had tried to look around at the surrounding terrain to ascertain her escape route should the opportunity arise. However, after a nice warm bath, change of clean local clothes and some hospitality by the poor village women, she was escorted back to her hut, which was also cleaned from inside during her absence, then locked from outside once again with the keys with Hazaar Khan. Before leaving for the day, Hazaar

Khan had ensured that his men take guard duty for the impending night, and other security arrangements were put in place.

Meanwhile, Sam realised from Baaz's gestures, his changing intention towards her and in order to somehow stay alive and make good her escape, she decided to entice him into freeing her—a long shot but worth a try nevertheless. For now she sent her thanks to him via Hazaar Khan, further confusing the militant's feelings towards her.

It is past Isha prayers[172] now as Baaz invites the local cleric of the village mosque for dinner. After their simple meal of pulses and naan, he decides to share his predicament with his guest. This imam gives a patient hearing to Baaz and then explains the religious stand on this.

'Islam is clear about marriage,' he continues, 'you can have a woman's hand in marriage as long as she believes in the scriptures. Hence a Jew and Christian woman is marriageable just like a Muslim woman. However, it is better if you marry a Muslim woman.'

Baaz, disregarding the last comments of the cleric, contents himself by focusing on the first part of his statement.

'So can I marry that prisoner of mine?' Baaz puts his next question across to the cleric.

'Yes, you can, provided she is a woman of belief—Muslim, Christian, or Jew,' comes the straight response.

Baaz smiles back at the cleric, a feeling of contentment going through his mind.

'But there is one condition,' blurts out the cleric, 'she has to be agreeable to this marriage and has to repeat three times, out of her own free will, that she agrees to this nikah.'[173]

'And what if she doesn't do it out of her free will!'

'Then it is not a legitimate marriage, and if the man consummates his marriage on an unwilling woman, then it is an act of rape . . . a sin punishable by death in this world and hell in the world hereafter.' the imam is clear in his mind about this topic.

'Can I consider her my war booty or slave and then do whatever I can with her?' Baaz makes a foolish attempt to find legitimate grounds to justify his lust but is stopped in his tracks by the cleric.

---

172   Night-time prayers. Last of the five mandatory daily prayers.
173   Marriage union contract.

'Baaz Jan, people justify their horrible acts within the garb of Islam, but let me tell you this . . . Your religion does not warrant any act of terror or cruelty on Allah's beings, be it under whatever circumstances and let there be no confusion about one thing,' the Imam musters up his courage to face an erratic commander, 'Muslims who still carry out heinous activities are condemned to hell . . . If you are a true Muslim, you will not undertake an act contrary to your religion's teachings.'

The Imam, seeing Baaz still patient with him, continues, 'If you ask me . . . you may have kept this woman here to save the local innocents from enemy bombs but kidnapping that woman and keeping her here against her will is itself not allowable in your religion.'

'That's enough!' Baaz's voice rises as he tries to control his temper. Cleric had crossed the line with his last comment, 'You restrict your answers to my questions only.'

Baaz did not like the outcome of this discussion. He believed he himself was leading the life of a Muslim warrior. He had derived his motivation from Islam to wage Jihad against Western forces occupying his country. All his acts so far, he justified as war against the enemies of Islam. But now his guilty conscience pricked him more on the thought of rebelling from the principles of his religion. He could not find any legitimate justification in imposing his will on his prisoner. Unhappy with his predicament, he asks the cleric to leave his room as he delves into the remote possibility of getting his captive's acquiescence towards a holy matrimony, thus keeping her here for good — an unlikely scenario but worth a try nevertheless.

*   *   *

Wednesday: 2200 Hrs — Military Hospital Attock Cantonment

Dhil reaches Rania's room. The florescent ceiling lights have been switched off for the night, and the room is mildly lit by a lone table lamp. The heartbeat monitor dutifully gives out beeps at regular short intervals, reflecting the steady beat of Rania's heart. While her physical wounds had shown improvement over the past week, it was her mental state that was still in a coma. Her position was changed today, and she was now made to rest flat on her back. However, doctors continued to remain non-committal about her condition, saying that she could either wake up today or remain in coma for a very long time, because they have done the best they could do. However, one thing the Army had assured Dhil that, unless he says otherwise, the hospital would not remove the life support system from her.

He reaches his wife's side and sits on the stool next to her. Rania's head is still bandaged, as is most of the rear side of her body. Giving a long deep look at her, he holds her hand in his hand and kisses it intently.

'You know what, I missed your prayers tonight when I left home,' he tries to speak to his beloved wife, who in turn lies motionless. 'It's the first time I'm going out on a mission, and I don't have your prayers with me,' he gives out a faint laugh.

'Kids are acting brave, but I feel they are running out of stamina . . . They want you back home,' he pauses before concluding, '. . . I want you back home.'

For a few more minutes, the mild clanking of the fan and the beep of the monitor try to show some life in the otherwise silent room as Dhil reminisces on some pleasant memories. Glancing at the wall clock, now showing half past ten, he gets up to leave, but before leaving, he kisses Rania's forehead for the last time.

'I'll be back in a couple of days, and when I come back, I want you awake . . . and that's an order, dear,' he smiles at his own order as he fixes his gaze at Rania. Taking a deep sigh, he then lets go of Rania's hand and leaves her room before firming up his facial expression for the outside world.

*   *   *

Thursday: 0000 hrs — Dhilawar's Unit, Attock Cantonment
Time to Mission two hours and counting down

Dhil had reached his unit a little more than an hour back. There he was greeted by his second in command, Major Rathore, along with his team member Major Dar. Dhil had then gone through the mission once again down to the last detail. Checking on his large size purpose built parachute, he had also ensured the serviceability of his weapons by rechecking his primary weapon, an AK-47 Kalashnikov automatic 'assault rife', along with his auxiliary weapons, a Beretta handgun, and contingency weapon, a compact P7 pistol, additional ammo checked, food ration checked, global positioning system (GPS) checked, first-aid checked, and communication system checked, his personal dagger checked. He had personally packed his baggage for the thirty-minute journey to the Pakistan Air Force Base at Kamra.

However, before their departure, he feels it important to have a combined prayer with his team members, seeking Allah's blessing and support to make yet another mission a success.

*   *   *

Thursday: 0100 hrs – Pakistan Air Force Base, Kamra
Time to mission launch one hour and counting down

In the dead of the night, there is only one large aircraft hangar that is lit up and abuzz with activity. Dhil is there with his six-fellow team members.

The mood is sombre as all are busy checking and rechecking their gear and going through the drill in their minds again and again. Dhil had carefully selected two officers, one junior commissioned officer and three non-commissioned officers to take with him for this mission.

They were selected for their knowledge of the area and related expertise in executing a combat rescue mission. Dhil had divided his team into three sections.

The first section comprised the 'sneakers', led by Capt. Samad Changezi, twenty-eight, a young and energetic officer from Quetta, the capital of Baluchistan Province of Pakistan. His Chinese eyes with a straight pointed nose, brown stubble and a long narrow moustache, on a fair-complexioned skin, gave him the look of a fearful Tartar. His colleagues often joked about his vicious looks being his biggest weapon. He was tasked with liquidation of any militants roaming the premises of the small village at night. With him, he had one non-commissioned commando, Sergeant Jamshed. These two muscular men specialised in neutralising the enemy with their bare hands and dagger in sheer silence. After having achieved their primary objective, their second task was to install time bombs on any vehicle they saw in the vicinity other than the two escape vehicles of Hidayatullah, granted by him to the Pak Army for this mission. Not wanting to take chances, the commandos wanted to ensure that they destroy the transportation capability of their enemies, rendering them incapable of pursuit.

The second section comprised two snipers Naik[174] Azam and Shuja. These corporals were under the direct command of Dhil. Camouflaged at strategic heights within a thousand metres in direct line of sight of Sam's hut, and the two guards in front, they were to be the first to fire their shots from their purpose built 'Steyr rifles' to neutralise the two guards on duty.

Major Dar was to lead the third team. He and his backup JCO,[175] Subedar Major Karamat Khan, forty-four-year-old, yet physically fit and a local of that area were tasked with the killing of the remaining four guards expected to be sleeping in the adjacent hut. Thereafter, Dar was to rescue Sam and bring her near Hidayatullah's house in the southern periphery, where Dhil would have secured the old Toyota Land Cruiser II and an old Jeep CJ7, of Hidayatullah to make good their escape, under rain and thunder, to two different rendezvous points about 100 kilometres from Bastikhel through the winding valleys, and from where they were to be picked up by the army choppers. The purpose of having the team spread into two on their exit was to deceive the enemy if a chase ensued.

With silencers fitted on their weapons, the team's primary objective was to stealthily sneak into their designated launch pad near to the village and silently go about their tasks without waking up the rest of the village or the militants holed up at the other end in their caves. Hoping the weather forecast remained accurate, they expected the rain and thunder to drown out any noise and make their job easy.

In case their plan went wrong and they were confronted with more militants, the contingency plan was to use all their weapons and abilities to fight their way out of the situation till the survival of the last man and his last bullet. Surrendering to the militants was not an option, an idea clearly inscribed in each commando's mind.

Dhil steps out of the hangar on to the tarmac in the open. In front of him is parked the CASA CN-235, medium-lift military cargo aircraft of Pakistan Air Force, especially flown to Kamra from Chaklala Base, to pick up the Pak Army commandos.

---

[174] Corporal.
[175] Junior commissioned officer.

As he stares at the aircraft thinking about the mission ahead, a dry gust of wind shakes him out of his deep thoughts. Looking up at the sky, he sees dark clouds arriving from the north-east, signalling an impending storm coming their way.

'You have selected quite a night for this adventure,' taunts Wing Commander Fawad Abbasi, officer commanding '22 Medium Lift Transport' Squadron of PAF,[176] standing behind Dhil. Abbasi, forty-one, belonging to the hill station of Murree, thirty miles from Islamabad, had known Dhil in their cadetship days when they both had spent their initial time in PAF College, Sargodha, together. Aware of the dangers of flying in this weather, but the necessity of undertaking this mission notwithstanding, he had volunteered himself to take these commandos to the drop zone. To his pleasant surprise, he saw his old course-mate Dhilawar leading the wolf pack to the D Zone.

Dhil finds the voice familiar. He turns around and finds the moderately chubby but pleasant-looking face of his old friend Fawad smiling at him. The boyish charm of this mild-mannered officer had not diminished over the years. The only addition to his face was a thin moustache grown over the years.

'Oye, Abbasi! What a pleasant surprise!' shouts Dhil, forgetting for a moment the sobriety around him. The two men give each other a bear hug.

'How long has it been . . . twenty-four years?' asks Dhil as they shake each other's hands vigorously.

'Yeah, mate, where have you been all these years?' The old cadetship memories go through Abbasi's mind.

'Well, long story . . .' replies Dhil as both of them take about fifteen minutes to update each other on their life stories.

'Sorry to hear about your wife, may Allah grant her recovery and health,' sympathises Abbasi after hearing out Dhil.

'But, bro, this is not the best of days to go flying. You know a strong weather system is coming from Kashmir side, and our ride will be very rough. I might then have to divert to an airfield near Bannu before the storm catches up with us.' Abbasi's smiling face turns a bit concerned about the safety of his plane and his passengers.

---

[176] Pakistan Air Force.

'Partner, this is what I need, the element of surprise in the worst of weather. I'm counting on you to drop us at our DZ,'[177] Dhil holds Abbasi by his shoulders and gives him a gentle shake, transmitting the energy into his old course-mate's body.

'Well, why do you think I'm here?' Abbasi smiles back at his towering old friend. 'Let's get the party started . . . wheels roll in twenty-one minutes.'

Abbasi quickly strides over to the dark grey bird as his crew gets about doing their jobs on seeing their captain coming towards them. Meanwhile, Dhil goes back into the hangar to get his men ready to board.

Time to Mission Launch: Thirty minutes.

*   *   *

Thursday: 0145 hrs — Inside CASA CN 235, Medium Lift Cargo Aircraft 14,000 feet above the tribal territory

Dhil and his six commandos are seated inside the big bird, which is lumbering towards the drop zone being expertly flown by Abbasi himself, his co-pilot and aircrew dutifully assisting him with the navigation. There are high winds at this altitude as the aircraft buffets up and down like a toy in the thick clouds. In the distance, Dhil notices the thunder and lightning, nature showing its fury and strength in all its magnificence.

Dhil then looks inside the cabin, where the mood is quiet and sombre. His men are dressed in black battle gear, faces painted dark, helmets tightly fastened to their heads, their weapons and gear clenched to their bodies in front, whereas their primary weapon and parachutes are buckled up at their backs. Dhil looks at Dar whose serious-looking face gives out a slight smile as their eyes meet. Dhil nods back at him reassuringly and then looks at each of his men one by one, who all nod back at him with respect and support, not wanting to let their honourable commander down. A special feeling of camaraderie run in their hearts as they silently acknowledge each

---

[177] Drop zone.

other's looks, assuring one and all that they are all meant to remain united.

Getting comfort from his men, Dhil then stands up and holding on to the overhead belts in the cabin of a bumping aircraft, he struggles to make his way up to the aeroplane's cockpit,[178] where Abbasi is busy steering the aircraft on course.

'How much longer, Bro?' Dhil asks Abbasi, having to literally shout to make his voice heard over the rumbling of the two turboprop engines of the lumbering bird.

Without looking back at Dhil, Abbasi raises his hand and signals five minutes and then gestures Dhil to get ready for the drop.

'Thank you, mate, stay in touch,' Dhil again yells back at Abbasi, and this time, Abbasi tries to turn around in his seat and look back at Dhil.

With his white helmet on and microphone reaching his mouth, Abbasi smiles back at Dhil and raises his right arm, signalling a thumbs up at his old buddy. 'Allah o Akbar!' he yells.

Dhil smiles back as he raises his thumb too and yells back over the rumbling noise of the plane, 'Allah o Akbar!'

He then straddles back in the main cabin where the load master is ready to open the rear door. The light overhead is still showing red. Seeing Dhil coming back, the master gestures all the commandos to stand up in one line and make their way to the door. Excitement coupled with fear of the unknown now creeping into their hearts, they try to slow down their racing heartbeats as all once again check on their straps and buckles, ensuring that all their gear is tightly fastened to them.

Dhil realises the emotions going through the mind of his soldiers. He makes his way to the front of the queue and looks back at them, addressing them in his commanding voice, for the last time before the jump.

'Soldiers! Our mission today is to rescue a hapless woman held hostage by terrorists. The very same terrorists who are tarnishing our religion and destroying our country. So let there be no confusion in your minds that Allah is with us, and we are doing this for the honour of our country. Remember one thing . . . ,' his piercing stare fixed on his soldiers who look back with a twinkle in their eyes as their morale

---

[178]   Pilot's control cabin.

gets boosted by the speech of their commander. 'we are one for all and all for one . . . I'll leave no one behind!'

At this, the serious mood in the dark bumping cabin of the aeroplane lightens up. Cashing in on the sudden burst of energy, Dar shouts out a customary army slogan, 'Naara e Takbeer!'[179]and the whole cabin responds with equivalent vigour, 'Allah o Akbar.' Following in on this, Captain Changezi continues with another army slogan, 'Naara e Haidri,'[180] and once again, the now boisterous occupants of the plane yell back with such gusto that their yells drown out the loud lumber of the aeroplane, 'Ya Ali!' [181]

Just then, the red light on top of the door turns green, indicating that the drop zone has arrived. The load master, who had already opened the door, gestures at the commandos to jump out into the dark clouds; suddenly the deafening noise of blowing wind and engines overtake all other noise.

Dhil volunteers to jump out first to set an example for the rest to follow and so he jumps from 14,000 feet into the thick blanket of grey clouds. The cold gush of wind and the moisture in the clouds chilling him to the bones, he tries to control his tumbling fall as he spreads his arms and legs in a free-fall position. Once stable, he looks up in the darkness to see whether others are following suit.

For Dhil, his mission had now commenced, where he had crossed the point of no return. His destiny now awaited his presence on the ground.

---

[179] Slogan of sovereignty.

[180] Slogan of bravery.

[181] O Ali, cousin of Holy Prophet (pbuh), and known to be one of the most fearless fighters of his time.

Chapter 15

POINT OF NO RETURN

Thursday: 0215 hrs — Near Bastikhel Village, Waziristan

It takes Dhilawar a few seconds before he exits from the clouds and sees the others following him. One, two, three, four, five, six . . . he counts the other members of his team, all dressed in black combat suits with their gear firmly strapped to them. With darkness underneath him, he waits for a few more seconds before he pulls at the chord to open his parachute. The large size chute dutifully opens, thus arresting his free fall with a tug. Crosswinds are still very strong beckoning the call of the impending storm. Dhil feels swept away in his parachute, a contingency they had kept in mind at the time of planning, and is barely able to control his descent atop his drop zone. On seeing the familiar tree as reference, he pulls on both his chords as he reaches close to the ground to make a comfortable landing at the designated area.

It takes him a little bit of effort to get hold of his parachute, which is being swept away in the high winds. Once secure, he looks around and locates the grey silhouettes of his comrades through his night vision goggles, within an area of hundred metres around him, similarly folding up their chutes.

There is darkness around their drop zone. The reason for sky diving from 14,000 feet rather than getting para-dropped from the standard 1,000 feet above ground level was to avoid the noise of the plane being heard by the militants; the rumble of a large transport aircraft would have been obvious. At 14,000 feet, the noise of the aircraft was hardly audible on the ground and that, coupled with the cover of thick grey clouds, gave Dhil and his team the element of surprise they so badly needed.

Their drop zone was about one mile south of Hidayatullah's house. It takes about ten minutes for all the seven commandos to tear up their parachutes rendering them useless, before packing them into compact bags and hiding them in the small patch of dense forests south of the village.

With the rest of their gear and weapons securely strapped to their bodies, they all huddle together for phase two of their mission. In the background, they hear the thunder and lightning within the dark clouds as the wind speed further picks up, signalling the coming of the storm they had so anxiously desired.

Once huddled, Dhil then looks towards young Captain Changezi, nodding at him on what to do next.

'Sir,' Changezi whispers in acknowledgment as he fixes the head set of his radio transmitter and signals his partner, the muscular Sergeant Jamshed, thirty-one, comprising the 'sneakers', to make their way towards Hidayatullah's house about a mile north from their position, under the cover of darkness. Radio was not to be used unless absolutely necessary. Changezi was to ascertain that Hidayat, who had rendered his assistance, was still willing and not in any kind of trouble. The danger of their mission being compromised could not be ruled out. Jamshed, following Changezi about twenty metres behind, was to cover Changezi in his contact with Hidayat.

As Changezi and Jamshed jog over the small cliff to the other side of the ravine, Dhil observes his two snipers, anxiously looking back towards him with their Steyr sniper rifles firmly in their hands. He then checks Dar and his Subedar Major Karamat who have taken guard, making a small perimeter around them, crouching in silence, looking out for any unexpected visitor — each minute seeming like an hour in this arduous situation. Different thoughts run silently in the men's minds, about finding themselves in the hornet's nest, their blind trust in their ex-army comrade, the reliability of Hidayat's vehicles, making good their escape as planned, and above all, making this mission a success. However, the presence of their leader and his assurance that nobody will be left behind gives them comfort in this precarious situation.

On the other side of the ravine, Changezi slowly makes his way towards Hidayat's house, prominently placed at a hillock on the southern end of the village strategically overlooking Sam's hut about 800 metres north and also at the militant's caves about 1,100 metres north-west. Sergeant Jamshed stops about fifty metres from the house and takes position atop a large boulder overlooking the periphery of Hidayat's house as Changezi alone makes the last stretch of the journey to the house; his heartbeat racing and his senses getting more alert, readying himself to face any impending danger. His Kalashnikov held tightly, he carefully walks around Hidayat's house, first ensuring on his own that there is no company around; he then finally reaches Hidayat's main wooden door. He gives a slight coded knock at the door, and within seconds, he hears a soft response from inside, presumably that of Hidayat.

'Who is it in this dead of the night?'

The plan was that Hidayat would not initiate anything on his own so as not to raise any suspicion among other villagers. Only when he would hear a coded knock from outside, he would ask the question with special emphasis on the phrase 'dead of the night'.

On hearing this query, Changezi responds with another coded knock. Hidayat gets assured that the commandos have arrived and slowly opens the door for Changezi, making sure that the overhead iron bolt does not make any noise when the door is opened. The young commando carefully walks inside the open courtyard of the house with his gun still held firmly in both his hands.

'Sorry, Hidayat Saab,[182] I need to look around just in case.' Without waiting for Hidayat's response, Changezi makes his way towards the four small rooms constructed side by side and all opening on to a covered veranda. Aware of the sensitivity of the situation, Hidayat accedes. Huddled inside two of these rooms, the youngster finds the sons, women, and children of Hidayat's clan, all fearful of the outcome should this operation go wrong. After ensuring that the premises are clear, Changezi whispers softly in his wireless set, 'Leopard 1 to Alpha . . . all clear, repeat all clear, over.'

A mile down from Hidayat's house, Dhil had been anxiously waiting for the call.

'Roger that Leopard 1, over,' he makes a brief response and then gestures at his two snipers to come with him.

---

[182] Mister, a term used out of respect by younger officers for their elder JCOs and NCOs.

Just then, a tremendous crack of lightning blinds them for a split second through their night-vision goggles. The flash of light is soon followed by a thunderous roar, revealing the distance left before the storm reaches them. Ten metres apart in line astern, Dhil and his snipers carefully jog towards Hidayat's house, all the while checking whether they are alone in this area. As planned, just short of the house, one sniper climbs over the large boulder where Jamshed lay down on his stomach earlier. This boulder is in direct line of sight and about 850 metres south-east of Sam's hut as well.

'All the best,' the tough-looking sergeant shakes his colleague's hand as he carefully descends from the boulder to join his captain.

'You too!' responds Azam, the sniper, now comfortably perched on the boulder as he fixes his sight on the first guard sitting in front of Sam's hut.

Meanwhile, Dhil and the second sniper carefully make their way into Hidayat's hut, where they are welcomed by Hidayat and his two sons, now out of their rooms and trying to hide their fear and look excited at the same time. These were big moments in their lives, but the fear of getting caught in the end by Baaz and his men never left these young men's minds.

Dhil then nods towards Changezi and Jamshed to proceed with phase three of their mission.

'Sir,' comes the response without a second's hesitation as they slowly creep out on their armed patrol on the assortment of huts placed in the middle of the village, ensuring that they neutralise any threat lurking in the corridors and then plant time bombs on all vehicles in the vicinity. Meanwhile, the elder son takes the second sniper on to the rooftop via the stairs in the veranda. This second sniper takes a comfortable position on a raised overhead water tank in direct line of sight with the second guard also crouched close to the first in front of Sam's hut.

'Bolt 2, position is secure, target to the left in sight, over,' the sniper Shuja softly murmurs into his microphone close to his mouth.

'Bolt 1, position is secure, target to the right in sight, over,' follows sniper Azam, earlier perched on the boulder, fifty metres south-east of Hidayat's house.

'Roger that, hold your positions,' comes the calm response from their commander who then waits for Changezi's call of confirmation about their task.

At the same time, Dar and his backup Karamat stealthily make their way from the south-eastern periphery of the village towards the northern end, right behind the hut of Sam and her captors. Their mission was to begin on the successful elimination of the two guards who would be taken out by the snipers. It takes them about fifteen minutes to reach their vantage point. Dar carefully points his machine gun at the guards as a contingency plan while Karamat keeps a watch around the perimeter, backing up his lead.

'Panther 1 and 2 in position over,' Dar softly murmurs into his radio transmitter attached to his helmet. From the night-vision goggles, he can see, at a distance of forty metres and with their backs towards the commandos, the two guards sitting on the ground, slouching forward with their thick woollen shawls draped around their bodies and covering their heads. These guards, completely oblivious of the danger lurking around them are in fact cursing their fates for being out there in the dead of the night. They don't look forward to getting drenched in cold rain coming their way while others sleep snug in the hut close by.

Just then lightning strikes again, and this time, the thunder follows almost simultaneously, clearly telling all that the storm has arrived overhead. Within seconds, all men hear the splatter of large raindrops falling on the ground as they see the heavy rain coming towards them. The wind that had increased earlier gets even rougher.

Dhil knows that there is no time to waste as he fears the guards may relocate themselves to avoid getting drenched. He gets a little impatient since the call from Changezi and Jamshed has still not arrived.

'Leopard 1, report your situation over,' he whispers into the microphone. There is silence on the other end.

'Leopard 2, report your situation over?' this time directly calling on Sergeant Jamshed. Again there is no response.

Little did Dhil know that Changezi and Jamshed had taken up positions to attack and kill the two guards guarding the five SUVs of Baaz parked in a compound next to a hardened shelter opening into the cave network. Their predicament was a young boy of not more than eleven years of age sitting with these guards entertaining them with Pushto songs. This boy was one of the trainee cadets brought out of the cave network to entertain these gruff militants. The humane commandos wanted to avoid killing him, but the danger of him yelling or running inside when they attacked the guards could also not be ruled out. At this moment, even a whisper could reveal their positions.

Rain reached them as well, which made the two guards stand up from their open-air location. While one of them gave a final look around, the other put his arm around the little boy as he had gestured to the other to follow them inside the hut, thus saving themselves from the killer daggers of the Leopard team.

With fear of having more militants inside the hut and the recurring lightning revealing their position, the Leopard team had decided to plant their explosives on the wooden fence semi-circling the vehicles around a periphery of about sixty metres in radius so that when they explode, they render the vehicles at least unserviceable, if not destroyed. After placing their five explosives, they had then slowly crawled back to the safety of the assortment of huts to subsequently respond to the preturbed calls of their commander.

'Leopard 1 to Alpha, contingency 1 deployed,' meekly confirms Changezi, feeling a little embarrassed at not having done his job properly.

Dhil arrests a moment of impatience fleeing through his mind. The last thing he wanted was a chase by Baaz and his men, but this was no time to seek an explanation or to demoralise his men.

'Alpha to Leopard 1, no problem, take your designated positions, over,' he orders. Once the perimeter is secured and properly rigged, the two commandos take up strategic positions in the middle of the village, stopping any militant from reaching Sam's hut from the caves. Conversely, they also have to stop any guard running from Sam's hut towards the cave for help.

Within three minutes, he gets confirmation from both commandos that they have taken positions at their vantage points. These men are now the only active guys in the village at this time of night. With the storm reaching on top of them, heavy rain pouring down with lightning, high winds and thunder to give it company, the villagers and even the militant guards prefer to stay within the comfortable confines of their small huts, bolting themselves from inside, giving the whole village a deserted look.

Within seconds, the rain becomes more intense giving way to hail as the wind becomes stronger bringing with it a wind chill that sends the temperature plummeting to shivery levels.

Dhil fears that this may be too much for Sam's guards, who may decide to take refuge in the hut as well thus waking up the others. With his RT system also crackling due to this weather system and lightning all around, he at once gives the order to his snipers.

'Bolt 1 and 2, open fire,' Dhil forcefully whispers in his microphone.

'Three, two, one, fire,' both snipers simultaneously fire their Steyr rifles at their targets just as both the guards get up to join their fellow guards in the hut.

This movement surprises the snipers, but the shots had been fired. As the two bullets pierce through the stormy winds at high velocity, one hits with pinpoint accuracy, blowing through the chest of its target, instantly killing him on the spot, and the other explodes in its target's abdomen a split second later.

'Aaaah!' the big-bodied guard winces in pain as his small intestines slit open, making him lose his balance and fall on the ground, losing his grip on his assault rifle in the process. His whining at that moment drowned in the noise of the storm, he holds his protruding intestines in his right hand, as he struggles to crawl on his back using his left hand, to the hut in the darkness and simultaneously screaming with pain. Without giving it a second thought, Dar leaps forward with his 'Rambo' style dagger in his hand, and before the injured militant can make sense of what is happening around him, Dar pounces on him like a bloodthirsty panther, slitting open his throat with one swing of his sharp dagger held in his right hand, while he puts his left hand on his victim's mouth.

'This is for beheading my comrades, you fuckers.' His eyes viciously light up as the sights of headless corpses of his fellow soldiers in Swat appear in his mind. His hatred for these terrorists now showing on his face, 'Go to hell,' he whispers in his dying victim's ear, who struggles to hang on to his life, which slowly drifts out of this once strong and sturdy body.

Dhil watches the proceedings from the roof of Hidayat's house through his night-vision binoculars. Seeing Dar cruelly slaughtering the guard sends a fleeting moment of regret through Dhil's mind that he then brushes aside to concentrate on the mission ahead.

'Guards neutralised, going for the rest,' Dar quickly murmurs in his earphone as he drags the dead body towards Sam's hut, all noise drowned in the ensuing thunder and hail. At the same time, Karamat again takes cover behind Sam's hut while pointing his gun at the door of the adjacent guards' hut just in case anyone comes out. All this takes not more than three minutes from the time the snipers fired at the guards. Once the second body is secured, Dar and Karamat turn their attention to the guards in the hut, wondering why no one has come out to check on their comrades. As if they thought too soon, they see the door opening and one guard coming out in the hail, looking down as he covers his head with a shawl. This time, Karamat, from a short distance of no more than twelve metres, fires a short burst of three bullets from his secondary weapon, a silencer-fitted Beretta pistol. This guard does not even know what hit him, and he falls on the ground without making a noise.

Three left against two, Dar under cover of Karamat, leaps towards the open door, and without checking on who's who, fires a salvo of bullets from his silencer-fitted Beretta automatic pistol on the three guards apparently sleeping on the ground. There is no resistance, as all proceed to their final abode without even waking up. Their torment does not end here; Dar takes out his dagger and slits each one's throat to make a statement against his enemies. He is bursting with adrenaline as his hatred brings out the beast in him. Karamat feeling a little uneasy at this act, and seeing precious time being wasted on this unnecessary slaughter, tries to stop Dar.

'Sir, I think that's enough now, they are dead already,' the elderly JCO humbly suggests to his young officer, who then looks up with madness in his eyes as if he has been consumed by evil. Karamat feels uneasy fearing that this man-turned monster may leap on him now, and he meekly continues, 'We should concentrate on the girl now, sir.'

As if jolted back into his senses from extreme rage, Dar responds as he gets up, a crackle of thunder and lightning reveals his white expressionless face for a second, 'Karamat Saab, they slaughtered my buddies and my soldiers in Swat. They take sadistic pleasure in beheading us. I just want to return the favour, so don't you stop me again, okay?'

Cleaning his blood-soaked dagger, Dar asks Karamat to look for the keys to Sam's hut while he walks out of the room into the hail and signals in the direction of Hidayat's hut. Dhil, to his relief, sees Dar waving at him with the thumbs-up sign.

Ignoring the protocol of army radio communication, Dar straight away pants into the microphone, 'Going for the girl,' he continues looking in Dhil's direction 800 metres away and then composes himself to meet the American damsel they had all risked their lives to save. Soon Karamat comes out of the room and shakes his head in the negative,

'There's no key in the room.'

*   *   *

It is nearing 0300 hrs in the dead of the night. Baaz is restless under his blanket. Even in the secure confines of his tiny room inside the caves, he can hear the thunder of the lightning and the patter of hail falling with ferocity on the earth.

Not fearful of the water coming into his cave network due to good sealing work done on it, his mind goes towards Sam, and he wonders how the white woman would be taking this situation all alone. The possibility of her hut caving in could also not be ruled out. He keeps lying on his back for a while listening to the storm outside. Despite wanting to stop himself, he finds himself going for his trusted lieutenant Hazaar Khan, who is fast asleep in the hall next door along with some other militants.

'Hazaar Khan!' he authoritatively calls on him but finds Hazaar sleeping like a log with his mouth open and saliva dripping from it, giving out faint snores in the process. Shaking his head, Baaz makes it to the exit of the cave with his lantern, towards the hut where the two guards, earlier watching over the vehicles, had entered minutes before, having just sent the boy to his small cave room to sleep with the rest of the under-trainee boys. Seeing their commander coming up at this hour of the night, with a hailstorm raging outside, shakes both of them out of their laxness.

'Salam, Baaz Lala!' They jump up from their squatted positions.

'You men are afraid of rain?' Baaz taunts his soldiers as both prefer to remain silent.

'Cowards,' Baaz continues with his taunt. He pauses for a moment and then asks, 'Have you checked with your comrades on the other end whether they are okay?' He inquires about the six guards on night duty at Sam's hut. Little does he know that these men had enjoyed a night of songs performed by an innocent young boy pulled out of his bed after curfew time for the pleasure of these guards.

Both the guards look at each other and lower their heads in shame, signalling their callous disregard towards their fellow men.

'Idiots!' shouts Baaz, beginning to lose his temper, 'Contact them now!' he points at the wireless set wrapped in a dirty red cloth with small mirror work and 'frill' sewed around it, lying on top of a steel trunk. One of the men quickly picks up this only line of communication with the men on the other side of the village. Pressing the wireless button to contact the guards, he calls repeatedly, 'Gul Zaman Khana, Gul Zaman Khana, are you there?'

Gul Zaman Khan was the leader of the guards over there, and his duty had been first watch. To the horror of the guard, he does not find any response from Gul Zaman Khan. He tries another name hoping, in front of his commander, that all has remained well over there.

'Kareem Mehsud . . . Kareem Mehsud?'

All remains silent at the other end as the two guards look at their fearful commander with bewildered eyes.

*   *   *

This was the last thing Dhil wanted to hear, the possibility of their plan going awry.

'Alpha to Panther 1. Break the lock with minimal noise, bring the girl to the exit pad,' orders Dhil as he fixes his binoculars at Dar. He then orders his snipers, 'Alpha to Bolt 1 and Bolt 2, scan the area for unwarranted movement and report.' He then races down to Hidayat to get hold of the escape vehicles and while climbing down the stairs, he commands the Leopard team to hold their position in the village until advised further, concerned that these two brave 'Leopard' commandos are right in the middle of the hornet's nest.

*   *   *

'Could it be the bad weather?' the elder of the two guards tries to act innocent in front of their fearful commander, Baaz.

'You jackasses!' yells Baaz at the two, falling into a fit of rage, 'You!' he points out at the person who is acting innocently, 'Rush to them right now and report to me from there.'

'And you,' he looks at the younger of the two, a boy barely out of his teens, 'go down and wake up the rest and get your weapons,' Baaz orders the other militant as he gets hold of the wireless set himself and tries to make contact with Sam's guards.

Something does not seem right. Baaz fears the worst. *Could it be the Pakistan Army or the Americans?* he thinks, *Or could it be my own comrades?* His mind goes towards his earlier meeting with his fellow militants who had come to take Sam away with them. In light of that confrontation, the possibility of other militants taking away his woman by force could also not be ruled out. Feeling betrayed and confused, he sets his first priority towards thwarting any unwarranted situation if it has cropped up.

*   *   *

Earlier, Sam had been lying motionless in her dark small hut. She was half asleep when the strong winds had started lashing at the structure, bringing with them the stormy weather and eventually hail. As she kept lying down, she began to feel the dripping of water inside from one side of the tin roof of her dilapidated hut.

'Ah, just what I wanted,' she cursed but stayed still, preferring water in her hut to frustrated guards. After a few minutes, apart from the thunder and lightning and patter of hail, she heard a different sound — the cries of a man rang out in the night for a few seconds before all fell silent again. These cries were of the guard who had finally been executed by Dar.

What could that be, she wondered, *deep in the night and in this storm?* A moment of excitement had run through her mind. Could there be a rescue party of US Army 'Rangers'? But then, the fear of being abducted by some rival faction of militants suddenly crept into her mind too. Unable to ascertain the situation and mindful of the dangers, she preferred to remain silent and let the situation come to her, rather than her going looking for it. Heart pounding and mind now fully alert, she fixed her stare at the steel door from where she heard someone trying to break open the big lock from the outside.

*   *   *

Back at the hardened shelter to Baaz's cave network, the elder of the two guards wraps his shawl around his head and gets hold of his AK-47 to head out into thunderous hail. His mind now thinking of his fellow militants, he quickly moves forward still in denial of any impending danger in these stormy conditions. The cold gush of wind and rain drenching him within seconds, he hardly acknowledges the presence of two Leopards seeing their prey walking in their direction.

Sure enough, alarm bells had started ringing and now the hornet's nest of militants would soon be swarming with more armed goons running around the village and in the direction of Sam's hut. But their first job was to stop this one from reaching the other end where Dar and Karamat were busy breaking the strong iron lock with a steel cutter.

Both Changezi and Jamshed are hiding in line astern behind the boundary walls of two huts, separated only by a small 'gully' passing through the middle of these huts. To quickly reach the other end of the village, the militant chooses to take this gully rather than the outer periphery of the huts. As he enters the gully, Jamshed being the closer of the two commandos, first lets the militant pass him by, and in the next second, he leaps on his prey from behind, putting his more powerful right hand on his mouth; pulling his head back, he shoves the large dagger in his left hand in the lower back of the militant, puncturing his kidney and intestines. The militant falls on his knees, his painful scream blocked by the strong hand of Jamshed, who rotates the dagger, once inside, to ensure that the militant does not retaliate. Seeing the strength seeping out of the militant's strong body, Jamshed decides to expedite the proceedings by taking the dagger out, and this time swiping the crisp blade across the dying man's neck, relieving him out of his torment, all under the close guard of Changezi, who looks around giving cover to his comrade.

Meanwhile, both the snipers continue with the surveillance of the area from their vantage points, ready to shoot down any impending danger approaching their fellow teammates. On the north-eastern end, Dar and Karamat finally succeed in breaking the big iron lock; unbolting the sturdy wooden door, they fling it open as Dar enters the room with his Beretta pistol pointed in front of him to handle any unexpected militant lurking inside—a safety precaution in such kind of exercise. Dar's torch is perched on his gun, as he had earlier taken off his night-vision goggles; he looks around only to see a feeble-looking white woman trying to cover her eyes from the oncoming beam of the powerful torch.

'Panther 1 to Alpha, all clear inside, package secured,' Dar updates Dhil on his RT after recognising Sam from the picture shown to the commandos during the planning stage, as Karamat maintains his position outside the hut, giving cover to his officer. For a minute, divorcing himself from the volatile situation around, Dar casually walks up to a crouched and confused Sam and sits down next to her. He puts the torch light on his face to make Sam more comfortable and, with a cool smile, tells his package in accented English, 'Don't be afraid, we've come here to take you home.'

Sam is stunned for a second; she marvels at the nerves of this guy and doesn't know how to react to his charm under such intense circumstances. She could hardly be expected to know that she was meeting Maj. Saifullah Dar, the Kashmiri heartthrob of the Pakistan Army. Trying to maintain her nerves, she responds, 'Who are you guys?'

'Don't worry, we're the good guys,' Dar stands up, 'Major Dar, Pakistan Army,' he extends his hand to greet Sam and help her stand up, 'Let's go.'

*   *   *

On the other end, Baaz is busy mustering his forces; a fighting force of a couple of dozen odd militants, who take a few minutes to wake up and get into their senses. Holding on to their weapons — an assortment of assault rifles, RPG rocket launchers and pistols, they rush out into the thunderstorm, trying to get their bearings. The first wave of ten men runs in the rain before dispersing into three groups. While six run straight ahead in the darkness towards the lurking Leopards, two break off towards the northern side of the village and over towards the assortment of huts, whereas the other two break to the right, coming in a south-easterly direction towards Hidayat's house. Meanwhile, others prepare to get into the SUVs to block the three exit points around the village in this small valley, thus blocking the assault party, if any, from escaping.

Changezi can see this dispersion through his night-vision goggles and seeing no other option but to open fire, this time he quickly yells on his RT, warning the others.

'Leopard 1 to Panthers, two militants heading your way from the north-west, repeat north-west,' he continues with his warnings, 'Bolt

1 and 2, two militants heading towards south-east, others coming straight at us . . . they are out, they are out! Opening fire!'

Changezi starts firing a salvo of bullets from his Kalashnikov while taking aim at the three militants running in his direction. He is supported in this action by his brave Sergeant Jamshed, who takes aim at the other three militants, who also fall to the bullets of these two commandos. At about the same time, Shuja, sitting atop the house of Hidayat, sees through the night-vision periscope of his rifle, on his left side, two militants crazily running in his direction. Their instructions were clearly to challenge any intruder lurking from the southern end. What they did not realise was that they were heading in a straight line directly towards their death. This sniper fixes his aim reticle on the person running a little to the right and behind the first one and fires his shot. Again with pinpoint accuracy, the bullet zooms through the air and pierces through the chest of this militant, instantly killing him on the spot. The militant in front, hearing only the faint swoosh of a bullet passing by, looks behind just in time to see his partner fall. For a moment, he stops in his tracks and frantically looks to his back and front. These three seconds give enough time for the expert 'Bolt' to reload and fire his next round at this shocked militant. Within the next two seconds, this militant is also dead, the bullet having gone through his abdomen.

'Bolt 2 to Alpha, both targets neutralised,' Shuja confidently shouts in his earphone, over the noise of the storm, for the rest to listen.

Back from the safety of his hardened shelter, Baaz sees, to his anguish, in the darkness of the night, the sparks of machine gun fire from inside the crooked alleyway between the huts and the shadows of his men falling about 200 metres in front of him. He goes mad and orders his two RPG[183] operators to fire their rockets at the twisted inner boundary walls facing each other in the gully of the first two huts in front, next to which the commandos had taken cover. Baaz is completely indifferent towards the lives of the villagers — the occupants of the tiny huts inside these walls, who had preferred to remain crouched inside, not wanting to get in any kind of crossfire.

In the next few seconds, the two RPG operators rush out into the rain, take their positions, aim, and fire their rockets. These rockets

---

[183] Rocket-propelled grenade.

zoom under the crackle of thunder and lightning towards their targets inside the gully, 200 metres ahead.

'In coming!' yells Changezi on seeing the trail of two rockets fired in their direction. Both the commandos jump quickly away from these walls, further back into the gully, empathising with the occupants of the huts inside. In the next second or two, the rockets hit these inner walls with a thunderous explosion, bringing down the whole walled structure and their adjoined huts, burying whosoever hid inside them. The detonation is large enough to also knock over the two tough commandos, as all falls silent in the rubble.

*   *   *

Dhil has, in the meantime, secured the escape vehicles. Both these vehicles had been parked about 500 metres north-east of Hidayat's house where the small valley narrowed down to a ravine before opening into another valley towards the east. This was the eastern exit of the village, away from Baaz's caves, which were on the western end towards Afghanistan. But what concerned Dhil now was the probability of flash floods that would soon start running through these narrow ravines with the ongoing storm. Deciding to deal with this challenge later, he looks north-westward in the direction of Sam's hut to see whether Dar, Sam, and Karamat are making their way towards him.

In the background, he hears the warnings of Changezi on his RT, coupled with rat-a-tat of machine-gun fire and yelling of people, hail now giving way to strong rain with gusty winds still blowing across in the dark night skies. Just when he gets the confirmation from Bolt 2 on having killed the two militants, he hears the yelling of Changezi in his earphone, almost deafening him in the process, 'In coming!' after which he hears a large explosion distinctly different from the recurring thunder in the sky.

'Damn it!' Dhil anguishes as he yells into his microphone, 'Alpha to Leopard 1, come in, over . . . Alpha to Leopard 1, come in, over!' There is no response from the other end. 'Leopard 2, report your situation, over.' All remains silent on the RT.

Knowing that the cat was out of the bag now and soon Baaz and his men will be swarming the village on foot and in their vehicles looking for his commandos, he reverts to Plan B. Getting hold of his remote-control detonator, whose frequency had been aligned with those of the time bombs, he goes for manual detonation of bombs earlier placed by Changezi and Jamshed around the fence of the vehicles and timed to blow up a few minutes later, hopefully by the time the commandos would have made good their escape.

In the next second, he hears five large explosions as all the bombs explode with high intensity, destroying men and material within a parameter of twelve metres around them. SUVs, even the two, which had managed to get out of the compound, do not escape the ferocity of the blasts. These, once the proud cavalry of Baaz's Lashkar,[184] are now damaged beyond repair; the ones still inside the compound turned into burning wrecks. His men, the proud soldiers of his cause, are there no more to fight. Baaz himself gets knocked back into his hardened shelter as the shockwave enters the darkened hut through the open door and window cracking the walls and mangling the tin roof before it all begins to cave in. Baaz loses consciousness as he falls on to his back on the mud-hardened floor; the back of his head hitting a steel trunk, his vision starts blurring, and a muted sensation goes through his ears. Motionless, he lies on the floor, as the last thing he sees before blacking out is the tin roof falling on top of him.

Just about that time, at the other end of the village, Dhil sees, through his night-vision goggles, the shadows of Dar, Sam, and Karamat briskly advancing towards his position in the pouring rain, their rescue job going as planned. The two militants advised of earlier by Changezi are not in sight yet. But seeing the Panthers safe and secure with their 'package', Dhil's mind at once rushed towards the rest of his men.

'Alpha to Bolt 1, give Panthers cover, over,' he commands Azam sitting on the boulder overlooking Panthers' escape route and its surroundings, just in case the militants jump on them.

'Alpha to Bolt 2, come with me and cover me,' he rushes back to Hidayat's house to collect Shuja before rushing towards the middle of the village. *I'll leave no one behind . . . I'll leave no one behind* — his own words running through his mind as he hopes that the commotion caused by the bombs exploding among the militants and the earlier destruction of the huts in the alleyway may enable him to reach his

---

[184] Army.

men undetected. He sprints away endeavouring to leave Hidayat's home and avoid revealing this poor clan's involvement in the mission.

As Dhil rushes past Hidayat's house, he is joined by Shuja, who has come down from Hidayat's rooftop. Behind him he hears Hidayat pleading,

'Please kill Baaz Jan, or he'll kill us all.'

A feeling of regret goes through Dhil's mind at not fulfilling the Army's promise to Hidayat in lieu of seeking his help, but first he must secure his own Leopards. 'InshAllah,'[185] he hears himself muttering at Hidayat to placate him for now.

Within a couple of minutes, Dhil and his sniper make it to the assortment of huts right in the middle of the village. As they pass through two alleyways, to their surprise, they see not a single soul creeping out of doors to see the happenings outside. Meanwhile, the two can see, in a distance further west of their position, Baaz's SUVs burning despite the rain, thus lighting up the area around it. Shadows of some of his men running around aimlessly could be seen; others sitting or lying on the ground, either dead or wailing in pain. Seeing no danger coming from the western end for now, Dhil arrives at the destroyed huts.

'Changezi . . . Changezi . . . Jamshed!' he whispers loudly, sifting through the rubble in the process as Shuja keeps a vigil from the side of Baaz's caves.

'Sirrr!'

Dhil hears the familiar voice coming from under a mud-hardened brick wall, which had fallen over as a result of the explosion.

'Changezi!' Dhil turns to face the fallen wall as he ascertains that Changezi must have taken cover next to it, which dislodged into three large pieces and fell on to him.

'Don't worry, we'll get you out.' Adrenaline gushing in this giant of a commander, Dhil is surprised with the strength in himself as he moves this large piece of hardened wall from over his young commando's back and tosses it aside in the process.

Changezi grimaces in pain as he feels his vertebra cracking and two of his lower ribs fractured, rendering him immobile. His hipbone also appeared dislocated along with superficial wounds on his body.

---

[185] God willing.

Dhil at once takes out his first-aid kit from his trouser knee-pocket and thrusts a pain-killing 'morphine' injection through Changezi's trouser into his thigh. This injection works its miracle as the youngster loses his pain and tries to get up, only to fall on the ground again due to his broken bones.

Meanwhile, Shuja finds Sergeant Jamshed's motionless body lying face down on the ground next to the rubble. A huge metal splinter, presumably from one of the rockets, had entered the rear of his upper back, going through his rib cage, puncturing his heart from behind, hence rendering him instant martyrdom.

'Sir, I've found Jamshed,' comes a sombre call from Bolt 2 as he looks with sorrow towards, what once was, his strong and courageous friend.

Dhil dashes towards Jamshed, hoping against hope that his soldier might be alive. Getting down on his knees, he picks up his strong comrade's body and turns it around but only sees open eyes on a smiling face looking up as if he had seen the heavens beckoning him in his dying moments. In the background, there is still commotion, but for Dhil, there is calmness around for a few seconds as he remembers Jamshed's association with him. He remembers his family, with two small children and his elderly parents who were dependent on their only son. Jamshed was originally from the same Infantry Battalion as Dhil. He followed his idol into commando training, after which Dhil brought Jamshed to his commando unit. Although Dhil was the commanding officer and Jamshed — a non-commissioned soldier, Dhil had ensured that like all his other soldiers, Jamshed got the respect he so rightly deserved, an ideology that earned for Dhil the unstinting support of all his men, including that of Jamshed.

'Inna nillah e Wa Inna Elieh e Rajioun,'[186] Dhil wishes heavenly abode for his fallen commando as he closes his eyes with his hand and composes himself.

'Nobody gets left behind,' he repeats his words again as he picks up the dead body of his fallen comrade on to his shoulder and gestures at Shuja to help Changezi walk towards the exit pad about 700 metres east of their present position.

---

[186]   To Allah we belong and to Him we will return.

'Alpha to Bolt 1, give us cover, over,' Dhil orders the sniper perched on the high boulder to secure their exit as he carries the dead body of Jamshed on his shoulder. The other sniper helps Changezi quickly walk forward towards the waiting Panthers with their package.

It takes them about five minutes to reach the rest of the party. Seeing a dead colleague in their centre suddenly takes the fun out of the yet another successful mission. But there is no time to break down in sorrow.

Dhil gives a passing look at the 'American agent' for whom he had just lost one of his soldiers. Sam nods back with a faint smile of thanks, assessing from the situation that this powerful towering personality must be the commander of this rescue mission. But Dhil has other priorities on his mind. The mission was only half complete and to make good their escape alive from Bastikhel Village with the recovered objective in this harrowing weather, with the danger of flash floods in their path and the possibility of other lurking militants ready to pounce on them, becomes Lt. Col. Dhilawar Jahangiri's next challenge.

Time after mission launch—one hour ten minutes.

Chapter 16

THE MISUNDERSTOOD ALLY

Thursday: 0325 hrs — Bastikhel Village

The intensity of lashing winds in the storm has marginally reduced, but the rain is still unrelenting. Meanwhile, much to the concern of Dhil, he sees through his night-vision goggles, water accumulating in the low-lying valley around the village as it flows down from the surrounding rocky hills, turning Bastikhel Village into a small island of sorts: such is the topography of this village and the outlying area. Dhil fears gushing water may block the path to their rendezvous points, but this was a possibility that had already been accounted for in their planning. In the distance, they can still hear the odd explosion and yelling of men. However, much to their relief, they do not find anyone coming to challenge them.

Another five minutes elapse as Dhil advises of the successful conclusion of the rescue phase to Haider, Rathore, and the rest at his Brigade HQ, and also seeks heli-support at the rendezvous points the moment the weather becomes favourable. Meanwhile, Azam also finally arrives from his observation post; Shuja joins Karamat and an injured Captain Changezi in the old Jeep CJ7. Dhil had respectfully placed the dead body of their fallen comrade Jamshed in the same Jeep after taking off his bulletproof vest and helmet, no more required by this martyred soul. In the end, Dhil, Dar, and the second sniper, Azam, sit in the old, yet operational Land Cruiser II along with Sam, who now wears Jamshed's protective gear.

As Karamat switches on the engine, Dhil quickly walks up to the elderly, yet physically robust JCO. Only three years older to him, Karamat was the son of the soil of Waziristan, belonging to a small village near Sheranni. Due for retirement from the Army within three months, Karamat had himself strongly volunteered for this mission on the pretext of honouring his respected CO one last time, by guiding him back from Bastikhel through the rugged tracks well known to him. Seeing his keenness and expertise of the area, Dhil also included him as an important member of the team. Now was Karamat's turn to prove his worth in leading his fellow commandos in the darkness of the night, under stormy weather, through mud and rain, across the winding ravines, avoiding floods and water streams in the process, and finally leading them up to their rendezvous point. Although he had been provided with a GPS, he did not take much fancy to the new technology and still preferred to navigate through his instinct and experience.

'Karamat Saab, the team is relying on you now . . . make me proud,' Dhil pats Karamat on his back, who has switched on the engine of the old Jeep CJ7, ready to take them into the darkness of the valleys lying ahead. Dhil then walks past Changezi, who is lying down at the rear next to his dead comrade; the pain not fully diminished, he pants trying his best to act calm.

'Hang in there, boy . . . We're going home,' Dhil reassures his injured young gun as he slaps the side of the Jeep to signal Karamat to start moving.

'Sir,' Changezi utters over his uneasiness as Karamat accelerates his Jeep with a jerk.

Dhil then comes and sits next to Dar, who had switched on the engine of their vehicle. As they allow Karamat to steer his Jeep a little ahead of them in darkness down the muddy, slippery track, driving over uneven tracks and rocks in the process, Dhil looks back at Sam, who is sitting on the middle bench as Azam covers the rear of the SUV clearing their tail.

So this is the CIA agent for whom we all risked our lives — he thinks, his remorseful expressions written on his face. Sam looks at the large-bodied mission commander wearing a black helmet, with black bloodied battle fatigue and black painted face, part of it washed down with rain water and weapons hanging around him.

'You okay?' Dhil curtly asks Sam, with a stiff facial expression.

'Yeah,' Sam responds, trying to feign a smile, relieved to be rescued and hoping that they make it back safely. Glad to have been asked of her condition by the mission commander, who then turns his face forward, fixing his gaze at the slow-moving Karamat's Jeep in front, she tries to make conversation with Dhil, 'Thank you very much, sir, for rescuing me. It means a lot . . .'

'It's okay!' Dhil abruptly interrupts Sam, raising his hand as a signal to stop, 'I'm just doing my job.'

He then gestures at a visibly uncomfortable Dar to start moving their vehicle after ensuring the required distance between the two vehicles had been reached.

Sam feels embarrassed at being rudely cut short in her gratitude. *That was nasty! I was just trying to be nice with this commander* — she thinks to herself. Looking at his imposing personality now concentrating on the GPS in hand as they start driving down on to the track, she wonders what is wrong with this guy. *Could it be the death of his compatriot? Could it be the situation? Could it be me?* Different thoughts run through her mind, but for now, she prefers to remain quiet, not wanting to distract the soldier from his work.

*   *   *

Thursday: 0345 hrs — Among the smouldering remains of Baaz's Cave network, Bastikhel Village

'Baaz Lala . . . Baaz Lala!'

A semi-conscious Baaz hears a familiar voice in his still numb mind as he struggles to regain his vision. His head still spinning from the fall following the explosion, his solitary eye tries to focus on the blurred image of his trusted lieutenant Hazaar Khan, looking over him, desperately trying to wake up his militant commander.

Hazaar, on seeing, in the light of a lantern, his commander opening his eye, feels a moment of relief together with fear. Knowing the volatile temperament of his boss, he readies himself to move out of the way when his commander gains full consciousness.

At the time of the explosion, the walls of Baaz's reinforced shelter had withstood the shockwaves, but the tin roof had not been so strong. While the gust from the shockwave piercing through the open door and adjacent window knocked Baaz over, it had also displaced the tin roof and its narrow wooden beams. Part of the roof caved into the room over Baaz, who had already blacked out as a result of hitting the back of his head from the fall.

Hazaar was among the five remaining militants left functional after the raid. With their vehicles destroyed, colleagues killed or badly injured, and command and communication in disarray, they had deemed it more important to rescue their respected commander first. Such was the faith and loyalty inculcated by Baaz into his men.

Baaz was lucky to have escaped the collapsing roof over him without breaking any bones. He is helped into a sitting position by Hazaar, who offers him some water to drink.

'Aaaah!' Baaz grumbles with pain as he rubs the part of his head that hit the steel trunk behind him. Now slowly getting back to his senses, he shakes his head, opening his eye fully, trying to fix his gaze on the smouldering wreckage right in front of him and outside the shelter. Rain having almost extinguished the fire by now, he can see in the faint light around, the wreckage of his once prized LR Defender, snatched from the Pakistan Army last year.

His mind at once goes towards Sam. 'Where's the woman?' he inquires as he tries to get up, while still holding on to the back of his head with one hand. Feeling dizzy, he again squats on the ground.

Hazaar looks in disappointment towards another militant who, in turn, only offers a silver glass of water to Baaz.

'Where is the woman?' this time Baaz yells at his men, more out of frustration than anger.

'Lala, they took her,' comes an uncomfortable response from Hazaar, a response Baaz was dreading to hear. 'Taj and Hashim just came back with the news that our six men are all killed, the lock broken, and the woman's hut empty,' he refers to the two under-trainee boys, who had earlier escaped the fight as they were kept inside the caves along with some other boys.

Baaz goes into a blinding rage as suddenly he retrieves all his senses becoming fully alert. He hurls a few expletives at the situation but then quickly tries to compose himself, realising that there is no time to waste if he wanted to get the woman back.

'Any idea who took her?' he asks the two militants as his mind goes over the various suspects. 'They kept us pinned down here while they took the woman from the other end . . . ,' he assesses the escape route of the rescue team, 'but they won't get far.' A sudden feeling of emptiness and anguish fills his heart, as the reality of losing out on the woman he had started fancying dawns on him.

But how can I tell this to my comrades around? He hits a quandary. *If they get hold of her, then they will take her, and my reputation will be ruined.* His ego not yet allowing him to share this news with other militant organisations around him, he decides to first attempt to intercept Dhil himself and stop his team from escaping out of the area.

'Hazaar! Get my satellite phone from my room,' Baaz orders his lieutenant. He then decides to call Qasim, his 'Section Leader', fighting with his group of seven men with a sister organisation near Bibi village, about seventy miles north-east of Bastikhel. Qasim was to immediately collect as many of his men as possible and start driving south-west through the rugged tracks to Bastikhel, expecting to intercept Dhil and his men midway before they cross the junction going further west, towards village Dree Khazay.

She is my woman . . . and I'll take her back—this thought repeatedly bounces inside Baaz's mind. Hazaar obediently walks down the opening into the cave network from inside the shelter with the lantern in hand, leaving Baaz in darkness and silence as rain temporarily reduces its intensity to a drizzle.

*   *   *

0415 hrs—On the way to the rendezvous points near village Dree Khazay, Waziristan

Dhil and his team of commandos exited the village about fifty minutes back. Passing twenty miles in an easterly direction through three smaller valleys, they now enter into a narrow gorge, a mile short of the junction where the main track from Bibi met this route. Here the flash flood was passing through the lower areas. In their planning, they had taken into account the possibility of flash floods passing through the low-lying areas, but now the danger of landslides made their journey even more perilous. Trying to cross the gorge and avoid getting stuck in water, Karamat climbs his Jeep up and on to the right side of the hill where a slightly tilted narrow track had formed for crossings in such weather. Just as he trudges carefully on the slushy ground to avoid slipping sideways into the torrential flash floods flowing through the lowest areas in the narrow gorge, the unwarranted happens.

Karamat's Jeep starts to skid leftward towards the edge of the tilted track and towards the roaring waters about six metres below. The JCO tries to accelerate, his four tires spinning madly, trying to find traction on the muddy track but to no avail. Engine screaming, the aged Jeep slides about a metre sideways, before its rear left tire hits a small boulder at the edge of the track, arresting its fall. Just as the occupants of the Jeep heave a sigh of relief, the unthinkable happens. To the horror of Dhil, he sees in front of him, the slushy track underneath the Jeep caving in. The whole track slides down into the water, taking with it the boulder, the Jeep, and its four occupants.

'Oh shit!' yells Dar as they see, in the headlights of their vehicle through the darkness and rain about twenty metres ahead of them, the Jeep tumbling down towards the gushing water. From their position, they are unable to ascertain the fate of their comrades.

Dhil springs out of his vehicle as Dar brakes it to a halt, thanking his stars that he did not yet climb up the track in this gorge. Tasking Dar with guarding Sam, he orders his sniper to follow him to rescue their unlucky commandos.

God, no more fatalities please—Dhil's heart pleads as he carefully runs towards the toppled wreck of the Jeep as it slowly sinks into the gushing water. The last thing he wanted right now was a mishap, and yet a mishap is what he encountered.

*   *   *

0430 hrs—Bastikhel Village

It is about twenty minutes since Baaz called in his reinforcements from up north. His section commander, Qasim Afridi, had gathered seven of his Lashkar men with their weapons and ammunition and had immediately started off for Bastikhel in an attempt to intercept his commander's prized prisoner midway. The path relatively less treacherous, and they being more abreast of the terrain, they expected to make this journey in about two hours.

Meanwhile, Baaz gathers his remaining few men—a group of foot soldiers, including Hazaar Khan. These six men had gotten hold of an old vintage refurbished 'Willies' Jeep from a villager and armed with Kalashnikovs, RPGs, a mortar, and smaller weapons, began their chase.

Baaz sees red in his eye. The anger of being attacked in his fortress and the taking away of his woman was unrelenting. Puffing with rage, he sits next to the driver, slapping on his driver's neck to drive faster as the driver slowly but surely navigates the muddy tracks under darkness and in wind and rain.

When I get my hands on them — Baaz visualises beheading the rescue party, be they whoever and making an example out of them for all to see. *Nobody messes with Mullah Baaz Jan and gets away with it* — this thought echoing in his mind again and again.

He expects to reach the junction for Bibi in about an hour's time, where he plans to join Qasim and his section.

*   *   *

0450 hrs — 25 miles east of Bastikhel in the direction of village Dree Khazay, Waziristan

The first rays of sunlight still have some time to create an orange glow across the eastern hilly horizon as the thick blanket of grey clouds blocks the sun from announcing the dawn of another day. The winds, which dropped down along with the rain, again pick up, not easing the misery of Dhil's team.

In the last twenty minutes, Dhil had been busy removing his fallen comrades from the toppled open top Jeep. In the tumble, Changezi appeared to have sustained further injuries as he had been unable to jump out of the vehicle. Karamat, also trying desperately to save the vehicle from rolling over, had held on to the steering wheel as it tumbled. With no protection of a hard roof, the front windscreen collapsed as the Jeep rolled over and, although Karamat had ducked to one side, the frame of the wind shield landed across his collar bone, cracking it; he also sustained fractures to the shin bones of both his lower legs, which had gotten stuck in the leg area, taking him down with the wreckage. Shuja, sitting on the left side of Karamat, was also unlucky in not making a clean jump as the Jeep had rolled over him while falling, fracturing his hip bone and breaking his ribs while simultaneously burying him in loose mud sliding down into the water. Now gasping for air, the sniper turns his desperate eyes towards his commander to save him from this ordeal.

Rain still pouring down on them, his one commando dead, three struggling to stay alive, a vehicle destroyed, and the path through the gorge all but washed away, Dhil makes up his mind that they cannot continue their journey towards their rendezvous points. He decides to go for the contingency plan. Looking south towards the higher grounds, climbing steeply to about 500 metres from his current position, Dhil decides to make a security perimeter there and wait for the weather to ease off before he calls in Heli support.

After recovering his injured comrades and giving them more morphine injections to kill their pain, he first sends Azam up the hill to ensure that the area is clear of enemies. It takes the sniper only a few minutes to reach the hilltop and confirm it to be secure from his RT.

'Dar! You stand guard here with the injured. I'll take Changezi up and send Azam down to carry up Shuja while I keep first watch over there,' Dhil pauses and looks up at the plateau.

'You guys then come up together. You'll bring Karamat. Once up, you keep watch, and I'll go down to get Jamshed's body. Get hold of all weapons and ammo you can manage to bring up there,' Dhil points at their projected security perimeter as he lays down his plan.

'Yes, sir!' Dar responds quickly, wondering what to do with Sam as Dhil then carefully picks up Changezi on his shoulders who, half dazed, grimaces with pain as Dhil struggles to carry him up the muddy hill with his weapons in hand, in unrelenting rain.

Dhil then assertively looks at Sam as he plans to get her to a safe place first and foremost. 'Give the girl a weapon and that ammo bag. She's coming with me.'

Sam quickly gets hold of Changezi's machine gun and pistols with the ammo bag and walks swiftly behind Dhil to keep up with him. The gradient of the 500-metre climb to the high ground is steep and rocky, making it difficult for Dhil to climb fast under this wet weather, with his weapons, ammunition, and Changezi slumped on his shoulders. Yet without stopping or struggling for breath, he reaches the top of the hill within minutes. On reaching, he slowly places Changezi on the ground and asks Sam to give some water to Changezi who struggles to take in air in his apparently punctured lungs. Sam quickly complies, feeling saddened for this well-built handsome young man now fighting for his life.

The grey daylight now taking over from the morning darkness, Dhil looks around their current high ground to ensure an unobstructed view in all directions before instructing Azam to go down and get his injured partner up along with the rest of the party. The sure-footed young sniper dashes down in seconds to get to his other partner.

At their height of approximately 2,000 metres, the winds were still strong and the rain but fierce. Dripping with a combination of sweat and rainwater, Dhil calls his brigade headquarters to seek heli-support as he gives the revised co-ordinates of their new pickup point.

'Alpha team to Base HQ, two hours is too long a time to hold on,' Dhil continues on the radio transmitter brought up by Azam. The frustration in his voice all but obvious. 'It's already daylight, and this place would be crawling with militants within an hour.'

To his anguish, he is asked to fight it out for another couple of hours before the storm eases sufficiently to enable the 'Puma' medium-lift helicopter to fly out to them.

'Roger that, over and out!' Dhil shuts the RT in disgust as he then looks down, trying to compose himself. On clearing the area around their plateau, he looks back towards Sam and Changezi to find Sam leaning over a seemingly relaxed Changezi. Not liking this situation, he walks towards them in the middle of their perimeter and first asks Sam to take his position to keep watch over his other comrades who were still at the gorge, waiting for Azam to join them.

'Hang in there, boy,' Dhil tries to put some water in Changezi's mouth to relieve him of his misery.

'Sir, please tell my father,' Changezi gasps for air with his bloodied lungs, 'I died with my boots on,' referring to a military lingo when a soldier goes down fighting bravely.

Changezi was the youngest son of a retired Major-General of the Pak Army who was a decorated veteran of Pakistan's two wars[187] with India. Changezi's 'Hero Daddy' was his role model, whose valour the young officer emulated, becoming a commando and volunteering himself for dangerous missions in trying to continue the family legacy.

'Don't you die on me, you hear?' Dhil softly admonishes Changezi, whose breathing has become erratic.

---

[187] 1965 and 1971.

Trying to smile even in this situation, the young commando struggles to speak, 'Tell them all that I loved them,' referring especially to his parents, his young wife, and a small daughter of one.

Dhil smiles back reassuringly. Dhil had so far experienced many such situations in his sixteen years of commando service, where his comrades had died in his arms. Knowing, despite denying that Changezi's end was near, his mind wandered again to what had been saving him over all these years. *Did he have a guardian angel guarding over him, was it the prayers of his loved ones, or was it simply not his time?* he would never know. But for now, he could see another one of his young officers reaching his end.

'La Ilaha Ill Allah . . . Mohamed ur . . . Rasul Allah,'[188] Changezi struggles to recite the first tenet of Islam as his gasps for air grow fainter, and he finally breathes his last. The pupils of his eyes dilate as his gaze fixes on Dhil's face. Changezi's lungs had been punctured, leading to massive internal bleeding. Drowning in his own blood, this brave young commando's soul leaves for the heavens with a smile on his face.

There is a moment of silence with only the patter of rain and blowing of the winds audible in the background.

'Inna Nillah e Wa Inna Eliehe Rajioun,'[189] Dhil observes a minute of silence as he looks towards the wet muddy ground before he closes the open eyes of his second 'Leopard' and solemnly recites the customary religious verse. Preparation of this mission and the sights of his fallen comrades come in front of his eyes; he laments the reason for being here.

Witnessing the whole sorrowful episode from her place, Sam feels sorry for this brave team of Pak Army commandos. She curses herself for having caused the death of three men so far, including that of Khattak, besides endangering the others who had risked their lives to save hers. Unable to keep to herself, she walks up to Dhil, who by now stands up after covering Changezi's face with his helmet, to save it from the downpour. 'I'm really sorry for your fallen soldiers,' she politely addresses Dhil despite his earlier snub.

---

[188]   There is no One (Sovereign) but God, and Mohamed is His Messenger.

[189]   To Allah we belong and to Him we return.

Dhil prefers to remain quiet, trying to control his emotional turmoil and wishing that the American would shut up.

'In fact, I'm really sorry for putting you all in this trouble,' Sam feels compelled to empathise with this commander.

Unable to take this perceived hypocrisy any more, Dhil sarcastically responds, 'Isn't it a little late in the day to feel sorry.'

Sam doesn't understand this snide response and looks inquiringly at this disgruntled giant of a soldier.

'You attack a sovereign country, kill tens of thousands of innocents in your search for a few terrorists, wreak havoc in our backyard, and then you expect me to believe that you are sorry!' Dhil cannot control his temper as he roars back.

'You twist our arm to fight your war, and look what it's done to us: friend has turned against friend, comrade has turned against comrade, bloody hell, our own reflection has turned against us . . . My once peaceful Pakistan has turned into a battleground!'

Dhil refers to the situation in his country.

Sam refrains from answering and lets the giant expend his emotions.

'War on Terror, War on Terror,' Dhil repeats sarcastically, 'this war on terror has made both our countries more dangerous than they were before . . . You wanted to kill one Osama, now you guys have hundreds of Osama's and we . . . thousands! . . . and unless we stop killing the innocent among them, we'll have more and more Osama's trying to kill more of us . . . This killing spree will never end, DON'T YOU GET THIS?'

Dhil's mind rushes towards his beloved wife struggling for her life back home as he screams hoarse at a stunned Sam, with nature complementing his fury through the lashing of the rain and gusting of the winds, supported by thunderous roars in the sky.

Suddenly feeling tired of his ordeal and lighter inside, Dhil quiets down, panting in the process; his mental state of mind, both for his wife and his teammates, taking its toll on his body. Silence prevails for a couple of minutes in the rain and then Sam responds to Dhil's tirade.

'My father was a pastor who only spread the love of God and peace around him,' she starts off softly, 'was it his fault that he was in the Tower on 9/11,' referring to the New York World Trade Centers that were brought down by terrorists on that horrific morning of 9/11 in the year 2001.

Dhil, who had by now taken his position, watching over his men struggling to climb up to their position, looks back at Sam as she continues with her thoughts, the rainy weather increasing the intensity in her speech.

'My brother Alex . . . he was only a photo journalist . . . Was this his fault that he covered the plight of Afghan widows in the War on Terror?' she pauses for a moment before completing her thoughts, 'he was ruthlessly killed by Taliban for taking pictures of these distressed women . . . These poor widows of their own soldiers, who could not go out of their homes under Taliban strongholds to earn a living . . . the same Taliban whom you considered your friends killed my brother because they deemed taking pictures a sin under Islam . . . an act punishable by death.'

Dhil notices the hurt in the tone of this American woman but then prefers to keep quiet, his personal tragedy too much for him to relent.

'I know you think these terrorists are your friends, and we are your enemies, but think again,' Sam admonishes.

But this time Dhil frowns at Sam. Arguing with women was never his forte. He does not know how to respond to this as Sam continues, 'Even if we would not be here, these so-called Jihadists would still have come on to you in Swat, in Dir, and in Buner.'

Sam refers to the districts of Pakistan where these militants had forcefully taken over control from the State in 2009, which was then recaptured by the Army in operation 'Path to Riddance'. Dhil is surprised at the level of knowledge this American had about Pakistan as she continues, 'These extremists would have still continued their march on your capital with the aim of bringing their . . . their austere version of Islam on the rest of you Pakistanis.'

Sam pauses for a moment as Dhil shakes his head trying to disagree, but before he can respond, Sam carries on, 'You may not believe me, but Americans mean well for Pakistanis, not those freakin' terrorists who use your kids as "suicide bombers" to kill your people! We are here to save you from those criminals just the way we came to help you in your earthquakes of 2005 and the super floods of last year.'

Unable to control her emotions, she continues, 'We assist your country financially from our hard-earned tax payers' money, while our own people suffer back home and still you call us your enemies? It's not them, it's we who are your friends, but you don't understand us,' she pauses for a moment to control her tears, before finally concluding, and this time her anguish truly reflected in her tone, 'Damn it . . . don't you get it? We are your misunderstood ally!' Sam finally breaks down as the toll taken by her for the past few days is too much to handle now.

Dhil prefers not to continue with this debate by responding to Sam. Her poignant outburst jolting him out his mindset, he suddenly feels like sympathising with her, but again holds back. Both remain silent while trying to compose their emotional states of mind before the rest of the soldiers reach their position.

Dhil's entrenched opinions have been jarred for the first time; he tries to focus on the job at hand as he fixes his gaze on the outstretched grey hilly horizon, trying to detect any unwanted company.

* * *

0530 hrs — 18 miles east of Bastikhel Village, Waziristan

Dawn has matured, but the intensity of wet weather is still unrelenting. The heavy downpour of last night in the storm created flash floods in all the low-lying areas of Waziristan, especially around Bastikhel and its adjoining areas. It has made commuting in vehicles even more dangerous as either the tracks are inundated with water or too slushy to be driven on. Baaz had crossed with great difficulty, the two valleys after Bastikhel and was a few miles short of the gorge where Dhil's mishap had occurred. Here, the antique Willies Jeep, struggling to cross the muddy tracks, first gets stuck in a deep muddy patch and finally breaks down when its driver overrevs the engine to pull it out of peril.

Seeing the steam coming out of his vehicle's bonnet as it conks out, Baaz directs a few more expletives at the stalled vehicle, hitting the dashboard with his hand.

'Get off, all of you! We're walking,' he shouts orders to his men as they look at him with fearful eyes, dreading the thought of walking under rain with their heavy backpacks for the rest of the journey; but nobody dares to challenge him.

Holding on to their AK-47s, RPGs, and the mortar with rounds, the six men trudge through the muddy tracks for another fifteen minutes, avoiding the roaring water passing through the low-lying areas next to them, in the direction of the gorge. As these men cross the opening of the third valley, they notice, to their surprise, about a mile ahead of them, a red-coloured speck conspicuous in the green grey surrounding. Anticipating trouble in the area, Baaz cautions his men. He is angry but still in his senses and does not want to take any brash action.

He tells his troops to take cover behind the boulders about twenty metres behind them before he surveys the entire area with his binoculars. From his position, he clearly sees the caved-in mud track having fallen into the flash flood still flowing down through the gorge, an overturned SUV and the red Land Cruiser II parked a few metres before the entrance to the gorge. The camouflage all but washed away, the red paint job of this abandoned vehicle, made it visible from miles away.

That bastard traitor — Baaz thinks about Hidayat as he recognises his vehicle — *I always suspected him . . . Wait till I get my hands on him.*

'They can't have gone far if they have injured,' Baaz assesses from the overturned vehicle half submerged in the gushing water below. Seeing the area around from his binoculars, he finally spots the soldiers struggling to climb up the wet rocky hill, rising from the gorge, with injured men and material on their backs; the men now almost reaching the top. On further exploring the hilltop, he finally spots another head: that is Dhil peering down at his soldiers. While still not being able to see Sam from his position, he ascertains them to be his foes that have rescued the American woman last night from him. Unaware of any fellow militants in this area at this time of the day, he then calls up his lieutenant, Qasim Afridi, on his satellite phone who himself is having a tough time driving back towards Baaz's position. Advising him of their location and the situation in front, Baaz seeks the current location of Qasim.

'Lala, we are still a few miles short of the junction, and once we reach there, the gorge would only be about three miles right, in your direction. Our drive is slow and tough, but we should reach the gorge within an hour,' replies Qasim.

'That's too late, they might be picked up by then,' Baaz yells back in his phone. 'Hurry up and once you reach the gorge from the northern end, call me.'

He knows that until he gets reinforcements, these five ragtag bunch of combatants is all he has. Not happy with the progress, Baaz, for the first time, then seeks help from another militant organisation.

He calls up his old friend and comrade Abdul Jabbar Khan—a militant commander based in village Kooza Khazay situated about seven miles further east of the gorge. Managing his own battalion of combatants similar to Baaz Jan, he keenly listens to Baaz's situation via the satellite phone system.

'Brother, the storm seems to be dying down, and soon they'll have helicopters coming to get them. They may also have gunships giving them cover,' Abdul Jabbar refers to the dreaded AH-1 'Cobra' helicopters. 'Out in the open, our vehicles will be exposed to them in daylight, and you know this is not how we operate . . . It is going to be very dangerous,' he contemplates.

'Yes, but if we start now, we can get to those dogs before their helicopters reach them,' Baaz finds himself pleading after a long time. The shock of losing Sam was too much for him to bear. 'The storm has not died down fully, and this is our only chance to get the woman back.'

There is a long pause as Abdul Jabbar contemplates sending his precious men and material on this unsafe expedition, but not wanting to let his old buddy down, he finally relents, 'Okay, brother Baaz, for you only . . . I'll send some reinforcements for Qasim.'

But Abdul Jabbar also estimates to reach the eastern end of the gorge within an hour's time, similar to the time when Qasim will reach the spot. Unable to wait for an hour, Baaz gets impatient and decides to take on the Pak Army commandos himself. He gets down to making a plan with his depleted resources at hand. Emotions overriding rationality, Baaz's ego starts taking control of his mind.

* * *

0600 hrs—Operation area, Waziristan

Dhil quickly reaches the base of the hill after Dar and Azam, the remaining operational members of his team, had brought up the injured Karamat and Shuja and then took up their positions on the hilltop. Dar keeps watch on the western periphery, whereas Azam covers the eastern side, scanning 180 degrees to the east across a wide span of rocky land, with ditches and caverns, looking out for any unwanted trouble. The rain beginning to ease off, they hope to be picked up by the helicopters within an hour's time from now.

Picking up his dear dead soldier on his shoulders and carrying another ammo bag in his strong left hand, Dhil negotiates his way up the wet steep climb on the rocky cliff, the vehement protests of Sam reverberating in his mind. Dhil had always thought of the US involvement in their backyard as the American hegemonic ploy to control the region and the cause of all the mess in Pakistan. But he also could not deny all the humanitarian assistance Pakistan received from the US whenever there was a natural calamity. He also could not ignore the financial aid that had come their way over all these years compensating their sagging economy due to this war. He felt his heart softening towards Sam's viewpoint. Although he still did not agree with Sam's strategies for countering the threat of extremism, he, at least, found sincerity in her feelings towards Pakistan. Feeling embarrassed at having unleashed his tirade on a hapless woman, who was just trying to be nice to him, he decides to make her feel more comfortable.

After all, my family sorrows should not come in the way of me representing my institution, he thinks to himself.

His mind then rushes to his beloved wife for whom he again prays to God for recovery. Thinking then about his children, he desires to reach home soon and take them all in his embrace. He feels guilty of neglecting them during the last few days. Looking at the weather now beginning to abate, he estimates the helicopter should reach them in an hour. But before all that, he focuses on ensuring the safety of his objective and the rest of the team and that they should prevail over any unwarranted situation.

Breathing heavily, he quickens his pace and reaches the top in a matter of minutes, where Dar and Azam marvel at the strength and stamina of their burly commander, who, even at his age, could give the youngsters a run for their money. As they again fix their sights towards their respective surveillance areas, Dhil slowly puts the dead body of Jamshed on the ground next to Changezi's and then walks towards Sam, who, crouching over an injured Karamat, is helping him to drink some water.

Dhil looks at his two injured soldiers first, leaning against a large stone also acting as their cover from the eastern side of the hill. Shuja is semi-conscious with the effect of morphine overriding the pain of his injuries, whereas Karamat is awake and manfully trying to bear his pain.

'Sorry, sir,' Karamat struggles to speak, 'I let you down.'

Dhil looks back at him with a smile and nods. 'Karamat Saab, no need to feel sorry . . . You tried your best, and I'm still proud of you. Just be strong for a little while more, we should be hearing those helis very soon.'

'I can still fight, please give me my weapon just in case,' responds Karamat.

Dhil just smiles back, shaking his head in negative and then looks towards Sam, who, by now, is checking on an unconscious Shuja, avoiding facing the angry commander again.

'Miss Albright, I'm sorry for the earlier outburst,' Dhil tries to make amends. He pauses before completing his sentence, 'I believe the pressure of this mission and some personal issues took their toll on me,' the low-pitched tone of his voice conveying the genuineness of his apology.

Sam, still crouched over Shuja, is pleasantly surprised to hear a mellowed-down Dhil. She looks up towards him before standing up and, while preferring to stay quiet, just gives out a faint smile acknowledging Dhil's remarks.

There is a moment of silence as Dhil also struggles to conclude this discussion.

'My mission here is to rescue you and take you back safely, and God willing, as long as even one of us is alive, we'll fulfil our mission,' he reassures her as he nods in the direction of his two brave commandos looking out, about twenty-five metres apart, guarding their positions overlooking the eastern and western ends of the hill.

'Thank you . . . Colonel,' Sam relaxes. A sense of calm suddenly going through her heart; for now, she looks forward to getting back to a warm bath in the safety of her heated apartment, but just then she hears Dar yell at the top of his voice.

'In coming! Take cover!'

Chapter 17

WHERE COMMANDOS DARE

0615 hrs — Battlefield, Waziristan

The intensity of the rain has died down to a mere drizzle, but the torrents of water maintain their flow down the smaller valleys, accumulating into flash floods passing through the gorge. Dark grey clouds in the sky have given way to lighter shades, enabling the sunlight to brighten the day a little more as the sun climbs further up from the eastern horizon, creating clearer visibility across the grey, green hilly landscape.

Baaz had waited impatiently for about forty-five minutes. His reinforcements, comprising twenty-one men, seven of his own and fourteen of Abdul Jabber's, with their weapons, including mortar rounds and RPGs mounted on four off-road vehicles, were about three miles east of the gorge. After his talks with them revealed they would reach the launch point in another ten minutes, Baaz decides to launch the first wave of offensive from his side.

Personally fixing the position of his 'mortar' lightweight cannon behind the boulder, he takes aim at the position of the commando party situated within a mile east and at an elevation of 400 metres from where he stood. Having five 60 mm mortar rounds with him, he orders his trusted lieutenant Hazaar Khan to man the mortar and fire the rounds at regular intervals; this would offer sufficient time for the rest of the party, comprising himself and four of his men, to run towards the gorge. The risk of getting shot down notwithstanding, Baaz had no other option but to launch his attack; his objective — to either get Sam back or kill her.

'If she can't be mine, she can't be anyone else's,' he mutters while wrapping his shawl around his face to cover himself with only his one eye protruding; he hardens his heart towards her as he orders Hazaar to fire the first round in the next two minutes.

* * *

At the hilltop, Dhil and Sam hit the ground as Dar yells for cover. They soon hear the whistling sound of an incoming shell before it hits the side of the hilltop within metres from their position and explodes with a bang. The incendiaries luckily get deflected from the side of the hill.

It takes a few seconds before Dhil looks up from his prone position.

'Everybody all right?' he yells as he looks around at his commandos and Sam; all seemingly okay but still covering their faces, except for Shuja who is unconscious.

'Yes, sir!' they respond almost simultaneously. Sam also nods back since she is crouched close to Dhil who then rushes towards Dar's position.

'Where did this come from?' he yells as he puts his binoculars to his eyes.

'Sir, I saw a puff of smoke from behind that boulder,' Dar points about a mile to the west in the direction of Baaz's position, and just then, they spot down on the plains, men running at full speed through the gorge towards them.

'Bastards! They have spotted us . . . It won't be long before we'll see more of them,' frustration written all across Dhil's tone.

Just then, they hear another whistling sound, this time coming from the east, informing them of the imminent arrival of another explosive projectile. Automatically, they all take cover on the hilltop, lying face down on the flat ground next to large rocks, hoping that they don't take a direct hit. Luckily, the shell falls short of their position and explodes harmlessly, the process startling them all out of their comfort.

Baaz had advised Abdul Jabber's men, from his satellite phone, of Dhil's position and, being locals to that area, they knew just where to target. Hence, on reaching about two miles short of the plateau, they affixed their two 60 mm mortar cannons on Dhil's position to eliminate the commandos or, at least, keep them pinned down so that they could not fire on the militants' infantry, who would soon be making their way up the hilltop. Meanwhile, Dhil quickly gets up and rushes for the radio transmitter.

'Alpha team to Headquarters . . . Alpha team to Headquarters . . . come in, over!'

'This is Headquarters to Alpha team, state your situation, over,' comes the calm response from the other end.

'We are taking fire! . . . We are taking fire! We have been spotted, and we need air cover, over!' yells back Dhil, marvelling at the calmness of the person sitting at the other end of this transmission.

'Rescue 1 will lift at 0620 hrs. ETA[190] 0647 hrs,' the calm voice continues.

Dhil looks at his watch. Its 0618 hrs; he estimates about half an hour before the heli would come to them.

'Twenty-nine minutes is too long a time . . . We need air support . . . we need Cobras, over,' Dhil exhorts for the helicopter gunship. Just then, he hears Azam's warning yell about an incoming shell, followed by another whistling sound, before a mortar shell from the east hits very close to them; this time, the splinters hitting the dead bodies, which were placed together.

As all again take cover to save themselves, there is a pause of about thirty seconds on the RT as well, which feels like minutes under the circumstances, and then a familiar voice resonates reassuringly over the RT, 'Affirmative on that Alpha, Cobra 2 is being dispatched. TOT is seventeen minutes . . . All the best Alpha team . . . Allah o Akbar! Over.'

Dhil recognises the voice to be of Rathore. A smile comes on his face. He heaves a sigh of relief, knowing that his trusted subordinate is now in charge over there, 'Roger that . . . over and out!'

Dhil quickly rushes to Azam's position to assess the situation at his end. Through his binoculars he espies three vehicles full of turban-clad, rough-looking, bearded men in dirty shalwar kameez, armed with various weapons, about 2,500 metres from their position, rushing straight towards the bottom of the hill. It will not be long before they start climbing on foot the 500-metre stretch to their position under the cover of their artillery. He assesses them to be still out of accurate range of their weapons and decides to hold his fire, as he does not want to expend his limited available ammunition.

---

[190] Expected time of arrival.

'Don't fire until I tell you to,' he quickly pats Azam's back before he rushes towards Dar's position, who is keenly tracking the movement of Baaz and his men sprinting across their hill from the east. Still about 1,200 metres from their position, Dhil holds on to his machine gun and takes a stance close to Dar to fire at this first assault party when they reach about 350 metres from his position. With danger of more mortar fire hovering above them, they are left with no choice but to fight these militants until help arrives.

'I'd like to help, please give me a weapon too . . . you know, I can handle firearms'

Dhil hears Sam behind him, pleading to assist in the fight. In the meantime, she had been helping the injured soldiers, Karamat and Shuja, get in-between two boulders to protect them against raining mortars. An excited smile shows on her face as she now feels part of this team of commandos fighting their way out of a militants' stronghold.

Dhil takes a couple of seconds to look around and feels no harm in handing her a weapon. He smiles back, gestures her to pick up the late Changezi's Kalashnikov, and tells her to take his position while he supports Azam who will be facing more enemies at his side very soon.

Just then, they hear two more whistles coming from both directions. While Hazaar has fired his third round from the western side behind the boulder, Qasim this time fires his first round, a 60 mm shell, from the north-eastern side. Both rockets land within a second of each other, compounding the mayhem. Qasim's rocket hits with more accuracy twenty-five metres behind Azam's position, and the splinters from the rocket hit Azam in the left hip, leg, and the armour-plated vest, which saves his torso in the process.

'Aaaaah!' Azam grimaces in pain, as Dhil, who ducked down while going towards Azam, crawls towards him under another salvo of mortar rounds; this time all coming from the easterly direction but falling randomly on the hillside.

'Azam!'

'I'm fine, sir . . . I'll manage.' Young Azam, from a small village of Punjab, tries to control his pain as he again gets hold of his sniper gun, waiting for the militants to come closer.

As soon as Dhil takes his position next to the injured Azam and focuses on the advancing party now at the base of their hill, he hears gunshots. Dar and Sam had opened fire on the first assault party comprising Baaz and his men coming from the west. A gunfight ensues as Baaz, along with his four men, climb up the hill from the gorge. Now reaching about 250 metres from the top, Baaz directs one of his men to fire an RPG explosive round up at Dar's position. Luckily, the rocket falls short of the higher ground and explodes in the wet mud, which absorbs the blast, sprinkling only mud all around.

Just then, Sam takes aim at the RPG holder and fires a salvo of bullets at him. Within accurate firing distance of her gun, the militant takes a direct hit and falls down. Meanwhile, Dar takes aim at the other two assailants making their way up a water trench under cover of Baaz's fire; Baaz prefers to stay behind with the last of his men to give cover to the other three. These militants do not even know what hit them as they succumb to their bullet wounds. At this time, the fourth mortar from Hazaar reaches the hilltop next to the injured commandos, who are luckily only moderately hit by flying splinters, the boulder blocking them from the bulk of the debris.

Two against two on this side, Dar takes comfort from Sam's proficiency with guns and her elevated position offering her the advantage vis-à-vis the militants. He advises her to take out the two remaining foes if they try to make their way up, while he goes to the other end to assist Dhil and the injured Azam. Just then, Dhil opens fire at the militants coming up the hill from his side, but in the next few seconds, they take cover as they hear another two mortar shells coming their way from the east beyond their visual range. Dhil counts this to be the tenth mortar fired at them. He wonders just how many more will the militants fire before their infantry comes closer to the top because then they will be under the direct artillery fire of their fellow militants.

As Dar gets up again to quickly reach the elevated position of Dhil, looking down the eastern face of the hill, they hear the crackling on the RT and the comforting voice of the Cobra pilot.

'Cobra 2 to Alpha, come in, over?'

Dar being closer to the RT placed directly in the middle of the two positions rushes towards it.

'Panther 1 to Cobra 2, advise your coordinates, we are taking heavy fire, and we have dead and injured, over.'

'Cobra 2 to Alpha team, TOT[191] less than two minutes, Allah o Akbar, boys, over.' The team gets ecstatic to hear the cool but firm voice of the Cobra pilot who had outsped the lumbering Puma rescue helicopter to reach the fight zone.

'Allah o Akbar!' yells back Dar in excitement as he glances towards Dhil, who for a moment looks back to hear the pilot.

Just then, Azam fires his Steyr rifle at one of the militants who has come within 200 metres of their position. Dhil again turns around and takes aim at the second militant behind the first one. A hail of bullets from his Kalashnikov takes out the militant. There are more militants trying to reach up the mountain from different places than the commandos can manage; caverns and boulders giving them natural cover as they crawl up the hill, but for now, the bigger danger for the commandos remains the enemy mortar shelling.

Taking cover from the raining shells, firing down on the crawling hoard of militants, trying to reach their position from the east, rat-a-tat of machine guns, injured men yelling with pain, and others busy communicating with each other, the scene on and around that hill-topped plateau is no less than that of a battlefield. The rain eases off, and the sun starts to peek through the dissipating curtain of clouds but hardly is anybody in a position to enjoy the cool breeze running through that area. As the gunfight ensues further at Dhil's end, where joined by Dar, the three of them gun down more militants, Sam notices through her small gap in between two boulders, the two militants coming out of their cover and slowly creeping up, presuming that there is no one on top guarding this end. She lets them come up, and it takes them another two minutes before they come close enough to recognisable distance. While she cannot recognise the militant closer to her, she is stunned to see Mullah Baaz, with his chequered cloth wrapped around his face, as the other one. Within a flash, she remembers the killing of Bilal Khattak, her abduction, and her subsequent ordeal, and then the acts of terror instigated by this beast towards the innocent Pakistani people. She freezes for a second, stunned at seeing Baaz, now less than twenty metres from her, slowly crawling up in a cavity with his AK-47 closely held. The other militant by this time is even closer to her. Adrenaline pumping in her body, a

---

[191]   Time on target.

rage of fury gushing through her mind, she gets up, partly revealing her head and upper body above the boulder and quickly takes aim at this militant, who is still unmindful of her presence and looking towards the commandos firing in the other direction. She opens fire.

A salvo of bullets pierces the militant's upper chest as he then looks in Sam's direction. She is the last thing he sees as he falls to his death. But this reveals her position to Baaz. At once, he gets up on to his feet and points his weapon at her; she simultaneously points her gun at him. Baaz relents for a second as his feelings for her take control of him, and that second is enough for Sam. A burst of 7.62 mm bullets exit the barrel of her Kalashnikov and pierce through the air before penetrating Baaz's broad chest, bursting it wide open. Shot down by the woman he loved, he falls back on the hill and tumbles down a few metres before his back hits a boulder, fixing the gaze of his eye at Sam. Stunned, she looks down at him from her higher position. Baaz shudders in pain as blood oozes out of his bullet wounds. The ultimate thing he sees before his vision fades is Sam's stone-faced beauty, as life slowly oozes out of his stout body.

Mullah Baaz Jan, who once was the terror of Bastikhel and a legendary warrior in the whole area, eventually succumbs to his only weakness; his captive white woman whom he could never make his own.

From a far distance, Hazaar, through his binoculars, sees this event as it unfolds and yelps in sorrow as his revered boss goes down from the hail of bullets fired by the woman he so keenly desired. With the last of the mortar rounds now left with him, he decides to fire this one. Just then, he hears the rumbling roar of a gunship above him. He jumps for cover in a small ditch next to his boulder as the Cobra flies over his position and makes its way north to attack the forces of Qasim and Abdul Jabbar from the north-south axis.

As Dar and an injured Azam continue pinning down the militants, Dhil runs back towards Sam, who remains standing, stunned after having killed the dreaded Mullah Baaz herself.

'Albright!' Dhil yells at Sam as he pushes her to the ground on hearing another whooshing sound coming towards them. This time the mortar shell falls right in the middle of the hilltop but does not explode, to the relief of all.

'You okay?' Dhil asks Sam as he takes a look at the smouldering shell.

'I killed him,' she softly replies. Getting back into her senses, she points in the direction of Baaz. Dhil moves closer to the edge and looks down in the direction where Sam has pointed and at once recognises Baaz, whom he had seen in pictures, his dead eye staring back at Dhil blankly.

'Good riddance . . . You've done a great job,' he reassures Sam as he remembers the recent terror attacks orchestrated by Baaz in Bannu and Attock. The condition of Rania fighting for her life whizzes past his mind as he again looks at the dead body of this dreaded militant commander. Anger seething into him as he yells, 'You deserve it . . . You bloody terrorist . . . go to bloody hell!'

This battle had become personal to Dhil, but he composes himself as their mission was not yet over. He also advises Sam to pull herself together. Sam takes her position at the western end, while Dhil joins Dar and Azam to fend off the militants coming from the east.

The men then see the Cobra pilot, a couple of miles away from their position, beautifully manoeuvre his gunship. As the gunner sitting in the front seat quickly takes aim at the mortar positions and fires rockets, which blow them all to smithereens, to the alleviation of the commandos, the mortars finally stop raining down on them.

'Naraa e Taqbeer,' yells Dar, ecstatic to be rid of the enemy artillery.

'Allah o Akbar!' cry out the rest, trying to keep up with Dar's morale.

As if spoken too soon, they hear an RPG firing in their direction as Azam cautions them on an incoming rocket. The rocket hits Dar's cover boulder with a bang, knocking him back and splintering the boulder in the process. On seeing their artillery destroyed, the militants now begin their march up the hilltop. Crawling in the cavities and natural trenches going all the way up, they gain ground under the cover of RPGs now being fired at the commandos' position from the vehicles at the base of the hill.

Just then, Dhil opens fire on two more militants who are about thirty metres closer to their position, slaying them both; but as he exposes himself from his cover to shoot at them, a militant from a range of thirty-five metres aft of Dhil, fires at him, and he takes a hit for the first time in this skirmish. As one bullet rips past his left upper arm, two others hit Dhil's armoured vest. Absorbing the velocity of the bullets, he falls back with a jerk; his lungs stop from the shock as he struggles to breathe. Endeavouring to stay alive, he tries to inhale, putting pressure on his lungs while trying to maintain his consciousness.

Just then, he hears the roar of the gunship cannon as it fires its explosive 20mm-cannon rounds on the vehicles now being driven in a figure of eight to avoid the bullets. Destroying two of them in the process, the gunship, for a minute, turns its attention on the side of the hill, trying to shoot as many militants as it can. Some of the militants hiding among the cavities and large rocks relent. Cannon rounds blowing their bodies apart, they fall down the steep climb like rats, while others try to take cover in the natural hideouts across the rocky cliff. Just then, a daring militant fires his RPG at the Cobra from the side of a boulder. The rocket narrowly misses the tail rotor. But in the process, he exposes his position and goes down in a hail of bullets fired in retaliation from the hovering gunship.

Some of the more daring militants also fire with their machine guns at the dreaded gunship but to no avail as it outmanoeuvres them and avoids being lethally hit. Seeing their inability to shoot down the Cobra, these determined fighters scatter around the hillside, trying to lie low and fend off the gunship, which fires another salvo of rockets on the hillside to attempt even more kills. Mortar positions taken out, vehicles destroyed, and a number of dead militants to its credit, but as it runs low on fuel, the Cobra makes its exit from the sector after playing its part in the destruction of the militants' artillery and cavalry, and just minutes before the 'Puma' is to arrive.

As Dhil struggles to get to his position overlooking the militant's assault, he hears the roar of the larger Puma helicopter behind him. Rescue 1 had arrived from the southern direction to avoid the militants climbing from the east. To the delight of all, it starts to descend to pick up its passengers at the southern edge of the high ground about fifty metres behind their position. The gunners with their LMGs perched on both sides ready to take down any attacker, one crewmember jumps off the hovering heli as it comes to six feet above the ground to collect their objective, Samantha Albright, the American national among them.

'You got to go to the helicopter first!' he yells over the noise of the helicopter as he quickly reaches her at the western corner of the hilltop.

'I'm not going without these men!' she yells back equally high, while pointing at Karamat and Shuja, to make her resentment felt on being preferred over injured soldiers.

With no time to argue on the formalities, the crew member, a Major from Military Intelligence, nods in affirmative and rushes towards the injured soldiers. Within seconds, both Sam and the Major pick up Karamat and Shuja and carry them to the hovering heli as Dhil and Dar continue to fight off the resilient wave of militants sneaking their way up. Baaz's trusted section commander Qasim is one of them, who after having lost contact with Baaz, wants to avenge his presumed martyrdom.

Once the injured are secured, the Major yells at Dhil, Dar, and Azam to join them. Dhil knows that the militants are close by, and one of them has to remain till the end. He first orders Azam to reach the helicopter. Azam gets up on his one leg and struggles to reach the helicopter. On seeing him limping, the Major himself comes down from the helicopter under the cover of the machine gunner and assists Azam to reach the hovering bird.

In the meantime, Dhil and Dar continue to fire down at the remaining nine or so militants who are resolute to reach the hilltop from where the heli will be a sitting duck for them, their dogged determination to avenge the death of their comrades and get back the American putting them on a daring face off with the Army.

'Partner, you're next, take Jamshed and Changezi's bodies . . . Nobody gets left behind, you hear!' Dhil orders Dar as he again looks down at any movement among the stone boulders; the remaining militants crawling up to their position now barely a few metres away from them.

Dar nods in affirmative, hands over his weapon to Dhil as backup and rushes back. Quickly picking up Changezi on his shoulders on his way, he rushes towards the helicopter where the co-pilot yells at him to hurry up. The helicopter crew now gets concerned about the safety of the living as they have been hovering in the area for close to five minutes, and it was already getting too dangerous.

Dhil scans down the 180-degree span of the hillside. Mindful of the depleting ammo with him he sparingly fires short bursts of bullets at regular intervals. He then takes a look back at the situation and sees Dar dutifully coming back fifteen metres from the heli to collect the dead body of Jamshed. As he sees Dar getting back up in the heli with

Jamshed's body, he ascertains that within the next few seconds, it would be time for him to make a dash for the helicopter whose roar of the engine had drowned out the rat-a-tat of guns and explosion of the grenade thrown down the hillside by Dhil. His job well done, he fires a final salvo of the remaining bullets down at the advancing militants who also fire back and then gets up quickly to rush back towards the helicopter whose pilot had already cranked up the engine to lift the bird further from the ground within seconds, giving just enough time to the brave commander to sprint back and jump inside.

Moments before, Hazaar, who had so far been hiding behind the boulder, trying to overcome his initial grief had gathered his strength out of rage towards Sam and the commandos. Sobbing with hiccups, but vengeance running in his blood, he had quickly put the last of the remaining 60 mm round in the mortar barrel aimed at Dhil's hilltop, from where it immediately fired up towards its impending target.

As Dhil gets up from his position to make a dash for the lifting helicopter, he hears, through all the noise, another whoosh of the flying projectile, before the sound suddenly stops. Dhil dreads the suspension of this sound. He knows the shell is coming at him, and he has less than a second to react. Unable to run to safety, he at once crouches as his natural reaction just when the shell hits the ground close to him and explodes in a fireball. The shockwave throws him a metre or two into the air before the burning flying splinters hit him all over his body, ripping his protective jacket and tearing into his flesh. Dhil falls back on the ground with a heavy thud. Clothes torn apart, bloody and wounded with his body badly burnt, Dhil grimaces with pain as he lies face down on the ground struggling to maintain consciousness. Bones fractured and his ear drums shattered, he can only hear a muted noise of the helicopter's rotors before he starts to black out; all his strength suddenly drained out of his battered body.

On the southern end of the plateau, the large Puma Helicopter buffets violently from the mortar explosion about thirty metres from its position. As the people inside see Dhil getting hit in horror and then brace themselves for the crash too, the pilot skilfully controls his large bird from toppling over from the shockwave. Avoiding the rotor blades from hitting the ground as soon as he stabilises the heli, Dar, who had earlier yelled with panic to see his commander getting hit, leaps off like a greyhound.

'Nobody gets left behind!' he yells as he frantically sprints towards his downed hero.

'Cover him!' the Major shouts at the gunner, fearing that very soon the remaining few militants climbing the hill would reach its summit from where Dhil, Dar, and everyone in the heli would be vulnerable to their fire, especially the RPGs.

He and Sam also get hold of weapons and point them in the direction of the drop behind Dhil's position, just in case the militants reach the top.

Within seconds, Dar reaches a badly injured Dhil, whose once strong body is nothing but a limp heap of flesh and blood right now.

'Get up, sir!'

He tries to pick the giant up and with adrenalin gushing in his body, this six feet tall commando generates extra strength in him succeeding in putting Dhil's flaccid body on his shoulders as he struggles to rush back to the hovering helicopter.

Just then, the others see, behind their commandos, the first couple of militants rising from the hillside.

At once, the heli gunner opens fire from his LMG at the same position, skilfully avoiding Dar and Dhil from getting hit by his bullets. One militant goes down in this volley of fire, the other ducks, but not for long. The Major gets the better of this militant, killing him with a quick burst from his MP5 submachine gun. Not to be left behind, Sam also fires her pistol randomly in the direction of the cliff from where she sees another militant popping out, keeping him down, just long enough to enable Dar to reach the heli with a semi-conscious Dhil. Dar quickly unloads Dhil from his back into the heli, and within the next second, the Major grabs Dar from the back and hauls him on to the hovering Puma, just as the pilot once again throttles up his engine to lift off the ground.

Gunners on both sides of the heli fire indiscriminately at the hilltop at anyone who moves, thus keeping them all pinned down to the ground.

'Rescue 1 to HQ, package recovered safely, but men are injured and need immediate medical assistance . . . ETA twenty-five minutes, over,' Maj. Hilal Shah, the helicopter pilot, gives the final call to the Base Headquarters before climbing beyond 5,000 feet over the rocky cliffs to avoid small arms fire from below, from where he sets his direction for Bannu Air Base. As the helicopter climbs, the crew notices some reinforcements heading towards the gorge to assist the downed militants, Baaz's other men and comrades, who had come to know of this incident from Abdul Jabbar Khan. But it's too late now, and they all live to fight another day.

Back in the helicopter, Dhil struggles for his life as Dar and Sam desperately try to control all the bleeding from Dhil's punctured body. Morphine injected into him to reduce the pain, Dhil is dazed with all his injuries and loss of blood. His strength slipping away, Dhil's mind starts to hallucinate, as the oxygen supply to his brain also diminishes.

Hallucinating with grey vision turning into a tunnel, he sees the blurred image of his wife Rania in Sam, who sits next to him smiling down.

'Rania . . . ,' he toils to speak as he tries hard to keep his eyes from closing.

'Tell the kids, I'm coming home,' voice barely above a whisper, he smiles as his eyelids close over his rolling-up pupils. Death starts to play hide-and-seek with this burly commando; Dhil finally seems to be running out of luck. Sam looks at Dar, who tries hard to stabilise his revered boss. The others look on helplessly as there is nothing much they can do in the absence of a medic.

To her own surprise, Sam finds herself offering comfort to this stranger, a man who had risked his life to save hers. She puts her hand on his battered and bloodied forehead and softly responds, looking down at him.

'Be strong, everything will be okay.'

All quiet down in the cabin after these few words of Sam. Only the noise of the engine remains audible as the rotating blades heave the bumpy helicopter forward towards its destination expeditiously.

*　　*　　*

0715 hrs — Dhilawar's House, Attock Cantonment

With the coming of dawn, the grey overcast sky is lighting up as the sun gradually makes its ascent up and over the horizon. Soon a beautiful rainbow emerges declaring the cessation of last night's storm whose fury has now ceased to exist.

The wet grey brick facade of Dhil's house had turned a few shades darker from absorbing all the rainwater during the night. This was in contrast against the thoroughly washed and neatly placed green plants around a perfectly manicured garden. Water dripping down their leaves, they ooze out a clean fresh look, making the whole environment in the area serene. The early-morning chirping of the sparrows adds charm to this peaceful ambiance.

Rania's father, the elderly admiral had offered his pre-dawn 'Fajr' prayers after which he had taken his usual morning stroll in the small driveway of Dhil's house. Now seated comfortably in the open veranda overlooking the garden, with a hot mug of tea in his hand, he hears the voice of his wife from inside the dining room, through the screen door, advising her grandchildren to be strong in the face of adversity as they try to munch on their breakfast before leaving for school. The overall mood inside the house still solemn, he prays for the lives of his daughter and son-in-law who were both facing their own challenges.

Just then, the phone bell rings, which catches the attention of everyone.

Who could it be this early in the morning? Is everything okay? Is that regarding Rania? Is that Dhilawar or is that about Dhilawar? Could this be good news? This could be bad news? Should I answer it or just ignore it? If I don't answer it, will it go away?

A plethora of tumultuous thoughts run through the minds of Ayesha, Taimur, and the elderly couple all at the same time. All are reluctant to pick up the phone, as they cannot afford to hear any more bad news.

Seeing all the elders in the house stunned, little Hamza jumps down from his seat and patters to the phone in the adjacent hall.

'Hello, Assalam u aliekum, who is this?' he greets in his usual sweet voice, shaking the others out of their shock.

Taimur, acting brave, reaches the hall and takes the phone from Hamza, 'Hello, Lieutenant Colonel Dhilawar's residence,' trying to act mature, he emulates his hero dad as he pauses for a moment to hear the voice at the other end.

Epilogue

Monday: 1900 hrs — Catherine's House, Jacksonville, Arkansas

It has almost been a month after the daring commandos of the Pakistan Army rescued Sam from the clutches of Mullah Baaz Jan in Waziristan. On her return, Sam was put on charge for breach of protocol, endangering the secrets of her organisation, causing casualties through her action, and on the whole, putting her country's interest in jeopardy. Dereliction of duty proven against her despite her positive intent, she was summarily discharged from service. However, her accomplishment of personally killing Mullah Baaz, a common enemy of USA and Pakistan, saved her from a prison sentence. Now back in her mother's home in Jacksonville, she recounts her experience of Pakistan as she sits in front of the television listening to the latest news circulating around the world. America had indeed erupted with joy.

Having heard the day before about the death of America's most wanted terrorist, she felt it was time for her government to revisit their strategy on the 'War on Terror'. Feeling compelled to write to her ex-boss, she switches the television off and gets up from the couch in the living room. Going to her room next door, she sits in front of her computer placed on a table next to the window.

She sighs, gives it a deep thought, and then starts typing.

Dear Sir, she addresses the letter to the CIA Chief.

I would like to congratulate you on finally tracking down and killing enemy number 1 of America. His death will certainly bring relief to all Americans, especially the ones who were victims of 9/11. This action was long overdue and finally justice has been done.

But this has also raised other questions. The fact that while we concentrated our search on the Af-Pak border area, he stayed nestled right under the nose of Pakistan's military without their apparent knowledge speaks volumes of the complexity we have to face in tracking down such criminals wherever they are in the world. The Pakistani State may not have known about his whereabouts but certainly it seems that he had a support network in Pakistan, who helped him stay below the radar for so many years. The question we need to understand is, who was in his support network in Pakistan for all these years, and why did they have sympathies with a terrorist.

In my short but intense stay in Pakistan, I met a lot of Pakistanis across the various sections of their society. In my interaction with them, I've come to realise that they are not bad people. In fact, they are just like us. They hate violence and terrorism just as much as we do. They have lost more than 20,000 civilians in approximately 3,500 acts of terrorism, including suicide bombings, in the last decade and about another 3,000 servicemen fighting these terrorists, and so far, they see no end to this spiral. While they also yearn for peace and security as much as we do, they don't like what we are doing in and around their country. Just as we value American lives, they value Pakistani lives, and just as we get inflamed when American lives are lost, they get equally inflamed and frustrated when their compatriots die needlessly. Here we need to assess who causes the deaths of normal Pakistanis, and as I see it, there are two main reasons:

First, the indiscriminate air attacks on their populace living in the border areas. While our drones successfully kill the intended targets, and I for one know because I was a drone commander myself, our missiles also kill others; women, children, and sometimes even the innocent men. These deaths are not acceptable to Pakistanis, and the extremists among them then begin to support the system of our enemies.

Second, the creation of terrorism among Pakistanis is a direct reaction to the first one. It is the killing of their friends and relatives by us, that convinces them to align with the extremists, who then mislead them into retaliating against innocent Pakistanis living in the semi-urban and urban areas, accusing them of being US partners. Thus, the phenomenon of the 'suicide bomber' is born.

Once these two reasons are eliminated, the terrorists will have no cause to garner support in Pakistan nor will we have the menace of suicide bombers.

Sir, the elimination of OBL has given us an opportunity to make a new beginning. I humbly suggest that we grab this moment to bring our military back from Afghanistan. They have fought bravely, and now they need to make an honourable exit.

Our men and women in uniform in Afghanistan need this from us. Our people back home need this from us.

With respect to Pakistan, I suggest that we reassess our strategy toward combating the cause of terrorism there. As someone said to me over there, 'Violence only begets violence and hatred only begets hatred.' The billions of dollars that we give to Pakistanis cannot make up for the economic losses they have faced so far from this war-like situation. The goodwill that so painstakingly is built up by our fellow Americans in Pakistan gets evaporated in a moment when we bomb their borders. Hence all the money we spend there cannot make us win their hearts and minds unless we stop killing their innocent people under the garb of defending ourselves.

Sir, we cannot buy their allegiance unless we listen to them as well. So let's listen to what our Pakistani allies have to say about this war. Let us sit down together and proceed with a mutually acceptable strategy. A strategy in which drone missiles do not indiscriminately kill, a strategy with which we can garner the support of common Pakistanis, a strategy with which we can alienate the terrorist elements from the masses, and a strategy with which we can build a long-term relationship with our ally: one of mutual respect, trust and friendship, because as I see it now, we both have misunderstood each other all along.

Looking forward to a brighter future for our generations ahead.

Yours sincerely,
Samantha Albright
(Ex) CIA

The rescue scene from Waziristan running through her mind, her eyes well up again on thinking about Bilal Khattak and the brave men who had rescued her from the terrorists. Now sitting in the comfort of her mother's home, her heart beats hard with emotions as she gulps down her sobs to press the print button of her computer. Getting her eyes off the printer, now printing her passionate letter, she looks up outside the window and sees in the glow of a setting sun, little children playing on the swings and merry-go-round in the park across her garden. These children prank gleefully, chuckling and laughing with excitement as they run around, completely oblivious to the plight of children halfway across the world. Seeing them enjoying life, Sam wishes the same kind of carefree environment for all the children around the world as she decides to send a copy of her letter to the President of the United States as well.

*   *   *

2030 hrs. 6 September – Pakistan Defence Day[192]
Lawns of Army Auditorium General Headquarters, Rawalpindi

It has been about six months since Dhil and his team of commandos undertook their daring mission to rescue Sam from Baaz. That particular battle might be over, but the war against the militants still goes on, where various contingents of the Pakistan Army and paramilitary forces are locked in combat with the militants in the border areas of Pakistan and Afghanistan. Rocket attacks on military patrols and suicide bombings across urban centres of Pakistan, in retaliation for the killing of OBL, are on the increase and showing no signs of abating. On the whole, nothing has changed for the Pakistani populace as they wake up every day with the fear of being caught up in the crossfire between home-grown extremists and the security forces.

In such circumstances, the Inter-Services Public Relations (ISPR) Department of the Pakistan Defence Forces have arranged a function to commemorate the valour of Pakistan Armed Forces in the war of 1965 with India. This year, the heroism of the brave men in uniform fighting the menace of extremism and militancy in their country is also being celebrated along with the memories of the 1965 Indo-Pak War. The stage is bedecked with the flag of the country and the insignias of the various military units currently fighting on the western front. On one large board, there are also pictures of the soldiers and officers martyred over the years. With 2,795 security personnel lost since 2001, the boards fall short given the number of pictures on hand. However, in one corner of the sprawling garden, a large memento is erected showing the names of all personnel, along with their ranks, killed

---

[192] On 6 September 1965, India attacked Pakistan across the international boundary in retaliation to Pakistani incursion in the disputed Jammu and Kashmir region, thus initiating a full-blown war between two warring nations. Despite being numerically inferior to Indian might, Pakistani forces held the Indian invasion off for two weeks before declaration of mutual ceasefire. This war is celebrated in Pakistan every year to celebrate the valour of the fallen heroes and living legends of that war.

in action. This list is never-ending and enough space is left for more names to be inscribed thereupon; such is the thinking of the State.

The Defense Minister of the country is attending the function, as the Prime Minister himself is preoccupied with other commitments. Some other senior ranking civil and military officials, including the chiefs of the three services are also present in their ceremonial uniforms, each displaying their medals of honour proudly perched on their left chest. A special guest at tonight's function is His Excellency Mr Daniel Redford, US ambassador to Pakistan. He along with his small entourage, including Col. Raymond Gaunt, US Military Attaché to Pakistan, have made it a point to attend this function and show their support for their ally's fight against terrorists. Redford is seated purposefully next to the Chief of Army on one side and Pakistan's Defense Minister on the other.

The function is underway, having started with the relevant verses of the Quran preaching that Islam is a religion of peace, where the death of one human being is tantamount to killing of the whole of humanity, and saving the life of one human being is tantamount to saving the whole of humanity. The Islamic scholar talks in depth, explaining that what the extremists are doing in the name of Islam is in fact contrary to the spirit and teachings, and how it is the duty of each and every Muslim to be steadfast in the face of terror and to advise the disillusioned to leave their violent ways.

His sermon is followed by some patriotic songs of 1965, which instil a spirit of camaraderie and loyalty towards the country and its people even to this day. Thereafter, the award distribution ceremony commences when some of the brave men of the Pak Army are awarded medals for their valour beyond the call of duty in the current war against the militants. Their smiling portraits, decked in uniform, are projected on to a large screen on one side of the dais as their feats are narrated by a particularly beautiful and articulate couple of celebrities, a man and a woman from Pakistan's showbiz industry; highly motivating the people sitting there and the viewers watching the live telecast of this function on their television sets in Pakistan and overseas via satellite transmission.

The whole environment exudes a spirit of patriotism, sacrifice, and perseverance in the face of adversity currently prevalent in Pakistan.

After another trip down memory lane of 1965 war and a couple of patriotic songs, performed by a chorus of children, the function enters the next stage, where a few officers or their kin are called to the stage to receive gallantry awards, but this time for the current war on the western border.

The show finally enters the phase where Dhil and his men are to be accorded gallantry medals by the governments of the USA and Pakistan, acknowledging their daring rescue mission. Ambassador Redford is here to personally hand over the medals on behalf of the US government to highlight the level of friendship between his country and Pakistan. Pakistan's Defense Minister who hands over Pakistani medals to the brave commandos accompanies him. General Malik also stands beside them to complete the troika. One by one, each commando's name is taken starting from the NCOs,[193] JCO[194] and finally the officers. The snipers, Azam and Shuja, who had both eventually recovered from their wounds, walk up to the dais one by one, albeit proudly, to collect their medals, whereas the mother of the deceased 'Leopard' Jamshed comes to collect his medal. Then Karamat, who had also survived the mission, comes up to the dais. Although on crutches, his head is held high as he proudly receives the medals for his bravery from the dignitaries. For the martyred 'Leopard' Captain Changezi, his father, the retired Major-General, takes the honourable stride up to the dais to receive bravery medals on his son's behalf. Late Changezi's graceful mother, charming wife, and cute little daughter are all there to attend this memorable moment. All of them control their tears as the elderly General talks about his son, his love for the country, and his eventual objective of dying for his country. This wish of his had finally come true, stated a proud father; holding back his tears, he concludes on the thought that this wish came much sooner than he, as a father, would have desired. The mood becomes sedate at the function as Maj. Saifullah Dar is invited over to collect his medals. Now married, on his return from the mission, he gets up and, unlike his jovial self, seriously walks up to the dais to collect his medal from the American ambassador before receiving his Pakistani medal from the Defense Minister; the coldness on the Major's face making his feelings towards Pakistan's allies all

---

[193]   Non-commissioned officers.

[194]   Junior commissioned officer.

too obvious, he walks away before causing any embarrassment to his superiors.

Finally comes the turn of Lt. Col. Dhilawar Hussain Jahangiri to be awarded with his medal of honour.

The beautifully attired hostess of the function begins her introductory sentence for Dhil. 'Ladies and gentlemen, the final award of the evening goes to the brave commando of our beloved Army who led this mission from the front. This commando was facing adversity at home: his wife being badly injured in a terror attack and fighting between life and death, his children needed him in such testing times. But he put his family challenges aside and led his mission with great conviction and intensity. The first to touch the battleground and last to leave from the battlefront, he followed the highest traditions of his honourable institution and set a great example for his men to follow. His deeds will be remembered in history for inspiration and motivation.'

She pauses for half a minute as she tries to overcome her emotions reached while reading for this brave son of the soil.

'This soldier is no more with us,' she struggles to conclude her sentence as the whole function enters into a pin-drop silence.

'He valiantly fought off the marauding group of militants climbing up his post while he ensured that the others, dead and living, first safely got to the rescue helicopter . . . It was then when he was about to make his exit that a shell fired by these miscreants exploded near him, fatally wounding him,' her voice echoes in the surrounding, carting all to the battlefront.

'Although bravely saved by Major Dar, Lt. Col. Dhilawar Hussain Jahangiri could not withstand the intensity of his wounds and attained martyrdom by the time the helicopter landed at Bannu Airfield.'

Choking on her own voice, she gestures at her male counterpart to complete the sentence. 'For his valour and accomplishment beyond the call of duty, the Government of Pakistan awards him Sitara-e-Jurat, whereas the US government has awarded our brave officer a 'Purple Heart', a gallantry award equivalent to Sitara-e-Jurat.'

He pauses as the people in the function subtly clap in tribute to their hero.

'May we now request his . . .' he looks down at the script and looks up again to complete his sentence, 'wife, Mrs Rania Dhilawar to come up to the stage and receive her gallant husband's awards.'

Rania had woken up from her coma in the early morning hours of that fateful day. The phone call made by the doctor to Dhil's house was received with relief, jubilation, and thanks to God in Dhil's household, all of who then rushed to see Rania being granted a new lease of life. Just when the boisterous children with their grandfather were coming out of the hospital after seeing their mother awake and in a stable but frail condition, the family had received the tragic news. Fate played a cruel game with the innocent children. While granting them their mother, it took away their father, whose comfort they would never again feel for the rest of their lives.

The whole crowd claps in unison as Rania slowly walks towards the dais. Not yet fully recovered from her own wounds, she grapples for the extra strength in her body to honour her late husband whose memories were still fresh in her mind.

One by one, she collects the gallantry medals from the Defense Minister and Ambassador Redford, and just when she is about to walk off, the host requests her to say a few words on this occasion. Rania was a simple schoolteacher and a housewife. Addressing a large gathering of people had never been her forte, but before she could decline, the 'show host' hands her the microphone.

The attendees quiet down to listen to her; silence prevails in the function for a few seconds as Rania struggles to find words over her choking voice. She then looks towards her children. Ayesha and Taimur subtly smile back at her and nod, encouraging their mother to say something. Her eyes well up on seeing the mental resolve of her children; even her little four-year-old keenly looks at his mother to say something. This brings out the strength in Rania to speak from her heart.

'Dhilawar was a caring husband, a loving father, and a sincere friend,' she begins, 'but above all, he was a great patriot. He joined the Army for the defence of his motherland and, indeed, laid down his life preserving her honour. Although I and my children will never be able to fill the void left by his departure, we are indeed proud of him and his services rendered in the protection of our country.'

At the end of this, Rania finds herself brimming with emotions, which makes her more confident as she speaks; this time in the English language.

'I remember the words of one American President when Pakistan conducted the nuclear explosions . . . Two wrongs don't make a right . . . and today, I want to give the same advice to our American friends.' Rania pointedly looks towards Redford who shies away from her gaze, looking in the direction of the people, as she continues, 'Acts of terrorism are certainly wrong, but to quell those by killing the innocent is equally wrong. Such violence on both sides only aggravates the situation around, resulting in loss of more precious lives such as . . .' She stops before taking her husband's name as she does not want to make it a personal woe.

Meanwhile, the senior-ranking defence secretary sitting in the front row starts to get uneasy on hearing Rania lashing out at the current policies. He looks back in the second row and finds a smiling Brigadier Haider sitting behind him.

'Can't you make her stop?' he whispers loudly, afraid that this philippic would agitate their American guests.

'Let her speak her heart out, sir, today is her day,' Haider shuts the bureaucrat up, who turns around angrily, helpless at the situation.

At this instant, Dar recollects the moment when he called Major Rathore in Attock from Bannu Heli Base. An absolute feeling of dismay had rushed through the unit on hearing the death of their comrades, especially their commander. Half of their unit had then made the three-hour journey to Bannu from Attock to personally collect the body of their martyred hero and take it back with honour to Attock. Such was the love Dhil enjoyed among his men. Dar's mind is then jolted back to Rania who continues with her tirade in English.

'Dhilawar was not the only martyr in this mission. There were two more brave soldiers who went down fighting for the esteem of Pakistan. However, they are only three of the very many uniformed personnel killed on our battlefronts in recent times. And let's not forget the thousands and thousands of civilian Pakistanis who have died in acts of terror and violence. How many more have to die before we realise that we are going nowhere with this policy.'

At this point, she sees the show's host, who by now was repenting his decision to hand her over the mike, slowly walking towards her signalling to end her address. She composes herself and looks towards the ambassador again as if addressing the US government, 'Please do not misunderstand our sincerity towards you but also understand our position towards this war.' Feeling that she has made her point, she concludes, 'Let us all step back and reassess our actions. I'm sure we can all sort out our differences and move on, making this world a more peaceful place for our children to live. They deserve a happy and carefree life, and we as their elders are obligated to provide them with that life.'

Rania hands the microphone over to the host, who, by now, was standing next to her ready to receive it. Silence prevails in the gathering as she slowly makes her way down the steps, and just then, the slow but audible claps of Taimur and Ayesha start reverberating on the lawn; these claps are soon joined by the clapping of others in the gathering as all wake up from their trance. Brigadier Haider, who had been passionately listening to Rania, gets up from his seat to acknowledge her heart-rending speech. Others follow his action as the whole congregation rises to give her a standing ovation. The environment on the lawns of the auditorium gets ecstatic as the graceful Ambassador, the Minister and the General also clap their hands airing their agreement with Rania's views. She hugs her children one by one, controlling her tears for her husband as all around her continue clapping, saluting her for her courage to speak out the feelings of her nation. The function ends on a hopeful note that things will change for the better in their beleaguered country.

*   *   *

Tuesday: 2300 hrs—Drone Operation Centre, Location Classified.
Nevada Desert—six months after Sam's rescue from Waziristan

A drone mission is underway as the pilot, sitting in the comfort of the Ops room, is flying his remote-controlled Predator at 20,000 ft, towards the predefined coordinates halfway across the world near the border into Waziristan.

His target is a house among a cluster of smaller huts in a small village situated close to Bastikhel. There had been reports that the remnants of LaM, including Hazaar Khan, were gathering there to select their leadership going forward after the death of their previous leader, Mullah Baaz Jan.

On another screen, the 'Eagle-eye' operator manning the drone cameras focuses the nose camera on the targeted house as the drone commander managing the whole mission stands behind his crew in the Ops room with his hands folded on his chest, scrutinising the images relayed on the various screens in front of him; several cameras on the drone giving them live feed of the drone's flight path, trajectory, target, location map, and the rest.

'We are nearing the launch point . . . time to launch Hellfire one minute and counting down,' the young blond drone pilot in his early twenties, with short hair and blue eyes, advises his commander as he flies the drone closer to the Af-Pak border.

'Copy that, maintain heading, and advise,' seriously replies the astute commander in his mid thirties, concentrating on the visuals of the area to be targeted.

There is silence in the room for the next minute, with only the mild noise of the overhead air conditioner making its presence felt before the pilot exclaims, 'Target locked, permission to fire,' a screen in front showing the aiming reticle moving across a house in the assortment of other huts as the drone pilot paint's his target with the laser beam.

The screens continue providing them with live feeds on different aspects of the mission underway. Just when the commander is about to give the order, all at once look towards the screen, showing a bunch of local kids playing soccer in close proximity of the house under their aim.

All remain silent as the commander contemplates seeing this development and then the 'Eagle-eye' operator abruptly cautions for the record.

'Sir! I see children . . .'

~~~

Edwards Brothers Malloy
Thorofare, NJ USA
March 2, 2017